MY RETIREMENT FROM THE AGENCY

A WOLFE ADVENTURE NOVEL

WALT BRANAM

abbott press

This is a work of fiction. All of the characters, names, incidents, organizations, and dialogue in this novel are either the products of the author's imagination or are used fictitiously.

Abbott Press books may be ordered through booksellers or by contacting:

Abbott Press
1663 Liberty Drive
Bloomington, IN 47403
www.abbottpress.com
Phone: 1 (866) 697-5310

ISBN: 978-1-4582-2199-5 (sc)
ISBN: 978-1-4582-2198-8 (hc)
ISBN: 978-1-4582-2197-1 (e)

Library of Congress Control Number: 2018908842

Print information available on the last page.

Abbott Press rev. date: 8/24/2018

Kirkus Reviews said about Branam's previous books *Hunting Evil* and *Nemesis Syndrome*:

> "An entertaining tale bolstered by outstanding characters, both recurring and new."

> "Full-tilt action drops recurring and new characters into a plot rife with gunfire and the occasional explosive."

ACKNOWLEDGMENTS

Although this book is a work of fiction you may find portions of it that are hauntingly familiar. That is because the technology described in this work of fiction exits and is being used today. Also, the current news headlines provided much of the inspiration for this story. My hope is that this work of fiction provides both entertainment and food for thought.

I wish to thank "Tony" who has made it clear that he is not my attorney!

I also wish to thank Tiffany for proof reading the manuscript. Without her keen eye this book wouldn't be readable.

Last, but most importantly, I want to thank my wife for her support and assistance in all segments of my life.

INTRODUCTION

My name is John Wolfe. No, I'm not the famous Wolfe with the military medals and high position in the FBI. That Wolfe is my younger brother. His name is Thomas Wolfe. I'm John Wolfe.

I work . . . er . . . worked for the Agency. That's how we who are imprisoned there under the guise of employment refer to it. Some people call it the No Such Agency. It also has a few other names—official and otherwise—depending on how bad it's screwing people at the time. This book begins on the day of my retirement party. Before it ends I lose one girlfriend, find a new one, cause my last supervisor at the Agency to have a fatal stroke, kill my arch nemeses, eliminate a swarm of mortal enemies, and begin a new quest to save the world. Read the book to find out more.

Speaking of reading the book, I recommend you buy this book and read it as soon as possible, because if the Agency has its way—and it usually does—this book may not be on the shelves for very long. Every employee of the Agency is required to sign a national security agreement. When I signed it, I acknowledged that breaking the agreement could result in five years in prison and a $250,000 fine for each offense. (My attorney, Tony, says there are allegedly hundreds of offenses in this book.) The agreement requires that I never tell anyone anything about the work I do . . . er . . . did. I may have crossed the line in writing this book, but that's yet to be decided in litigation.

I tried to explain to Tony that my position in writing this book is that since my retirement party didn't take place until a full week after my final day of work for the Agency, I'm free to tell you everything about that day and forward. I argued I was only telling a story about a day in the life of a retiree. Unfortunately, I can't tell you what Tony said—attorney-client privileged conversation, but mostly civility. I can say we went round and round and finished off a whole bottle of high-end scotch that night.

The short version is the Agency intends to file charges, or sue me, or something. You never know which it will be with them, since they consider even their soiled toilet paper as ultra-top secret (eyes only) that must be disposed of using classified methods. (And you wonder why government spends so much money.) So I recommend you tell your friends to buy a copy of this book while they still can. If the JATAs (jerks at the agency) get their way, both the book and I will disappear very soon.

Enough preambles. My story begins the morning of my retirement party, one week after my last official day at work.

1

BREAKFAST OF CHAMPIONS

There was perfume in the air when I woke. The fragrance was strong—almost too strong. It made my nose itch so I turned over and saw the blonde head sticking out of the covers. Janet was my off-and-on-again girlfriend. (Yes, I meant it that way.) She was a thirtysomething who worked at the Agency. She supervised the Cryptology Lab that breaks unbreakable codes and unscrambles computer-encrypted messages. I can't say too much about her without getting in trouble with the censors. I will say she was hot in bed and we'd been covertly breaking each other's codes for a couple of years.

Janet was snoring lightly. Give her a break; I was very hard on her last night.

I carefully rolled out of bed so I wouldn't wake her and shuffled to the toilet where I performed my morning ritual.

As I was finishing up, I glanced out the window of my cramped little condo off Twenty-Third Street NW in the Foggy Bottom area of DC. The same gray Toyota was there, with the same bored-lifeless man sitting behind the wheel. He'd been there last night when I went to bed. I know it was the same guy because I took his picture with my telescopic, night-vision camera before I went to bed. I usually made files on the actors who imposed on my privacy so if I ever needed to address the problem, I could work with information.

Before, I described this poor guy as "bored-lifeless," but right now, he looked as if he was really cold and miserable. Someone had left the guy out here alone all night. Didn't they relieve their people? He must work for

Homeland Security, unless the Russians or Chinese were still watching me. All three had about the same caring attitude for their employees.

Whoever he worked for, didn't they know I was retired? I expected this when I was active, but this was silly. I'd been retired for a full week. Why would someone be watching me now?

It was winter here in DC, with a couple of inches of snow and ice on the ground, and I thought he must be freezing his ass off. Then I noticed the steaming exhaust pipe: the engine was running. He probably had the heater on full blast—real covert and stealthy.

He must've been a new guy. I felt sorry for the poor bastard for a moment. You always sent the new guy on the shit details. It was not uncommon for some a-hole supervisor to send the new guy on a detail the experienced guys refuse. Maybe I'd invite New Guy to join me for coffee this morning. Or maybe not.

This was why I kept a condo in DC. I didn't want spy scum soiling my real home—a hundred-acre estate in the Shenandoah Valley, Virginia, located southwest of the DC Power Belt. I usually only got home for long weekends and vacations, but now that I was retired, I expected to spend more time at my Old Rock House. That was what I named it because it was built in 1796 from rocks carried in wooden carts from the Blue Ridge Mountains of northern Virginia. There had been a dozen renovations since 1796, so my Old Rock House was now a modern five-thousand-square-foot manor with a detached six-car garage, plus an aircraft hangar on the back of the property.

You may ask how a civil servant could afford such an estate.

It is better you don't ask.

I gave New Guy one last look to ensure he was staying put and then went back into the bedroom. Janet was wide-awake and sitting up in bed with the blanket covering her breasts. She always slept naked.

I liked that.

She was giving me *the look*.

What the hell? I thought. *It's my retirement celebration day.*

I climbed back into bed and threw the blanket off so I could see all of her. Her body was one reason I liked her—a thing of pure beauty.

Yes, for you who think I'm a chauvinist—a throwback to an ancient generation—you're right! Worse yet, I'm proud of it. I love women. I enjoy women's bodies and the naughty things men and women can do together. If the woman feels the same, we have an accord.

If you don't like gratuitous sex, romantic innuendos, a complicated plot sprinkled with action, and a lot of killing, maybe you should stop reading.

Good-bye.

For those still with me, Janet and I spent the next forty-five minutes enjoying each other's bodies in almost every way you can imagine or have seen if you've watched a good porno movie.

Now thoroughly exhausted, we were taking a shower—together to save water, of course. We played more games under the water, doing some things that should only be done in the shower.

Finally, I stepped out and grabbed a towel.

That's when she announced, "I won't be seeing you again. This was our last time."

"Why?"

"Does it matter?"

"Yes, it does! You wake up in my bed, suck all the energy from my body, take a hot, sexy shower with me, and then standing there naked, unbelievably sexy, and dripping wet, say, 'Dear, *John*, this was our last time'?"

I threw the towel at her—a little harder than normal—then grabbed one for myself. There would be no dry-each-other-off games this morning.

She laughed. I liked her laugh, even when she was laughing at my pain. "Well, I wasn't going to tell you *before* I sucked all the energy from your body."

"Why?"

"The real reason? I guess I owe you that. I've been flirting with a new cryptologist in R Section. I'd like to know him better. Your retirement gives me a good breaking point to go our separate ways. Sorry."

"You're not sorry," I grumbled. "And copulating with a subordinate in R Section could turn into sexual harassment later."

She smiled and finished drying off then playfully threw the wet towel at my face. It smelled nice. By the time I'd hung it on the rack, she was back in the bedroom and had on her panties and bra. She was fully clothed in less than two minutes.

She really means it.

"Based on this announcement, I'm assuming you don't want to stay for breakfast," I said, standing in the center of the room. I was facing her and still fully naked.

Janet treated herself to a leisurely look, as if she were memorizing every part of my body. Then she slithered up to me, like a cat in heat, and stood as close as possible without us being back in bed. She tilted her head up to my face, and we kissed. It lasted long enough that I was beginning to think she'd changed her mind and I was going to be breakfast.

Finally, she stepped back for one final look.

I hated my body for its reaction. Little John was betraying me—out of control—even after all he had been through last night and this morning. What made it worse, it was a good-bye kiss!

She continued to press her body against mine while she looked deep into my eyes. "This hurts me too, John. I'll miss your hard, muscular body and those deep-blue eyes that burn with passion, the way your curly black hair falls so casually across your forehead . . . and your cruel smile." She playfully tapped her finger against my lips.

"But you're still leaving me," I retorted.

Janet gave me one last, quick kiss and slinked to the door. Her hand curled around the handle as she turned and looked back. I could see the amused twinkle in her eye.

"Au revoir," she said, chuckling as the door closed quietly behind her.

2

NO GOOD NEWS THIS MORNING

I watched Janet through the bathroom window as she exited my building and strolled down the street. She knew I was watching her. She tossed a quick kiss at my bathroom window and then popped into her bright-green Mini Cooper with the two white racing stripes running from bumper to bumper. She started the spunky little four-cylinder engine and jumped into the morning nightmare that DC calls traffic.

I was still peering through the window as the Mini Cooper disappeared around the corner, but I really wasn't watching Janet. True, I was a little depressed—maybe despondent—she had dumped me, but primarily I wanted to know if New Guy, sitting out there all night with his engine running to stay warm, was watching Janet or me. If New Guy followed Janet, I'd call her cell, warn her, and then it wasn't my problem anymore. On the other hand, if New Guy stayed put, I would have a different reaction.

New Guy stayed put. He was watching me, and I couldn't even begin to guess why.

I retrieved my binoculars and zeroed in on the front seat of the Toyota. From the way he was wiggling around, either he hadn't brought a bottle to relieve himself in or he'd already filled it up during the long, cold night. Either way, *he didn't have a pot to piss in,* as my grandmother used to say.

I didn't feel too sorry for him because he was watching me, and in my experience, that indicated somebody who wasn't on my side and was up to no good. I decided I might have to hurt him.

Next, I opened a hidden closet where a fireproof safe contained a collection of toys and personal documents. I selected an aerosol spray can of special formulated clear latex and gave my hands a heavy covering. The spray dried in about thirty seconds and blocked fingerprints and DNA. It didn't wash off without acetate, so it would last all day.

Then I selected a nice little .40-caliber semiautomatic and two extra magazines. As an afterthought, I pocketed two tiny surveillance devices that transmitted video and audio signals using cell phone technology.

I was about to leave the condo when my landline telephone rang—probably a telemarketer or solicitor. I intended to let it ring, but my little voice had a different suggestion.

Pick it up.

I answered. "Hello!"

"John, this is Janet."

"Back so soon?"

"This is serious. I just got a call. Jimmy Trang was found dead in his car this morning in the employee's parking lot at work. It looks like suicide, but they haven't ruled out other possible scenarios."

"You mean murder?" I asked.

She was silent for a moment then said in a quieter voice, "They've blocked the local cops from the investigation—handling it internally. Sprout says there's no need for an autopsy. He says the cause of death is obvious."

Sprout!

I have this little voice in my head that runs a constant commentary about what's happening around me. It's sometimes distracting and nags me, but it also keeps me alert—warns me of trouble. My little voice is not always right, but it's right more than wrong, so I listen to it. Right now, my little voice was screaming, "*Cover-up.*"

Or, *frame-up!*

"How did he allegedly kill himself?" I asked.

Janet said, "He was shot once in the head. The bullet traveled left to right. The car doors were locked, engine off. The pistol was found on the floor inside the car."

"Keep me informed," I said.

"I will. I'm going to the site now," she said, and the connection went dead.

Jimmy Trang is . . . was a second-generation Vietnamese descendant, born in the U.S. His parents had escaped Saigon in 1975. I liked Jimmy. He was smart and energetic—a lot like me my first couple of years in the Agency. Jimmy was also willing to take chances, which is another reason I liked him. I recommended him to take my place after I retired. I briefed him on all my projects, so he could take over seamlessly. Jimmy was also naive and trusting.

On my way out the door I switched on the covert CCTV system that utilized cameras disguised as mundane objects, placed strategically inside the small condo. The cameras do not run constantly but are activated by motion detectors. The system alerts me via an app on my smartphone if there are any intruders. I can see them in real time on my smartphone. I don't always activate the system when I leave, but today I was feeling insecure.

As I walked down the stairs to the underground garage, I replayed Janet's phone conversation in my head. She said the bullet had entered Jimmy's head on the left side and exited on the right. That meant he shot himself holding the pistol in his left hand.

Jimmy was right-handed.

3

BREAKFAST OF ANOTHER KIND

I pressed the keyless start button on the bright-red 1967 Corvette Stingray with a 427-cubic-inch, fuel-injected-and-blown V-8. The 650-horsepower engine roared to life. It is actually a 2017 Corvette with an aftermarket, fabricated '67 body, built by this guy who only does that type of work. The relic 'vette cost me more than two new ones would cost, but it was worth it. If you're asking how a civil servant can afford such a high-end, custom-built sports car, I already told you—don't ask.

I pushed the remote to open the one-car garage door and taxied between the canyon-like walls of the condo complex. I was probably waking up my late-sleeping neighbors as I inconsiderately enjoyed the deep, echoing rumble from the threatening exhaust pipes. There were three possible exits from my condo complex, but I made a point of taking the Twenty-Third Street NW exit. I made a conspicuous right turn directly in front of New Guy, who was still squirming in the Toyota. The poor guy was wiggling so violently he almost missed me, so I raced the engine as I passed to ensure he noticed my passing. It wouldn't do to lose him before I found out who he worked for and why he was watching me.

New Guy made a quick U-turn in the middle of the block—illegal in DC—and raced after my Corvette. I also saw a black Mercedes, driven by a red-haired beauty wearing a fur hat. She was discreetly following two cars behind the Toyota. She looked interesting.

Is she following the Toyota or me?

Regardless, I needed my morning coffee. Without it, I'm kind of a bear—real grouchy—especially after just being dumped by my girlfriend. Also, New Guy would probably appreciate me stopping, since I'm sure by now he was reaching the pissing-panic point. I didn't know about the mystery woman in the Mercedes, but I couldn't keep tabs on everyone following me.

I spearheaded the parade of vehicles; taking them directly to a Starbucks located about two miles from my condo. Yes, I passed three other Starbucks before getting to this one. Like most cities, there seems to be a Starbucks at every intersection, but I liked this particular Starbucks because there is a late-twenty to early-thirty, dark-haired beauty who works there. Michelle had a near perfect body, sparkling eyes, and a beautiful smile that melted even my cold heart. More importantly, she knew exactly how I liked my coffee, and she always spent an extra few minutes talking to me.

At least in my mind, this seedling romance had been germinating for the past few months, and I believe she really saw me as a possible stud bull—not just another steer to shove through the coffee-customer chute for slaughter. I had considered asking her out for more than coffee, if you get my meaning, and now that Janet had officially released me from any obligation, I was thinking of bringing up the subject with Michelle this morning.

What? Were you expecting me to pine away because Janet dumped me? Don't be an idiot!

Available parking in DC is only a myth, so I stopped directly in front of the coffee shop, blocking the fire hydrant, and ambled into the Starbucks.

I looked around for Michelle but didn't see her, so I stood in the middle of the store, seriously disappointed. Maybe she was working in back or had gone to the ladies' room. I waited. All the customers ahead of me cleared the line. I continued to wait.

An eighteen-or nineteen-year-old boy was currently taking orders. He had a shiny face and a huge, mindless grin. He also looked like he hadn't exercised since his freshman year of high school. He was just standing there looking at me, apparently anticipating that I would step up to the counter.

I ignored him. I was waiting for Michelle.

At that moment, New Guy came into the Starbucks and rushed directly to the restroom. I pretended not to notice him. He pretended not to notice me. We didn't make eye contact—Basic Spy Craft 101.

It had been almost five minutes now since I had entered the Starbucks, and I was still waiting for Michelle to appear. New Guy emerged from the restroom and saw me standing in the center of the shop—right where he had left me. I don't think he expected that, because now he looked confused. He timidly walked up to the counter.

Shiny Face asked New Guy, "How's your day going so far?"

"Better now. I'd like a grandé mocha latté with whipped cream and cinnamon, please."

"Low-fat or whole milk?"

"Skim, please," answered New Guy. "I'm trying to cut down on my calories."

I studied New Guy closer. He was maybe five years older than Shiny Face, about five-ten, 170 pounds, with brown hair. He wore a dark-brown ski jacket, Dockers, and Nike running shoes. He looked nervous. Maybe this was his first real solo surveillance job and he didn't want to screw it up. Like I said, I almost felt sorry for him—almost.

New Guy walked over to the pick-up area and waited for his morning dessert drink.

Shiny Face decided it was time to force my move. He asked me, "Can I help you?"

I approached his station, but before I could say anything, he asked, "How's your day going?"

The same exact words he used on New Guy.

By now New Guy had gotten his dessert coffee and was pretending to peruse the newspaper rack, but he was actually listening to my conversation with Shiny Face. I wanted him to underestimate me—think I was just an old, grumpy, retired codger. I didn't want him to worry that I could be dangerous.

"You don't care how my day's going. You're just paid to act like you care while taking my money. If I told you I just turned forty-five, I have no job, no purpose in life, that people no longer appreciate my contribution to society, and my girlfriend left me for a younger man, what would you say?"

Shiny Face blinked, dumbfounded.

"I thought so. So just pour me your largest size coffee—hot and black." I tossed a five-dollar bill on the counter.

"You want sugar, cream, whipped cream, or any flavoring with it?" Shiny Face was a robot, programmed to follow a specific routine. There would be no deviation.

"Didn't I say black?"

"Yes, sir." Shiny Face looked like he was about to cry. I almost felt sorry for him.

New Guy, on the other hand, had just moved up a notch on my evaluation scale. He was smiling.

"By the way, where is Michelle this morning?" I asked.

"Who?" Shiny Face was easily confused.

"Michelle. She usually gets my coffee. Is she here this morning?"

"I . . . ah . . . she no longer works here . . . she got married last Saturday and is on a honeymoon. I'm not supposed to give out . . ."

She got married? I thought she was interested in me . . . damn!

"Never mind! Just get my coffee."

At that exact moment, in walked a long-legged redhead. She was wearing a full-length black winter coat, Russian-style fur hat, black leather gloves, and black leather snow boots. Everything else worth inspecting was covered up, but from what I saw she looked like fifty billion dollars. I wanted her.

I warned you earlier that I like women. You ask, "What about pining away for Michelle, or even Janet?" Well, one dumped me; the other got married—remember?

New Guy was watching the redheaded beauty too.

She walked directly to the counter without acknowledging I exist.

Shiny Face asked her, "How's your day going so far?"

"Fine. I'll have a large black coffee, please." She laid four one-dollar bills on the countertop.

I walked over to New Guy, nodded in the direction of The Fifty Billion Dollar Woman, and said, "My kind of girl."

New Guy looked like he was going to faint.

"So which agency do you work for, and why are you following me?" I asked, pressing a compact .40-caliber pistol hard into his kidney.

New Guy either passed gas or messed his pants. I'm not sure which.

4

GETTING TO KNOW YOU

"It's better you don't make a scene," I advised him.

"Better for who?" asked New Guy.

"It's better for Shiny Face, working behind the counter, but mostly better for you."

"I don't understand?"

"Well, Shiny Face will most likely have to clean up the mess if I pull this trigger and disappear in the confusion. You should be smart enough to know why it's better for you."

He almost dropped his desert drink and made a little choking sound.

I continued. "Why don't we go find your car and have a nice private chat? If I like what you tell me, I let you go, and all's well."

"What happens if you don't like what I say?"

Is this really Amateur Hour?

I whispered in his ear, "I'm not here to give you on-the-job training. Let's go!"

The Fifty Billion Dollar Woman walked directly up to both of us and said, "You two want to be alone, or can we do a three-way?" She held a cup of very hot coffee in one hand and a sexy little pistol discreetly in the other. I think it was a .380.

"Your place or his?" I asked without hesitation.

"Mine!" She was smiling. It was a very seductive smile. Now I really wanted her.

A short time later, we sat in her Mercedes: New Guy and me in back, The Fifty Billion Dollar Woman in front. The windows were tinted very dark, so I doubted a casual passerby would notice us inside.

But she'd made her first mistake: sitting in front required her to awkwardly twist around to keep us both covered. It would slow her ability to react.

Everyone was still armed—even New Guy. I bumped him on the way to the car to make sure. So this could get deadly real fast.

I could see my relic Corvette blocking the fire hydrant in front of Starbucks from here. The Fifty Billion Dollar Woman had talent—unlike me, she had found a legal parking space close to the coffee shop.

"So who are you?" I asked her.

"I'd rather not tell just yet. Let's both ask Squirmy who he works for first."

She'd observed New Guy squirming in his car, too, only she'd given him a different nickname. I liked the one she'd given him better. More importantly, that told me she may be following him—not me—but I needed to be sure.

We both stared at Squirmy.

He said nothing.

So I asked him, "What's your name?"

He didn't answer.

I continued. "There's no harm in telling us your name. Otherwise, we'll make up names for you, and in the meantime we'll hurt you."

Squirmy remained silent.

The Fifty Billion Dollar Woman leaned over the seat and almost purred as she whispered in Squirmy's ear, "Darling, if you don't tell us what we want to know, I'm going to hurt you real bad, and I like punishing bad little boys."

My little voice warned me, *Careful, you could fall in love.*

Squirmy whimpered. He really looked scared, but he still didn't speak.

"There's no harm in telling us your name," I repeated.

Squirmy's eyes bounced back and forth between me and The Fifty Billion Dollar Woman. He looked scared and confused, but I had to give him credit: he still said nothing.

I began, "You do speak English don't—"

But The Fifty Billion Dollar Woman interrupted me by jabbing a Taser into Squirmy's neck and holding it there for a full second. His body jerked and trembled in spasms to the sound of the electrical crackling of the Taser. The interior of the Mercedes filled with a mixture of burned flesh and a rotten aroma from his sphincter muscle. Squirmy dropped to the car floor, stopped shuddering, and moaned softly.

I felt a pang of sympathy for him.

I pointed my pistol at The Fifty Billion Dollar Woman's face and said, "Give me that Taser. I don't want you getting the idea you can do that to me."

"You wouldn't shoot me," she purred.

"Really . . . you sure?"

Her dark green eyes glistened seductively. An enticing but snarly smile crossed her full, red lips. Her Taser hand slowly but deliberately closed the distance to my neck. She had a seductive-hypnotic gift. I bet that combination of skills had worked many times for her. I secretly nominated her for the title of "Most Gorgeous, Seductive, and Potentially Dangerous Woman of the Year." Her demeanor promised me a cornucopia of wild sexual pleasures, just waiting around the corner if I would succumb to her charms. I could hear my small voice saying, *let her have her way with you—it'll be fun.* I watched passively, almost in a trance, as she slowly moved in for a promised kiss—a black widow's kiss. You could clearly see she was convinced her wicked charms were working on me.

I shot her.

No, I didn't kill her, but I sure blew a nice little hole in her shoulder—on the side holding the Taser. She dropped the Taser and fell back into the driver's seat. The gun blast had been eardrum-shattering inside the Mercedes but probably muffled and almost silent from outside the car. However, her back hit the steering wheel horn and woke everyone in the neighborhood. At least she didn't flounder around, or scream, or yell. She was in shock and just moaned quietly.

I pulled her off the horn and let her lay quietly across the center console. Then I picked up the Taser and slipped it into my pocket. Next, I reached over and retrieved her pistol. It was a nice little Smith & Wesson Bodyguard .380, colored black and blue—very space-age and sexy. I liked it. Next, I liberated Squirmy's pistol from his belt-clip holster. He carried a .40-caliber Glock compact—not as sexy, but deadly.

I slipped my two new pistols into pockets and then returned my attention to Squirmy. He'd been sentient enough to know I'd just shot one of the most beautiful women on the planet. That was good, because now he'd have no doubt I'd shoot him too.

I had to hurry. Someone may have taken an interest in us because of the horn honking.

"Enough fucking around . . . what's your name?" I shoved my pistol into his eyeball just deep enough to make him worry he'd lose that eye.

"Planter! My name is Planter—David Planter. He almost shouted it.

I let off a little pressure on the eyeball. "Well, that wasn't so hard, Mr. Planter. Now tell me who you work for and why you were following me."

"I can't. I'll get fired."

He said fired, not killed. That most likely meant a government agent but not the Russians or Chinese—they don't talk like that. He could work for some private enterprise. I decided there were still too many possibilities. I needed to narrow it down.

I grabbed the back of his head and pulled him in tighter against the pistol that was still inserted into his eye socket. "Tell me who you work for or you'll be fired permanently—just like her." I nodded to the front seat.

"Okay, but please let up on my eye. I don't want to go blind."

"Talk!" I hissed, without letting up.

"I work for the Agency—for Sprout. He said to watch you, report your activities, until you showed at the luncheon today. That's all!"

Bingo!

Planter was with Sprout—how poetic. Sprout was the division chief over electronic intelligence gathering at the Agency—my last supervisor before retirement last week. I seriously disliked the bastard. He'd been a factor in me pulling the plug early. He had attempted several times to have me discharged over the past five years. But why would he want to have me followed now? I was out. What was the point?

"Why does Sprout care what I'm doing now, and why only until my retirement luncheon? He hates my guts—calls me a relic from a forgotten past."

"I don't know. He didn't tell me why. Just said to watch you until the party . . . to make sure you made it."

I pressed the barrel a little deeper into his eye socket. I think it was maybe a little too deep, but I didn't care. "Tell me the truth, Planter, or lose your eye."

"I swear!"

"He's telling the truth." The Fifty Billion Dollar Woman was now sitting up, pushing a handkerchief into her shoulder wound.

How would she know? asked my little voice.

"You work for Sprout too?" I asked her.

"No, work for the other side."

"Other side? You mean the Chinese?"

"No," she said.

"Then who?" I asked.

Instead of answering, she pulled her coat back and inspected her wound. "You bastard! I'm bleeding like a pig. The bullet missed my vest. I think my shoulder's broken."

"It's not broken. I purposely missed the bone." Then what she had said registered with me. "You're wearing a bulletproof vest?"

I'd missed that. Maybe I'm slipping.

"A lot of good it did me," was her answer. "I need to get medical attention."

"In time . . . just sit quietly for a moment," I said. "Try not to get too excited. It'll make you bleed more."

I saw a meter maid stop next to my Corvette in front of Starbucks. *Shit!* In DC blocking a fire hydrant is a tow-away offense. I needed to get over there ASAP and stop her from calling it in, but I had my hands full here.

The Fifty Billion Dollar Woman saw it too, and from the twinkle in her eye I could see she knew time was working for her.

Unless she bleeds out first.

"Okay David Planter, you can go back and tell Sprout I'll be at the luncheon this afternoon, and I'll give him an opportunity to tell me why he sent you to watch over me. He better be there, or I'll come find him. You can tell him that too. Now get the hell out of this lady's car!"

Planter unsteadily opened the door.

"No, wait!" I said. "Do you know anything about Jimmy Trang's death this morning?"

"I never heard of him."

I didn't recognize David Planter, and he claimed he'd never heard of Jimmy, but he works for the same Agency I had. That was puzzling. Or maybe Planter really is a new guy.

"How long you been with the Agency?" I asked.

"I just got out of training. This is my first assignment on my own, and I screwed it up."

I glanced at The Fifty Billion Dollar Woman. We exchanged a knowing smile. "Okay, get out of here and don't follow me ever again."

Planter crawled out of the Mercedes but didn't close the door or walk away. He stood on the sidewalk, rubbing his eye while holding onto the Mercedes's roof for balance. I guess he was still shaky from being Tasered. I think he was feeling sorry for himself too. He stuck his head back inside and asked in a pleading voice, "May I have my pistol back? I'll catch hell for losing it."

I felt sorry for the kid, so I pulled his pistol, dropped the magazine, removed the round from the chamber and said, "Give me all your spare mags. I don't want you reloading and going Wild West on me."

He complied and I returned his empty Glock. The Fifty Billion Dollar Woman and I watched Planter wobble down the sidewalk, apparently to wherever he had parked his gray Toyota.

The meter maid was making a cell phone call. I had to hurry.

"Okay, beautiful, what's your name, who do you work for, and why are you following me? Quick, before you bleed to death."

"You mean before the meter maid tows your flashy sports car away—don't you?"

I looked down the street. The Corvette looked worried. It probably thought I had abandoned it. I had to finish the interview and rescue my car—fast!

"Tell me what I need to know, and I'll get you to a hospital. Stall and I'll let you bleed out and just pay the fine to retrieve my car from the police pound. It'll be a little inconvenient for me, but not as much as for you."

"You bastard!"

"Time is running out along with your blood. Let's start with a name—your real name, not a cover name."

"Mary Killigrew."

I said, "You're joking—Mary Killigrew? Your parents must have had a real sense of humor, naming you after a woman pirate."

"Not too many people know about the sixteenth-century woman pirate, but it's true," she answered.

"So are you related to her?" I asked.

"That's the family legend, but I never tried to establish it."

I was enjoying this. "If that's really your name, I bet you were teased a lot in school."

Mary didn't seem amused. "Not really. Most didn't know about the woman pirate, and the ones who did didn't bring it up twice to my face. I don't take well to being teased."

"I can imagine. Okay, Mary, you say you don't work for the Chinese. Who do you work for and why are you following me?" The meter maid wasn't talking on her phone any longer. She was just waiting—a bad sign.

"Who I work for is confidential, but I can tell you I was supposed to make contact with you and determine if you'd be interested in a new job now that you're no longer with the Agency."

"A job offer? I'd want to know who I was working for before I could answer."

"So you may be interested?" she asked.

"If the terms and money were right, it's possible."

"That's not really an affirmation."

"It's not a turndown, either, and you're bleeding. Who is my potential employer?"

"I can't tell you that until you commit to the position," she said.

I chuckled. "I'm not committing until I know who I'd be working for." *Stalemate.*

"Can you tell me why are they interested in me?" I asked.

A police car pulled up next to the meter maid. He turned on his strobes. *Shit! There goes the Corvette.*

She pressed the bloody cloth against the bullet hole in her shoulder as she spoke. "They are interested in employing a cyber-attack master. They liked what you did to China in 1997."

"The 1997 China Reversion Disruption Project was considered a failure. We were supposed to sabotage the Reversion. We didn't."

A tow truck appeared.

She continued. "It wasn't a failure for my people. They made a lot of money on it, and they know you caused the US disruption plot to fail on purpose."

I thought I'd covered it up better than that.

"That was a long time ago. I'm not the same guy now."

"How about the 2003 Shenshou? That time you successfully stopped China's Man-on-the-Moon Project."

"Well—"

"Or in 2011, when you frustrated China's attempt at Mars?"

I grinned. "You make me sound so negative—stopping progress like that."

"No, I'm making the argument that you are a cyber-attack master—possibly the best in the world today." Then she asked, "The Chinese are making another attempt in partnership with the Russians at the Mars project. The launch is this morning—Yinghuo. Did you work your magic on that one too?"

"I don't kiss and tell." Then after a moment of awkward silence, I added, "So I assume you're *not* offering me another government position."

"No, I'd say pretty much the opposite," she said.

"Criminal?" I asked.

"One man's criminal is another man's hero," she quipped.

"I'm not Robin Hood."

Why is she droning on and on, wasting time, while bleeding all over her precious luxury car?

She shot a quick glance at my Corvette being hooked up. "Being Robin Hood is not expected of you. In fact, we will pay you a lot of money for your services. You've demonstrated a high level of skill at the Agency. Now you can make a lot of money using that skill for us," she said.

"For who?" I asked again.

The tow truck pulled away with my Corvette. The meter maid and cop exchanged some parting words and then were gone.

Damn!

Mary dispassionately studied the tiny but steady dribble of blood leaking from her shoulder. "I think you nicked a vein. I need medical."

"It's not life-threatening," I replied.

"Get me to the hospital and we can discuss your future after I'm properly doped and stitched up."

She had been stalling until they towed my car—but why?

Mary really was a pure professional. She wasn't crying or ranting and raving because she'd been shot. Still bleeding rather messily, she had stalled until I was minus my car and then just said, "Get me stitched me up and we'll talk about your new job." All very professional.

I reached for the door handle. "Move over; I'll drive. There is a hospital four blocks away."

I got out and walked to the driver's side, half expecting her to lock me out and drive away, but she didn't, so I opened the door and slipped in behind the wheel. There was a small puddle of blood on the seat. Try as I might to avoid it, by the time we arrived at the hospital my pants were stained.

5

YOU'RE GOING TO BE OKAY

"I'm required to report all gunshot wounds to the police," said the woman doctor with a very heavy Indian accent.

"I am the police," I replied and produced my Agency picture ID and a nice gold badge that said I was a federal agent.

The badge is a forgery. I had it illegally commissioned several years ago. My job description didn't authorize me to carry either a badge or a gun. But I'd found both were sometimes convenient, so I'd spent $1000 to have the badge discreetly constructed. The cost was high to insure discretion and credibility. It was worth every dollar. I had successfully used the combination of badge and ID for everything from weaseling my way out of traffic tickets to crashing investigations I wasn't supposed to be on. Once, a police officer saw the "print" of a pistol under my shirt. He confronted me since only politicians and police can legally carry concealed weapons in DC. I used the badge and ID combination to convince him I was a fellow police officer, entitled to carry a concealed firearm. If you're wondering how come I still had my real ID after retirement, give me a break. Don't you think I could have found a way to acquire a duplicate?

The doctor took a quick look at the badge and ID and said, "Okay, thank you very much."

"Can you tell me how serious Ms. Killigrew's wound is?" I asked her.

"Fortunately, the bullet was slowed by the shoulder strap on the Kevlar Vest she was wearing and didn't hit any arteries or bone. There is only superficial muscle damage. We are keeping her overnight for observation, but if she's doing well in the morning, we can let her go home."

"Will she have any permanent damage?" I asked.

"I expect her to fully recover with no permanent damage except a scar."

"Can I see her?"

"Only for a moment. She's still feeling some shock and needs to rest."

"I won't be long." I smiled at the doctor, but she didn't smile back. She really didn't seem very friendly. I guess guns and badges do that to some people, or maybe I'm not as charming as I think I am.

Mary Killigrew's eyes were closed when I entered her room. At first I wasn't sure whether she was sleeping, but she opened them as soon as I approached the bed. "You still here?" she asked.

"I wanted to be sure you were properly taken care of," I said shyly.

"Well, you have. You can go now."

"I also wanted to inform you I will be borrowing your Mercedes." I rattled her key ring, which included the key fob for the Mercedes.

"Bastard!"

It was eleven in the morning. I had to get moving. "Well, I don't want to get Mr. Planter in trouble by not showing up for my own retirement party. The doctor tells me you're going to be fine after a day's rest. I'll fill your car with gas before I come back tomorrow and take you home or wherever." I turned to leave.

"Wait . . ." she called.

I turned back and asked, "What?"

"Your pants have blood on them."

"It's your blood—from the front seat," I answered.

"Try some hydrogen peroxide. It may clean it off."

"Thanks." I turned to go again.

"Don't wreck my Mercedes, and clean up the blood inside! It's my personal car," she snapped back.

"You shouldn't drive your personal car for work. Only heroes in the movies drive their own cars," I said.

"You were driving your private car—the Corvette."

"I'm retired! That gives me an exemption." I turned to leave again.

She called after me. "Watch your back. There are some people who are not happy with you."

"But I'm retired . . ."

"That only makes you an easier target."

"Why were you really interested in me?" I asked.

"I told you. I was supposed to offer you a job."

"Somehow I don't believe you."

She was silent for a moment then said, "My employer wants some software you developed."

"What software?" I asked.

"I don't know much about it. I'm not a technical expert. I was only supposed to contact you—arrange a meeting with someone who knows more than I do."

This doesn't make sense.

"What software?"

"I wouldn't know. I do know they're willing to pay you a lot of money," she answered.

"Are you working for The Major?"

The Major is a legendary figure in the intelligence community. There have been rumors of The Major since post–World War II, like a campfire story told before bedtime. The legend states that he—or she—watches over all the intelligence agencies to insure they don't get out of control. The Major's position was allegedly created to keep tabs on the newly formed CIA in 1947, because President Truman didn't trust such a large and powerful organization. As other intelligence agencies were created and gained power, The Major expanded his scope to include them. The Major's identity is an absolute secret from everyone—the government even denies the existence of the position. But The Major supposedly has vast resources available. He is funded privately by gold taken from the Japanese after their surrender (who had stolen it from conquered countries all over Asia). Legend states that President Truman had decided there was no practical way to identify individual ownership and return the gold to the rightful owners, so the United States kept the treasure. The treasure had never been accounted for in the official government books, but it had been invested wisely. The vast riches have been frugally spent on intelligence projects since. Anyway, that's the legend. In my opinion, The Major is a folktale told by World War II veterans to inspire awe—a myth.

Mary said, "No, I don't work for The Major. Hopefully he doesn't even know I exist."

I had meant the question as a joke, but she had taken it seriously. Maybe she knew something I didn't. I decided to pursue that issue again at a later time, but right now I needed to be somewhere else.

I turned to go.

"Could you stay a little longer?" she asked with a seductive smile.

She was trying to engage me in long conversation—interrogate me from her hospital bed.

"Why?" I asked.

"I'd feel safer." Her eyes pleaded and then promised a reward.

She's something else—one minute angry, the next seductive.

"I must go." I had to leave before she could seduce me further.

I heard her expel "Bastard" again as I cleared the doorframe.

If this was her in shock, I'd hate to see her at full capacity.

6

WHO IS MARY KILLIGREW?

I sat in Mary Killigrew's Mercedes, in the hospital parking lot, and considered my next move. I had three hours before the luncheon—plenty of time—and I wanted to know more about Mary. I wasn't buying that she had been sent to offer me a job. Why bring a Taser and a gun and wear a bulletproof vest to offer me a job? Why the covert surveillance? Why not just call me up and meet me for lunch? Trust me, if she'd just asked me out for a drink, I'd have been there—job or no job—and I wouldn't have shot her either. No, she wanted something darker. Right now I was thinking she worked for either a foreign government or a criminal organization. I needed to find out which.

But first things first: Mary had said this was her personal car—stupid for her but maybe helpful for me. I opened the center console and found some change and a small bottle of water. The glove box had the usual stuff: a leaking pen, a small box of women's hygiene pads, the car registration, proof of insurance, and a pistol. This one was a heavy, short-barreled, .357 Magnum revolver, made by Smith & Wesson. I pocketed the pistol and the car registration and proof of insurance. I wouldn't need the feminine hygiene products.

I was accumulating a nice gun collection.

I searched the trunk, under the seats, and everywhere else I could think of but found nothing that gave me any working information. I did learn she was single, lived in a townhouse about two miles from my condo, and was a member of a twenty-four-hour gym not far from her townhouse. It wasn't enough. I needed to know more about Mary and especially the people she represented.

She seemed to know a lot about me. Most of it was classified—especially my projects involving China, my area of expertise in the Agency as you may have figured by now. The Agency hired me directly from college and sent me to the Language School at Presidio of Monterey to learn Mandarin, which used up over a year of my life. After that, I attended a very restricted spy school in Maryland and then studied advanced and very specialized subjects at several private universities and trade schools. In the past twenty years, I have probably spent a third of my life in one school or the other. Mary somehow knew this. That wasn't good. If she knew, others did too.

I was especially concerned about the Chinese finding out. The Chinese can be vindictive. If they learn I'd been the biggest thorn in their space-program saddle for the past twenty years, they would have no compunction about squishing me like a bug—retired or not.

I had to find out who Mary represented and why they wanted me. I needed to evaluate the level of danger I was exposed to, so I decided to follow the trail in front of me. I had her address, her key, and time to look through her townhouse.

Mary lived outside the Beltway in an exclusive area. She probably had a few senators for neighbors. The guarded community sat behind a locked gate. I drove up to the entrance where an armed guard was talking to a carpet-cleaning van with two workers, apparently there to clean a residences' carpets. Deliveries and service venders would need to check in with the security kiosk to enter; however, residents could drive directly in, gratis a transponder attached to their cars.

I stopped in front of the resident entrance, the gate automatically swung open, and I drove in. It was just that easy. It took me another few minutes to find her townhouse. I stopped in front and sat quietly for several moments, studying the neighborhood and her two-story, brown-brick townhouse. There was a two-car garage. I saw no cars parked on the street. That probably meant residents didn't park on the street and my doing so could draw unwanted attention, so I pulled into her driveway, found the garage door controller, and drove into her garage.

From there it got easier. She had not bothered to lock the connecting door leading inside the townhouse. My only concern was a possible alarm system. I stood at the connecting door and fretted for at least thirty seconds before deciding it was getting me nowhere, so I opened the door and stepped into a laundry room which in turn lead to the kitchen. I quickly looked around for an alarm panel, found it, and determined she had not set the alarm before leaving this morning. I was in.

You want to learn about someone, find their pile of mail, especially the junk mail that everyone receives every day. Of course, you look at the bills and any personal correspondence, of which there is very little in today's age of online banking; electronic mail; and social media. But the catalogues and solicitations for denotations from charitable organizations can also tell you a lot about people. For example, a gun enthusiast receives catalogues about gun supplies, ammunition, camping, hunting, and military surplus. If you donate money to the Trail of Tears Foundation to help the plight of the American Indian, soon other charities begin sending you solicitations for donations, such as Save the Animals. Donate to Planned Parenthood and soon you're receiving requests from . . . well, you get the idea. These items tell you about the person.

Mary had no mail stacked anywhere—nothing. That meant she was either the neatest single woman on the planet and tossed the junk mail as soon as it came in, or she wasn't on anyone's mailing list, which is highly unlikely. It could mean she didn't get mail here. Maybe she has a post office box.

I searched the entire downstairs of the townhouse, looking for any clues about Mary and who she represented, but found nothing. It was sterile—like a model home. I walked upstairs. There was a master bedroom, a master bath, and a second bedroom she'd converted into a small office.

I sat at the computer and stared at the dark screen. It was worth a try. I turned on the computer and waited for it to boot. Of course, it asked for the password. I had no idea. There was an icon button—forgot your password?—to click to receive a hint of the password. I clicked the icon. The hint simply said, "On the monitor."

So I began entering what I saw on the face of the computer, one item at a time:

HP—no.

Intel—no.

Windows 10—no.

I was worried the system would soon freeze up because of the string of wrong guesses. Then I saw a small pink heart sticker—the type a child might put on the computer to decorate it. I typed "pink heart" but was rejected. Then I tried "LOVE," all caps. The computer screen went blank and then flashed, "Welcome Mary." I was in.

I spent the next half hour searching her files and even got into her email account. She was permanently signed on, silly girl. I found her online banking records and searched the source of her income. I learned that she received a respectably-sized transfer of funds once per month from a corporation I'd never heard of: Panzram, Inc.

I heard a noise. Someone was downstairs, and he wasn't being particularly quiet. Maybe it was a boyfriend? I didn't need that. I shut down the computer and quietly eased to the doorway to peek out, but I couldn't see anything. I slipped down the hallway and peered over the staircase to the bottom floor. I saw two men. Neither was a boyfriend—I was sure. They were dressed in blue coveralls with a logo printed on their backs—carpet cleaners, the truck that had been at the guard kiosk when I drove into the complex. But they weren't setting up any cleaning equipment. They were searching the townhouse. I heard them opening and closing the closet doors and pulling out drawers. They were looking in all the places I had, but they were very noisy.

One guy was large—I mean big around. He easily weighed over two hundred pounds without being over five feet six inches. His partner was tall and skinny—over six feet—but probably weighed less than one hundred seventy pounds. I called them Mutt and Jeff. You younger readers may not know that Mutt and Jeff was a popular comic strip in our fathers' and grandfathers' times.

Anyway, Mutt—the shorter guy—must be the boss, because he told Jeff to go upstairs and look around.

I hustled to the bathroom and hid in the shower. As soon as I stepped into the shower I realized it was stupid. Anyone walking in would see my form through the frosted glass. I hadn't been thinking straight, but it's what I'd done and I was stuck with it. It was too late to change now. I heard his footsteps in the hallway.

Just go with it.

Jeff had a heavy footstep. He went directly into the office, fumbled around for a few seconds, then came out and called down to Mutt. "I found her computer."

Mutt shouted back, "Box it up, and anything else that looks informative."

"I don't have a box!" Jeff shouted back.

"Do I have to come up there and do it for you? Use your brain," Mutt shouted back.

They're having a lover's spat.

Jeff was mumbling to himself. I heard him open the closet door and rummage around. I decided to act.

I'm not like my younger brother Tom Wolfe, who is a natural-born fighter. I never took to fighting. I'm more of a thinker and a lover than a fighter. But that doesn't mean I can't do what has to be done. I stepped out of the shower and slipped across the hall into the office. Jeff had his back to me with his head bent over in the closet. He'd found a cardboard box and was just straightening up when I stepped in behind and swung just as hard as I could with my pistol, hitting him on the back of the head. I didn't want to kill him—just knock him out—but I didn't want him to just be hurt and start yelling either.

He fell to the floor and didn't move. I used a lamp cord to "hog tie" his hands and feet, stuffed a washcloth into his mouth, and then locked the cloth in place with some clear plastic tape I found in the desk.

I listened but couldn't hear Mutt downstairs. That bothered me. He'd been noisy before. What was he doing? I slipped to the staircase and looked over to the ground floor but didn't see him, so I dashed back to the office. I quickly searched Jeff and found a 9mm Beretta, a leather sap filled with lead buckshot, and a wallet. Inside the wallet was a license to carry the pistol. There was a matching driver's license and several credit cards. His real name wasn't Jeff, but that's not important right now.

I heard Mutt coming upstairs. If Jeff had a heavy footstep, then Mutt was a T-Rex.

"What the fuck you doing up here? Smelling her panties?" cried out Mutt as he ascended the stairs.

I dashed across the hall, back into the bathroom and into the shower again. I know it was stupid, but it's what I did.

I heard Mutt enter the office and say, "What the fuck?"

I dashed across the hallway and hit Mutt across the back of the head with Jeff's leather sap. He screamed, blood splattering around the room. It was messy. I guess you need to practice this stuff if you're going to depend on it.

Mutt turned on me and charged head down, like an angry bull protecting his lady cows. I hit him three more times with the sap, directly on the top of his head in rapid succession as I backed up. Mutt finally fell at my feet. His legs trembled for a few seconds then he was still. A puddle of blood began spreading from his skull. I quickly searched him and found another Beretta and a wallet. He also had a license to carry, and his name wasn't Mutt.

By this time the blood had made quite a puddle. It was messy, and the copper-like smell filled my nostrils. After a few deep breaths to compose myself, I tied and gagged Mutt.

Jeff stared at me with hateful eyes. He was trembling. His gag didn't allow him to verbalize, but I could see he really wanted to express himself. Now was the time to have a little talk, before he composed, so I ripped off the plastic tape and removed his gag.

Jeff screamed, "You fucking animal! You killed my partner."

"You two were close?" I asked.

"That's not your business," he shot back.

"Well, your partner is not dead yet, but if you want him to live you'd better cooperate with me."

I have to give Jeff credit: he calmed down and asked, "What do you want to know?"

"Who do you work for?"

"We're security employees for the Panzram Company."

"What does the Panzram Company do?"

"What do you mean?"

He can't be that stupid.

"Why does Panzram exist? How does it make money?" I explained.

"I don't know. We just do odd jobs. They tell us to do something, we do it, and they pay us."

"You don't expect me to believe you don't know what they do?"

"We're just contractors."

"You said you were employees a moment ago—now you're saying your contractors. Which is it—employee or contractor?" I asked.

He stared at me like I was speaking Greek.

"All right, let's try something easier. What were you looking for in here?"

"We were told to pack up her computer and any files or paper documents she had and bring them in. If we found a safe, we were supposed to clean it out too. Everything—money, insurance papers, anything we found."

"Did they tell you why?" I asked.

"No, except that she's in the hospital and wouldn't be coming out—she's terminal. We've done this before after a Panzram employee has been fired or dies. The company doesn't want anything that leads to them for others to find."

Her wound is superficial.

"What do you mean she's terminal?" I asked.

"I don't know. It's just what I was told."

There's little more to learn from this guy.

I needed to learn more about the Panzram Company, and about Mary. Also, I wanted to know why Sprout was having me followed. There was only one place to go—the Fort.

"Okay, here's what going to happen: I'm leaving you tied up. I'm taking her computer and papers. I'll call 911 and get an ambulance sent here for your partner. The front door will be left open so they can get in. You can yell and direct them upstairs when they arrive. After that you're on your own. Maybe you can talk yourself out of this."

"You bastard!" he hissed at me as I carried Mary's computer out.

Everyone's calling me that lately.

7

THE OFFICE

There's no better place to learn everything about anyone on earth than Fort Meade. That was my next destination.

I negotiated the heavy morning traffic. The Agency's building complex is located just over the border, in Maryland. There are no signs to indicate that it is there, but once you see it there is no doubt you have found it. While I crept along the toll road, I subconsciously listened to the world's problems on the car's radio and wrestled with my own.

Is that what the younger generation calls multitasking?

I started paying attention to the woman announcer midsentence.

". . . reported that the Chinese-Russian space mission, Yinghuo 34, failed to launch this morning from the Baikonur Cosmodrome in southern Russia. Yinghuo 34 is part of the joint Chinese and Russian space program to construct an orbiting launch platform for the manned Mars mission in 2020. Reports coming in are sketchy, but it is believed that all four astronauts on board—two from China and two from Russia—are unharmed. The rockets failed to ignite, and it is rumored the guidance system failed to come online. Sources are reporting that all the electronics onboard the spacecraft failed. If true, this represents a massive setback for the joint mission to put men on Mars. Both the Chinese and Russian space agencies have refused to comment on the failed launched . . ."

The irony of it all made me smile. It meant that my Trojan Terminator program worked as designed, but I'm not supposed to tell you about that— it's super–high classified. I wondered whether this was the program Mary's people wanted me to give up. If so, they must know the trick isn't the program but the method of delivery. Any talented high school kid could probably design the program, but getting past the security, performing a proper installation, and executing the program without leaving a footprint takes a considerable amount of skill and sometimes luck. That is my expertise. That's what makes me a cut above.

My mind turned back to the news.

". . . In another story, sources say multibillionaire William Kincade, who was found dead at his home in Virginia this weekend, apparently died of a heart attack. William Kincade is the grandson of the founder of the Kincade Bank and Great Eastern Kincade Railroad. Kincade was also the CEO of Kincade Broadcasting. He was 87. In sports . . ."

Another billionaire bites the dust. I guess money can't buy immortality.

I parked in the visitor's lot at Fort Meade because the employee's lot was completely blocked off and full of federal police vehicles. They were still investigating Jimmy's death. I saw no local police cars.

First rule for a government cover-up: don't let the locals get involved.

I exited Mary's Mercedes and walked along the wide walkway that leads to the main entrance of the massive black building. When I officially worked here, I would enter via the employee entrance, located on the side of the building, using a magnetic card key. Employees pass through an airport like security station with body scanners and armed guards even though they have a card key. Today, I would enter through the main lobby. After all, I'm supposed to be retired.

As I walked along the wide sidewalk, I kept my face pointed at the ground so the cameras couldn't get a decent fix on me. It was a habit reinforced over a lifetime of training and practice. I also changed my gait and posture in an attempt to at least confuse the Fort Meade surveillance computers—maybe slow them down in identifying me. The effort was meaningless. The computer would have me identified before I made it to the front door.

Today, the Agency's Human ID Recognition Software—HIRS—is science-fiction-level scary. It is so powerful that no amount of sunglasses or hooded sweatshirts can hide your identity. With today's technology, being able to hide your identity by covering up your face is a myth. The new software not only recognizes body language and facial expressions to identify people but also predicts their intended behavior. HIRS can predict if a person intends to do something illegal with ninty-five percent or higher confidence level. HIRS even predicts the precise illegal act that is being contemplated—theft, kidnapping, robbery, etc. Someone known only as Shaman allegedly developed the current system. I don't know if there really is such a person or not, but that's the rumor.

Like many of the Agency's secrets, the existence of HIRS has been kept from even Congress and other agencies. What surprises me, in this age of purported cooperation between agencies, is that the Agency doesn't make the software available to Homeland Security and local police agencies. If used properly, the software could stop rapes, robberies, and terrorists in advance. HIRS exists, but the Agency doesn't want anyone to know, so it is grossly underutilized.

And that's the intelligence community's mindset in a nutshell . . .

I entered the building. The main lobby is meant for VIPs: senators, congressmen, and the occasional Boy Scout troop. Primarily, it is designed to look good to those who control the budget. Ironically, the real public is rarely allowed in the lobby, and never allowed inside the work area of the building. Tourists are politely turned away. Even so, the lobby is the Agency's public face.

The first thing most people notice when they enter, high on the wall, is a very large marble plaque with the Agency's official mission statement engraved in gold lettering. The statement is a long, rambling paragraph of misleading crap that no one who works here ever pays attention to—most have never read it, or did their first day of orientation, then they promptly forgot it—so I won't bore you with it now.

In reality, the Agency's mission is to: Learn everyone's secrets and maintain a technological advantage over all other nations—friendly or not—by any means necessary.

Like most large organizations these days, the Agency also has a publically stated set of values. The Agency displays its "official" values in four-inch black lettering, welded to a huge, silver plaque. The plaque is bolted high on the opposite wall from the Mission Statement, and is the second thing most visitors notice. The Agency's officially stated values are:

+ Honesty
+ Respect for the Law

- Integrity
- Transparency

The official values are a prime example of misinformation. I learned early in my tenure with the Agency that its true values are:

- Misinform Everyone About Everything.
- Deny Everything—Even If Caught Red-Handed.
- Learn Everyone's Secrets Anyway You Can.
- Trust No One.

I walked across the large, open lobby to the security-screening chokepoint. The uniformed armed guard recognized me and nodded as I swiped my magnetic card key across the plate.

"Good morning Mr. Wolfe," he greeted me. "I thought you retired."

"Not quite yet. Just one last time . . . I need to clear up some old business and say goodbye to a couple people," I answered with a smile.

My picture, with APPROVED inside a green bar, flashed for the guard to see. He pushed the button to allow me entrance to the scanner airlock that was more sophisticated than used in airports. The scanner didn't set off any alarms so I was cleared to pass. I had left the pistol and other forbidden objects in Mary's car.

Are you wondering how I got in so easy?

Well, I had a valid ID. I know you're thinking when someone retires, management takes away their security passes and IDs—right? But I told you earlier I had furtively filched a duplicate security pass and ID. If you don't remember the encounter with the doctor, then you haven't been paying attention. Obtaining a duplicate ID was a trick my first training officer put me onto. He was old school, grandfathered into the Agency when the US Army had disbanded the ASA—the army's own private version of electronic intelligence collection—in the early 1970s.

You may be asking why the security computer didn't reject my ID as a retiree. Well, it had only been one week since my last day at work. The IT people hadn't taken me out of the computer yet—lazy government workers—and the guard was still used to seeing me, so my entrance wasn't challenged.

As I waited for the elevator to arrive, I rehashed the radio news account about this morning's failed Russian-Chinese launch. My mind drifted back to my beginning at the Agency, when I was still very young and idealistic. I had just completed the Electronic Intercept School in Maryland. My first assignment was to "monitor" the Hong Kong "Reversion." That's what the Chinese were calling the process to bring Hong Kong back under the Communist Chinese control after the ninety-nine-year lease expired in 1997. The Chinese desperately wanted the process to go very smoothly, with no violence or miscommunications. They wanted to prove they could be civilized. There were no planned executions or land seizures—at least not immediately. The British, wanting the world to believe they were true gentlemen, had agreed to assist in that goal. However, for some reason not told to me, the American Administration did not want the Reversion to go smoothly, but, of course, they couldn't announce that openly.

I was just one member of a large team that was monitoring the Reversion's progress from a classified location. But my duties migrated when my supervisor instructed me to electronically cause problems for the transfer of power. I was to find ways to "disrupt and distort communications." The goal was to create a severe international incident. It was just the type of skullduggery the Agency does all the time, but since it was my first real assignment I didn't know that at the time.

I decided what the Agency wanted to do wasn't right, so I performed some skullduggery of my own. I was able to make contact with a beautiful Chinese Agent, named Hong Li, who was loyally performing her duties, both in and outside the bedroom. Together, we made sure the Reversion went as planned—with no problems. Because the American administration had wanted the Reversion to fail, and it didn't, my assignment was considered a failure. But since I was just a worker bee—new to the Agency—my supervisor took the hit for the failure. His career went in the toilet and mine continued on. As far as I know, even to this day, no one has ever suspected I had anything to do with my supervisor's failure except possibly Mary's employer. The failure became known in the secret whisperings of the Agency's hallways—and in the toilet stalls—as "The 1997 Chinese Fiasco."

The elevator arrived, and a few moments later I stepped out onto the sixth floor. My ex-boss's secretary was posted nearby in what passed for a reception area. She was the gatekeeper for the executive floor. I had been hoping she wouldn't be in yet, or maybe making a run to the powder room, but luck just wasn't with me.

"Oh, hello Mr. Wolfe; I didn't know you were coming in today?" Her forced, phony smile was legendary in the Agency.

"Good morning Ms. Dingle ..." (Not her real name—at Tony's insistence). "...Yes, I had a couple of things to clear up . . . thought I'd do it before the party this afternoon."

"Should I call Mr. Sprout? I'm sure he'd like to see you."

"He's not in? Too bad. No, that's not necessary. He's a busy man, and I'll see him at the party later. Have a nice day!" I returned her phony grin and briskly walked to my old office.

Encountering Ms. Dingle reminded me how risky coming here was, but I had little choice if I wanted answers. Sprout was having me followed (remember New Guy/Squirmy—Planter). Why, I couldn't guess. But there had to be a reason, and I needed to learn it. I planned to wire Sprout's office so later I could sit at home and monitor what was going on. I had to get Ms. Dingle away from her workstation for a few minutes to accomplish that.

Unfortunately, it wasn't quite that simple. I couldn't just place a transmitter bug in Sprout's office. The Agency's facility was swept regularly for such things. Plus, the walls were sandwiched in a copper-wire grid that was alive with a fluctuating, electric current that randomly changed wavelengths, and power levels, at irregular intervals. The wiring created a barrier that no unauthorized cell, radio, or other wireless signals could penetrate. Even the windows had the thin wire mesh to block electronic transmissions in both directions.

But there are ways . . .

I entered my old office and was greeted by the mess, which was just like I'd left it a week ago. I guess I'm not a very neat person. There were still papers and knick-knacks scattered throughout the cramped little office. What can I say? It looked—and felt—lived in.

I powered up my former computer. It was an older model that still used *Windows 7* and was overloaded with programs. Also, its memory was full, so it took a minute to boot up.

While I waited for the terminal to come to life, I crossed over to a small wall safe. The safe was there to store classified documents and flash drives, but I had used it to store a few more exotic items I had managed to covertly collect over the years—all completely unauthorized. The safe's combination had not been changed. I opened it, stared into my toy box, and then quickly filled my pockets with gadgets that weren't inventoried to me. They were still here because there were security checks when leaving the building. Therefore, opportunities for smuggling items out of the building were limited. Today, I intended to make a special opportunity so I could take my toys home.

However, there was one particular item I planned to leave here—a small black plastic capsule called a Remora. The Remora was invented by an Agency employee twenty-five years ago and is still being used today. It was named after the small sucker fish that attach themselves to sharks and other sea life. The remora feeds off the leftovers from the larger fish, enjoying a commensal relationship. The Agency's Remora attaches to the input cable of a computer monitor and records everything displayed on the monitor. It then encrypts and burst-transmits the data every twenty-four hours to a designated server, using the host computer's email account but without leaving a record of the data being sent. Even if someone finds the encrypted data, it would appear to be a typo hidden inside an authorized transmission. I can receive the data either on a computer set up specifically for this purpose at my Old Rock House in Shenandoah Valley or on my smartphone.

This Remora was for Sprout. It was the item I needed to get into his office without Ms. Dingle's knowledge. I slipped the Remora into my pocket.

The IT people had not removed my computer ID and passcode, either, like they should have, so I was able to sign into the secure system with no problems. My clearance level, along with the authorization access codes I knew, gave me full access to all Agency data-gathering systems.

I began a full-spectrum check of Mary Killigrew. The Agency uses proprietary search-engine software I'll call Oversee. My attorney insisted I not reveal the real name of the program, lest I go to jail. Oversee can unearth just about everything there is to know about anyone on the planet.

It only took a few minutes to learn all about Mary, including her bank information, which confirmed she received a sizable electronic payment each month from Panzram, Inc. I learned everywhere she had traveled in the past two years, who she'd traveled with, where she'd bought gas, and her medical history, including prescription drugs and the type of contraceptive she used. I learned where she shopped, including what groceries and clothing she bought. I discovered what satellite television programs she watched, plus a hundred other small details about Mary Killigrew's life that she probably didn't even realize about herself. This could be the last time I'd have this level of access so easily, so I decided to make a flash-drive copy of all the data. There was a large amount, and it took several minutes to download.

I know what you're thinking: what I just did is illegal. The government can't obtain that information without getting a warrant signed by a judge. Medical information is even covered by a special provision of law—giving it extra privacy—right? Wrong! Remember the Patriot Act of 2001, amended in 2006? The Patriot Act gives the government authority—a loophole—to learn whatever it wishes to learn.

Next, I signed into the X-Key Essential Program—another very powerful, classified program I'm not supposed to tell you about—and downloaded all social media contacts, emails, and internet hits Mary had made in the past three years. It also listed all the websites she had visited, even the ones where she deleted the history. I downloaded her texts and printed a listing of who she talked to on the telephone. Then I downloaded computer-generated texts of her telephone conversations. The data was substantial, and I'd probably never go through all of it, but something specific could be accessed later. This data was sorted by date and physical address from where it originated. More importantly, the X-Key Essential Program allows me to link her phone, text, and email to my personal phone so I can listen to and read all future communications in real time. Each time she called or came online, I would be notified.

I searched for the Panzram Company. I learned Panzram was a privately held, not-for-profit company organized out of Canada. I pulled the incorporation papers and learned the names of the corporate officers and their addresses and then searched the backgrounds on each of them. They were all prominent billionaires. The corporation's stated purpose was "to further the human existence," whatever that means.

By this time I was accumulating a massive amount of data. It would take me weeks to sort through it if I did nothing else. I didn't think I had that kind of time. I found a flash drive and filled it with data. But there was still more data, and I had no more storage drives with me.

(Note: my editor tells me that I'm throwing too much technical detail at the readers and I will lose most of you. I think not. Please prove me right and keep reading. We'll sort out any confusion later.)

By this time, I still hadn't learned why my own people—er . . . ex-people—at the Agency would be following me. Why not let me go quietly into the darkness of retirement? I decided to find out, but the Agency has an absolute firewall feature on its computers that forbid any remote invasion of Agency files. I needed to find out what was on Sprout's personal files. To do so, I had to physically access it from his terminal. That's why I had the Remora. It was time to sneak into Sprout's office.

That meant I had to motivate Ms. Dingle to leave her post. Also, it wouldn't do for Sprout to walk into his office while I was performing my skullduggery. I had to be sure no one would interrupt me for at least fifteen—preferably thirty—minutes.

I needed a fire drill.

8

FIRE DRILL

I departed my former office and turned the corner and walked toward the restrooms. I casually nodded good morning to several people who recognized me. No one asked why I was back or what I was doing or said, "I thought you retired." Remember, it had only been a week, and they were still used to seeing me around. Also, the culture of the Agency is to keep everything secret and compartmentalized, so others don't know what you are doing. Therefore, people didn't ask a lot of questions about one another's work.

There was a fire control station next to the men's room. I unlocked the door (yes, the Agency taught me that skill too). Inside was a state-of-the-art control panel. There was also emergency equipment: first aid kits, fire clothing, tools, and other gear hanging on the walls. I activated a fire signal for the fifth floor, west corner. I heard the fire alarm activate. I waited one minute and activated the fire alarms for the fifth floor, east corner. I waited thirty-seconds then set off the general alarm for the full fifth floor. I waited a few more seconds before activating the alarm for the sixth floor. I was simulating a fire that was a hot and fast-moving.

The automated system would call a full response fire alert and fill the building with carbon monoxide to starve the fire of oxygen. Of course, everyone would be evacuated and made to stand outside while emergency personnel took a roll call and the firefighters searched the building for the fire. Even after they determined there was no fire, they would look for the reason the false alarms activated. It would be a minimum of an hour before the "all clear" sounded and the workers were allowed to return to work.

I selected an oxygen mask, an orange jacket, a white fire helmet, and then grabbed a long, heavy flashlight. As an afterthought, I buckled on a utility belt that carried a few hand tools—crowbars and such. Now I looked like an official emergency building coordinator—like I was supposed to be there during a fire.

I waited another full minute before stepping out into a deserted hallway. I could hear people scrambling down the stairwell—no elevators during a fire drill. Their voices sounded like a million hornets buzzing.

I knew the cameras would still be recording my every move. I would need to make a stop in the basement before leaving the building today.

Ms. Dingle had evacuated like everyone else, and following Agency protocol she had locked her desk and Sprout's outer door before leaving. Again, the lock presented no real barrier, and I was able enter Sprout's office within seconds. I sat at his desk.

There's not a loose piece of paper or personal item anywhere.

Sprout must be a cyborg. He had no personal items anywhere in the office. Also he apparently never left scratch pads or loose papers carelessly lying around. The office looked like it was not occupied.

He'd get along fine with Mary.

While the system was booting up, I unplugged the monitor feeder cable from the monitor and attached the Remora at the neck of the plug. The Remora looked like it was an extension of the plug itself and was exactly the same color as the cable. Whoever happened to look at the monitor cable—why they would do that I don't know—would probably not notice the inconspicuous capsule. Even if someone did notice it they would think it was an integral part of the input cable, unless they were a highly trained, cyber-spy expert.

I would now be able to see everything that was done on this computer. The device had a forever life-span. The only way it would ever be detected was if the security geeks knew it was there and looked for it, or when the monitor was physically replaced—not the computer. Even if one of those events occurred, it would still be a dead end. The Remora capsule was an Agency device. Using an Agency device to spy on an Agency employee was not unusual. The Agency spied on its own all the time. Remember how this started? New Guy had been following me. It was a closed loop.

Spout's computer had an upgraded operating system, which, ironically, made it easier for me to breech (never mind the technical details). I went in the backdoor as a system administrator; the same way your computer at home is automatically updated without you having anything to say about it.

Next, I connected the X-Key Essential Program to Sprout's computer and cell phone number, so I could be alerted to any phone calls, emails, or text messages to or from him.

Finally, I scanned his email inbox. Almost immediately I found a message from Sprout two weeks before my retirement. I caught it so fast because it had my name in the subject line. It was addressed to the Agency's director, not Sprout's boss, which is curious, because the director is two levels above Sprout in the food chain. Sending the director an email without going through the chain of command is a major breech in bureaucratic decorum, which is usually not good for one's career.

It was classified CONFIDENTIAL—EYES ONLY.

The email read:

> Senior Intelligence Officer and Bureau Chief (China Desk) John Wolfe recently intercepted verbal communication referencing the Order of the Golden Squirrel. The intercept was between the Deputy Chairman of the People's Republic of China Space Agency and a ranking member of the Order. The topic was American space-program technology.
>
> I am concerned that Wolfe may be conducting a covert investigation on the Order. If so, the outcome has the potential of being adverse and undesirable.
>
> Awaiting instructions.
>
> T. S. Sprout, Chief
>
> Electronic Surveillance Division

A typically cryptic government message with poor grammar, but I was used to that after twenty years.

Is this why I was under surveillance?

Sprout had been riding me like a tick on a hound dog since he had wormed himself into the Division Chief position five years ago. Now he wanted to screw with me one last time, and since I was gone, the only punishment available would be sending me to federal prison and causing me to lose my pension.

And people call me a bastard.

But more interestingly, the email hinted at some internal conspiracy that included Sprout and the director, cutting out the normal chain of command. The Chinese had been trying to steal American technology for decades, but this sounded like the Agency was helping them. It also referenced something called the Order of the Golden Squirrel. Squirrels? Give me a break. It sounded like some kid's club. Why would some juvenile club be an interest—forget about a threat—to either China or the United States?

Focus! The email said you intercepted the verbal communication—a phone call.

At first, I didn't remember the elect-intel Sprout was referencing. I searched my memory and then vaguely remembered a telephone communication that had been intercepted and immediately discounted about a month ago. Could that be the "verbal communication" Sprout was referencing? I remembered laughing about someone in China talking to someone in the United States about squirrels. I briefly considered that "squirrels" could be a code word for something sinister, but I was already closing down operations, in anticipation of my retirement. So I sent a note to Jimmy Trang, and promptly forgot about it. I didn't follow up. Obviously, Sprout had a stake in this squirrel conspiracy and was concerned I had followed up.

Is that why Jimmy was killed?

The irony is if Sprout hadn't done anything, I would have gone into retirement quietly, and his precious secret would have remained safe. But not now. Now, I was interested and wanted to learn more—a lot more.

I initiated a search for references to the Order of the Golden Squirrel. At first, I found nothing, which was surprising. I thought, *maybe it isn't real,* so I dug deeper and finally found a thread. There were no official documentation about such an organization, but I did find several electronic intercepts in the database referencing the Order of the Golden Squirrel dating as far back as 1968.

In the 1960s, a lot of oversees communications were monitored by the Army Security Agency—ASA. The ASA was dissolved in the early seventies and their best people were transferred to the Agency. I learned that the first references to the Order of the Golden Squirrel were discovered by ASA.

I also discovered that two corporate officers from the Panzram Corporation were noted in a 1968 ASA report on the Order of the Golden Squirrel. Texts of their telephone communications were scattered throughout the ASA interceptions between several different foreign military personnel.

However, what really got my attention was a much more recent intercept: a telephone conversation between a staff member of US Senator Fetterson and, of all people, T. S. Sprout. Fetterson is a senior US senator from Washington State who chairs several very powerful committees. The conversation referenced both the Order and Panzram Company, but always in some vague, foggy way. I needed time to dig deeper and digest the information, and time wasn't something I had much of at this time. So I began downloading the data for study at a later time.

My flash drive signaled full. I looked around for a spare, but Sprout had followed Agency rules to the letter. There wasn't one to be had. I needed this information, and I couldn't print it out and carry it out of the building. Even a fire drill wouldn't give me that much leeway. I might be searched. I would need to depend on the Remora to pick up what I'd displayed on Sprout's monitor and burst-transmit it to my server. However, my hacking into Sprout's computer would show up on the security audit that was done daily. I had to erase any trace of my snooping around. My head began spinning on how to do damage control. There were too many ways they could know I had been here snooping around.

I must destroy the archives.

9

TECHNICAL SERVICES DIVISION

I'd been skulking around Sprout's office too long. The firefighters would be here at any moment, looking for the fire. It was time to get out before I was caught with my hand in the skullduggery cookie jar.

Because of the fire alarm, no one except firefighters and security personnel were supposed to be in the building, but I was dressed like a fireman and should have no trouble. I took the stairs to the basement level. On the third-floor landing I encountered three real firemen coming up—apparently physically checking each floor for evidence of a fire.

The lead fireman stopped me and asked, "What are you doing here?"

"I was inspecting the executive level. I'm security; making sure all the big shots are out safely. They have a tendency to ignore fire drills and hide in their offices. I'm supposed to round up the strays."

"So everyone is out?" he asked.

"Yep—all clear." I answered.

"You see any evidence of fire?" he asked.

"Nope—I saw nothing up there." I was trying to be unmemorable.

"Okay, get out of the building!"

"That's my intention," I answered as they brushed past me.

The Agency's basement level is where Technical Services Division—TSD—is located. For you spy movie buffs, TSD is roughly equivalent to Q Branch of the popular James Bond movie series. The tiny electronic gadgets used to spy on others are issued from TSD. TSD is also the keeper of the Agency's Big Momma computer, which is so powerful I can't even begin to tell you what it can do without sounding like a science fiction novel and losing all credibility—you wouldn't believe me. The Agency's secure server network is also located in TSD, which is different from Big Momma. TSD is responsible for internal security and providing the espionage equipment for the Agency. So the basement is like a big box store at Christmas for spies.

As soon as I stepped into the main room, I saw two security guards standing post; watching over the Agency's secrets.

Damn!

Like I indicated before, I'm not my younger brother, Tom. I'm a lover and a thinker—not a fighter. I don't have the temperament to stand toe-to-toe with a tough guy and put him in the hospital. I'm sure my younger brother would have just walked up to these thugs and beaten them senseless within a few seconds, but I don't work that way if I can avoid it.

I approached them and said, "Hi, guys! I came down here to tell you you've been ordered to evacuate to the parking lot. You're in danger down here. I'm supposed to go through and make sure everyone is outside and everything is secure, and then I'll be directly behind you, so let's go!"

They stared at me: blink-blink.

It's not working.

One of the men must have had a brain, because he asked, "Why didn't they contact us directly?" He clicked on his two-way radio and began to call for confirmation.

Oh well, sometimes there's no choice.

I hit the radio guy with the heavy flashlight. He went down without a sound. His partner went for his sidearm too late, because I caught him next. It happened so fast even I was surprised. They lay in a pile at my feet.

Maybe little brother's way sometimes has merit after all.

I knew I had very little time.

One of the fallen security guards had a key ring. I liberated it and immediately went to the nasty-tricks room. I already knew what I needed and exactly where it was. I'd known about this weapon for two decades, but I had not been authorized to be issued one. I was looking for a compact aerosol spray can, similar in appearance to a small can of pepper spray. Only this spray—invented by the Russians four decades ago—discharged a highly refined mixture of toluene and manganese derivatives combined with a catalyst agent that, when breathed in sufficient quantities, causes a stroke.

There were three cans locked inside a glass cabinet. I used the key ring to open the case and took all three cans. You never know.

Next, I needed to sabotage the DVD recordings from the security cameras in and around the building. I'd been skulking around—up to no good—for almost an hour now, and it had all been recorded. I knew there were the main recorders and simultaneous backup recordings being made in a separate room, so that meant two sets of disks had to be destroyed.

I stood in front of the banks of DVD machines. There were two-dozen recorders running at the same time. I opened each DVD recorder. They were all empty.

What the . . .?

Standard procedure is to keep the machines recording 24-7. I went to the backup room and looked, with the same results. The DVDs were all gone! Who had removed them? Had they been removed before or after they had recorded my skullduggery?

Something is seriously wrong here.

I was about to exit TSD—thinking there was nothing I could do about it right now—when I had a haunting thought. I really wasn't an expert in this technology and didn't know whether these machines digitally stored the most recent hour in the DVD recorders—similar to my satellite DVR at home. At home I could play back programs on my television for the most recent hour. The programs were saved digitally, without the need for a disk. The Agency prided itself on having the most cutting-edge technology. If these machines had that digital feature, the security people would still be able to pull up the most recent images from the temporary digital recordings. And there I'd be—performing my skullduggery, all on video. I couldn't take that chance. Also, the Agency's server would have the audit trail of me using Sprout's computer while he wasn't in the office.

I need a real fire.

After all, the fire alarms had warned everyone. I found a gallon of denatured alcohol in the supply room. I think the techies use it to clean electronic equipment, but I know for sure that it is very flammable.

I splashed the alcohol all over, under, around, and through the recorders in both rooms. Next, I found a spray can of air freshener in the women's toilet and a lighter in a nearby desk. The jet stream fire from the can of air freshener would be as hot as a flamethrower and would project a stream of fire several feet. More importantly, using an aerosol spray would allow me to stay at a safe distance when the flame hit the denatured alcohol. The effect was explosive. I still had to jump back several feet not to be engulfed in the flames. It was a perfect way to completely destroy the electronics in TSD. I had used up the full can of air freshener by the time I'd finished burning the backup recorders. The carbon monoxide fire suppressers kicked on, but it was too late. The denatured alcohol fire had already done its work.

Then I remembered the server.

I ran to the opposite end of the basement where the Agency's server is located. The door was locked. It was a heavy-duty, fireproof vault door. I wouldn't be able to kick it open, and the lock wasn't within my capability to pick.

Damn!

Then I remembered the guard's key ring. Yes, one of the keys fit the lock. I was inside seconds later, pouring more alcohol into the server, and then I repeated the air freshener–flame thrower process, using a second can of freshener I'd found in the other rest room. The smoke and carbon monoxide fire suppressers were now so thick I could barely see the exit. If it hadn't been for my oxygen mask, I would have asphyxiated. Plus, the air was being burned up, so I left the vault door and stairwell door open so air could feed the flames. The fire was so hot, and burned so fast, I knew the damage I hoped for was done.

It was getting very hot in TSD. I had to leave. Then I remembered the two security guards. I'd left them unconscious in the main room. I didn't intend for them to die. I went back and dragged them out to the stairwell. They were both unconscious but alive. They would be safe out here until the firefighters arrived.

As I approached the main exit, workers had begun to trickle back into the building complex as a result of an "all clear" order, but within seconds the fire alarms began blasting anew. The mixed message created complete chaos. The security personnel were just as confused, but focused on repelling the workers trying to reenter the building. As a result no one paid much attention to one emergency coordinator leaving the building. The confusion made it easy for me to exit.

Outside, I found a fire captain and told him, "I think there are two security guards overcome by smoke in the basement stairwell. You need to get someone to them ASAP!"

The captain turned to another fireman and shouted, "Take a team downstairs and find those men!"

I slithered away before he could ask who the hell I was.

When I reached Mary's Mercedes, I stripped off the emergency coordinator's costume and left it on the ground in the parking lot. A few minutes later, I was slowly driving the Mercedes through the fire trucks and other emergency vehicles. I followed all the traffic laws as I slipped onto Interstate 95 South, and within minutes I wasn't even in Maryland anymore.

So ended my nostalgic return visit to the office.

10

THE BLACK SUVS

Like I've told you, I have this little voice that advises me from time to time. It usually whispers from the back of my mind, and I can ignore it if I foolishly choose to do so. This time the voice was shouting at me.

Look in the rearview mirror!

There were three very big, black Suburbans traveling in convoy formation and tailgating me.

I foolishly argued with my little voice: *They aren't following me.*

You should make sure.

I exited the expressway at a travel stop, and they followed—not very subtle. I drove directly back onto the expressway, and they still followed. They didn't care whether I knew they were following.

Being followed twice in one day?

Again, I had no idea who it could be, or why they were following me. There were a lot of people who didn't like me. I needed to clear this up, but I couldn't just stop at a coffee shop and manhandle three Suburbans full of soldiers.

Shit!

It wasn't my decision any longer. The head Suburban pulled in front of me and cut me off. The second Suburban pulled alongside and began to crowd me over to the right shoulder of the road, while the third nearly bumped my rear bumper. I only had one direction I could go—to the shoulder of the road. I moved to the edge of the pavement. They continued pressing me until I was in the dirt. The three worked together as if they had done this many times before. They brought me to a full stop on the shoulder of the expressway.

Where are the cops when you need them?

Now the Suburbans were flashing emergency strobe lights I hadn't noticed before. It all looked official, as if they were the cops! I sat in Mary's Mercedes and waited.

Maybe they're after Mary. Was this a case of mistaken identity? The windows are tinted very dark—they wouldn't be able to see who was inside.

I'd know soon.

Men poured out of the front and rear Suburbans. They were carrying exotic little submachine guns. I didn't recognize the brand. One of them tapped on the passenger-side window with his gun barrel. I was seriously outgunned and decided to try dumb and innocent—at least at first.

I rolled the window down. "May I help you?" I was smiling.

I think me smiling under the circumstances threw him. He didn't expect that. He backed up a step, looked around at his buddies, and then returned to the window. "Out!"

I couldn't open the driver's-side door because of the roadside Suburban was nearly touching the Mercedes. So I scooted across the front seats and opened the passenger-side door. As soon as I did, two big bullies grabbed me and dragged me all the way out. This wasn't going to be civilized. They spun me around, searched me, and found my and Mary's pistols. Fortunately, Mutt and Jeff's pistols, the spray cans, flash drives, and the other cute little gadgets I'd stolen earlier at the office were locked in the trunk. Someone slapped a pair of cold steel handcuffs on me from behind, and two men began shoving me toward the front Suburban.

"Am I under arrest?" I asked.

No one answered my question. They didn't even grunt.

I wondered whether the Agency had somehow caught me for my skullduggery this fast, but I didn't have time to dwell on the question before I was pushed into the back seat of the Suburban and two huge bullies climbed in on either side of me. Within a minute the caravan was moving again. One of the thugs drove Mary's Mercedes.

11

MEET THE MAJOR

A thug slipped a black hood over my head. I was now blind and handcuffed, with huge knuckle draggers bracketing me. Nothing today was working the way I had anticipated when I woke this morning.

"What's the problem fellas?"

No one answered.

"If you tell me what you want, I'll cooperate."

Still—silence.

Maybe they don't know how to talk.

We drove silently for some time, and then the vehicle stopped. A window opened, there was an electronic beeping sound, and a man's speaker-voice said, "You're cleared." We were entering a secure facility—I heard a loud jet taking off—near an airport.

We made a series of turns, drove over a speed bump, and then stopped. No one moved or spoke. It was spooky. They could put a bullet in my head right now, and I wouldn't stand a chance. Just as I was about to try something foolish, one of the knuckle draggers removed my hood. We were inside a large building with no windows, possibly a hangar, maybe underground. The Suburban's door opened, and the talking knuckle dagger growled, "Out!"

Four very large men were waiting for me outside.

"This way," ordered the knuckle dragger who had learned to talk. He led me and the others through a steel door and down a narrow, poorly lit hallway. We passed several closed, unmarked doors. We finally stopped in front of a closed door that looked the same as the others.

The talking-model had also been trained to turn doorknobs. He opened the door and said, "In!"

Maybe eventually he'll learn to speak in whole sentences.

We now stood inside a plain room with no furniture or other decorations. The walls and ceiling were concrete. There was a drain in the center of the floor. My hands were still handcuffed behind me, and there were still four very large men watching over me. I felt panic edging. I thought of running, but there was nowhere to go, so I waited.

"Wait here!" said Talker.

He went through another door on the far side of the room, leaving his nonspeaking clones to stand guard over me. They stood six feet away and never took their eyes off me. I thought I'd test my theory about their ability to speak.

"Hey, guys, did you see the football game last night? I think we saw one of the teams that will go to the Super Bowl this year. What do you think?"

They just stared at me. No one spoke. No one smiled. No one even looked puzzled.

The Talker opened the door and said, "This way!"

I followed him into the next room. The non-speakers remained outside, my first break—the odds were improving.

We passed through a smaller room. This one had furniture and a male receptionist guarding an entrance on the far side apparently leading to another room. The receptionist looked very tough, and I could see the bulge of a gun under his sports jacket—a shoulder holster. His eyes never left me as I walked across the room. Talker opened the door and nodded for me to enter.

Sitting behind a large glass-top desk was possibly the largest man I'd ever seen, at least in circumference. I had no idea how tall he was. The chair he sat in had to be custom-made to hold the massive amount of weight and accommodate his size. He had fiery-red hair that was thinning on the top, but he had allowed it to grow long on the sides. His face had deep scarring, probably from a severe burn sometime in the distant past. His pale-almost yellow-hazel eyes were small for his head, but they were also hard, focused, and penetrating. I could see no humor in them. I soon discovered he always appeared intensely angry. His expression never varied. The total effect gave him a bizarre, almost clownish look—an evil clown that children would run away from. I know I felt that way.

"Hello, Mr. Wolfe. I am sometimes called The Major. Have you heard of me?" His voice was deep, and he spoke at a slow, determined pace.

"I've heard the stories told around intelligence agency coffee rooms and campfires at night—stories told about The all-powerful Major to scare the new kids," I replied.

He sneered, didn't laugh. It wasn't a pleasant sound. "Very good! Keep your wits about you and don't show a weakness to your opponent. I like that in my agents."

"I'm not your agent!" I snapped back.

"Not yet, but that's why I asked you here. I'd like to offer you a position in my organization."

Another job offer or is this Mary's employer?

"Does Mary Killigrew work for you?" I asked.

"I'd rather talk about your potential position with me," he answered.

"You don't waste any time with small talk," I said with a guarded voice.

"Our time on this earth is limited."

"Is that a threat?"

"Nonsense, it's merely a fact of life." He chuckled, but it sounded more like a grunt and a cough.

"Then why am I handcuffed and guarded by these knuckle-dragging Neanderthals?"

He emitted another stifled chuckle. It didn't convey humor. "I was wondering how long it would take you to ask to be released. I just wanted to see." He nodded to Talker. "Remove the cuffs and wait outside. I think Mr. Wolfe and I can have a civilized conversation. Isn't that true, Mr. Wolfe?"

"For the moment," I agreed.

The talking knuckle dagger removed my cuffs and quietly closed the door on his way out.

I asked, "How do you know I'm the right guy for your position?"

"Please sit down. May I offer you refreshment? Anything you wish—coffee, tea, water, beer, wine, whiskey?"

"No, thanks. So why offer me a job—why now?" I stayed focused on my point.

"I first became aware of your talents during the 1997 China Fiasco, Mr. Wolfe, and I've been watching you closely ever since."

"That was my very first assignment. I was a new guy then."

"Yes, I'm aware of that, and for a new guy on his first assignment, you managed quite a trick: Stopping the all-powerful Agency from sabotaging the Reversion and then framing your supervisor to take the hit for the failure. It showed real potential."

How does he know this?

"So, why didn't you hire me at that time? I was not happy then and would have accepted without hesitation."

"Possibly, but you weren't worth much to me then. You were more lucky than talented that time. You needed experience and seasoning. So I waited and watched your progress from a distance. And I must say, you've come along nicely in the past two decades. I was particularly impressed with the way you ended China's 2003 *Shenzhou* flight early, causing them to bring their man home after only fourteen orbits due to technical difficulties. Of course, they never admitted it. They called it a success, but we both know better. They had planned on leaving him up there for a full thirty orbits. Your little interference set the China manned space flight back two years by evaporating their confidence and requiring them to redesign all their electronics. I was particularly impressed that their astronaut was not harmed and that China never suspected the United States for its complicity. After that, the Chinese partnered with the Russians, and you stepped in again and completely shut down the 2011 launch of Yinghou. You know, the Russians and Chinese still blame each the other for the failure—brilliant!"

I was getting bored listening to him talk about me, so I cut in. "Yes, the United States couldn't have their two biggest competitors joining forces in space, so I was tasked with shutting it down. I was able to disable almost all the electronics onboard, and the launch never left earth's gravity due to total electronic failure. The rocket remained in low orbit for about two months and then crashed back to earth in January, 2012. End of lecture."

"Yes! That's why I want you. You destroy things and nobody knows who is responsible. When Yinghuo 34 failed this morning, I assumed it was your work?"

I think he meant the last sentence as a question.

"I'm retired."

"Of course, but your work still functions, and because of that the Russians and Chinese are again suspicious of each other. This distrust slows their progress in space. You are the master, Mr. Wolfe!"

"What do you need of me?" I asked.

"I have need of your skills."

"What would I be doing for you?"

"Primarily, you would be doing deeds similar to what you did to create the China Fiasco in '97 and again for this morning's launch of Yinghuo."

"Against who? I asked.

"Our own intelligence agencies with an occasional exception of a foreign intelligence—"

I cut him off. "I'm retired . . . moving on. Besides, I'm not a traitor."

He cut me off. "We express our gratitude, and openly express our respect, by paying much better than the Agency, and you won't be subjected to the jealousy and bureaucratic petty-mindedness you've suffered there for the past two decades."

"Under what authority do you operate?" I asked.

"I am responsible directly to the President of the United States. I was appointed by the first Bush to replace my predecessor, who was the original Major, appointed by President Eisenhower."

"Was your predecessor fired?"

"No, he passed away."

"Legend says President Truman created The Major—not Eisenhower." I said.

"Misdirection by Eisenhower," The Major explained. "He blamed Truman so he didn't have to take the heat for spying on our own spy agencies. Eisenhower didn't trust the power the CIA was already amassing, or what he referred to as the 'Military-Industrial-Congressional Complex.' He wanted a tool to keep the greedy, power hungry amalgam in check."

"I'm listening."

"Traditionally, The Major is appointed for life—similar to Supreme Court justices. The Major's original mission was to oversee all the intelligence agencies of the United States—to insure they were not running rogue or operating contrary to the interests of the United States."

I asked, "You said original mission; has it changed?"

The Major smiled for the first time since I had entered the room. It looked ugly.

I like him better angry.

He continued, "Currently, I watch over the intelligence agencies, government bureaucrats, and sometimes even private individuals. My mission is to detect whether they are acting contrary to the best interests of the United States. I report the deviations and unauthorized actions to the president. If he agrees, he orders the delinquent party to cease actions or to change policy accordingly."

I was thinking of a few covert operations at the Agency that I suspected weren't sanctioned. I knew from experience the intelligence community could be very willful about their pet projects—sanctioned or not. I asked, "What if the agency doesn't comply?"

The Major paused before answering. "That's when you will earn your fat pay check. Your job will be to enforce compliance. I am offering you the position of Chief Compliance Officer. You will be responsible only to me, and I in turn to the President of the United States."

"What if it's the president who is acting contrary to the best interests of this country?"

The Major sneered, but continued talking as if I hadn't asked the question. "You will have a highly classified but written presidential executive order, giving you carte blanche license to take any action you deem necessary to bring delinquent individuals or agencies into line. Your only mandate is that your actions must be completely covert and cannot be traced back to you, to this organization, or to the president."

I was dumbfounded and speechless. "What if someone has to die?" I asked.

"It would be best if their death appeared to be natural causes or self-inflicted, but again, that is at your discretion."

"By 'natural causes' you mean stroke or heart attack?"

"An accident or suicide would also be acceptable."

The Major studied me for a moment and then asked, "So Mr. Wolfe, what is your answer?"

My little voice was warning me, *Careful . . . I've heard too much. I need to delay and find a way to stall the decision . . . find a way to get free of here . . . find time to think.*

"Could I take a few days to consider this? My attention is spread pretty thin right now. A close friend died this morning."

The Major interrupted. "Yes, Jimmy Trang. I hear it was apparently suicide."

How does he know?

"And I have a retirement party to go to this afternoon. Later tonight, I am having a few close friends over to my residence, in Virginia."

"You mean your Old Rock House?"

The Major had done his homework. I said, "Yes, you're invited if you wish."

"I rarely go to such things, but I agree; no one should make this kind of decision impulsively. I will give you until this evening, Mr. Wolfe. On your way out, ask Pit Bull for a business card."

"Pit Bull?" I asked.

"The receptionist who guards my office. Asking him for a business card is how he knows to allow you to leave alive. If you simply walk out of here without asking for one, you wouldn't make it to the second doorway."

This is a take-it-or-die offer.

I was again blindfolded and driven off the base to Mary's Mercedes. The knuckle-draggers set me free without ceremony or talking.

He said I have until this evening. I should have asked, does that mean he's going to show up at my house tonight?

12

THE OFFICIAL PARTY

I hate government service retirement parties, including my own. The function always lasts too long and is full of small-minded people making speeches no one wants to listen to. The speakers always feel obligated to present the retiree with a joke gift or two—worthless crap, such as a wristwatch with no hands or the meaningless Congressional Certificate signed by a representative who never heard of you before and will never meet you in person. Only retards ever hang their Congressional Certificates on the wall or read them more than once. It's a redundant ritual, almost identical for every government retirement party. By the time the party is over, almost everyone there would gladly sever a finger to leave early.

I expected my party to be even worse. I had only two friends at the Agency; one had allegedly killed himself in the employee parking lot this morning, and the other broke up with me before breakfast. It'd been a tough morning. It's not easy being me. Maybe I need to cultivate better people skills and then more friends.

Oh, don't worry; there will be a lot of people attending my party—mostly career-political attendees, not true friends. If someone really likes you and is your friend, you'll continue seeing them after you retire, so they don't need to say goodbye at an office function, right?

Who are the career-political attendees—the hobnobs? They are people vying for an advantage back at the office. Some think the retiree was "someone" in the Agency, and if they are seen at their retirement party, they also must be important—maybe moving up the line. A subcategory of this group is the brownnoser: those who show up to rub elbows with the top brass. These little shits believe brownnosing will improve their chances for a promotion.

Then there are the sheep people who come because they feel obligated to be there. For them it's a work function. They didn't care that much about you when you worked there, and they won't really miss you once you're gone. They only showed up because it's marginally better than being at work and they aren't strong enough to just say no.

Others are the escapees. They attend because it gets them out of the office for the afternoon and gives them an excuse to get drunk in public during working hours. Related to the escapees are previous retirees bored beyond repair. They no longer have any purpose in life and would attend a feces-burning festival just to have something to do.

Also, there are a few old flings that show up—those little indiscretions you'd rather forget about. It's always awkward when you see them again. You both know this will be the last contact, and you're not sure how to act. Do you shake hands, hug, or maybe engage in a quick brother-sister kiss? It can be awkward.

Finally, the boss, and sometimes his boss, attends. Many times the big shots are also there out of some vague sense of obligation. For them it's a work function—they are attending because they are expected to. It's that simple.

Except Sprout. He was coming to my retirement party for another, darker reason, and I wanted him there. In fact, Sprout is the reason I wanted to have the party.

I know what you're thinking right now: that I have a bad attitude. It's one of my major flaws. I know, I've been told that before.

I arrived at the restaurant a half hour early and parked in the far corner of the almost-empty parking lot. I got out, looked around, saw nothing noteworthy, and opened the Mercedes's trunk. The Neanderthals had returned my and Mary's pistols after the interview with The Major. I deposited my pistol in the trunk next to Mutt's and Jeff's Berettas, but I had no intention of attending the party unarmed. I checked Mary's sexy, two-toned Smith & Wesson to ensure it was loaded and then slipped it into my belt-clip holster. If you need to shoot someone, it's always best to use someone else's gun. I wasn't concerned with fingerprints or DNA because I'd sprayed my hands this morning, remember?

Next, I selected a very expensive-looking ballpoint pen, slipping it into my jacket breast pocket. It was actually a video camera that also records sound. You never know. Then I selected one of the aerosol cans I'd picked up earlier from TSD and slipped it into my coat's side pocket. Like I said before, you never know.

The Agency almost always used this same restaurant and the same dining room for its parties. It is humorous that the world's most powerful and advanced electronic spy agency is so predictable—using the same room time after time—making electronic espionage easier for its enemies. I could only hope that the Agency had sent a crew to sweep the room earlier this morning.

From previous visits, I knew that everything in this restaurant is overdone in understatement, including the dark mahogany wood on the walls, ceilings, and floors. It is so dark inside that I almost needed a flashlight to find a table in the private banquet room. I entered and looked around. The room smelled musky and foul. There were hints of alcohol, tobacco, mildew, and vomit. I doubt the wall-to-wall carpets had been cleaned in a year. Maybe management was waiting for Spring.

There were already a few people present from the Agency. There was a middle-aged woman sitting at a folding table near the doorway to check arrivals against her prepaid guest list. The luncheon costs each person thirty dollars, which included the meal and a nonalcoholic drink. There was a bar in the far corner of the room, where you could buy your own alcoholic drinks. I smiled and said, "Hello!" I couldn't remember her name.

She apparently didn't know me either, because she asked me, "Name, please."

"I'm the guest of honor—John Wolfe."

"Oh, I'm so sorry, Mr. Wolfe. It must be the low lighting in the room. I apologize."

I drifted into a corner near the restrooms. Like I've already said, I don't have that many friends. Some people were setting up decorations. Some were just standing around with a drink in their hand, chatting. It all seemed very cordial.

A young agent I'd seen around the building came up to me. "Congratulations, Mr. Wolfe. Twenty years, and we're losing one of the last master spies. You will be missed."

Which is he: Genuine respect, escapee, or career-political?

"Thank you . . ." I couldn't remember his name.

I should work on my interpersonal skills.

"Collins, Lee Collins," said the young man.

"Well, Lee, I appreciate your kind words. Thank you."

"You're no master spy!" Sprout growled as he approached. He'd apparently overheard the exchange. He addressed Collins. "Don't listen to Wolfe. If you do, your career will end up like his—in the toilet."

I cut in. "Lee, if you take Sprout as a mentor, you'll learn to spout off about everything and still know nothing. Remember, you can't rise very high when you're floating in bullshit."

Sprout had been in the Agency five years, but he'd never been an agent. He had been the leader of the GSA consulting team, brought in by a political appointee to find ways to make us more efficient. However, the consultants weren't cleared for the super-high, top-secret-crypto level information, so we couldn't disclose to them what we did or how we did it. The result was that only meaningless, superficial opportunities for improvement were identified. For example, one of their suggestions was to add more pencil sharpeners in the room, so we didn't have to walk as far to sharpen our pencils (Remember—almost all our work is done on a computer.) During the course of that project Sprout somehow managed to convince the top brass to bring him in as division chief over the Electronic Surveillance Division.

We soon learned that Sprout believed a manager didn't need to know the technical details of the work he manages. Sprout believed he only needed to know how to supervise people. Therefore, five years later, he still didn't know the details of what we do or how we do it. However, he is just smart enough that being ignorant of the work made him feel insecure, especially around the technically savvy and experienced agents. Sprout expresses his insecurity by trying to put down anyone smarter than him.

Which is almost everyone at the Agency.

Lee Collins took a step back, his head snapping back and forth between Sprout and me. The young agent stammered. "I'm supposed to help with the decorations. Please excuse me." He turned and hurried away.

Maybe Lee Collins had been drafted to set up the decorations—another category of attendees I failed to note earlier.

I turned to face Sprout directly, so I would have a clear picture for the pen recorder in my breast pocket. I casually reached up and pushed the on button. The digital device would record for ninety minutes. I wouldn't need that much time.

Sprout was wearing a sports jacket—bright green with thin yellow stripes. Looking at the jacket almost burned my eyes.

Poor taste in clothing—another of his shortcomings.

Sprout repeated, "You're no master spy, Wolfe. All the real master spies went out fifty years ago. You're just an old fart whose time has passed."

He considers forty-five to be an old fart?

"You're going to miss me, Sprout."

"No, I won't, Wolfe."

"Yes, you will. You'll miss trying to get me fired by soliciting and falsifying sexual harassment claims from the female workers, even though none of them would agree to sign the complaint. It's ironic that you asked the same women *you* actually harassed. Or how about the time you sent me on the shit mission to the South Pole to accomplish something that wasn't even my section's area of responsibility? But my favorite attempt was when you ordered me to bug a private conversation between the President of the United States and the Russian Premier, and then told the Secret Service I was doing it without authorization. You would have had me that time, except I recorded our conversation of you ordering me to do it. I still don't understand why you weren't fired for that."

Sprout grunted, "You have lived a charmed life, Wolfe . . . up to now."

What's that supposed to mean?

As you may have guessed, I had let Sprout get under my skin. It was personal.

I need to let go—move on.

I took a deep breath and said, "I only have one last question for you, Sprout."

"What would that be?"

"Who are you going to treat like shit after I'm gone?" I flashed him the biggest grin I could manage.

"Nobody will ever replace the special spot I've reserved for you in my heart, Wolfe."

It's personal for him too.

I said, "Dog turds and maggots!"

"Pardon?" Sprout asked.

"I said dog turds and maggots: that's what I'm looking at."

"Are you calling me a dog turd or a maggot?" Sprout looked confused.

"Actually, you're a maggot," I answered.

"Really?"

"Yes, dog turds are dropped on the sidewalks forcing normal people to find a way around them—they're filthy obstacles to our life."

"Really?"

I continued. "Yes! And the maggots feed off the dog turds. Without the dog turds maggots couldn't exist."

"I don't get it," said Sprout.

I explained, "Dog turds are created by large government; those stumbling blocks put in the way of progress: bureaucracy, rules, regulations, and taxes. The maggots are parasites that exist to live off the dog turds. They eat the dog shit, grow bigger, and multiply. They thrive in it. You are a maggot, Sprout. You don't really improve life. You're just a burden—an obstacle to progress."

"That's rich! You were one of those maggots for twenty years, Wolfe.

"No, there are some legitimate government functions and workers who perform those functions. The maggots I speak of are people like you—middle-level bureaucrats who do nothing to make things better. They read and write reports, shuffle papers, and make up rules to slow things down."

"I'm the Division Chief of—"

"You're a bureaucrat who never even bothered to learn the work of those who work under you, Sprout."

Sprout trembled as he said, "I can't express how happy I am you're leaving the Agency."

"I've gathered . . ." I was smiling because I knew he'd hate it.

Sprout sneered and turned to walk away.

I called after him. "Why did you have David Planter follow me?"

Sprout stopped and looked back. His expression was as if he'd bitten into a dog turd and couldn't find a way to spit it out. "I never heard of David Planter."

"So you didn't task Planter with keeping an eye on me and insuring I made it to this party?"

Sprout looked directly into my eyes. "I told you; I've never heard of Planter. And why the hell would I care if you came to the party, anyway?"

I believe him. That means Planter lied to me—if that's even his real name.

At that moment Janet appeared. She'd gone back to her place after leaving my condo this morning and changed into her professional work clothes—very conservative, very sharp. She looked great. I would miss being with her.

She wedged herself between Sprout and me. "Hello, Mr. Sprout. That's quite a sport jacket you're wearing today. It really stands out." Her tone was very professional and cool.

"Thank you," replied Sprout, looking a little confused.

Then Janet turned to me and said, "Congratulations on your retirement, Mr. Wolfe. The Agency will seriously miss you."

"I'll miss some things at the Agency," I answered.

Sprout must have felt the need to degrade the conversation to something less civilized, because he asked, "So what perverted plans do you have now that you're no longer employed?"

"Well, besides a couple of very lucrative job offers that I am considering, I thought I'd look into an organization that calls itself the Order of Squirrels or something like that. I think it is either a very nasty gang of criminals or a kid's fraternity gone wild—maybe both. Either way, the squirrels need to be brought into the light so everyone may see whose nuts they've been eating."

I can't adequately explain to you the paleness that flooded across Sprout's face or how good it felt for me to watch it spread. He was speechless—a rare event.

Janet saw it too. I think she suddenly realized something profound was going on. She decided to add her tools to the conversation. "John, did you hear that the investigators are saying Jimmy committed suicide this morning?"

"No, are they sure it was suicide? He seemed such an upbeat guy," I answered with a straight face as if I didn't already know about it.

Janet and I have always worked well together.

"The Agency is keeping the investigation in-house, so I guess we'll learn soon enough," she answered with an equally straight expression.

Sprout looked like he was going to swell up and explode. "Wolfe doesn't work here anymore—talking to him about an ongoing Agency investigation is a security violation."

"Using the toilet at the Agency without checking for microphones is a security violation. Besides, Jimmy was a friend," I said.

"Well, your friend should have been careful what he stuck his nose into."

Both Janet and I asked together, "What does that mean?"

I unconsciously glanced at my pen.

Hope you're getting this.

Janet may recognize the covert recording device because she is adept at her tradecraft, but as I indicated earlier, Sprout most likely didn't even know recording pens existed.

"We had to protect others from getting splattered," Sprout shot back.

Janet asked, "What do you mean, 'protect others from getting splattered'?"

"And who is 'we'?" I added.

"I just meant Jimmy stuck his nose into something he shouldn't have."

Janet asked, "What do you know about his death?"

"Yes, tell us more, Sprout," I said.

"It's obvious! He shot himself," said Sprout.

Janet pressed, "Jimmy was right-handed. Why would he hold the gun in his left hand to shoot himself?"

Smart and sexy . . .

"How did you know that?" Sprout stammered.

It was my turn. "Come on, just because you never bothered to learn any tradecraft doesn't mean everyone else is stupid and illiterate. Answer our questions, Sprout. Why did you say Jimmy should be careful what he sticks his nose into?"

"I'm not saying anything here—too public."

"Then let's go somewhere that's not so public," I suggested.

"I'm going nowhere with you, Wolfe." Then he said to Janet, "And I thought you were smarter than this. Why are you siding with this cave dweller? Think of your career."

"Actually, I *am* thinking of my career. If you can kill Jimmy all of us are in danger."

Sprout started, "How did . . ." then stopped himself.

Got you, bastard!

"Tell me about the squirrels," I added.

We were throwing multiple questions and topics at him, rapid-fire, trying to confuse him, and it was beginning to work. If we could keep the pressure on, he may say something else spontaneous, something he didn't mean to—something he shouldn't. The technique was to press hard, create a crack, and then to pick at it until you learned something important. It was a more civilized way to unravel secrets than waterboarding.

I repeated, "Tell us about the order of squirrels.

Janet asked, "Why did you kill Jimmy?"

"I know nothing about the Order of the Golden Squirrel. What do you mean why did I kill Jimmy?" Sprout looked worried.

We had him.

"I never said golden squirrel; I just said squirrels."

Sprout snapped back, "Doesn't matter. I never heard of it, and you can't prove what I just said. This isn't an official interrogation. You can't prove anything!"

He was rattled because he knew he'd been busted and was trying to bluster his way out. I decided I'd push harder. "I know you're lying, Sprout. I read the email you sent to the director about the Order of the Golden Squirrel. You're worried someone will learn about it, like me."

Sprout looked shocked. "What? You've hacked my email? You'll go to jail for this, Wolfe."

I chuckled. "Nonsense; you left your computer on, and I just happened to walk by and saw it. That's your security violation—leaving your computer up when away from your office for anyone to see. You're the one going to jail."

Janet snapped at him before he could recover. "I want to know why you said Jimmy should have kept his nose out of other people's business. Did he stick his nose into your business? Is that why you killed him?"

Whoa! Where is that coming from?

"Who said I killed Jimmy?"

I stepped in. "You did a moment ago."

"I didn't say kill—Janet did." But Sprout didn't sound sure of himself.

"Come clean, Sprout, you'll feel better," I said.

Janet tagged in. "I went directly to TSD this morning first thing—before the fire. By the way, did you set that fire, Mr. Sprout?"

I'd set that fire, but no one here needed to know that—especially with the recorder pen working.

"Don't be stupid! Why would I set a fire in TSD?" asked Sprout.

"To destroy evidence . . ." I chimed in. I almost felt ashamed—almost—but then I thought of Jimmy. If Sprout knew something about Jimmy's death, I was justified if I could learn what he knew.

Janet said, "It didn't do you any good, because I had already removed all the surveillance DVDs before you burned the place down this morning, Sprout."

Janet took the DVDs. That's why the recorders were empty. How did she get past the security guards?

"That sounds like another security violation," Sprout proclaimed, but he sounded rattled.

Janet said, "I had a chance to scan the recordings for the parking lot at the time Jimmy was supposed to have killed himself. Guess what I saw?"

Sprout was quiet. So was I.

She continued, "A man walked up to Jimmy's car just as he parked and tapped on his window. Jimmy apparently knew the man, because he immediately rolled down his window. The man shot Jimmy in the head, threw the pistol into the car, opened the car door, rolled up the window, turned off the engine, locked the door, and then casually walked into the building, using the employee's entrance. I'm sure once we run the video through HIRS we'll discover the killer's identity. Identification will be easy, since the killer must be an Agency employee. But I already know who the killer is—even without HIRS—don't I, Mr. Sprout?"

"How?" mumbled Sprout.

Janet said, "Because the killer wore a bright-green sports jacket with thin yellow stripes. It looked exactly like the one you are wearing now."

Didn't I say she's smart?

13

GOODBYE MR. SPROUT

"You'll never pin it on me; besides, it was sanctioned. I was following orders from the director. If you try to prosecute me, you'll be the ones who go down." Sprout was gloating.

I hope my pen-recorder got that.

"Was it sanctioned by the director or the squirrels?" I asked.

Sprout laughed. "It's the same . . . the two of you would be smart to disappear. Once I make a phone call, you'll end up like Jimmy. He got too close to the Order. That's why he had to go. Now you're getting too close." Sprout reached into his pocket for his cell phone.

Janet and I exchanged a knowing glance. We had him. I had it all on the recording. The arrogant bastard thought he was untouchable, but he was wrong.

I couldn't let him make that call. I turned off the pen-recorder and produced Mary's pistol. "Put the cell back into your pocket, and let's go powder our nose, Sprout."

Janet said, "No, let's take him in—do this legally."

"You heard him. Legal won't work. He's covered from above. They're all part of some conspiracy, operating under a guise of being legal. There are some very powerful people in this conspiracy. Sprout's right: he will get a pass, and we'll end up like Jimmy."

Janet was silent. I took that as agreement.

"Let's go, Sprout." I nodded in the direction of the toilets.

Sprout looked to Janet. "Are you going to let him do this?"

"Do what? All I heard was, 'Let's go powder our nose.' Maybe you two have something going on—you know: Don't Ask, Don't Tell."

I really love her.

We walked to the restrooms. Janet led the way. Sprout was second. I brought up the tail with Mary's pistol jammed into Sprout's spine.

Janet walked directly into the men's room without hesitation.

I placed my free hand on his shoulder and whispered, "Wait, Sprout."

We stood just outside the door. Sprout was being surprisingly cooperative. I don't think he really understood what was coming.

Janet returned and announced, "It's empty."

"Inside, Sprout," I hissed.

"You can't just shoot me in the men's room of a public restaurant and walk away free. They'll hang both of you for this," Sprout said, but he didn't sound as convinced as his words.

Janet said, "He's right, you know. We can't just shoot him. That pistol doesn't have a silencer. People will rush in here before we can get away, and we'll be toast."

"Not a problem," I said. "Hold the pistol on him. Only shoot him if necessary." I handed the pistol to Janet.

Like I've said, I'm not my brother. I'm a lover and a thinker, not a fighter, but once in a while there is only one solution to a problem. I had decided this was one of those times. Sprout was corrupt. He was evil. He'd killed Jimmy this morning, and now he was threatening Janet and me. When you look at it that way, it was self-defense.

I extracted the aerosol spray can I'd taken earlier from TSD, disguised to look like a small can of self-defense pepper spray. The can discharges a highly refined compound of toluene and manganese derivatives, combined with a catalyst cocktail agent. The longer someone breathes the spray the more damage it does to their brain. A short blast only causes a state of confusion, loss of balance, and short-term memory loss—maybe unconsciousness. A longer blast can bring on death from a full-force stroke. In the latter case, when an autopsy is performed, there will be no traces of the highly refined compound found because it breaks down into harmless base elements after doing its damage.

I walked over to the paper-towel dispenser and removed several sheets, then wet them at the sink. I handed Janet half of the wet paper towels. She knew what was about to happen. Like I said before, she knows her tradecraft.

Sprout, on the other hand, had no idea what was in the aerosol can because he never bothered to learn anything on the technical side of how we worked. He is a desk jockey that reads reports, signs off on them, and passes them on to others who do the same. It's important to repeat myself: Sprout doesn't believe you need to know the technical details of the work if you know how to boss people around. So he never dirtied his hands with doing any fieldwork or learning any tradecraft. Sprout is a true—corrupt—bureaucrat.

This morning he'd been promoted to murderer when he'd killed Jimmy.

I nodded to Janet. She placed the wet towels over her nose and mouth and stepped back, just in case.

Sprout stood there, unknowingly and passively watching his imminent death unfold—a complete idiot. "Is that pepper spray? What's that going to accomplish? Nothing but piss me off and add assault to your crimes."

"Whatever," I said.

No more talking.

I sprayed Sprout in the face—my arm fully extended—aiming at his eyes, nose, and mouth. I emptied the small can. The compound takes about a minute for the full effect, so I had to manage his reaction to being sprayed until the compound did its work.

In the training class, I learned that the target typically doesn't understand what is happening at first, so there is not much of an immediate reaction. According to the trainer, it is only in the last ten or fifteen seconds that the target realizes something very bad is happening and may become violent or attempt to get help. That's when it's important to manage the scene to insure against "negative forensic evidence."

I waited.

"What was that?" Sprout shouted, brushing away the overspray with his hand. He involuntarily took in a second deep breath of the spray in some instinctive act of trying to identify the scent.

I needed to keep him calm for a few more seconds. "Oh, I'm sorry. I was just spraying some air fresher. I've been suffering from indigestion and didn't want to offend you, or Janet, with my gaseous expulsions."

Sprout shot me a puzzled look. "Well, watch it! You sprayed me directly in the face, and it doesn't smell much like an air freshener. He sniffed in the remaining overspray one last time to verify his opinion then said, "That's not an air freshener. It smells like some hideous chemical. What . . . was that . . . real . . . ly?" The last syllable trailed off into slurred mumbling.

It's starting to work.

The end came much faster than I expected. Sprout's left arm slowly dropped and hung limp along his side. A few seconds later, his left leg buckled, and he gently lowered himself to the floor. I had been prepared to wrestle him for a few seconds to keep him under control, but it was not necessary. The end was almost peaceful. One moment Sprout was a sentient human being—a traitor and a murderer, who had been threatening Janet and me—the next, he was staring at us without any comprehension of what he was seeing. He raised his head up once as if he were going to saying something then laid it back on the floor and was still. A puddle of urine grew underneath his body and a strong odor of feces filled the room.

Janet and I stared at the body for several seconds then we stared at each other. It was the first time I'd ever done anything like that, and I'm sure it was the first time she'd ever witnessed such an act. We were both in a mild state of shock. I know you're thinking Sprout was in a much deeper state of shock, but you're wrong. Sprout was dead. He had died of a massive stroke, and that would be the findings of the autopsy—if there was one.

"I think we better go back out to the ball room and be seen acting normal until someone finds the body," said Janet.

I was still holding the spray can. The thought came into my head: *I've already started working for The Major.*

"You should put that away before someone sees it." She indicated the spray can as she wiped off the pistol with soap and water and then dried it with paper towels. I assume she was removing her fingerprints and DNA. She returned the "scrubbed" pistol to me, wrapped in a dry paper towel, not touching it directly.

I slipped the pistol in my jacket pocket and tossed the paper towel into the wastebasket. I wasn't concerned with fingerprints or DNA because I'd sprayed my hands with the latex this morning. Next, I planted a tiny transmitter, I'd had with me, in the corner of the room near the ceiling. It would send sound and images for up to twenty-four hours.

I asked Janet, "Can I buy you a drink?"

She smiled. "No, you're the retiree. I should buy you a drink."

"As you wish!"

14

IT'S A HORSE RACE

We sat at the bar and ordered drinks. Heaven knows we both needed one. It was reasonable for us to be seen sharing a drink while waiting for my retirement party to officially begin. We spoke in whispers. In reality, we were waiting for the brown stuff to hit the fan.

Janet took a long sip of her gin and tonic before announcing, "You know, back at the Agency they are already whisperings that you killed Jimmy Trang. The investigation is drifting that way in case the suicide story doesn't hold up. You're the backup plan—you're being set up to take the fall."

"What would be my motive?"

"So you could have his wife. Have you been a bad boy, John?" she asked.

"Have his wife! That's nuts! Jimmy was killed because he was snooping around and asking questions about the Order of the Golden Squirrel. You have the parking-lot surveillance video to prove Sprout killed Jimmy. I have a recording of him admitting he did it!" I indicated my recorder-pen.

"So you weren't sleeping with his wife?" she asked.

"You should be asking something more important: Who—high up in government—is a traitor? Jimmy must have learned who the traitor is. That's why Sprout killed him and tried to make it look like a suicide."

"There are two traitors: Sprout and the director," said Janet.

"There must be more. They couldn't make this happen alone."

"Hope we live long enough to find out," said Janet.

"Yeah . . ." Then I asked, "You still coming to the party tonight at my Old Rock House?"

"Of course, my dear, I wouldn't miss your real party for anything." She was quiet for a moment and then added, "I'll be there tonight, but I expect my own bedroom."

Women can be cold.

It didn't take long for someone to find Sprout's body. Lee Collins—the new agent who had been helping set up decorations—found Sprout in the men's room. Collins came out; face pale and drawn, shouting for someone to call 911. Apparently he didn't trust himself to make the call. After several people ran into the men's room to see whether they could help, a waitress finally made the call.

In a few minutes there were half dozen emergency first responders on site. The police showed up after the paramedics, and then there was total chaos. The police pushed the growing crowd back out of the men's room as paramedics and firemen rushed back and forth between the body and their vehicles. I have no idea why.

Apparently, someone had the authority to declare Sprout dead on the scene and did. After that, the urgency was over and routine settled in. The paramedics and firemen simply picked up their toys and left, leaving the scene in a state of shambles for the police to handle.

I was curious, so I peeked through the door of the men's room. The scene looked nothing like it had been when Janet and I slipped out. Sprout's clothing had been ripped away to expose his chest—I'm guessing for the defibrillator. The floor around his body was littered with used antiseptic wipes. Apparently the medics had cleaned Sprout's face and mouth with the wipes prior to inserting a plastic resuscitation device down his throat. The one-time use-and-throw-away, plastic resuscitation device was lying next to the body, being ignored. I breathed a sigh of happiness. If there had been any "negative forensic evidence," it was obliterated now.

"Anyone with him when he fell?" the police sergeant asked the assembled group gawking through the door.

No one answered. Janet stood farther back—away from me, as planned—and also remained quiet. We would only speak if spoken directly to.

The sergeant sighed and said, "Okay, no one leaves until you've been interviewed—no one."

Of course, my official retirement party was cancelled, which really didn't upset me, but I had to make a show of it. So I moped around. I asked the lady supervising the decorations whether the party was cancelled. She gave me a look that communicated, *I can't believe you'd ask that,* but said nothing.

The director of the Agency showed up—not because it was my retirement party but because Sprout had died. He was asking everyone who would pay attention to him questions about what had happened. He finally came over to me. "Mr. Wolfe, can you shed any light on what happened here?"

"No, sir, I was having a quiet drink at the bar when someone found his body in the men's room. I don't know anything else."

"Some people said you and Sprout were arguing before he died. What was that about?"

"To be honest, sir, we never got along. We always argued about everything. It was just the nature of our relationship. It didn't mean any more today than a hundred times before," I answered.

The director nodded and studied me.

"Mr. Sprout often seemed angry," I added as an afterthought.

"Well, all right, but if you think of anything, let me know, will you?"

"Of course, sir . . . does this mean my retirement party has been cancelled?" I asked again.

From the expression on his face it was obvious the director thought I was a moron.

Which is the reaction I wanted.

The interviews with the local cops were short and sweet. Currently, they were interviewing Lee Collins, the young agent who had found Sprout. I slipped as close as I could get without seeming suspicious. I could hear him tell the officer that Mr. Sprout seemed agitated but that he saw nothing unusual. After a few more questions Collins was released. As far as I heard, Collins didn't mention my name during the interview, but someone had or the director would not have known about our argument.

The same officer decided it was my turn. He asked me whether I knew the deceased. I told him Sprout had been my supervisor at the Agency. Then he asked whether we had been arguing. There was no point in hiding the argument—several people had witnessed it—so I answered Sprout and I had never got along. I said Sprout was a high-strung individual who often yelled at his subordinates. This time was no different than a hundred times before, but when we parted he was okay. I told the officer I went to the bar for a drink and I didn't see him again. He asked whether I saw who was last with the deceased. I said no. After a few follow-up questions, the officer let me go.

Janet was still waiting to be interviewed when I left the restaurant. As agreed, she and I didn't talk to each other anymore—we would stay very arms' length and all business.

In the parking lot, I stored the expended aerosol can in the trunk of Mary's Mercedes. I'd need to dispose of it in a way it could never be traced to me or identified for what it is. Maybe I should burn the aerosol can.

I'm beginning to think like a firebug lately.

As I was getting into the car, my cell phone sounded an alert. The X-Key Essential Program was alerting me that someone was emailing Sprout. I hit the icon for the app and read the message. It was from someone calling himself Agent M. The subject line was Mary Killigrew, so I read on.

Team prepared—on the way to hospital.

Whoever Agent M was, they had not deleted the original message that they were responding to via the "Reply" function. So I read the original message sent by Sprout earlier today.

Subject: Mary Killigrew
Location: Mercy Hospital, South DC, Room 307
Mission: Terminate immediately, any means necessary

A recent picture of The Fifty Billion Dollar Woman was attached.
She looks good even in this "kill her" picture.
How did Sprout know Mary Killigrew? Why had he ordered a hit on her? Who was Agent M? Had Sprout worked for the Panzram Company on the side? I didn't know the answers to these questions, but maybe Mary did. If I got there in time, maybe I could save her life and convince her to tell me.

Then it hit me: Sprout had been a really nasty character. He had killed Jimmy this morning, and then turned around and ordered Mary Killigrew murdered—all before lunch. If I had felt any remorse about his "stroke," I didn't now.

I started the Mercedes and checked the car's navigation system for the fastest route back to the hospital. According to the navigation system, the journey would take nearly an hour—DC traffic. I merged into the snail-paced, high-blood-pressure/heart-attack environment of Interstate 95.

I prayed that Agent M—whoever that was—would also face the same traffic to reach the hospital. In addition, I was hoping he was professional enough to spend time on-site to study the hospital and then set up the hit properly. Even if that were all true, I still had to hurry, because his email had said he was on the way. That was thirty minutes ago.

It's a horse race.

15

BACK TO THE HOSPITAL

I bent a few traffic laws and arrived at the hospital forty-five minutes later. I quickly parked and walked into the building, then stood in the crowded lobby and considered the scenario. I had several problems. Everywhere I looked I saw potential assassins, and they had a clear advantage. I didn't know what the killers looked like. I didn't know whether they would be disguised as staff or visitors. I didn't know whether they were already here or whether I'd gotten here first. I didn't know how many assassins there were. It occurred to me there were other things I didn't know. In fact, I didn't know what else I didn't know.

I briefly considered notifying the hospital security but then decided against that. By the time I explained the situation to them and they began to act, it could be over. Besides, explaining how I knew would expose me. So there was only one tactic I could employ. I would ride the elevator up to Mary's floor. It was shoot-from-the-hip cowboy time.

I stepped onto the elevator. Everyone in DC must have been riding that elevator at that moment. I was becoming weary from all the crowds. I was wedged in between some old guy with a walker and a fat woman coughing her head off. On the opposite side of the prisonlike cube was a young woman with two small rug-rats who were constantly fussing and hitting each other. She reprimanded them to be still. They ignored her and continued. She slapped the kids, and they began crying. Now it was worse. In the other corner was a woman dressed in purple scrubs from head to toe—some kind of medical staffer. She was fiercely staring at the floor numbers overhead, trying to pretend she was alone in the elevator. Two men, wearing business suits and ties, stood in the center of the cube. They looked fit.

Surely professional hitmen wouldn't show up looking like the movie version of professional hitmen.

There were two more women standing against the wall. They both wore the same solid-purple scrub pants and slipover tops as the medical staffer staring at the floor-indicator lights. Although it was obvious from their tight-lipped smiles they didn't like being trapped inside the crowded cubical, they chatted with each other as if no one else existed. I decided they belonged here. The one common trait that everyone in the elevator shared was that they looked hopelessly trapped and miserable. No one enjoys riding in a crowded hospital elevator—not even assassins.

Could one of these people be the infamous Agent M—an assassin?

The doors opened to Mary's floor, and most of us got out. The floor was teeming with hospital staff, wandering patients, and visitors. There was a janitorial crew slowly threading their way through the throng of people. They were pushing a laundry cart toward the elevators. I thought that odd. Didn't the janitorial staff do their work in the middle of the night when there was minimal traffic? The laundry cart appeared to be filled with soiled sheets, blankets, towels, and similar material. I stopped, pretending to be disoriented. As the three-man crew passed, I studied each closely.

What do janitors look like?

These guys were dressed in blue coveralls. They were all trim and muscular—athletic—not a potbelly among them. They were all in their mid-thirties and had expensive haircuts. I studied the nearest man's hands. His fingernails were trim and clean.

Don't janitors have dirt under their torn nails? Maybe one of these guys is Agent M.

Moving through the hospital disguised as janitors would allow them to go almost anywhere and to carry awkward equipment in their utility cart—like guns. Later, witnesses would only remember the janitor uniforms but not the men. It was a perfect disguise for a killer in the hospital. I decided I had my assassins.

The janitor with the perfect fingernails looks Hispanic.

"Buenas tardes, senor," I said. My accent sucks, but I got the words out.

Perfect Fingernails stopped and turned to me. "What did you say, mister? Are you some illegal alien or something?"

A second janitor rudely shoved the cart past me, giving me a disdainful look as if I were a pile of turkey dung. The third guy acted like he didn't know I existed. He was checking out a nurse in tight pants who had just exited from a nearby room. I agreed with him. She had a nice figure.

Get your mind back on business.

Maybe I was wrong about Perfect Fingernails, so I said, "Sorry, I thought you were someone else—someone I knew."

I guess I'm not the deductive-reasoning mental giant I thought I was.

I didn't bother trying to guess who any of the other people were as I walked directly to Mary's room.

I glanced back down the hallway before entering. The janitor crew was now waiting at the elevator. Standing next to them were the same two guys, dressed in suits and ties, who had ridden up the elevator with me. If I didn't know better I'd think they were with the janitors, but that couldn't be, right?

I stepped inside Mary's room and found the bed empty. I stepped into the hallway and double-checked the room number. I was in the correct room, but Mary wasn't here. I went back inside and touched the sheets. They were warm, so she hadn't been gone very long. Her purse rested on the nightstand next to the bed. Women don't usually leave their purses lying around unattended.

The bathroom door is closed. Maybe she's inside.

I still had Mary's blue-and-black-colored Smith & Wesson .40-caliber pistol. I drew it and pressed it alongside my leg as I cautiously approached the door. I knocked lightly, "Mary, are you in there?"

No answer.

I knocked again then tried the door. It wasn't locked. I slowly pulled it open and looked into the closet-size lavatory. It was empty.

I turned back to the room and looked for any clue of what had happened. Everything seemed as it should be, except for Mary's purse sitting unattended and the fact that Mary was missing. I pocketed the pistol, stepped out into the corridor, and looked in both directions. I saw nothing suspicious, except the three janitors were pushing their cart into the public elevator at the far end of the corridor. The two suits followed them in.

Don't hospitals have a service elevator for maintenance and janitorial staff?

You're an idiot—those guys aren't janitors!

I ran down the hallway, almost knocking an older gentleman over who had been racing along with tortoise-like speed in the same direction as me. I caught him from falling, excused myself, and sprinted away. A medical assistant called after me to slow down. I waved and increased my speed.

The lady in purple scrubs, who had fiercely stared at the floor numbers overhead, followed the janitors and the two suits into the elevator.

Are they all in it together?

I arrived just as the doors shut. I had been too slow.

Damn!

16

THE MORGUE

I stood there, helplessly watching the floor-indicator lights above the doors. The elevator was going down. My head spun like a cartoon character, looking for the stairs. There they were: back in the direction I had just come.

Double damn!

I shoved my way past several people who were taking up the entire width of the hallway in a gaggle—moving like they had all day—rudely oblivious to anyone else's needs.

As I wedged past, the lady barked, "Well, excuse me!"

"No problem, lady. I forgive you," I responded as I ran toward the stairs.

I could still hear her complaining to her companions, "Did you see that?" as I vanished through the doorway.

I took the stairs down two at a time.

The assassins were taking Mary to the basement—I was sure of it. This time I would listen to my little voice. I didn't know what I would do once I reached the basement, but I was sure they were taking her down there.

Hurry! They have a head start.

I made it to the lobby level and was forced to stop. These stairs didn't go to the basement. I ran to a candy striper, sitting peacefully behind her information counter. She was talking to a lady, answering a question. I pushed the lady-visitor aside and was nearly shouting between breaths, "How do I get to the basement?"

"I'm sorry, but the basement is for hospital staff only," answered the candy striper indignantly.

The lady I'd shoved aside cut in. "Do you mind? I was here first."

I glanced at her with my *I'll kick your ass if you say anything else* look. Then I turned back to the candy striper. "Look, lady, it's very important I get to the basement fast. Someone's life is in danger. Just tell me where the stairs are—now!" I realized I was shouting.

Not productive.

Other people began looking at us. A security guard, dressed in a pair of dark-blue slacks, a white shirt with badge, and a two-way radio, began walking slowly in our direction. I was drawing an unwanted crowd that would only slow me down.

I took a deep breath and forced myself to regain composure. I produced my phony badge and duplicate government ID. "Look, I'm a cop. I'm trying to stop a murder. If you don't cooperate you could be charged with obstruction of justice—maybe even accessory to murder."

Sounds pretty official.

The candy striper glanced over my shoulder. I knew she was watching the approaching security guard and was thinking he'd take care of everything. "To your left," she pointed.

I turned and rushed to the indicated door. There was a small plaque that read "Staff Only." I didn't bother to look behind me. I was sure the security guard would be following.

I took the stairs two at time and stopped on the bottom landing, allowing my breath to settle. I drew Mary's pistol again and checked that it was ready to fire. I did that more as a way to collect myself and prepare for what was to come than being unsure it was ready. I slowly opened the door and looked into a large, open-spaced room, with cement-floors and walls. There were large pipes attached to the ceiling overhead. The room was actually a corridor, stretching as far as you could see, but I couldn't see any people. There was a row of laundry carts lined up on the opposite wall from the door. They all looked exactly like the cart I'd seen the "janitors" pushing upstairs. I stepped through the doorway and allowed the door to click closed behind me. I stood very still for a long moment. Everything seemed quiet except for the drumming and roaring of the building's environmental equipment.

There was a metal plaque on the wall with arrows giving directions. To the left was the morgue. To the right was laundry and maintenance. Even though the "janitors" had been pushing a laundry cart, I doubted that was their destination. There would be people in maintenance and the laundry. If these men were planning to murder Mary, or already had, they didn't want witnesses. Besides, where better to take a dead body than the morgue? I moved to the left.

I knew I needed to move quickly. They had several minutes' head start, and if they were real professionals, that would be more than enough time to do their job. The morgue was almost two hundred feet from the stairwell, and I felt the need to stop at the various intersections and look both ways before crossing. Also, there were several closed doors that I didn't feel good about passing without checking. Therefore my passage took time—precious time Mary probably didn't have—but if I got killed on the way to saving her, I wouldn't save her anyway. So I moved with rapid caution.

The morgue had huge double metal doors with vertical, narrow windows running halfway down so you could see through to the other side before pushing them open. I peeked through the window and immediately saw the "janitor crew" talking to the two suits. They had all been in it together. I could see a woman's form exposed in the laundry cart, but I couldn't tell whether she was alive or not.

I heard a two-way radio squawking from behind me—the security man. I had to hurry. I pushed the door open and took aim at the nearest suit.

"No one move!" I shouted.

They complied.

I was trying to decide how to best disarm them and retrieve Mary safely when the door slammed opened behind me and that stupid security guard dashed in yelling, "Okay, what's going on in here?"

Things happened very fast after that, and I don't remember exactly how it went, but here's my best recollection: The guy I'll call "Janitor 1" drew a large-caliber pistol from under his coveralls and began firing. I'm not sure whether he was aiming at me or the security guard, but he hit the security guard square in the chest—twice.

I shifted my aim and fired at Janitor 1. I must have hit him, because he fell. I turned just in time to shoot Janitor 2—once in the stomach—who had also pulled a pistol. Janitor 3 produced a pistol but ran for the far door, firing over his shoulder as he dashed off. Acting from some dark instinct, I shot him in the back, and then turned back to the two suits, who had ducked behind a set of metal examination tables. They had guns too.

Everybody has guns in a city where it's illegal to carry a gun!

I pushed a heavy stainless steel gurney over so that it lay on its side and took cover behind it. We had a standoff.

As best I can estimate, only six seconds had passed since the security guy burst into the room.

I decided to try diplomacy. "If you haven't killed the woman yet, you can leave peacefully. I won't stop you."

The Suit's answer was elegant: he fired three rounds into the gurney I was hiding behind. I was surprised to see that the bullets punched nice clean holes all the way through. This gurney wasn't going to give me any cover—only concealment. Eventually, they'd get me if they shot enough holes in it. But then it was a two-way street. I fired back. They were stupidly hiding behind a table with open space beneath—not closed off. I could see them crouching down there. I hit one suit in the leg with the first try. The wounded suit began limping for the rear exit. I let him go, because Suit 2 was still punching holes in my gurney.

I felt a presence behind me. Just as I turned to see what it was, the woman in purple scrubs, from the elevator, hit me with a metal stool. I felt the world spin and darkness began closing in. She raised the stool again to finish the job.

I shot her. The bullet hit her directly in the heart. She was flung backward several feet, crashing into a cement wall. She left a blood smear on the wall as she slid to the floor. The metal stool she'd used as a club was slung across the room. It made a loud clanging as it landed. I turned back to readdress Suit 2 and saw that he had joined his partner—the suit with the bullet hole in his leg—and they were both disappearing through the far door. I fired at their disappearing backs, out of reflex more than logical thinking, and missed. The two suits had gotten away.

I told you I wasn't my famous brother—the expert shooter.

Blood was trickling down the back of my head, and I felt dizzy. But I forced myself to stand up, using the turned-over, bullet-perforated gurney for support. I stood quietly for a few moments to gather myself, but my eyes constantly swept the room. I saw no more threats, so I unsteadily walked over to the laundry cart and peered down at Mary. She was either unconscious or dead. I couldn't tell which by just looking at her. To be truthful, I was a little afraid to find out. What if I hadn't gotten here fast enough? I'd feel bad forever, but she'd feel even worse.

No she wouldn't. She wouldn't feel anything.

I hated my little voice when it said things like that.

I placed two fingers on the side of her neck and felt for a pulse. It was there—strong and steady. She was alive! I inspected her for any wounds or bleeding but found none except the one I'd given her earlier—the reason she was in the hospital. I decided she'd be okay for a moment.

Start thinking.

First the pistol . . . I wasn't concerned too much about my DNA and prints because, if you remember, I'd sprayed my hands this morning. But I wasn't sure whether Mary's, or possibly even Janet's fingerprints and DNA were still on the pistol (remember, she'd held it on Sprout earlier, even though she'd washed it off afterwards).

Fortunately, we were in the morgue, with resources to clean body fluids and DNA. I walked over to a stainless steel sink and turned on the hot water. There were antibacterial soaps and blood cleaners on a shelf above. I scrubbed the pistol inside and out—bullets and all. It took a couple of minutes.

Mary groaned, attempted to rise up from the laundry cart, and then fell back. She'd be fully awake in a moment.

I thought about the security guard. He was dead—shot by one of the assassins. I might as well make him the hero. I placed the Smith & Wesson in his hand. Then I ejected the magazine and pressed his fingers on it—fingerprints and DNA. I returned the magazine to the pistol, put it in his hand, and fired until the magazine was empty, aiming in the general direction where the bad guys had been standing. There would be bullet holes all around the room, and powder residue on the security guard. Also his fingerprints and DNA would be on the weapon. The angle of trajectory for the bullets might be off, but it would work. Maybe he had shot from a prone position. The investigators would think he'd shot it out with the assassins. I made him a hero. They would posthumously forgive him for carrying an unauthorized weapon on the job, which would make him even more of a hero. In my experience, the police like the evidence pieces to fit a nice neat pattern. They generally accept at face value the clues that fit the pattern that supports their working theory for the crime. They would decide the security guard had shot it out with the others and had been killed in the process. The pieces fit close enough. It's unlikely they'd look further.

You better stop patting yourself on the back. This only works if you and Mary are not here when more security guards, or the cops, show up.

It was that little voice of mine again, but this time he was right.

I had one more task before we slipped away: I wanted to have information about what would happen when the cavalry arrived, just in case. I stood in the center of the room and turned 360 degrees, studying where the ceiling and walls met. In one corner of the room was a gaggle of pipes growing out of the wall. I pulled a chair over to the corner and climbed up. Then I reached into my pocket and removed a small camera, turned it on, and stuck it in the corner. The pipes would hide it from even reasonably discerning eyes.

If you remember, I'd brought it with me this morning from my condo. The tiny camera transmitted the picture and sound via cell phone technology. It had an adhesive backing that would stick to almost anything. Once activated, it would send pictures and sound to a cloud server for me to download and watch at my leisure. It was motion-activated, so I wouldn't have to sort through hours of nothing. Later, I could review the video to see where the cops' investigation was going. It would record twenty-four hours of action, which should be enough.

I scooped Mary up, who by this time was conscious but not yet steady.

Her first words were, "The bastards came into my room, hit me on the head with a leather sap, and tossed me into the laundry cart."

A leather sap—same as the guys in Mary's townhouse.

"You've been avenged. The security guard came in and shot them all except the two guys in suits who managed to escape," I answered.

"Not true—I saw you shoot those guys, not the security guard," she said.

"Well, let's keep that our little secret, shall we? Right now we need to put some distance between us and this shooting scene."

I pulled a white lab coat off a hook on the wall, and told Mary to put it on. It wouldn't do to have her wearing a paper dress as we walked out of the hospital. Then I found a pair of surgical paper slippers for her feet. It also wouldn't do for her to be walking around barefoot.

We exited the same door the two suits had escaped through a few minutes earlier. Luck stayed with us as we rode a freight elevator to the lobby, where we found chaos: Several uniformed police officers were talking to the candy striper; other police officers were talking to potential witnesses. Luckily, no one paid us any attention, so we hurried through the main doors and out into the parking lot.

By the time we reached the car, Mary had regained her full composure. "Let me clean that gash in your head," she offered.

She was referring to the ugly laceration where the purple scrubs lady had hit me with the metal stool. Mary removed the small bottle of water from inside her center console and then opened the glove compartment and extracted one of her feminine hygiene napkins. She wet the napkin with water and began dabbing it on my gash.

"Hey! What are you doing? I'm not having a period!" I yelled.

"Be quiet! These are made to soak up blood. There's nothing better, and you need to clean up."

I shut up and sat still as she pressed the feminine napkin hard against my wound to stop the bleeding. I kind of liked her fussing over me but didn't say so.

After a couple of minutes the bleeding had stopped, and she announced, "There, now you're suitable for public consumption."

"Thank you," I replied meekly.

She reached inside the glove compartment and snapped, "Where's my Smith & Wesson? It was here."

I pled guilty. "It's in the trunk. I went through your things."

"I want it back!"

I laughed. "Not until I feel I can trust you."

"You can't trust me! What do you mean?"

"Give me a break. I have no idea why you were following me or what you're intentions are. You won't even tell me who you really work for."

Then she said, "My purse—I need to go back inside and get my purse!"

That was a quick change of subject.

"Forget your purse. I'll buy you a new one," was my response.

"No, my purse has something in it I need—something important. I'm not leaving without it.

17

THE PURSE

I heard myself saying, "You stay in the car. I'll go up and get your purse."

My will won over.

"Get my street clothes too, will you?"

I left her in the front passenger seat but took the car keys. I removed my overcoat, so I would look at least marginally different. Then I retrieved my own .40-caliber pistol from the trunk and briskly walked back inside the lobby, setting course directly for the elevators. But there were a half dozen uniformed police playing Keystone Cops in the lobby, and they were checking everyone. It got worse.

The candy striper saw me and shouted, "There he is! There's the man I told you about!"

Two uniform police officers approached me.

Double damn!

I had my pistol and bogus federal police identification, but I didn't want to use either, if possible.

"We want to talk with you."

"What can I do for you, Officer?"

"Were you in here earlier, threatening that lady?"

"I just got here. She must be mistaken. You saw me walk in just now."

"Let's see some identification," demanded the officer.

I produced my civilian driver's license from Virginia and nothing more. He studied the license for several moments then handed it to his partner. The partner made notes in a small notepad. I was now on their radar. That was not good, but alone it was still manageable. It would only become a real problem if they discovered anything else that connected me to the shootings downstairs.

"So what are you doing here, Mr. Wolfe?" asked the officer.

"I was coming to visit a friend of mine, Miss Mary Killigrew."

"What room is she in?" he asked.

"I don't know. I just got here, remember?"

"Don't be a smart-ass," the cop shot back at me.

"I'm not! I just walked into the lobby when you stopped me. You saw me come in! What's this all about?"

The officer called to the candy striper, "Could you come over here please?" When she arrived he asked, "Is this the man who threatened you? You must be sure."

She studied my face.

I smiled as big as possible, and stood straight up, not bent over her counter like before. I was trying to look different from stressed and angry.

Several seconds passed and she still said nothing.

The officer asked again, "Is this the man?" There was an edge to his voice.

"I'm not sure ... he said he was a policeman and he wore a heavy coat. This man seems taller ... I'm not sure ..."

The police officer sighed. "Okay miss, you can go back to your work station." He exchanged looks with his note-taking partner, and then looked back to me. "You can go, but we know who you are and we can find you if we need to."

"Sure . . ." I mumbled.

They gave back my license and let me go. As I stepped into the elevators, I saw four cops entering the stairwell leading down to the basement. It wouldn't be long before they locked the hospital down tight. I had to hurry.

I stepped onto Mary's floor and weaved my way through the crowds of staff, patients, and visitors. As I walked past the central nurse's station, I saw Mary's purse sitting on a desk behind the counter. Someone had taken it out of her room and placed it there. That meant several things: They knew she was missing; they probably expected foul play, since women don't leave without their purses; they may eventually tie Mary to the shooting in the basement; I had used her pistol to shoot those men; and it may be traceable.

The cop in the lobby has your name and knows you're here to visit Mary, which will connect you to her and therefore to the shooting. You're toast!

I was beginning to really dislike my little voice, but he was right.

But I was here to retrieve Mary's purse and clothes, if possible. I decided the direct way was best. First, I went to her room, opened the closet, and grabbed a plastic bag with panties, bra, shoes and other miscellaneous items. Her coat and dress hung on a hanger, so I grabbed them too.

I walked back to the nurse's station. For the moment no one was there, so I slipped behind the counter, just like I belonged there, and snatched Mary's purse. Then I casually walked to the stairwell. The stairs are quicker—and healthier—than the elevator.

Amazingly, everything went smoothly: I arrived in the lobby without any incident and was able to walk out through the main doors unchallenged. Maybe my luck was improving.

On my way back to the car, I quickly searched Mary's purse to find what was so important that I had to risk my freedom to retrieve it. I found nothing obvious.

Except a flash drive.

18

FINDING TRUST

Just as I reached Mary's Mercedes, two fire trucks and two paramedic trucks rolled up. *Paramedics responding at a hospital?* The firemen and paramedics were followed by several police vehicles. They found the bodies.

Surprisingly, Mary was still waiting in the car. I started the Mercedes and promptly but slowly drove out of the parking lot. I'd just made it. As I drove past the front of the building, I could see they were closing it down—no one in or out.

I turned onto the expressway and headed south, staying in the slow lane. I didn't want to be noticed by anyone. I'd be taking an exit to the west in another couple of miles. I wanted to get off the expressway with its surveillance cameras and state troopers.

I tried not to look at Mary as she changed back into her street clothing: bra, panties, and all. It took all the will power I had not to look. She, on the other hand, didn't seem to care whether I was looking or not, because she took her sweet time dressing. Only after she was fully clothed did I openly inspect her. I thought she was still just as beautiful as I thought when she entered the Starbucks this morning. The only flaw was the bullet hole in her clothing and the blood stains.

I'll have to spring for a new outfit to compensate her.

We drove several miles with no conversation. It was becoming uncomfortable, and I needed to know a few things. I needed to chip some ice off the edges of our relationship, so I asked shyly, "How are you feeling?"

She glared at me. "I'd feel better if you hadn't shot me."

"You were going to electrocute me with that zapper. It was the only thing I could think of at the time."

"Yeah," she muttered.

Another mile passed before she said meekly, "Thanks for getting my purse."

"What was in there that's so important?"

"A USB drive."

"What's on it?" I asked.

"Some personal stuff—nothing you should be concerned with."

"What kind of personal stuff?" I pressed.

She had her head turn away from me, watching the countryside pass by. "It's personal—not your concern," she repeated.

"I risked everything to go back in there. What's on the USB?"

"I told you." Then she asked, "So where are we going?"

Changing the subject, avoiding answering my questions.

"To my Old Rock House, in the Shenandoah Valley region of Virginia. You'll be safe there.

"Your old rock house? I don't like camping. Let's go to my townhouse."

"We can't. It's been trashed. Whoever is after you sent a team there too."

"How do you know?" she asked.

"Because I was there. I caught them stealing your computer and personal papers."

She looked pale. "Did they get them?"

"No, I talked them out of it. I have your computer and files in the trunk. I left the carpet cleaners—that was their disguise—tied up in your townhouse, and then called 911. Right now, they're probably trying to explain what they were doing tied up in your townhouse."

"The old carpet cleaner scam," she said with a chuckle.

"Right . . . they said they worked for the same employer as you—the Panzram Company."

"You had a conversation with them?" she asked.

"Of course, but why would your employer want you dead, and what would you have on your computer, or in your papers, that they wanted?"

. . . and why won't you tell me what was stored on the flash drive?

But I didn't ask that—not yet.

She closed her eyes, took a deep breath, and leaned her head back against the headrest. "I'm not sure."

She's lying.

We were now driving on a narrow, two-lane road.

She asked, "Can I have my pistol back?"

"No!"

"Why not?" She looked so sweet and sexy. Her voice had just the right tender edge to it.

"Because I don't want you shooting me." I was weary of her holding back information and lying. "You want my trust; you need to tell me what's going on. Stop keeping secrets. Stop lying."

"How did you know where I live?"

She's diverting the questioning again.

"That's my secret for now. Answer my questions first."

"I need the information on my computer," she said.

"What do you have on your computer that your employer wants to kill you for?"

She fell quiet again.

I never took her for the sulky-type.

I'd had enough. I needed her to talk to me even if it meant saying something not pleasant for either of us. "You need to talk to me. If you don't . . . well, use your imagination."

She let out a long sigh and said, "Okay, what do you want to know?"

"Let's begin at the beginning. You said you were supposed to recruit me, right? Recruiters don't wear bulletproof vests and carry a Taser and a pistol, and they aren't targets for assassination by their own employer. That's extreme, even in the spy business."

She looked directly at me, "What's your point?"

"Why are you armed for World War III? Why does your employer want you dead? Who are you really?" There was an annoyed edge to my voice.

Mary studied the passing farmlands before answering. "Okay, you're right, I'm not a recruiter. I contacted you for help. I have information about the Order, and I wanted your help."

The Order again.

"You mean you want to give me information about the Order of the Golden Squirrel?"

"Yes, the secret organization you have been investigating . . . building a file on," she replied.

I said, "I've been investigating . . . but I haven't . . . I didn't know anything about these squirrels until this morning. When I first heard of them, I thought the name sounded like some kid's club, invented by a nine-year-old. I have no file."

Then it hit me. "Wait! If you have information about the Order, is that why those guys were in your townhouse, and why the hit team came after you at the hospital?"

She didn't miss a beat. "I have something they want. I thought I'd covered my tracks, but somehow they knew."

Ah, maybe a grain of truth . . .

She continued. "They've done this before. Panzram sends a team in, takes everything that could have any connection to the Order, and then the person disappears, dying a natural death or by accident."

"Or commits suicide?" I asked, thinking of Jimmy.

"Sometimes," she answered.

"This doesn't make sense. Why would Panzram Company want you dead for knowing about the Order? There's something you aren't telling me."

She sighed. "It's a long story."

". . . long drive," I retorted.

19

THE ORDER OF THE GOLDEN SQUIRREL

We stopped at a coffee shop and purchased coffees and sandwiches. While I was waiting for the food to arrive, my security phone app dinged. Someone was breaking into my condo. I watched the smartphone screen as three men dressed in dark clothing ransacked my condo. They found my hidden closet and took all my toys—the bastards! They even took the bath towels that Janet and I had used that morning, placing them in large evidence bags. They finally left. I didn't contact the cops because I didn't want them involved. This was my project.

I decided to check the video file for the little camera I left in the men's room where Sprout died. I activated the feed and watched. The director of the Agency was there, giving orders. It was unheard of that someone of his rank would be involved personally. I watched in amazement for a while, then shut down the feed and pocketed the cell phone. I'd seen enough. I had no idea why they wanted to cover up Sprout dying from a stroke, or why they had tossed my condo. It didn't make sense. I would have to let Janet know so she could cover her own ass—just in case.

The food arrived, and we got back on the road. We ate in silence as I drove and I speculated about why anyone was interested enough in me—a retiree—to burgle my condo. It didn't make sense.

After a few quiet miles, I asked Mary, "So tell me, what you know about the Order of the Golden Squirrel?"

"I don't know much," she said. "They're very secretive."

She's still evading questions.

"Tell me what you do know. It could make a difference—maybe save both our lives."

Mary seemed to be considering her words before she spoke. She talked slowly at first. "In the 1960s—during the antiestablishment days, the Vietnam War–protest days—a group of college students formed an off-campus fraternity because they were denied permission to form an official, on-campus fraternity. They were a rebellious bunch and decided to take revenge against the fraternity system. One of the ways they did that was to name their fraternity the Order of the Golden Squirrel, instead of using the Greek alphabet like traditional fraternities do."

"That name sounds so immature."

She nodded. "Well, at the time, they were young—still in their late teens or very early twenties."

"How many of these frat brothers were there?"

"I don't know, but enough to cause trouble for the legitimate fraternities on campus. At first, they just made midnight raids on the other frats—simple vandalism and harassment. They also raided women's sororities—stealing panties and bras and keeping them as trophies: all adolescent misdemeanors—nothing too serious. Besides vandalism and petty theft, there were a few cases of assault and battery, but from what I know that was pretty much the extent of their mischief in college."

"How did they get to be killers, and how does the Panzram Company fit in?" I asked.

Mary studied me before answering. When she spoke, her voice was quieter, more thoughtful. "As the frat brothers moved into the real world, they became successful in both private business and government. Some even entered politics. But they stayed in touch and each year met in a luxury resort to party and reminisce. At some point they realized they had the foundation for a potentially powerful organization. They could use their connections to become rich and powerful. That's when their annual meetings became serious business."

She stopped talking.

She's still holding something back.

"Go on . . ." I said.

"Now they use the meetings to plan future, coordinated activities to make themselves even more powerful and wealthy."

"Yes?" I was becoming impatient.

She gave me a sideways look and sighed. "What are you going to do with me?"

"I told you. I'm taking you to my private residence in Virginia to protect you from your employer."

Mary's voice took on a devilish tone. "Why are you taking me to your country home? Are you some kind of bondage serial killer? You going to tie me up and have your way with me?"

She doesn't sound worried about it.

I laughed. "No such luck for you. I'm having a party there tonight, and you have just been invited. There'll be fifty-sixty people. Hiding in a crowd will be the safest place for you right now."

"Oh." She sounded disappointed.

"Tell me more about your squirrels," I said.

"Today these frat brothers are a collection of the most powerful and wealthy men on earth. They control, or at least strongly influence, every major country. They are the heads of government, members of Parliament, US senators, CEOs of large corporations, oil sheiks, Muslims, Christians, Sunnis, Shiites, Democrats, and Republicans. They're all fabulously wealthy and powerful—the true ruling class—and they covertly work together to shape this world how they want it to look."

How does the Panzram Company fit into this?" I asked again.

She fell silent.

"Come on," I said.

Mary sighed and said, "They use the Panzram Company as their public face."

"And . . ."

"That's all I know."

"Who are these squirrels? What are their names?" I asked.

Mary was silent.

Mary is a professional. Change tact. Going back for her purse at the hospital wasn't just a girl thing. What is on that USB drive?

I asked, "What is on that USB drive? Why did I risk going to jail to get it?"

"It has information that could bring it all down for them."

"What?" I asked.

"It contains financial information about the Panzram Company and the identities of the original frat brothers."

20

THE FLOPPY DISK

For reasons unknown to me, Mary began opening up. I couldn't stop her from talking. Her words flowed out in a torrent.

"Apparently, at least one of the founding members had a bookkeeper's mentality. He kept an accounting of the members, the money they contributed, how much each paid into the slush fund, and the not-so-legal purposes they used the fund for, from the beginning up to today. The others realized the mistake of keeping such detailed records that could send them to prison and told him to stop doing it, but he didn't. He began storing the information on what used to be called floppy drives."

"You mean the two-and a-half-inch-floppy disks?" I asked.

"No, I mean the really old disks—the four-and a-half-inch floppies from four decades ago," she said.

"That information would be interesting for background and foundation, if we could read it, but it seems to me the statute of limitations has run on something that long ago," I offered.

"Not for murder and treason or for income tax evasion."

"Treason?"

"Of course. They work internationally and sometimes not for the benefit of the United States if they can make more money helping another country's defense or military goals."

"So you got hold of the original four-and-half-inch floppies?"

"Yes, I found them in a founding member's ranch in Arizona. He was entertaining me that weekend . . ." Her voice trailed off.

"You little devil—screwing one of the bosses. What is his name?"

"William Kincade," she said.

I said, "William Kincade . . . where do I know that name?"

"He was a presidential candidate about twenty years ago."

"I remember him. He's old money; his grandfather was in railroads and oil. He inherited much of his money and tried to buy the presidency but was squeezed out of his party's nomination by insiders. You're saying he is a member of the Order of Golden Squirrels, or whatever they call themselves?" Then I recalled the radio broadcast this morning. William Kincade had died of a heart attack over the weekend. I was about to mention the fact when she continued.

"There's more."

"I'm listening."

"I have it," she stated flatly.

"Have what?"

"He was fast asleep by nine o'clock, and he'd given the regular staff off that evening. There were only two security guards, but they were drinking beer and watching some movie in the theater. I had the run of the house. I found where Kincade stored the old floppies in his den. They were in a plastic box that was covered with half-an-inch of dust. It looked like they'd been sitting on that shelf for decades, forgotten. I connected his obsolete computer (there aren't too many computers still functioning that can read four-and-half-inch disks) to my laptop and saved all the data onto a USB drive."

The USB drive I went back into the hospital for!

I asked, "Was there current information on his computer?"

"Yes, and I downloaded that too." She continued. "I was putting everything back like I found it when Kincade came in and caught me. He had a gun and threatened to kill me. He was careless enough to let me get close, so I was able to grab the gun. We struggled."

I waited for her to continue, but she fell silent. "Well, what happened?" I asked.

"I had my Taser. I hit him with it several times. I guess he had a bad heart or something, because he died," she answered.

"That's why they are trying to kill you? Revenge?"

"No, they're after me because I got his computer files containing information about all the members—current and past—and the projects they used to make themselves so rich and powerful. It's all on that USB drive."

"Did you make more than one copy?" I asked.

Mary looked at me as if I'd just said something she'd never considered before. She finally said, "I only have the one."

"What happened next?" I asked.

"Luckily, I managed to escape with the USB drive before the security guards knew what happened."

"So the Order is after you for murdering one of their founding members. But you work for the Panzram Company, which is a front for the Order. If you work for them, why did you risk everything to get this information?" I asked.

"I wanted insurance to protect myself. I knew that sometimes the Order's employees disappear. That's obviously what they were intending this morning in my townhouse—make me disappear. I wanted something to hold hostage to protect myself."

Something doesn't fit here.

I said, "Seems to me you just made yourself a bigger target."

Mary said nothing. We drove in silence for several miles.

Her story doesn't add up.

21

THE RUSSIAN

My cell vibrated. It was an incoming call. I answered. "Yes?"

"Make a right turn at County Road 12, about two miles ahead, and follow the map I'm sending you." It was Janet.

"How do you know where I am?" I asked.

"Don't play naive."

She had linked to my cell GPS and had been keeping an eye on me. She might even be watching me via satellite.

"What will I find there?" I asked.

"I want you to meet with The Russian," she answered.

The Russian was another legendary figure in the espionage world. He had been responsible for a dozen security leaks and failed operations over the years that I knew about. He had no allegiance to any nation. He would sell information to the Russians, Americans, Cubans, Chinese—anyone that had the money. I'd always wanted to meet him.

"What's your part in this?" I asked. I didn't want to appear too eager. There would be others listening to our conversation.

Janet said, "I've been temporarily appointed to Sprout's position."

Janet had been promoted because of Sprout's death this morning. Ironic was insultingly inadequate to describe my thoughts. I chuckled and asked, "Why me?"

"The Russian asked to meet with you."

"Me ... personally ... by name?"

"Yes. Do you know why?" she asked.

"I have no idea."

Janet said, "Sounds like grounds for a treason charge."

"That and five dollars will buy you a cup of coffee at Starbucks," I answered. "Why does he want to meet me?"

"He claims to have proof that high-ranking US officials and politicians have been trading top secret information with the Chinese. He wants to sell us the traitors' names and provide proof we can use in court."

Could this be about the Order?

"I'm retired. Send someone else."

"Normally I'd agree—good riddance—but he insisted he'd only tell you and no one else."

"Why me?"

"I don't know why anyone would ask for you," she answered.

She's playing the "keeping a distance role" because someone is always listening in.

I played along. "Don't be insulting—acting like Sprout—just because you're in his position now."

She snorted over the phone. "Don't start insulting me just because I've taken Sprout's place."

I laughed. "I'm really not interested. I'm retired." I wanted to go and I would go—she knew it and I knew it, but we needed to play this out for those listening, or those who may review the recording at a later time.

She came right back with, "If I remember correctly, you've wanted to meet this guy for the past decade. Here's your chance. Besides, he's just a few miles over the next rise in a farmhouse. He's expecting you."

I pulled over to the side of the road then asked, "I assume this is official?"

"Yes, you're back on the payroll, at least for now."

"I want a raise. Make me a private contractor—at contractor rates, not civil service pay."

Janet said, "We'll talk about that if you come through with the goods."

Mary sat in the passenger seat, giving me a puzzled look. She was unable to hear what Janet was saying, but she could tell from my end of the conversation and my expression that something important was happening.

I took a couple of deep breaths before saying, "If I agree, as a contractor, what do you expect from me?"

"Find out what information and proof The Russian has and what he wants in return." Then she added in a quieter tone, "I would expect you'd treat him with respect—the same respect you gave to Sprout here at the Agency."

She wants me to kill The Russian?

I played along. "I'll give him the respect he deserves. How will I know if he's giving me good information?"

"We'll vet it later."

We'd played the game long enough. "Okay, I'll meet him, but I want backup in case this gets nasty."

"There's no one available. Between Jimmy's apparent suicide this morning and Sprout's stroke, all the Agency operators in the DC area are tied up. Besides, The Russian insisted you come alone."

I thought of calling my brother, Tom. "What about the FBI? They could have an HRT standing nearby."

"This stays in-house," she answered simply.

There was nothing more to talk about, so we hung up.

Meeting The Russian could get terminal real fast.

"What was that about?" Mary asked.

"The Agency wants me to visit The Russian."

"Who's The Russian?"

"The rumor is he sells defense secrets freelance to anyone with the money. He has no political or national allegiances. He's a thorn in everyone's butt."

The Russian is expecting me but not Mary.

I turned to Mary and asked, "Do you feel up to something tricky and maybe fun?"

"Always," she replied.

Bad idea—you can't trust her.

I decided not to listen to my little voice this time, which is usually a mistake.

Looking back on it, I guess I'll never learn.

22

THE SURPRISING FARMER

I studied the map Janet had sent me. It indicated that the farmhouse was not far away. After I had memorized the details, I turned off my phone and removed the battery. Then I removed the SIM card. Out of pure paranoia I put the battery and SIM card in separate pockets. I didn't even want them touching each other. Now I was reasonably sure the Agency couldn't track me—maybe. I exited the car, opened the trunk, and surveyed the toys stored in there.

Mary came around and immediately saw her Smith & Weston .357 pistol. "Hey! I want that back!"

"Take it!" I said.

She checked her revolver professionally and slipped it into her purse. "What's our plan?" she asked.

I didn't answer right away. Instead, I considered the second aerosol spray. When Janet said that I should pay the Russian the same respect I had Sprout, she was suggesting I kill The Russian. Maybe I could give The Russian a stroke. No, before I got into the same room with The Russian I would be searched. Anything resembling a weapon or a communication device would be confiscated—probably forever. I wrestled with the variables for several minutes.

Slowly, my plan came into focus.

I spent the next several minutes explaining my idea to Mary. She asked more questions than I had answers for, which actually helped because she brought up issues I hadn't thought about. It forced me to create solutions. In the end, Mary seemed to grudgingly agree.

Soon, I was driving alone, along the country road.

Janet had been right—our destination was just over the rise. It took less than five minutes to reach the wooden gate leading into the farm. But there were three tough-looking guys and a four-wheel-drive pickup truck blocking the entrance.

I rolled down the window. "Hi, guys! I was told to meet The Russian here. Hope I have the right address."

"Out!"

The three knuckle draggers searched and then re-searched me, taking turns, lest one of their comrades had missed something. They were very through. After the traditional pat-down, one guy used a scanner to check for transmitters, while his buddy started pulling my clothing free to see if something was secreted in the folds. They made me remove my shoes and closely inspected them, and then one of the guys must have had a foot fetish because he gave me a foot massage to see if I had anything hidden in my socks. The whole time a third guy stood watch, pointing an AK-74 at me.

After they were assured I had no toys or modesty left, the leader barked, "In the truck bed!"

Two of the knuckle draggers climbed in the back with me. Mary's Mercedes was left at the gate. I was instructed to sit quietly for the short, bumpy ride in the truck bed.

The dirt road led over a rise to reveal a farmhouse sitting in the center of a small valley. We stopped in front of the modern, two-story structure with shutters and gables. There were no rusty tractors or pickup trucks to be seen. Everything looked newly painted and well-maintained. The driveway circle in front of the house was paved and spotless—no oil stains. The house clearly belonged to a gentleman farmer, not a hardworking farmer with dirt under his fingernails.

Two more tough-looking guys with AK-74s were waiting for us on the veranda.

The leader barked, "Out!"

I climbed out of the truck bed and stood on the circled driveway.

We waited. I soon found out why.

New Guy—David Planter—appeared from inside the house and stood on the veranda. "Hello, Wolfe. Looks like I'm in control this time." He snapped at the leader. "You searched him for electronics?"

"Yeah."

I studied Planter with fresh eyes. He had fooled me this morning. Planter had told me he worked for Sprout, and I'd believed him. I had dismissed Planter as an amateur—New Guy—but right now, he seemed to be pretty competent. He was apparently working for The Russian. Maybe it was time for me to retire if a young punk like him could lie to me and I believed him.

Planter commanded, "I want him searched again!"

The leader began, "Not necessary—"

Planter cut him off. "Do it anyway!"

They found no additional contraband, but I think they did remove some navel lint that was missed the first time.

Planter had apparently regained his confidence after this morning's experience.

He's confident because his friends are backing him up.

"I see you brought some friends this time," I quipped.

Planter ignored my comment. Instead, he stepped back a few feet so his friends could have a clear line of fire as I entered the farmhouse—just in case.

"Inside!" Planter snapped at me.

All five shooters escorted me inside. Planter followed last from a safe distance. I was taken directly to a large, modern kitchen that would be functional for a medium-size restaurant.

I asked, "Are you The Russian?"

"Sit at the table." Planter snarled, still keeping his distance.

I guess he's a little gun shy after this morning.

I sat and waited quietly, but not for very long.

I had no preconceived idea of what The Russian would be like, but I was still surprised when I saw him. "Dapper" was the first word that came to mind. He wasn't particularly tall or short—maybe five eight. He was dressed in an expensively tailored, dark-blue, pinstriped suit with a maroon tie and black, highly polished Oxford shoes. His hair was clearly shaped by a high-end stylist, and he obviously spent time each day keeping his body trim and his muscles toned. A wave of energy preceded him into the room, and an aura of vigor surrounded him. His dark-brown eyes sparkled with excess energy. He must have a high metabolism. When he spoke, somehow each word had emphasis as if it were important.

"Mr. Wolfe, so glad to finally meet you." He spoke with an educated English accent. His words came crisp and fast.

I don't like him.

I agreed with my little voice. It was some feral thing I can't explain, but I decided, given the circumstances, that I should act civil—at least for now.

I replied, "I always thought you were a myth. I didn't think I'd ever meet you."

"I never thought I would meet you face-to-face either, Mr. Wolfe. You've been a thorn in my foot for over a decade. I am very happy to learn you have decided to retire. I wish you well."

I felt a primitive urge to punch him in the face. "Then why this meeting?"

"Because I have one final business proposition for you—one you may find very profitable."

"Do you mean me personally, or the Agency?" I was playing dumb.

He ignored my feigned stupidity and said, "I want to obtain the access codes and frequencies for the Perfidious Mountebank Program."

23

PERFIDIOUS MOUNTEBANK PROGRAM

The Russian continued. "In return, I will happily compensate you most generously and then send you off to live your golden years in peace and luxury, wishing you a *bon voyage.*"

The PM Program is the most secret program in the United States' military arsenal.

"I don't know what you're talking about," I said, trying to sound sincere.

"Yes, you do. I know that you were the primary designer for that nasty little program, and that in the past decade it has been installed in every military aircraft the United States has sold to any foreign country, even its closest allies. I want to buy its activation codes and frequencies."

"Gee, sounds interesting, but I still know nothing about this Prime Minister Program or whatever you called it."

The Russian chuckled. "Perfidious Mountebank Program: It means treachery and deception—an apt name for it—and let's stop playing the stupid game, please."

Mary should be in the building by now. Stall a little longer.

"Maybe it'd ring a bell if you told me what this program is supposed to do. We may call it something else in-house." I tried to sound sincere.

He studied me for several moments, and then sighed. "Very well, I'll play along for one more minute. The PM Program involves a hidden code in all military aircraft the United States has sold to foreign powers in the past decade. The code is hidden deep inside the avionics utility programs and virtually undetectable unless someone knows what to look for. Once activated by satellite signal, the program will cause the engines to shut down, the flaps to go to landing position, and the aircraft to plunge vertically to the earth and crash."

"Sounds deadly," I said.

"It's absolutely evil. But it does allow the pilot to eject—at least you showed some civility there. The PM Program is designed to be used if a foreign power attacks the United States, using the aircraft sold to them by the United States. The very genius part is that each individual aircraft has its own code and frequency, so you can select individual aircraft to bring down . . . such irony."

"What do you mean, 'such irony'?" I asked.

"That the United States has created such a perfect terrorist weapon . . .'"

"Impressive if it's true," I said.

"Don't pretend ignorance. I know, as a fact, that you were the designer for the Perfidious Mountebank Program."

Where's Mary?

I continued stalling. "Rumors are you were old-school KGB and went private when the Soviet Union disbanded. But you look too young to be ex-KGB, and you have a distinctive British accent."

"I take very good care of my body and went to school in England—spent my teens and early twenties there. You are not going to gain anything by prevaricating. How does one hundred million dollars sound?"

One hundred million!

I didn't hesitate. "Of course, but I don't have the codes and frequencies with me."

"Can you access them online?"

There was no point in pretending any longer. I shook my head. "No, the PM Program is the highest classified weapon in the US arsenal. You can only access the program by physically being in the room with the computer—it's stand-alone technology."

"So where is this computer?" asked The Russian.

"There's one in the Pentagon, another in the White House crisis bunker, another in the Colorado bunker—"

He cut in. "This isn't helping. I guess I don't need you after all—"

I continued. ". . . and I have a duplicate set of the codes and frequencies at my Old Rock House in Virginia."

At that moment Mary stepped through the doorway from farther inside the house. She wasn't armed, but she wasn't handcuffed either. Two knuckle draggers entered behind her. One of them tossed her revolver on the table. The .357 landed with a heavy thud. Then he tossed the five loose rounds. The rounds rolled around, and a couple fell off the table's edge and bounced on the floor.

"We found her sneaking around behind the house, trying to find a way inside," explained one of her guards.

Mary looked scared. She faced me and said, "I'm sorry, but they were onto me the moment I crossed onto the property. I had no chance."

There goes your backup plan.

"What's this?" asked The Russian.

"She's with me. I thought I'd leave her outside, but looks like that's not an option now," I answered.

The Russian seemed privately amused about something. "She's with you?"

"Yes."

Mary's eyes shifted to me, then to The Russian. I thought I saw something pass between them, but it could have been my imagination. "She shouldn't be in the room while we discuss our business," I said.

The Russian shook his head and said, "I think she should stay where she is, so we can keep an eye on her."

"We better do as he says," said Mary.

The quick look that had passed between them, plus her statement, set off alarms in my head. I asked her, "What exactly would you recommend I do?"

I could see her face turning red. She realized she'd just screwed up.

There's more going on than I know.

I turned back to The Russian and said, "All right, come to my Old Rock House tonight. I'm having a party—my retirement party for close friends and people I trust, but you're invited anyway. We can complete our business there. I assume you have some way for me to verify the transfer of funds?"

The Russian became still for a moment and then said, "This is too easy. Why have you given in so quickly?"

"Well, you have a half-dozen assault weapons aimed at me, and I am your prisoner in the center of a farm where my body could be buried and never found. But maybe more convincing, as a retiree I will be on a fixed income, and a hundred million is a lot of money."

He asked, "How do you reconcile your lack of patriotism?"

Don't overplay your hand.

"Now that you brought that up, I do have one question: how do I explain this meeting to the Agency? If you remember, you contacted them to arrange this meeting, so they know we're talking. How do you propose I get over that little speed bump?"

The Russian laughed. "I like smart. You are, of course, correct. The speed-bump solution is I will give you the names of the founding members of the Order of the Golden Squirrel, along with proof they are at this very moment selling China highly-classified information from America's space program."

"I assume the information you have is accurate and verifiable," I said.

The Russian was smiling. "Of course! I will provide the proof and their names, and in return the Agency will pay me one hundred million in gold. On the backside of the deal, you give me the Perfidious Mountebank Program codes and frequencies, and I will discreetly transfer the Agency's one hundred million, US dollars directly to you."

"Where's your profit?"

"Later, I can sell the PM Program for several times the hundred million."

"So this is a three-way. You get the PM Program codes and frequencies; the Agency gets the identities of the key people in the Order of the Golden Squirrel, with proof they are trading secrets to China; and I get the money."

"Essentially," answered the Russian.

"So in effect, you get the US government to pay me one hundred million dollars for giving you the PM Program?"

It was smart.

The Russian's smile had evolved into a smirk.

I really don't like him.

"What about her?" I nodded to Mary, still standing in the center of the kitchen.

"I will take care of her. She means nothing to you, does she?"

"Well, she's very attractive—"

Mary snapped at me, "Hey, what the hell does that mean?"

I continued, "I'd like a chance to know her a little better, if you know what I mean."

Mary's face had now turned a serious shade of red. "That's not happening! Some nerve! You shoot me this morning, then you leave me out in the middle of the country to hike into this farmhouse and play commando, setting me up to get caught . . . now you're thinking I'm some sex toy!"

The Russian was chuckling at our exchange.

"Don't forget I saved your life at the hospital—"

"Not enough! I wouldn't have been in the hospital if you hadn't shot me, sweet pea!" The words flowed in a torrent of genuine, heartfelt anger. If she was putting on an act, she should receive an Academy Award for her performance. I was beginning to doubt my doubts about her.

The Russian laughed and said, "I'll keep her with me. Call it insurance that you'll keep your word. I'll bring her to your rock house tonight, and you two can reconcile your differences. In exchange, you can take Mr. Planter with you. We can exchange our hostages as we complete our transaction. Say about eight this evening?"

I said, "I'd rather not have Planter."

"I insist!" said The Russian.

Mary blurted out, "Don't leave me here with these animals—please."

She is beautiful.

I considered my options while The Russian and I stared each other down. The silence became awkward.

"Well, your answer?" asked The Russian.

I grunted. "I don't want Planter hanging around, spying on me. He's an amateurish pain in the ass at best."

"It is not negotiable if you wish to leave here at this time. I need someone keeping an eye on you," declared The Russian.

"I don't like it," said Planter.

"Neither do I," said Mary.

"Me either," I said.

We have an accord.

The Russian said, "Good! It's settled!" Then he added, "I expect you to return Mr. Planter in the same condition he is now. I will, of course, do the same with your lady friend."

"Wait! Don't I have any say in this?" asked Mary.

The Russian and I spoke as a single voice. "No!"

"I want my car back!" she said.

She doesn't give up easily; I'll say that for her.

I said, "You can have your car back tonight. I promise to take good care of it."

"Yeah, right!" she said.

"I told you not to use your personal car for work," I said.

"She drives her personal car for work?" The Russian asked.

"Yeah, can you believe it?" I answered.

24

THE CONVENIENCE STORE

A short time later, I was driving the back-country roads in Mary's Mercedes, sans all my weapons and gear in the trunk. They even took the expended spray can I'd used on Sprout—goodbye, evidence. They had my cell phone, so I couldn't call Janet to report on the meeting. Planter was sitting next to me, sulking. I'm not sure why—he had his gun and cell phone, while I had neither. Yet he was supposed to be my hostage. It was a strange situation.

After an hour of driving with no conversation, I told Planter, "I have to stop at a convenience store to pick up some supplies for tonight's party."

"You don't have servants to do that for you?" His tone was packed with sarcasm.

"No, asshole, I don't."

Except for my full-time grounds keeper, Jackson.

Planter didn't need to know about Jackson, but he did need to know something else. "There will be a large number of people coming to tonight's event, and I recommend you behave yourself. Some of my guests aren't as civilized as I am. If you insult them they'll hurt you or maybe just make you disappear. They won't feel bound by my arrangement with your boss." I was smiling, so I don't think he believed me. He should have, because I was serious.

There is a general store about five miles from my estate. Over the years I'd fostered a relationship with the owner, who I will call Crockett. Our bond began as a strictly business relationship. Crockett agreed to open a line of credit so Jackson could drop by and pick up needed supplies to keep the property maintained, and so he could feed himself. After Crockett learned that I paid my bills on time with no complaints, and I learned he was an honest store-keeper who didn't overcharge me, we became more trusting of each other. I learned Crockett was a retired Special Forces sergeant, who served during the Vietnam Experiment in the late sixties and early seventies. I told him about my career with the Agency (leaving out classified details). That's when he asked whether I knew another Wolfe—a master sergeant named Thomas Wolfe. I told him that was my younger brother. With that exchange of information we opened a new chapter in our relationship.

I told you my brother was famous.

"Once Special Forces, always Special Forces," Crockett said. He had maintained his contacts inside the Special Forces community. As a result, he had a virtually endless list of Spec-Ops supplies and services at his disposal, including some very deadly men who would do favors for him. (The price would vary, depending on the type and length of the job, but sometimes they'd work for beer.) Crockett had proven to be a very valuable person to know in my line of work . . . er ... I mean my former line of work.

I pulled Mary's Mercedes into the parking lot of the general store. With the motor still running, I took a moment to study the area. We were in an area of the state that had resisted development since the beginning of time. Besides the store, there were only two buildings in sight: a gas station directly across the street and an old—but still operating—US Post Office about fifty yards down the road. Otherwise, only trees were visible in all directions. There were two other vehicles in the general store's lot. I knew the jeep belonged to Crockett but didn't recognize the second car.

I turned off the Mercedes and opened my door. Planter didn't move.

"You coming in?" I asked.

"This isn't a grocery store. It's a camping-gun-fishing store," he answered.

"It also sells hardware, food, and liquor. We're going to need a lot of food and liquor tonight. My friends are always hungry and thirsty. Come on in. They sell girly magazines. You can ogle them while I shop."

Planter didn't look happy, but he climbed out of the car.

"Recommend that you watch your manners in here. The owner doesn't take any shit from anyone," I advised him.

Crockett is a medium-size man, but he doesn't need to be big because he isn't the punch you-in-the-face-and-knock-you-down kind of fighter. He is a gunfighter. I've seen him shoot, and I think he'd give my famous brother a run for the marksmanship title. I don't recall ever seeing Crockett miss a shot, even at impossible distances and under impossible circumstances.

Crockett was setting up a beer display near the entrance when I entered. He straightened up and thrust his hand forward. "How the hell are you, John? Haven't seen you since the Fourth of July when you and that gorgeous woman—what was her name . . . Janet . . . when you and Janet came home for the holiday. How is Janet, anyway?"

"She dumped me. Guess I wasn't doing the job," I answered with a shy grin on my face.

"Damned women . . . same happened to me when I was a buck sergeant. I've never got too close to a woman since. I just rent a woman when necessary now."

"That's probably a better arrangement," I mumbled. Somehow acknowledging that I lost Janet was bothering me more than I had realized.

Crockett nodded and said, "Renting is cheaper in the long run. And you can tell them to leave when you've had enough, and working girls don't get offended."

I laughed despite myself. I had thought I was a chauvinist until I'd met Crockett and learned what true male chauvinism was. I looked around for the owner of the second vehicle parked outside. Then I saw the old-timer. I'd seen him around over the years. He was a World War II vet—one of the last of his breed—living out his final days in the same forest he'd been born in over ninety-six years ago. He saw me and waved with a huge smile. He was looking at the fishing gear in the rear of the store.

Don't worry about him.

Planter entered the store. His expression conveyed disgust with the archaic concept of a general store. I'm guessing he's a big-city boy, who enjoyed high tech chain stores, big box stores, loud restaurants, and crowded cocktail lounges. He wasn't shy about showing his aversion to being in the sticks either. His expression said he detected a foul smell in the store. Planter seemed on the verge of turning around and going back outside.

Crockett studied Planter. "Is the fed with you?" He had purposely asked loud enough for Planter to hear him.

I answered in a soft voice, "Yeah, but he's not a fed. He belongs to some gangster, and he's part of the reason I'm here. I need someone to babysit him this afternoon and then bring him to my party tonight. Of course you're invited. I'd feel incomplete—vulnerable—if you didn't attend tonight."

Crockett made another assessment of Planter, who had drifted to the magazine rack. He ask in a confidential tone, "What are the rules of engagement?"

"None; I'm thinking he has a limited shelf-life anyway."

"Consider him on ice," Crockett said almost theatrically loud as he walked around the counter and picked up a landline telephone.

I added in a softer voice, "He's armed."

"I assumed as much." Crockett reached under the counter and slipped a Colt Model 1911 pistol into his belt. His call went through. "Ralph, can you come over to the store? I have someone I want you to contain for me . . . no, not particularly gentle . . . fine. I'll keep him occupied until you get here." Crockett hung up and grinned at me. "Ralph will be over in five minutes. He likes doing this kind of work. There will, of course, be a nominal storage fee."

I said, "That's expected."

My back was toward Planter at the magazine rack, but Crockett's expression told me Planter was drifting in our direction. I turned around. Planter was standing just a few feet away. I looked directly into his hateful eyes.

Crockett pretended to ignore Planter. He said, "How about beer and chips, Mr. Wolfe? I also have some very good salami. It's a little spicy, but if you cut it into small bites, it'll go good with this cheese I just got in. There are also a variety of tasty crackers. If you wish, I could provide a prime rib roast—cooked and ready to eat. It's in the oven now. Come with me, I'll show you." Crockett began walking toward the food section of the store.

"What's this talk about putting me on ice?" asked Planter as his hand slithered inside his jacket.

I warned Planter about his manners.

At that instant, Ralph walked through the front door. He isn't a particularly tall or husky-looking man. In fact, Ralph is thin. But I knew him from several of our deer-hunting trips. Ralph is very wiry and very— almost inhumanly—fast. In addition, he has almost superhuman stamina. He once carried a 150-pound deer in a fireman's carry, along with twenty pounds of gear, three miles back to camp. When he arrived at camp, he found Crockett and me sitting around the campfire, drinking beer. Ralph had a huge smile on his face as he casually tossed the large carcass on the ground and said, "I hope you guys didn't drink up all the beer while I was bringing in the meat." He wasn't even breathing hard.

Ralph now stood in the general store's doorway, appraising the atmosphere. After a few moments, he shouted, "Hello, Crockett . . . Mr. Wolfe." Then he faced Planter. "Who's your friend, John?"

"I'm not his friend," said Planter. His hand had completely disappeared inside his jacket.

I answered, "This fine upstanding piece-of-shit is David Planter. I'm his quasi-hostage, in that he is keeping an eye on me until his boss arrives at the party tonight. After that I have no idea what he intends to do."

"That doesn't sound friendly," replied Ralph.

Planter apparently didn't like being talked about as if he weren't there. His hand moved much faster than before. His shoulder rose up almost to his ear—telegraphing his intentions—as he drew the pistol.

Like I told you before, Ralph is wiry and immeasurably fast. His iron like grip wrapped itself around Planter's gun arm and twisted before Planter's pistol had cleared leather. I'm sure I heard a bone snap, and I certainly saw Planter sink to his knees in pain. He had clearly given up any thought of shooting anyone. Ralph slowly and carefully retrieved Planter's pistol and slipped it into the side pocket of his dark-green cargo pants.

Ralph was grinning as he slipped a zip tie around Planter's wrists. I could see Planter wincing as the zip was pulled tight. I'm sure Planter's forearm or wrist was busted. From his expression it must have hurt like the devil. Ralph lifted Planter to his feet and expertly searched him. He found Planter's cell phone and removed the battery and SIM card. He pocketed the battery and now-useless phone and then laid the SIM card on the front counter and produced a fast-opening knife. He stabbed the SIM card so he could hold it on the tip of the blade. Then he extracted an old-fashioned, engraved Bronson cigarette lighter and set the SIM card on fire. After melting the SIM card on the blade's tip, he tossed the distorted, melted plastic lump into an ashtray on the counter. Then Ralph turned back to Planter and said in an almost gentle voice, "Come with me, sonny. We're going to spend a quality afternoon together. I have a massive collection of DVDs—almost any movie you can name. We'll have a beer or two and watch a few movies together."

"I'm supposed to stay with Wolfe until my boss arrives at the party," Planter whimpered.

Ralph laughed and said, "Don't worry about that." He looked at me. "How long do I keep him?"

"Bring him to the hangar after dark. I want him available and under our control when his boss arrives."

Ralph nodded and said to Planter, "You won't miss the party, I promise."

Ralph laced his fingers through the zip tie that bound Planter's wrists and pulled. "Come along."

Planter whimpered but followed.

At least Ralph didn't poke out Planter's eye with a gun barrel.

My little voice was being a smart-ass.

Crockett and I followed them outside to watch the show.

Ralph shoved Planter into the bed of his black, four-wheel-drive pickup truck. He had spent a small fortune sexing up the truck. It had a full roll bar; a string of LED aircraft landing lights strung across the top, pointing forward and rear; raised beefed-up suspension; Big Horn off-road tires and wheels; and a cowcatcher that covered the front grill. There were also at least four antennas sticking out of the roof and from other places, and a stainless-steel toolbox bolted in behind the cab.

Ralph said as he closed the tailgate, "There is no civilization between here and where we're going, so it won't do you any good to scream for help or jump out of the bed and try to run away. I'll just catch you, and next time I won't be so gentle. You behave yourself, and I'll treat you well. You create any problems, and this will be the worse day of your piss-ant-fucking life. You got that?"

Planter looked scared, but he nodded.

I shouted to Ralph as he climbed into the truck cab, "See you at the party tonight!"

"Wouldn't miss it!"

We watched Ralph slowly drive away with Planter sitting meekly in the open bed of the pickup truck.

Crockett and I returned inside the store.

"What else can I do for you today?" he asked.

My eyes swept the gun rack behind the counter as I answered. "I need to stock up for tonight's party. I'm expecting some old friends and a few enemies, so I'll need support."

"I'm planning to attend. I'll come prepared if you like."

The Russian will not come alone.

You also invited The Major.

Yeah, but The Major said he doesn't often attend such things.

But he didn't say no either.

I stopped arguing with my little voice and told Crockett, "That sounds good. I'll meet you in the hangar at about 2200 hours. I'm expecting my brother and his wife, plus Jackson is there."

Crockett chuckled. "Your brother and his wife? You don't need any more shooters. I'll just bring body bags and shovels."

I had to laugh—couldn't help myself. "Well, I still need hors d'oeuvres and alcohol for the party tonight. That prime roast sounds good too!"

The World War II vet, who had stayed back with the fishing tackle until now, ambled up to the front counter. He was carrying a plastic bag full of live bait—worms. "You guys are pretty good at taking out the trash, but in my day we didn't babysit them. We'd just burned their Nazi asses."

"The worms are on the house, Colonel," replied Crockett.

"You fellas have a good day." The old-timer was laughing as he ambled out.

MY OLD ROCK HOUSE

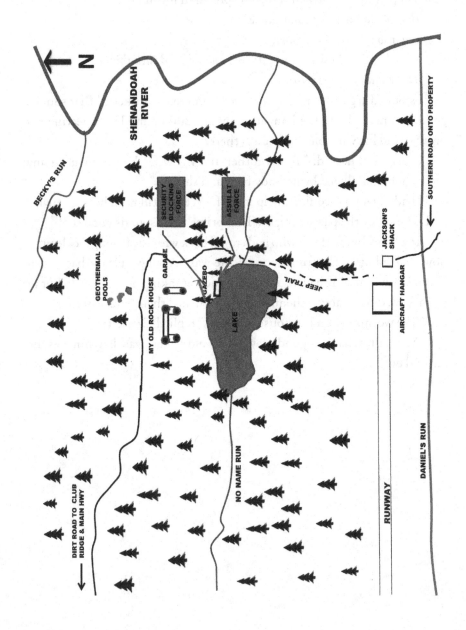

25

MY OLD ROCK HOUSE

You can find my Old Rock House about a mile's drive down a private gravel road after leaving the main highway. The private road takes you through tall pines, hardwoods, and other varieties of trees and brush. The land stays green year around. That's one of the things I like about this area. Driving in, it's not uncommon to see deer, fox, all manner of birds, or an occasional black bear ambling through the trees. I'm always amazed after I've been gone for a while how the house looks like an enchanted castle hidden deep in the forest.

I came around the last turn into full sight of the main house. There was a light dusting of fresh snow from last night that made everything look so clean and untouched.

It always feels good to come home, no matter where you've been or how humble home is. In my case, my Old Rock House is not exactly humble. In fact, I sometimes feel it's a little pretentious—a little over the top. The Old Rock House began as a very modest rock cabin in 1796, and over the centuries it has been added to and reconfigured a dozen times, until today it stands as a castle-style structure, complete with turrets on each of the four outside corners. Even the detached, six-car garage has turrets on each end. The walls are about two feet thick and made of solid stone, so the house stays cool in the summer and warm in the winter with minimal heating or air conditioning required. My brother Tom commented once that the thick walls were probably bulletproof, which he considers a plus.

Geothermal water is piped through the stone floor from deep underneath the earth, keeping the house warm even when there is snow on the ground. The original owners had discovered geothermal-heated pools on the property and had built the original stone cabin near them for that purpose. As technology advanced, so did the use of the natural heating from the pools.

For whatever reason, the house has remained a single-story structure over the centuries, so the current five thousand square feet is spread out over a generous piece of land. That just makes the building appear more impressive, and I always thought that when I get older, I won't have to worry about walking up and down stairs with my feeble old legs. The building does have a basement though. I put an indoor shooting range down there with a modest armory—just a dozen of my most favorite handguns and rifles. Whenever my brother Tom and his beautiful wife Terry visit, they always spend a measurable amount of time (and ammunition) downstairs on the range, but I don't mind—Jackson replenishes the ammo and keeps the weapons in good working order. He also does his share of target practice.

I parked the Mercedes between the garage and the main house and crawled out. I stood silently for a moment, stretching and smelling the sweet pines and other scents.

It's good to be home.

I saw Jackson working in the garage. He put down the object he'd been fiddling with and walked out to greet me. Jackson is a large man—especially for a former jet-jockey—maybe six feet three inches and two hundred thirty pounds. He flew a US Air Force A-10 Thunderbolt II, also known as the Warthog. The Warthog's primary role is to support ground troops and attack ground targets. Rumor is Jackson was one of the best Warthog pilots in the air force. His call sign had been "Rocket Man," because he had been so effective in placing rockets into the enemy positions where the sun doesn't shine. He'd reached the rank of major during his five-year stint and could have made a career in the air force, maybe even becoming a general, except his career was cut short by a court-martial.

Jackson had dropped a full load of unsanctioned incendiary bombs and then emptied his 30 mm Gatling guns into a few hundred Al Qaeda assholes that had been attacking a platoon of US Marines in Afghanistan.

When I first heard about his act, I thought, so what's the problem? Jackson's a hero, right? However, the mission wasn't sanctioned. (*Enter the micro-managing politicians and bureaucrats: "We aren't fighting a war—it's a political action."*) Even though Jackson saved a platoon of marines and probably single-handedly broke Al Qaeda's back in the region, he didn't have the green light to engage, so they court-martialed him. However someone, hidden in the bowels of the Pentagon, must have recognized that Jackson had saved thirty marines' lives, so they declared Jackson crazy, giving him a "Less Than Honorable Medical Discharge" instead of sending him to Leavenworth for twenty years.

I didn't know there was such a thing as a "Less Than Honorable Medical (mental) Discharge." I think someone invented it (took a personal risk) to help Jackson.

In any event, the Pentagon Fairy did Jackson no favor. With that kind of discharge Jackson can never fly again, and he's also denied most other careers he has skills for.

Tom had introduced Jackson to me. He'd said Jackson was an orphan. He had no family, and my brother was concerned that if Jackson were left to his own resources, he'd become homeless or maybe worse—end up in prison or dead.

So I offered Jackson the comfortable little cottage behind the aircraft hangar on my property—it's a shack, really. I told him it was his home as long as he wanted it. In return, he keeps an eye on things when I'm not here and performs some minor handiwork. If something needs fixing that he can't handle, he's authorized to call a repairman. As a side note, he's also a deadly shot with almost any kind of weapon. The bottom line is I've grown to trust Jackson completely. He's like a second brother to me.

Later, I'll show you the project Jackson and I have taken on together that I never would have dared alone. I keep it in the aircraft hangar. You'll like it!

Jackson smiled at me. His breath frosted in the air as he said, "Crockett called—said you were coming in. Said there may be trouble?"

"Yeah, about usual," I answered.

Jackson laughed. His laugh was closer to a growl—deep and gravelly. "I was hoping things would get more normal now that you're retired."

"They're trying to pull me back into it," I said.

"They keep humping your leg, huh?" Jackson grinned. "Maybe you should push their faces in a little—make them leave you alone."

"Well, I did a little. That's one reason it could get rough tonight. Some of the injured players, or their associates, may show up to push back."

Jackson laughed. "You're not worried about a few limp dicks are you?"

"I can handle the limp dicks. It's the hard ones that worry me. By the way, there are some supplies in the Mercedes for tonight's gathering. Could you take care of it?"

"That your new ride?" asked Jackson.

"No, belongs to a lady friend."

"Janet?"

I sighed and said, "No, Janet dumped me this morning, so I'm in the market for a new girlfriend."

Jackson shook his head and said, "That's too bad. I liked Janet. I was hoping she would work out."

"Yeah, so did I."

Jackson nodded to the Mercedes and said, "I'll get The Mule and shuffle the supplies to the main house and set things up in the game room—sound good?"

"Perfect!"

The Mule was one of several Polaris ATVs we used to get from one place to the other on the property. The one we'd named The Mule had a flatbed in the back—like a miniature pickup truck.

I added, "I'm going to the armory. I seemed to have lost my side arm earlier today. I recommend you kit up for tonight too."

"I was already planning to," Jackson replied.

"Has anyone showed for the party yet?" I was expecting several people who were traveling from faraway places, so they could arrive at any time.

"An Asian panther showed—said her name is Hong Li. She arrived early this morning. At present, I believe she's in the library drinking your good whiskey and listening to your CD collection."

Hong Li is the former agent from China who had helped me perform the skullduggery to ensure the 1997 Chinese Reversion went as planned. If you recall, I told you earlier the American administration at that time had wanted the Reversion to fail. Hong Li and I had made a great team, both inside and outside the bedroom. We made sure the Reversion went without a hitch. What she did for her country was patriotic—she probably got a medal. What I did was treason. But we both did the right thing. The result became known in the secret whisperings of the Agency's hallways as "The 1997 Chinese Fiasco." I have always had a crush on Hong Li. She is one of the most beautiful and exotic woman I have ever known.

I asked Jackson, "Is she still as beautiful as ever?"

"Gave me a woody just helping her with her bags."

"Good thing you didn't try to help yourself to anything else—she's deadly," I said.

"I assumed as much," answered Jackson.

I studied the main house for several moments, took a deep breath, and watched my breath frost into the late afternoon air. "What bedroom did you put her in?"

He said, "I gave her the Blue Bedroom—"

"Next to mine?"

He grinned. "I thought you'd appreciate that."

"Normally, but not today; I was thinking of putting Janet in the Blue Bedroom."

"You just said you and Janet broke up?"

"It's complicated."

"Roger that!" Jackson laughed.

I sighed again and said, "I guess I should go say hello. It's the proper thing to do."

I turned toward the main house.

Jackson held up his hand. "Ah . . . There are also two others . . ."

I stopped and waited for him to finish.

"A tall, Nubian beauty who calls herself Kay and a fiery redhead named Marie."

"They traveled here together?" I asked.

"Hell no! They showed up about thirty minutes apart—airport shuttle and a taxi. The three obviously don't get along with each other. They all started pissing fire . . . didn't even pretend to be polite to each other," answered Jackson.

"No, I wouldn't expect them to," I said.

Jackson said, "I will say they're all heartbreakers and life-takers—real fire-panthers."

"They always were," I said and then sighed again. I needed to get my game face on before I went into the panther's den.

Jackson added, "One more thing—they're all armed. That's why I'm holing up here. I didn't want to be around when the shooting started."

Yeah . . . I'd expect that . . .

I nodded, but said nothing.

Jackson added, "As a precaution, I spread Kay and Marie out in the opposite wing from your bedroom."

"Have you given them a tour yet?" I asked.

"Just the main house," Jackson answered. "Figured the less geography they knew the better."

"Good!"

This is what I was saying earlier about retirement parties: the part about not knowing how to act when former lovers show up—in this case all three of them . . .

There will be more . . .

My little voice was stating the obvious again. I turned toward the main house as Jackson called out, "Here, take a two-way so we can stay in touch—just in case."

"Thanks." I took the tiny radio and slipped it into my pocket, then added, "We should provide radios for Crockett and Ralph when they arrive tonight."

Got it!"

I took my time walking across the gravel driveway to the main house. I wanted to compose myself.

26

OLD LOVERS AND ALLIES

I entered the main entrance and stood quietly for a moment. There was no sound coming from anywhere. The library was to my right—in the front turret. It also had a modest bar. Jackson had said Hong Li was in there, drinking whiskey and listening to my CDs. I didn't hear any music, so I slowly walked along the stone-floor hallway toward the library turret. I stopped outside the heavy oak double doors and listened—still no sound from inside.

Oh well, there's one way to find out.

I gently pushed open the doors, stepped across the threshold, and was shocked by the scene: all three women were warming themselves by the fireplace and drinking brandy. There were no dead bodies on the floor.

"Hello, ladies. Jackson said he got you all settled in bedrooms and showed you around. I apologize for not being here to greet you personally."

Kay was the first to react. She slithered across the room with her powerful athletic stride and pressed her firm body against me.

Kay is a true intelligence operative in a world where self-proclaimed agents are either mercenary killers at one end of the spectrum or bureaucrat paper-shufflers at the other end. Kay is a field agent for MI-6, which stands for Military Intelligence, Section 6. MI-6 is also known as the Secret Intelligence Service—SIS—or if you're a James Bond fan, the British Secret Service. Kay had been recruited from her birthplace in Kenya at the age of fifteen. She had been an orphan and welcomed the opportunity to escape the deadly environment where her life expectancy was less than ten more years. Her British masters took her to England and trained her until she was ready to become operational at the age of twenty-two. She had been assigned to Afghanistan to gather intelligence on the Taliban for the 2003 invasion. She helped identify military targets and key people to take out during the first few days of the invasion. She was one of the very first people the American intelligence services hooked up with when they arrived in Afghanistan. As such, she became the primary liaison with the American forces. Once it became known by the locals she was an MI-6 agent she had to be reassigned, so she moved to Benghazi. Within six months she had become deeply imbedded with the Brotherhood. It had been Kay who warned the CIA three days before the fall of the embassy in Benghazi that it was going to be hit, but no one apparently believed her, or maybe they didn't care.

I'd first met Kay about ten years ago when we'd bumped into each other in Hong Kong. Unfortunately, I can't tell you about that occasion because of my attorney's health. The incident is still highly classified, and telling you about it would give Tony apoplexy, as my grandmother used to say.

Kay is tall: About two inches shorter than me when barefoot, but today she was wearing heels. She wrapped her powerful arms around my waist and pulled me in so tight that her flat, hard stomach and warm loins were crushing me. She slowly kissed me . . . and kissed me . . . and then kissed me a little longer.

My body began to respond.

Kay stepped back and glanced down to appreciate the results of her effort. The smile on her face was testament to her satisfaction. Her eyes slowly returned to my face. "I missed you, John. Why did you wait until you became an old man before inviting me to your home? This is a wonderful place." I liked her accent. It was a mix of Kenyan and English. She sounded both very proper and very sexy at the same time.

"I didn't think you wanted to see me again."

Two years ago, Kay and I had spent a summer together in the hottest, most sinister center of intrigue in the world today—Washington, DC. She had contacted me for help. She was working as the chief of staff for a senior US senator. It was a cover, of course. MI-6 had become interested in the US senator when he began selling British secrets he'd learned as a member of the Senate Intelligence Committee. She had contacted me for help in exposing his illegal activities. In the end, the powers in Washington would not allow the attorney general's office to prosecute a powerful US senator; he was quietly removed from the committee, and he agreed not to run for reelection. However, Kay and I had managed to prosecute each other to the fullest extent of our abilities and imagination for about six months that summer.

Kay purred in her throaty voice, "I've missed you . . ."

Marie—the fiery redhead—suddenly appeared next to us. "Don't be rude. I want to say hello too."

Marie is shorter—about five foot six—but she's all gorgeous woman. She speaks seven languages so fluently that even natives of the countries cannot tell she isn't one of them. As far as I know she is still employed by the CIA, but I have no idea what her current position is. I'm guessing by now she must be pretty far up the food chain—at least a senior case officer, maybe higher. I won't ask, and she won't tell me, because even her job title is classified, just as it was when she and I first met.

She was working in the United States Embassy in Moscow at the time, and I had been brought in for the purpose of infesting certain sections of the Kremlin with electronic spy devices the Russians couldn't detect. It took me nine months to complete the job. I had actually completed the work in seven months but stayed on an extra two to fine-tune the system—that is, to fine-tune Marie's and my sex life. We had begun fine-tuning each other the second week after I had arrived in Moscow. I finally had to go home; my boss in DC (Sprout's predecessor) had recalled me. To be honest, I was secretly grateful because Marie had worn me out and I couldn't keep up with her needs any longer.

I'm just mortal after all.

Marie slipped past Kay and slid her hand around the back of my neck. She gently pulled my face down to hers and kissed me. I could feel her gargantuan breasts pressing against my chest. By now I was uncontrollably aroused. At present I couldn't understand how I could have felt worn out in Moscow.

I stepped back to take a breath and looked at the two women. "Jackson told me you two weren't getting along."

Kay answered first. "That was before we talked—compared notes."

Oh my God!

I glanced across the room to Hong Li. She wasn't going to echo their performances, but I could tell from the subtle smile etched across her lips that she had something planned for later. That made me nervous: it could be good or bad for me. She was unquestionably a contender for the title "Most Dangerous Person in the Room." In any case, I could see she was enjoying my current predicament.

The next couple days are going to be hard.

There's my little voice again, stating the obvious.

27

TOM AND TERRY WOLFE

People underestimate how competent and dangerous my brother Tom can be. It's not until they experience him in action that they realize their mistake. He projects a humble shyness as a first impression. He is very athletic and powerful, but those qualities are not evident until you see him move. I was a second-string tight end, in my senior year, when Tom tried out for the football team in high school. I was there when he walked onto the playing field as a freshman. He wasn't particularly large or intimidating, standing on the fifty-yard line in his gym shorts and T-shirt. He was only about five feet eight inches at the time and weighed maybe 145 pounds (he was much larger by his senior year). There were smirks and crooked smiles by everyone, even the coaches at first, but that all changed when he was given a chance to move on the field. Soon my little brother was the go-to running back. Tom Wolfe became the MVP all four years he played on the varsity team. He was clearly a superior competitor, but when he went to college, he never even went to a football game, even as a spectator. I asked him once why he didn't try for college football, and he simply said, "Been there, done that—interested in other things!"

Tom is as tough—or possibly tougher—as anyone you've ever met or even heard about, including in movies and fiction novels. Tom is currently the assistant director overseeing the FBI's tactical forces—SWAT, HRT, and the Quick Reaction Force. His people are required to be ready to go anywhere to resolve any crisis within four hours of notification. Tom's not a bureaucrat/desk jockey. He got to where he is by a long, convoluted trail involving twenty years in the military and being awarded almost every decoration possible. His most recent accomplishment was last year when he hunted down and brought to justice an evil billionaire who had unlimited resources.

Tom's wife, Terry, had been right in the middle of that hunt and had done more than her share to help. She is not someone you would underestimate in any fashion, even at first glance. First, she's the most gorgeous woman I've ever met face-to-face. There is no physical aspect of her—from her deep-green, sparkling eyes to her perfectly formed toes and everything in between—that does not say *drop-dead, movie-star gorgeous*. Yes, I have a crush on her. I think most men who meet her do, but what makes her so very unique is her intelligence. She is undoubtedly the smartest woman I've ever known, except possibly Janet.

Also, Terry is an expert martial artist and highly skilled with almost every type of small arm. She saw her parents killed during a home invasion when she was very young and vowed never to be a victim. That home invasion has been the source of her drive. I've never personally witnessed her in action, but I've been told that on more than one occasion, she has crushed seriously evil men and women using those skills.

Together, Tom and Terry's exploits are legendary.[1]

So, right now you're probably thinking I've got a case of hero worship for my little brother and I'm in love with his wife. Well, you'd be correct on both counts, but it's all proper, known to them both, and maybe more importantly, deserved. They are a force to be reckoned with.

Why am I telling you about my brother and his wife in my story? Because Jackson has just informed me of their pending arrival. He called me via the little two-way radio and said they are driving up the private gravel road.

Jackson seems to have a sixth sense about things that are happening on the property—it's almost magical. I've always meant to ask him how he does it. Maybe I will later.

---

[1] Read the Adventure Novels of Tom and Terry Wolfe, by Walt Branam, where they tracked down and disposed of the evil billionaire Vernon Crassman in *Alaska Gold, Hunting Evil*, and *Nemesis Syndrome*.

I responded immediately, "Got it," and went to the window to watch for them.

It wasn't long before a black sedan with blacked-out windows appeared on the gravel road. It came to a slow stop and sat with nothing happening for several moments.

Jackson stood outside the garage, watching the sedan.

Finally, the driver's side door opened and a fit-looking man with black hair, dressed in jeans and a heavy sweatshirt, climbed out. He said something to Jackson, who laughed and walked over to shake his hand. Then the passenger door opened, and one of the most gorgeous women on the planet climbed out and walked around to greet Jackson. She also wore jeans and a sweatshirt. Her outfit showed just enough of her perfect figure to make me stare in wonderment. She finished off her outfit with a short-brimmed, black cowboy hat and snow boots. My brother and his wife had arrived.

I opened the window, letting the cold air rush in, but I really wanted to hear what they were saying.

"Long time since I've seen you two. Welcome!" I heard Jackson say as he helped himself to a hug with Terry.

"Good to see you, Jackson!" said Tom Wolfe.

Terry added, "You still look the same as the last time I saw you. You have to tell me your secret to not aging."

Jackson chuckled. "Are you kidding? You're just as beautiful as the first time I saw you—maybe more so. When the words *A Beauty to Behold* were first uttered, I bet the speaker was looking at you."

"Careful there," said Terry. "I have a very jealous husband." She winked.

All three laughed.

Jackson is a charmer.

My brother asked, "So where's John?"

"I think he's in the house trying to reconcile three former lovers who have just met each other for the first time. He's got his hands full," answered Jackson.

He didn't have to say that!

I glanced back into the room to determine whether any of the three women had overheard Jackson. They were standing together in a tight bunch, next to the fireplace on the other side of the room, talking quietly—heaven only knows about what.

Through the open window, I heard my brother quip, "Maybe I should go help him."

Terry Wolfe rested her hand on her hip and said, "Wait a minute, mister. I'm not so sure I'm going to let you have a free hand with three beautiful women who are angry at your brother. One of them may decide to get even by stealing you away."

"Well, maybe we should both go rescue my brother," I heard Tom suggest.

"I'm coming too. Don't want to miss this," announced Jackson.

I closed the window and waited in the library with Marie, Kay, and Hong Li. I was feeling the way I imagine a man does on death row, just before the guards come to get him for the strap-down and lethal-injection procedure.

A few moments later my brother, sister-in-law, and Jackson entered the library. I could see from their smiles they were sharing some private joke at my expense.

All things considered I was happy to see Tom and Terry. "You made it!" I declared, realizing as I said it that I was stating the obvious.

My brother replied, "Yeah, got away from Quantico for a couple days. Besides, I wouldn't miss your retirement party for anything."

Terry stepped forward and said, "Who are all these beautiful ladies, John?"

She got right to the roasting.

"Ah, they're former business associates . . . friends that came to wish me well in my retirement." I knew I sounded feeble as I mumbled the words.

Marie reacted first. "Business associates! Just friends! Is that what you think of us?"

Kay was only a half-beat behind. "I agree! You make us sound like hookers. What kind of business did I transact with you, anyway?" Despite her angry sounding words, she hooked her hand around my arm and pulled me close. Marie did the same on the other side. I was captured—trapped in the middle.

On the other side of the fireplace, Hong Li stood quietly with that irritating-but-beautiful, subtle grin and a glistening sparkle in her eye. She was clearly enjoying me being boiled alive.

So was Terry.

My brother just smiled—no help at all.

Jackson stood near the doorway, arms crossed over his chest, quietly chuckling. When I caught his eye, he said in a sotto voice, "Looks like the fire-pissers have joined forces."

Just what I need: three former lovers allying with my closest friends and family—and all plotting against me.

"Anyone want a drink?" I managed in a squeaky whimper.

28

ANOTHER GUEST ARRIVES

We were on our second round of excellent brandy that I had saved for this exact occasion. Everyone was beginning to let a coil or two out of their knotted rope, including me. I had even begun to appreciate the humorous side to three of my former lovers here at once, getting into the game of abusing me—having fun at my expense—and thinking maybe this could be a fun party after all when Jackson announced, "Someone is coming."

I looked out the window and saw no cars arriving.

How does he know?

A few minutes later a perky, bright-green Mini Cooper with the double-white racing stripe running from bumper to bumper slid to a four-wheels-locked stop in my gravel driveway.

Thanks a lot! Now I'll have to pay for the gravel to be re-leveled and repaired.

Janet had arrived. I looked at my watch—five thirty. I hadn't noticed before, but the sun was setting.

It had been a long day, and her arrival reminded me that it could be an even longer night.

I was guessing that Janet had gone back to the office, put in some time, got herself promoted, called me, learned what she could about Jimmy's death and Sprout's part in in it, and then drove here. It had been a busy day for her too.

Then I thought, *Janet's arrival puts four former lovers together.* Life was getting more complicated. It wasn't only that they were former lovers but that each was a world-class intelligence agent and they knew how to know stuff, so there would be no hiding anything.

However, despite the fact she had broken my heart this morning, I was glad Janet had arrived. I wanted—no, make that *needed*—to know what had been going on back at the Agency. I also needed to brief her on my meeting with The Russian.

To be really honest, I missed her.

I excused myself from the others in the library and walked outside to greet her.

"Hey there, handsome. Did you miss me?" Janet stood with her hand resting on a hip that jutted to the side, showing off her perfect, round shape.

"I thought you were dumping me." I sounded whiny even to myself.

"Well, after all, it's your special day. I should have waited until tomorrow morning to tell you. If you'll allow me, I'll make it up to you tonight. That is, if there's any room in your bed." Her eyes quickly darted to the library window as if she knew the other women were watching.

How can she know?

Jackson appeared next to me and announced, "Your special guests have arrived at the hangar." For once, Jackson's announcement of seemingly magical awareness was welcomed, but I still have no idea how he knows these things.

"They came early," I said.

"Apparently . . ."

Janet became serious. "I have something very important to tell you. You need to hear this now . . . before you greet anyone *special*."

"We can talk on the way to the hangar. You can ride with me and my brother and his wife."

"I can't have civilians hearing what I have to say," she hissed at me.

I grunted and said, "Tom and Terry are not civilians. You've never heard of my brother?"

"Should I?" she asked.

"Yes, and trust me, you'll be happy he's in the loop. Besides, it's important that we prepare for tonight's party. Part of that is briefing those who need to know what they need to know," I answered.

I took her silence as agreement and said, "Follow me. If you're nice, I'll introduce you to your competition for my affection."

I could hear Janet grumbling as she followed me back into the house.

29

OFF ROAD TREKKING

In the library, I made formal introductions all around, followed by another round of brandy with Janet added to the drinking club. Then I interrupted the party and explained we needed to prepare for tonight's events. I love this group of people, because they all got on board without a lot of stupid questions.

We migrated out to the garage where I had two Polaris utility vehicles, plus two quads. We were going to the hangar. Everyone—Janet, Marie, Kay, Hong Li, Tom, Terry and Jackson—opted to ride in the Polaris utility vehicles because they were more comfortable than the quads. The utility vehicles looked like sexy golf carts with light bars, a back seat, and roll bars. I drove the lead vehicle with Janet riding shotgun and Tom and Terry in the backseat. Jackson drove the second Polaris, staying about fifty yards behind. He had my three former associates/lovers with him. I wasn't worried about him stealing away one or more of them—actually, I hoped that he would. If he did, he'd deserve what he got. In any case, I already had too much on my plate to sample any more desserts, if you get my meaning.

Soon we were threading our way through the thick forest of trees on the jeep trail that led from the house to the hangar. It's a very scenic route that takes us over a couple of small streams and past a small lake that is contained on my property. I've always thought that my property must look very much like it did four hundred years ago when the first Pilgrims settled here. It takes about fifteen minutes to make the trip to the hangar when we're not in a hurry. Jackson claims to have made it in two minutes.

I believe him, because I remember paying the repair bill on the quad. The cold evening air rushed past and threatened to freeze us. The Polaris didn't have a heater. Even if it did, it would do no good in the open-air vehicle.

Janet couldn't wait any longer. She turned in her seat to face me, her arms folded across her chest to stay warmer. "What I have to tell you is top secret—for you only," she announced as she glanced back at my brother and sister-in-law.

I grunted. "First, I would tell Tom and Terry anyway, so you might as well cut out the middleman. Second, Tom is an assistant director of the FBI, and Terry is one of their top analysts. Both are cleared for top secret and beyond. Besides, he has a need to know. I'm putting them both in the loop, so let's get to it. What do you have to tell me?"

She hesitated for a moment and then began, "Well, as we already knew, the Agency is covering up Jimmy's death. They're calling it a suicide and employing one of our own doctors to perform the autopsy."

"Keeping everything in-house—the fix is in," I said.

"Yes," she replied.

Tom broke in, "Why do they want to keep such a tight control over someone committing suicide?"

I answered, "Because he didn't commit suicide—he was murdered. The murderer tried to make it look like suicide."

"How do you know?" Tom asked.

Janet was now all in with sharing information. "I have the security DVD of the killer doing the deed."

"Do you know who it is?" asked Tom.

Janet and I answered in a duo, "Sprout!"

"Who's Sprout?" asked Terry.

I answered, "Sprout was my supervisor at the Agency. He was also Jimmy's supervisor."

Tom paused before saying, "I could pick him up—put him in the FBI's custody if you wish."

"Can't do that," I answered.

Before Tom could ask why, Janet added, "Sprout died this morning too—an apparent stroke while attending John's official retirement party."

I cast a glance at Janet. I'd hate to play poker with her. If I didn't know the truth about Sprout's death, I'd believe her.

Terry asked, "Do you think he was murdered too?"

"What do you mean?" I asked.

Terry said, "I don't believe in coincidences—the murderer just happens to die of a stroke the same day he kills someone. It's the first rule of assassination: kill the assassin so he can't tell who ordered the kill."

This time Janet glanced at me. I think that rattled her. Then I realized we had actually helped in the cover-up. By killing Sprout we'd protected whoever ordered the hit on Jimmy.

Damn!

Janet didn't miss a beat. "That leads me to the next related news: The Agency is also taking full control over Sprout's death, and the same Agency doctor is going to perform that autopsy. The rumor is he's already written the autopsy reports for both deaths—cases closed."

"Who's calling the shots?" I asked.

"The director, personally," Janet answered.

It was my turn. "That meshes with what I learned. I have video feed of the director controlling the scene of Sprout's death. I left a video camera in the men's room where Sprout died, so I could keep an eye on things. The director showed up and started giving orders. He apparently has a federal court order giving the Agency jurisdiction over Sprout's death. He sent the local police packing. The Agency security agents cleaned up everything— left nothing that could be construed as evidence. Also, earlier I found an email from Sprout, addressed to the director, referencing the Order of the Golden Squirrel. He was concerned I knew of it and that could be a problem for them."

Janet frowned at me. "You *found* an email? How did you get into Sprout's or the director's emails?"

I gave Janet a *Do you really have to ask?* look.

She faced forward and fell silent.

"One more thing," I said.

"What?" she asked quietly.

"Did the Agency search my condo this morning?"

"Not that I know of ... why do you ask?" she answered.

"Because my home security app sent me an alert. I watched a team of experts go through the condo. They didn't miss anything. They even put the bath towels from this morning into plastic evidence bags and took them."

She'd know I was telling her they would learn she'd been sleeping with me.

"Perverts!" she grumbled.

"My thoughts too."

Janet looked pale—rattled. She hadn't known about the break in.

My sister-in-law broke the silence. "The director must be giving the orders. He's the next higher link but not the top guy."

"Why do you say he's not the top guy?" asked Janet.

Terry said, "In my experience the top kingpins rarely do the dirty work themselves. They almost never show up personally and give orders to the worker bees. They never directly send and receive emails, or phone calls, or other communications that could incriminate them either. They use a cut-out—someone who can be eliminated or sacrificed, if necessary, to protect themselves."

"Then who is the top man? And what is this squirrel order? And why did they break into John's condo?" asked Janet.

I didn't answer, but Terry did. "Those are questions to ask your director."

The Polaris crashed into the icy-cold water of a small creek. The creek has no name, but it drains from the lake on my property and merges with another stream off my property that eventually joins the Shenandoah River. The water splashed over the side of the Polaris, and everyone got showered. Exposure to the elements can be one of the disadvantages to using these particular vehicles, especially in the winter. Sure, I could have been more careful—driven slower—but crashing through the creeks is one of the little pleasures I allow myself when I'm driving on this trail. Call me immature if you like.

It was cold.

I used the distraction to refocus the subject. "Janet, you've been appointed as Chief of the Electronic Intelligence Division—right?"

"Yes, I've taken over Sprout's job—at least temporarily until they pick a permanent replacement. Why?" She was shivering.

"I need you to task a full workup on the Panzram Company. I think Panzram plays a prominent role in all this."

"What's Panzram?" asked Janet.

"That's what we need to learn." I spent the next few minutes giving them a brief overview of breaking into Mary's townhouse, my little raid at the Agency, the visit to the farm to meet The Russian, and his proposal to make me rich if I gave up the PM Program. However, I neglected to tell them I started the fire at the Agency, or that Mary claimed to have a floppy with detailed information about the leadership of the Order of the Golden Squirrel, or about The Major and his job offer, and especially left out the details of Sprout's fatal stroke. You have to keep some of your cards to yourself. Regardless, the narrative was vividly entertaining, because they all remained silent until I finished, which is saying something with this particular mix of people. I ended with, "We don't need to share most of this with the others—need to know and all that rot."

It was my brother who said, "You've had quite a day."

"Something tells me it's just starting," I answered between my chattering teeth. I came to a stop outside the hangar none too soon. I think I was edging up on hypothermia, or maybe it was just nerves.

30

THE HANGAR

I crawled out, rubbed my hands together, and regarded the last light in the western sky. Dark clouds were moving in from the northwest and the evening air was near freezing.

Jackson rolled to a stop seconds later with the three women. They sat quietly in the second vehicle for nearly half a minute.

I eyeballed the prefab steel building and the surrounding terrain. Everything appeared normal. You may think that I was being overly dramatic. But it had been an eventful day, and I was expecting it to be an even more exciting evening, so I didn't want to take anything for granted.

I could see Ralph's black pickup truck and Crockett's jeep parked at the front entrance of the hangar. The motion-activated halogen floodlight was burning brightly, which meant someone had been walking underneath it within the past few minutes. It wasn't us because we had stopped out of its range. I didn't think any of my invited guests would have been out for an evening's stroll. So I stood quietly, just listening and watching.

I studied the landing strip that can accommodate anything short of a full-size commercial jet. I'd inherited the hangar and landing strip when I bought the property. At the time I wasn't that much into aircraft, but having the facilities had gotten me interested. I've taken some flying lessons but have never gotten around to getting my pilot's license. Maybe I'd do that now that I have more time—being retired and all—but that isn't really part of this story.

I swept my eyes along the tree line that was cut back fifty yards or so, but I saw nothing unusual. All was quiet in the quickly darkening landscape surrounding the hangar.

"Let's go in," I announced.

My brother didn't agree. He leaped from the Polaris, and seemingly using magic, produced a Glock pistol and dropped behind the vehicle for cover. Terry mirrored his action, dropping next to him with her own pistol. I don't know guns well enough to tell you what kind she had, but hers was more compact than her husband's.

Jackson apparently sensed something too, because he slipped from his vehicle and drew a full-size Beretta from under his jacket, taking cover behind his vehicle.

I knew that none of these people are easily rattled into rash actions, so I ducked behind the Polaris without being told to do so.

Tom said, "There's someone hiding in the tree line—there—he pointed to the nearest clump of trees adjacent to the road, leading in from the south. We had come from the north.

I reached inside the Polaris where I kept an AR-15 concealed under the driver's seat. I pulled back the charging handle and squatted next to my brother.

We waited.

Finally, Tom shouted to the tree line, "Come out and show yourself, or we will open fire!"

There was no reaction.

"Last warning . . ." my brother shouted.

Then a figure dressed in woodland camouflage and holding a scoped hunting rifle stepped into the open. He was almost invisible in the quickly darkening landscape. The figure approached slowly, holding his rifle in one hand dangling at his thigh—clearly demonstrating he was not a threat. As he came closer, I recognized Crockett. He'd apparently been keeping watch outside the hangar, just in case.

Crockett grinned at me and said, "Hey there, Mr. Wolfe. Sorry to give you an alarm." Then he turned to my brother and asked, "You haven't lost your skills. Thought I was well hidden. How did you see me?"

Tom answered. "The woodland camouflage you're wearing doesn't quite blend with the current vegetation. Even in this dim light, I saw the pattern move when you shifted your weight from one leg to the other. Next time wear a ghillie suit, or better yet, cut some branches from around you and tie them to your arms, body, and hat. They'll break up your outline and allow your color and pattern to blend in with the surrounding vegetation."

Crockett laughed.

I said, "You should know better."

Kay asked," Who's this—Daniel Boom?" purposely mispronouncing the name.

"Actually, my name is Crockett—not Boone. People get us mixed up all the time," answered Crockett, chuckling.

Marie said, "Oh, he's a comedian."

Marie and Kay have teamed up.

"I think I should make introductions before this goes any further." I introduced Crockett to the group and then asked, "I assume Ralph has our guest inside?"

"Yes, and the poor city boy hasn't stopped complaining all afternoon. He's a real crybaby. I don't think he appreciates our hospitality."

I laughed. "Shall we go in?"

We entered the hangar through a man-size side door. The building was constructed of steel in a half-cylinder design, forty yards long and twenty-five yards wide. The top of the cylinder-domed ceiling was thirty feet high.

Sitting prominently in the center, and using up most of the large room, was my F-100 Super Sabre—a two-seater first flown in 1961 and decommissioned in 1971. Jackson and I rebuilt it with the idea of flying it someday. In its heyday the F-100 could break the sound barrier in level flight and carry either air-to-ground or air-to-air combat systems. Last year, I spent a small fortune to recondition the Pratt & Whitney J 57 Turbojet engine. We'd painted the original silver body a flashy red, white, and blue with a white United States Air Force star on its side. To my knowledge it is the only F-100 in the United States still able to fly.

Jackson had installed a 20 mm Vulcan Gatling gun and had somehow obtained one thousand incendiary rounds for it—very deadly and destructive. The six-barreled, electric Gatling gun was mounted underneath the jet's fuselage, just below the cockpit. It didn't belong there and looked out of place, but Jackson was a Warthog pilot and wanted it. It was possibly the only F-100 ever fitted with the powerful M-61 Vulcan Gatling gun.

My brother asked, "What's the rate of fire on the Gatling gun?"

Jackson answered, "About six thousand rounds per minute."

My brother, the wet blanket, studied the F-100. "You know, the F-100 is a death trap . . . one of the most dangerous aircraft to ever fly in the US arsenal. During the Vietnam War, the United States lost hundreds of F-100s because of breakdowns and design flaws. They weren't shot down by enemy fire—they just crashed on their own. More pilots were killed because of the faulty designs than from all enemy contact combined. Chances are you'll take it up and die on the maiden flight."

Jackson shook his head. "I've taken her up three times so far, and you're right: the original design of the F-100 did have a tendency to yaw and roll when the jet accelerated too fast, tried to fly too slow, or went into a sudden dive. The first time I flew this bird I almost lost control, but think I have that problem licked. It's mostly a matter of becoming familiar with the aircraft."

Tom asked, "Does that gun interfere with the avionics?"

Jackson smiled and patted the fuselage with his hand. "I haven't test-flown her since she was fitted with the Gatling gun, so I'm not one hundred percent on the current handling characteristics. I was thinking of taking her up after the party—maybe tomorrow."

We all silently stared at the powerful red, white, and blue F-100, sitting majestically in the center of my hangar. It looked odd, retrofitted with the Gatling gun. The F-100 was a fighter plane—not a Wart Hog.

Tom was the first to shrug and walk away. The others took that as their cue to follow.

At the far end of the building, I'd pieced together a bar. Ralph and David Planter were already sitting at the bar, each with a draft beer. Ralph's beer was half full. Planter's was apparently untouched. A bar stool separated them. At first glance the scene appeared to be very sociable until you looked closer. Planter was holding his right arm in a peculiar angle, tightly against his stomach, and the entire left side of his face was a blue-black color and swollen several times its normal size. Planter looked miserable.

We crossed the concrete floor and fanned out around the two men.

I announced, "This is Ralph, career Special Forces, then Delta for three years, and now retired, except for an occasional special job requiring extreme precision." I indicated Planter. "And this fine, upstanding piece-of-shit taking up space next to Ralph is David Planter. Ralph is babysitting

Planter until Planter's boss arrives. After that I have no idea where events will take any of us . . ."

Planter was doing his best to impale me with his hate-filled eyes, but everyone could see he was under Ralph's control and not a threat, so they ignored him.

"Nice bar," said Terry. "It looks professional."

The bar was the most-often-used feature in the hangar. It got its life here when a local bar down the road went out of business because of the recession. I managed to purchase the furniture and stock for a fraction of its true value. The seller threw in the beautiful hardwood bar and matching stools, gratis. Over the past couple of years the bar had become an underground local watering hole, known only to close friends and neighbors. I asked that if people used the facility they either drop a twenty in the cookie jar to pay for their drinks or bring booze to restock. If someone wanted to use the hangar bar for a private party, they were asked to let Jackson know in advance so there'd be no misunderstanding. So far, the arrangement had worked. I didn't make any money on it, but everyone around for several miles appreciated it being here. It had proven a good method for bonding with my neighbors.

I stepped behind the bar and announced, "Saloon's open!" then spent the next few minutes mixing and pouring drinks.

My brother took his beer and quipped, "If this were California you'd get your ass sued by one of the neighbors for having a dirty glass, and then the state alcohol tax and control people would raid you and throw your ass in jail for operating an unlicensed—and more importantly, untaxed—drinking establishment."

"Well, it's a good thing it ain't California!" I replied as I took a pull on my beer.

"On that we agree," said Tom.

We clicked glasses.

I raised my voice over the group's murmuring. "It's time to talk about tonight. Everyone take a chair and be comfortable."

The group pulled chairs around the tables clustered in the area. After a moment of chair shifting they fell silent and waited for me to begin.

"You are all people I can trust," I glanced at Planter, "with one exception. Also, each of you has a stake in what happens tonight to one degree or another. I'm expecting maybe fifty-sixty people tonight. Most will be here for the party and to celebrate my retirement from the Agency. However, at least one subgroup may be here for something much less pleasant. They may attempt to do us harm."

I took a sip of my beer as I waited for any reactions.

Jackson and Ralph didn't display any overt response. They just pinned me with their stoic glares. Marie, Kay, and Hong Li sat off to the side, curiously watching the others, not me. They seemed of a single mind. Janet, on the other hand, impatiently tapped her fingers on the table-top as if I were taking too long to make my point.

She thinks you're being too dramatic.

Too bad.

On the other hand, my brother and his wife were both smiling as if they thought this would be fun, which made me nervous.

"The faction we need to be concerned with is The Russian and his thugs." I paused again, measuring the reaction to hearing this.

My brother said, "Are you saying The Russian is coming to the party tonight?"

I said, "I believe so. He's pressing me hard to make a deal, the details of which aren't too important at this time."

Hong Li spoke for the first time. Her words, although soft, came across with strength. "I believe there are several people in this room who would gladly put an end to The Russian."

Marie nodded, "I agree!"

Kay was quietly nodding her head.

I glanced to Planter, who appeared to be sulking. It was obvious he didn't want to be here, and he sure didn't want to be part of a plot to make his employer disappear. It was clear to me he was thinking, with some justification, that hearing the plan could only lead to bad things for him later.

I said, "Well, that may be true, but regardless we need to prepare for what is likely going to be a very unpleasant time later tonight."

I went on to lay out my plan. I won't bore you with the details. Suffice to say that, like most plans, this one didn't unfold the way I anticipated. In fact, the enemy wasn't even who I thought they were and didn't come for the reason I had anticipated; so the plan fell apart immediately and isn't worth telling now. I had my first hint the plan was a lost cause almost the instant I completed laying it out to my associates.

I ended with, "Are there any questions?"

Jackson said in a loud voice, "A large armed force has invaded the property in three Humvees! They came in from the north and are swarming the main house and garage now."

I still don't know how he knows this stuff.

Ask him later!

Instead, I asked, "Could it be my guests beginning to arrive?"

"Not unless you expect them to be dressed in black and carrying submachine guns."

Tom asked, "How large is the party?"

"Maybe a dozen," answered Jackson.

31

PARTY CRASHERS

The intruders arrived in four military-grade, black Humvees. They were dressed like modern-day ninjas. Each man wore black BDUs, black ski masks, black leather gloves, and black body armor. Their eyes were covered with carbon-fiber shock-shield goggles. They all carried the same weapons: a 9 mm, fully silenced Uzi with four spare thirty-round magazines, and a 9 mm Beretta in a shoulder holster. They communicated with the latest generation of miniature, two way radios wrapped around their heads. They moved fast and professionally—at least initially. They had most likely rehearsed this raid several times, but it did them no good. Nothing ever goes like you plan it, and they made mistakes, especially after they met my friends and family.

Their first mistake was the reckless speed they approached on the private road. The black nights in Virginia's wilderness are unforgiving and they drove with their headlights off. There are no streetlights in the forest, and the trees create a canopy overhead that blocks moonlight or starlight. So they were driving almost blind on an unfamiliar road.

The lead Humvee carried two men, and was moving too fast to make a sharp right-hand turn on the dark, icy road. The Humvee slid sideways into a large hardwood tree that had been growing since before the Civil War and had no intention to giving way to some punk driving recklessly on this dark night. That mishap took the two men and the vehicle out of the game before they even arrived at the main house. The three trailing Humvees stopped to help their comrades and to regroup. Seeing their comrades broken in a car crash before they even went into action disheartened their methodology, taking the steam out of their night attack. They spent precious minutes caring for the injured men and determining that the crashed vehicle was a write-off. Finally they crowded the injured men into the remaining Humvees and resumed, albeit at a slower pace.

I didn't learn about the crash until later, but I thought it appropriate to tell you about it here.

While their drama was playing out, I confidently proclaimed to the assemblage of veterans and intelligence agents, "Follow me!" and led them across the hangar to what appeared to be an oversized, shallow, metal footlocker bolted to the floor near the wall.

Ralph stayed back with Planter. He called out, "What about Wonder Boy, here?"

Planter was still sitting on the barstool, cradling his broken arm, and being uncharacteristically quiet.

I opened a machinist's tool chest, extracted a pair of gunmetal-blue handcuffs, and tossed them to Ralph. "Cuff him to the landing gear strut of the F-100. He won't go anywhere if he has to drag the jet behind him."

Ralph had a true sadistic streak. He cuffed the broken arm to the strut, so each time Planter moved it would hurt. "That should keep you until we return."

Planter looked truly miserable, sitting on the cold concrete floor, leaning against the aircraft tire, his broken arm chained against the strut. I almost felt sorry for him—almost.

I opened the metal footlocker. There were a few rags and blankets lying inside—misdirection. I scooped them out and pushed a hidden switch located just inside the lip. The bottom slid aside to reveal a metal ladder that descended to a sublevel. "Jackson and Tom, come with me. The rest of you remain up here. There's not enough room down there for all of us."

The three of us descended the ladder. I found the light switch, and the eight-by-eight tomb exploded in LED overhead light. This was my armory— my real armory. I had been squirrelling away weapons and ammunition for the past fifteen years. They were all stored here. I kept all my deadly toys in this single basket, and tonight there was a good chance we would play with them.

My brother took over the process from there, selecting a variety of assault rifles and pistols for the group. He selected two military-issue assault rifles with electronic sights and announced, "These will be perfect for Terry and me. She loves the M-4."

"Looks like you do too," said Jackson.

"Well, I'm familiar with it," my brother answered with a shy grin.

Then Jackson said, "I think we'll give each of John's former girlfriends these H&K .223 rifles with night-vision optics. They're perfect for a dark night like tonight and easy to use."

Jackson selected a very compact, lightweight, duel-magazine, 12-gauge pump shotgun. Each magazine held nine rounds, so with one in the chamber, the total capacity was nineteen rounds. But that wasn't the real treat. He had secreted away some highly classified ammunition from a visit to Fort Bragg's Special Operations Training School a couple of years ago. The rounds were high-explosive fragmentation grenades that would fire from any 12-gauge shotgun. The explosive rounds had a one-meter killing radius. The rounds didn't arm until they had traveled five meters out of the barrel, so it was unlikely the shooter would accidently blow himself up by shooting something too close. The shotgun carried a night-vision, wide-angle, close-combat scope and an infrared spotlight that brightened the darkest night out to one hundred meters, which is the maximum effective range of the weapon anyway. I selected a handgun: a never-before-fired Colt .45 LC single-action Peacemaker—the gun that won the west. It was one of a matched set that I had. I stored its twin in my vault in the main house. (I'll tell you more about the vault later.)

My brother called me on the choice right away. "That's just a toy. You should select a modern firearm—a rifle or shotgun."

As I loaded the Peacemaker, I replied, "I'm not going to need it with all this firepower around me. Besides, I just love this particular pistol. I've never had a chance to shoot it, and I've always wanted to. It'll be fun."

I could tell by the way he shook his head that he didn't approve of my logic.

Too bad! This is my party, and I'll carry what I want to . . .

(Author's note: Looking back on the night I should have listened to my brother. Until then I'd never been in a real gunfight and didn't have a clue—a real amateur.)

We carried the assembled arsenal up the ladder and passed out the weapons. It was like Christmas. Everyone spent the next few minutes becoming familiar with the mechanisms, loading, and checking the spare magazines. They were all experienced agents of various backgrounds and had no problem familiarizing with the weapons. Crockett and Ralph had brought their own toys to play with, so they just observed the little ceremony with amusement.

After I figured they'd had enough time, I shouted "Let's go!" and moved to the door.

I led the way outside, and we loaded up in the four vehicles: Ralph's pickup truck, Crockett's Jeep, and the two Polaris'.

32

THE PERFECT ASSAULT PLAN

As I've already said, the best conceived plans never go as envisioned—for good guys or bad. Reality has a way of extinguishing fantasy and changing happiness into misery. But looking back on the evening, and considering all angles, we weren't as bad off as the ninja-clad intruders. They were drowning in a tsunami of confusion and mediocre leadership. Compared with them, we were wired together and ready.

We raced up the jeep trail in a single column as fast as I deemed it was safe to drive with our lights off.

Jackson reported, "They're out of their Humvees and floundering around the gazebo and the surrounding forest."

Why the intruders had congregated around the gazebo I couldn't guess. And I still didn't know how Jackson knew all this detail, but now wasn't the time to ask.

We raced into the darkness. It was only my intimate knowledge of the jeep trail that kept us safe.

I slowed to a stop just before crossing No Name Run. We got out and spread. Most took a knee and watched the dark trees for threats. Like I said earlier, these people were all experienced operators and didn't have to be told to be quiet and to not clump together.

That's when I saw the black Humvee hung up on the top edge of the five-foot waterfall that is located on the downstream side of the jeep trail. Apparently, the bad guys had traveled too fast—not having learned their lesson from earlier—and the lead Humvee had lost control when it crashed through No Name Run and diverted downstream, leaving the trail. Eventually, the force of the running water would push the Humvee over the falls if it wasn't winched back to safety. At that moment, I decided these raiders were not that bright, or maybe they lacked experience fighting in the boonies—probably both.

Jackson nudged me and showed me his smartphone. It displayed a video feed of the gazebo. I saw several armed men dressed in black, apparently looking for us. They did not have night-vision optics, so they were stumbling around in the dark.

We watched the bad guys tripping over rocks and tree branches. They were almost comical.

I mumbled in a low voice, "So that's how you do it!"

"Do what?" he whispered back.

"Know what's going on all over the property."

"Of course! What did you think? I'm psychic, or something?" He chuckled. "I have an app that feeds from cameras I've placed all over the property. Motion activates the cameras and alerts me so that I can watch the feed on my phone."

"That must have cost a small fortune," I said.

"Not to worry. You paid for it out of the maintenance fund." I could see his smile even in the blackness.

"So they're at the gazebo right now?" I asked.

"Think so . . . looks like there's about ten shooters . . . at the lakeshore and gazebo," Jackson answered.

"Why are they down there—not at the house?" asked Tom, as he joined us.

"No idea," answered Jackson.

I knew what we had to do. I motioned for everyone to move in close and laid out the new plan. Again, I won't bore you with the details because this one didn't go as I intended either.

Right away Terry, my sister-in-law, said, "Why are you separating the men from the women in your plan?"

But I was ready for her. I puffed up, just a little, and replied, "Because I know you ladies are all accomplished shooters. We need a security force to block the bad guys' retreat. We'll be chasing them to you. You need to be precise where you place your shots so you don't hit us. Your job isn't easier than ours. In fact, it's more difficult and more technical. We'll be making a lot of noise and herding them to you. You need to get into position before we begin, so let's stop the feminist bickering and get to it!"

"Should we try to take them prisoner or just shoot them?" asked Terry.

"I don't know if they'll give you a choice, but adjust to the moment," I answered.

It took fifteen minutes to get everyone in place. By then the bad guys had apparently decided there was nothing for them at the gazebo and were moving back to the two remaining Humvees parked on the dirt trail. It seemed their goal was the hangar next. That wasn't going to happen. Tom, Jackson, Ralph, Crockett, and I opened fire, punching holes in the radiators and engine blocks of the parked Humvees. I had to give it to the bad guys: they dropped to the ground and began returning fire almost immediately—very professional.

For a few minutes it was a standoff, but then one of the bad guys got hit—not dead, just wounded. I knew because he was a crybaby. I was betting they could hear him yelling all the way back to DC. Then a second bad guy caught a round, and he just stopped firing—maybe dead, maybe not—but at least he was quiet about it. The final straw was when my brother fired a long accurate burst, pelting dirt and rocks into one of the bad guys' faces. That bad guy lost his nerve, jumped up, and ran away from the fight—right past his buddies. His buddies stood up and quickly joined him. I guess they weren't being paid enough to die, or maybe they didn't want to engage in a fair fight with shooters of equal or better skills. In any case, suddenly the whole troop of bad guys picked up their marbles and ran back toward the main house, right to where Terry, Janet, Kay, Marie, and Hong Li had been patiently waiting for them.

They encountered deadly cross fire from Terry on the far-left side and Hong Li on the far right. Janet, Kay, and Marie were in the center, lying in the cold snow and laying down a wave of lead. It was nasty. The cross fire caught the entire assault group at nearly point-blank range—cutting them down.

A few of the bad guys fired back, but they were standing in the open while the women were all prone, or hidden behind trees. The gunfight was very much one-sided. For a few seconds, the thunder and flash of gunshots filled the dark, snow-dusted forest. Then the firing suddenly stopped, leaving only stillness in the cold night air.

It almost wasn't fair. At least that's what I thought during a very brief moment of elation. But like I said earlier, well-laid plans often do not pan out, and I was soon to learn that the night was still young.

Apparently, their leader and two of his operators had stayed at the main house. When they heard the shooting, they had slithered down the gradual slope toward the lake and gazebo . . . and walked right up behind Janet, Kay, and Marie lying prone on the cold, snow-dusted grass.

The three women were focused toward the gazebo—oblivious to the approaching danger from behind.

"Hello, ladies," said the leader. "Please lay your weapons on the ground and slowly stand."

Again, I learned about this later. I also learned that several things happened at the same time.

My sister-in-law was covered behind a tree on the far left-hand position of the firing line. She quietly faded into the darkness before any of the bad guys saw her. At the same instant, Hong Li, who was on the right, did the same. Instead of following orders, Janet, Kay, and Marie rolled over, face up, and point their rifles at the three bad guys, who had not been prepared to shoot it out with the women.

It was now a standoff.

The leader realized his error and angrily jammed his submachine gun toward the three women for emphasis and shouted, "Put down your weapons!" Then he shouted to his two men, "Take their weapons!"

By this time, only five seconds had elapsed since the leader of the bad guys had said, "Hello, ladies."

It was at this point that chaos and hell erupted.

Both sides opened fire on each other.

Terry fired from the dark tree line. Her accuracy is legendary, and she proved it again tonight. She dropped the leader and one other shooter with her initial burst.

Hong Li fired a single round from behind a large hardwood tree, dropping the remaining bad guy as he sprayed the ground at his feet.

By the time we (the men) arrived, the gunfight was over. Only the grisly aftermath remained: clouds of burned gunpowder drifting over the snow-patched landscape and the bodies.

I don't know if it was the scene or the cold night air that brought on the sudden chill, but I began shivering uncontrollably. I found myself standing over the leader. I noticed a black stain still growing underneath his body. In the dark, his blood was spreading on the earth and in the snow. I was mesmerized as I watched his body shutter violently—the death rattle—and then become still. I turned away.

But there were bodies everywhere. They were twisted and contorted into positions a human being would never assume while still alive. Several bad guys were still alive. There was no problem finding the living, because they all seemed to be making noises of various varieties and volumes. I walked around the battlefield and calculated that most were dead. I knew because they made no sound.

The dead are silent. Where had I heard that before?

Terry Wolfe and Hong Li drifted into view from opposite sides of the battlefield. They both held their rifles at the ready. Kay and Janet were now standing, but they stared down at Marie, who remained on the ground—unmoving.

I walked over.

There wasn't a question: Marie was dead. There was a pencil-size hole in her once-beautiful face, just below the right eye, and a fist-size exit crater in the back of her fiery-red head. Her blood and brain matter were sprayed onto the ground underneath her skull. Steam was rising from the gaping exit hole.

I looked away, fighting the urge to vomit. Then I forced myself to turn back and kneel next to her body. I cradled Marie in my arms and tried to think of some way to bring her back.

Dear God, would praying help?

Finally, I stood and wiped my bloody hands on my shirt, then walked into the dark tree line to get away from the others. I needed to hide the tears running down my face. I had loved Marie. There had even been a time when I'd considered quitting the Agency and marrying her.

I was still trying to compose myself when I heard Tom say to the others, "Go around and disarm all the shooters, even those who appear to be dead. Check for hidden pistols and knives. We don't want anyone suddenly coming back to life and making trouble."

Experienced and practical at this sort of thing, that was my brother.

I took a couple of deep breaths and rejoined the living. I would mourn Marie's death later in my own way.

33

THE SHERIFF

We had stacked the bad guys' weapons off to the side, away from the bodies, then performed first aide on the four bad guys who were still breathing.

We needed to know who these ninja-like men were and why they had attacked us, so Hong Li and Terry Wolfe volunteered to ask the questions. The two women proved themselves to be an irresistible interrogation team.

I didn't watch, but I don't think they used torture. Although after they were finished, both had blood splattered on their clothing. They assured us they only used feminine charms and trickery to get the weakest man to talk. He happened to have a stomach wound and was in considerable pain and losing blood rapidly. With some persuasion, he told the women that the ninja-like bad guys worked for the Panzram Company as independent contractors. He said they had been sent to kill me and anyone else who may know anything about the Order of the Golden Squirrel or the Panzram Company. I guess the act of confessing was more than he could bear, because he stopped breathing just moments after he had given up the information—another death.

There will be more.

Learning those details relieved our collective conscience about killing them and clinched our strategy about what we would tell the sheriff. We convened a short meeting and agreed on one little white lie—we would all swear that the bad guys had fired the first shot. After that we would follow the pure path of honesty. After the conference adjourned, Jackson called the sheriff and we waited patiently to tell our story.

Lucky for us Jackson's brother-in-law is the county sheriff—Buford Boone. Yes, I know it seems unbelievable, but Sheriff Boone is a distant relative to one of America's first folk heroes—Daniel Boone. Remember, the Old Rock House is in a remote region of Virginia's wilderness, and Daniel Boone had done a reasonable amount of stomping around in this area after the Revolutionary War. In fact, Daniel Boone was instrumental in converting part of Virginia into Kentucky. Daniel Boone had even been an elected member of the Virginia Assembly and a prominent figure in Virginia, Kentucky, and Tennessee, so the name Boone is commonly found in this part of the country.

Sheriff Boone arrived with four police units, and after a brief, friendly greeting with his brother-in-law, he and his deputies became all business, taking complete control of the scene, including relieving us of our weapons. They didn't search each of us, but relied on our honor to turn over our weapons, so I didn't give up my Colt Peacemaker. It stayed tucked in the small of my back under my jacket. I was okay with that, since I hadn't fired the six-shooter yet. I also observed Jackson slipping away with the shotgun and then returning without it.

They separated us for interrogation.

I sat quietly alone in the gazebo, waiting to be interviewed, and reflected on how the gun battle had gone. I was proud of how my retirement party guests had performed. Then I thought of Marie again, and the pride turned to grief.

I heard a deputy grumble, "Jesus, these three guys are bleeding to death, and another dozen are already dead. This was a slaughter!" He keyed his radio and called for medical units. He ended the call with, "Hurry—Code 3 all the way!"

Definitely a retirement party to remember.

That was my little voice again.

Eventually, a deputy approached me and said, "I need to ask you some questions. Your name is John Wolfe, is that correct?"

He didn't read me my rights.

"Yes," I answered.

He asked, "Is Tom Wolfe your brother?"

"Yes."

"To your knowledge is Tom Wolfe an assistant director of the FBI?"

- 165 -

"Yes."

"Is this shooting the result of an official investigation by the FBI?"

"No."

The deputy sighed and then recited the Miranda Rights paragraph that everyone who has ever watched a TV detective show has heard. Then he said, "Perhaps you should tell me what happened here tonight."

I stuck to the truth, except I neglected to say who shot first. If he didn't ask, I wasn't telling. I ended with, "I thought for sure I was going to die!"

After the interviews were over, the sheriff said we were free to go, so I thanked Crockett and Ralph for being here and said they wouldn't be needed any longer tonight with the sheriff here and all. They disappeared within minutes, glad to be gone.

Boy was I wrong about not needing them.

The flashing red-and-blue strobe lights remained on my property for the rest of the night and most of the next day. Unfortunately, the sheriff and emergency medical personnel being there didn't stop the events from their downhill slide.

34

THE PARTY

I wasn't quite accurate earlier, when I said the Old Rock House is built all on a single level. Technically, it's a split-level structure. The west turret is where I have the game room. To enter requires walking up a staircase to a level that is about six feet higher than the main house. My part-time hobby has been to collect arcade games and recondition them when I'm able to. I started long ago by collecting the pinball machines of old. Then I graduated to the first generation of computer arcade games, like PAC-MAN, Space Invaders, Pong, and the like. Later, I added the newer generation of computer arcade games. So as you walk into my game room the walls are lined with each successive generation of arcade games right up to the more recent retired versions like Quick Draw, 911, Off-Road Racing, Moto Cross, and Terminator. In the center of the large room I have a pool table. It was constructed in 1890. I also collect old guns, swords, and other weapons. They are mounted on the walls. There is a huge rock fireplace centered on one wall and a fully stocked bar and snack center against another. The octagon-shaped room is large with plenty of seating, so besides playing games, guests can relax and have a civilized conversation, if they please.

By the time the sheriff released us to return to the house, most of the other guests had arrived and had settled in the game room; however, some were outside, gawking at the red-and-blue strobe lights that decorated the gazebo and lake area downhill from the house. I could hear a low-level mumbling that filled the cold night air as we walked up the icy slope to the main house.

Most of my guests are real friends who wanted to wish me well and maybe get drunk at my expense tonight. They are harmless and provide energy and background noise for the real event that was yet to take place. So when they saw us, blood-splattered, some of them were concerned they had gotten into something they didn't want to be in. But after some preliminary introductions and a short explanation about the police, fire trucks, and ambulances, most relaxed and followed me into the game room where most had already gathered.

You might ask why am I still having a party after what just occurred? Well, keep reading and find out.

When I arrived in the game room people were playing the arcade games, shooting pool, or engaged in conversations. Almost all of them were eating the food and drinking my booze. That's okay—it's why I provided it. Laughter was a regular background sound as the buzz of their voices blended together in the large room. Everyone here seemed to be enjoying the gathering, and they all got along—at least for now. I had intended to invite only the good people from my past. Most knew and trusted each other and had a common background. They were here for friendship, not politics or personal gain.

Well, almost everyone.

I was standing near the fireplace, letting the flames warm me and contemplating the mess the evening had turned into, when Sue sashayed up to me and said, "Hey there, I've been here for two hours, and you haven't pinched my ass even once. Is that blood all over your shirt?"

"Yes," I answered quietly.

It's Marie's blood.

Sue works in the Communications Security Division at the Agency. CSD is responsible for protecting the phone calls, emails, texts, Twitters, open-voice communications, and any other coms at the Agency. Her job title is Equipment Review Manager. Her job is to set the schedules for the periodic checks made on all equipment to insure they have not been bugged. She doesn't personally check or inspect anything herself. She just sets the schedules and sends out an email informing the tech-teams where to go next. After the sweeps, she receives reports on the results of the equipment reviews and then sends a summary report to someone else. So Sue meets my definition of a bureaucrat who lives off the taxpayers.

More importantly for our story, Sue has been chasing my butt for the past two years. I'm partially to blame for why she has the hots for me. Two years ago, at the "Annual" party—the PC Police won't let us call it a Christmas Party or even a New Year's Party, although it is held one week before Christmas—I'd gotten a little drunk and made a pass at her. She was drunk too and accepted. It turned out to be my faux pas of the decade, or at least for that December.

The "Year End" party was being held in the Ocean Front Hilton, in Maryland. The Ocean Front is a very high-end hotel, far from work and home, and most of us had reserved a room for the night. Sue had reserved a very expensive suite on the top floor, so there was both motive and opportunity for us. We'd disappeared into her room where I'd had the intention of getting a fast thirty-minute union and then slithering back to the party. If done well, no one would miss us.

Of course, that was too much to hope for—we were surrounded by intelligence agents—everyone missed us, and they weren't bashful about telling us. Especially Janet, who'd made it quite clear that I wouldn't be joining with a second woman that night, especially Janet. We made up later, but it was a long, costly reparation for me. (That's another story.)

Sue, on the other hand, took our brief encounter as the opening to my inner sanctum of intimacy and the signal that we were now a couple. In other words, she wanted to shack up with me full-time.

I had no intention of doing that, although she is a physically attractive woman and had skills between the sheets, I couldn't stand her constant prattle about whatever thought was flowing through her head at the moment. By the way, that's a very unusual trait for agency folks who are normally very close-mouthed. Her constant dribble drove me senseless. Even in her suite that evening, while breathing hard, all hot and sweaty; rolling around in bed, on the floor, and in the bathroom; and doing things the censors won't let me put on these pages, she constantly talked. It almost spoiled the ending I had been seeking, if you know what I mean. I realized just seconds after I finished that I had made a mistake (strange how I didn't think that way before). Within five minutes I was disinterested in her nonstop prattle and wanted to get back to the party.

Right then I knew I had to put an end to this before it went any further, so while pulling on my pants I diplomatically said, "This was a mistake, Sue.

We're not right for each other, and it's bad for our careers. We should just go back to the party and pretend it never happened."

If you have any experience with women, you know how that suggestion was received. It took another twenty minutes of consoling before she was ready to go back downstairs. I know that seems quick, but I finally just cut her off by saying, "That's how it's going to be." She was smart enough not to make a scene—at least in public. Unfortunately, in private she never gave up the pursuit of our relationship. She has sent me suggestive emails at work and other little "gifts" ever since.

Now here we were at my retirement party. Somehow Sue had showed up (I don't remember inviting her) and was maneuvering for a replay of that night in the Hilton, probably hoping the long-term outcome would be different this time.

"I'm glad you could make it, Sue," I said with my best false smile.

"What do you say we go to your room and clean you up?" Sue was persistent.

"I'm sure it'd be an experience of a lifetime, but we agreed not to do that again. I have other commitments—"

She cut me off, "I can see that. There are so many beautiful women here. Which ones have you bedded? And more importantly, which ones are yet to be bedded tonight?"

"That's not something a gentleman discusses," I replied.

"It's only fair to tell me who my competition is. Besides, you're no gentleman." She touched my chest where Marie's blood had yet to dry. She pulled her hand away and studied the small stain on her finger.

"Whose blood is this?" she asked.

"Someone I cared about deeply."

Somehow the act of Sue stealing Marie's blood from my shirt made me angry. "There's really no competition for you to be concerned with, because we aren't a couple," I said firmly.

At least, I hope it sounded firm.

Before Sue could reply, Kay slithered up to us with a sly grin on her face and a twinkle in her ebony eyes. She was carrying a cardboard box a little larger than a toaster. She wedged her considerably powerful, but perfectly formed body between Sue and I, and then gave Sue a long, scrutinizing once-over before turning back to me—ignoring her. "I have a gift for you, my love."

At this point, even I knew Kay was rescuing me from Sue, so I played along. "Should we go to my bedroom for it, or is it something you can give me here with everyone watching?"

"You're turning into a dirty old man," Kay said with a smile.

"I've always been a dirty-minded man; now I'm just getting older," I quipped.

Kay laughed. "I like that!"

Sue began, "I was here first—"

Kay cut her off, "And you may leave first too, my dear. John belongs to me tonight. When I'm done with him, he won't have enough strength even for your skinny little ass, my dear . . . I promise you." There was no doubt Kay was ready to knock Sue on her butt.

It wasn't necessary.

Sue looked to be on the edge of tears. She gave me one last hopeful glance but saw no reprieve in my expression, so she turned away and silently walked off. To be honest I felt bad for Sue. It was my fault. I had been weak and had succumbed to her seduction two years ago. I'm sure she believed we could be a twosome when she bedded me before. I felt like an asshole then and again now. I didn't want to be with her, but I didn't want her to be sad either. I had no idea how to resolve the dilemma.

I think Kay read my mind because she said, "Don't worry, my dear, little Sue will be bedding someone else before you and I have a chance to go to your room. I've been watching her, and she's hit on almost every unattached man in the room tonight. She's not a victim, she's a predator—trust me, I know."

I hope Kay's right.

"So what is it?" I asked.

"What?" Kay asked.

"What's in the box you're carrying?" I asked.

For an answer Kay handed me the box and said, "Open it."

It was heavy. I sat the box on an end table nearby and pulled the lid off. Inside, was a statue of a black squirrel standing on its hind legs. The bushy tail curled in a question mark, and it was holding a walnut in its front paws. I removed it from the box. The statue did not have a smooth finish. The surface was pitted with broken-bubble craters. The texture felt like plastic, but the squirrel was heavy—too heavy to be plastic.

"What is it?" I asked again.

She said, "Something to assist in your quest to expose the secret organization that got away; the Order of the Golden Squirrel."

What does she mean? I just became aware of the Order of the Golden Squirrel this morning.

Kay continued, "Be sure to read the care and feeding instructions pasted on the bottom."

I began to turn the statue over, and she stopped me with her hand. "Later dear, after everyone else is gone."

"When we're alone?" I asked.

"Yes, after the others are gone. I will give you part two of my gift."

I could see great energy and passion burning in Kay's dark eyes. She moved in very close, snaked her arms around me, and kissed me slowly on the lips. I could feel her soft, full breasts pressing hard against me and smell the musky, sensual scent of her body. She stepped back.

There was a small blood stain on her blouse—Marie's blood rubbed off from me—but for some reason I wasn't angry this time.

She said, "Later my love," then slowly moved away.

Suddenly, Janet had appeared in front of me. She was holding a tubular container, about four inches in diameter and maybe four feet long. "I also have a present for you, dear."

I set the black squirrel on the fireplace mantle and accepted the cylinder.

"Open it," she said.

I opened the end and extracted a double-edged, silver-and-gold sword with an ivory handle. I touched the blade's edge with my finger. It was razor-sharp and had engraving along its full length. The engraving was in Latin—a language I never bothered to learn. "What does it say?" I asked.

"It's the Sword of Saint Gabriel—patron saint of communications. Actually, Marie was planning to give you this, but I'm sure she wouldn't mind me being the courier on her behalf. She said it was an appropriate gift for an old Agency retiree."

We looked deeply into each other's eyes and were quiet until it began to feel awkward. Janet had just broken up with me this morning, and now she was standing here, giving me an expensive gift and looking like one of the most seductive and gorgeous women on the planet. I was beginning to feel melancholy. That wouldn't do at all, so I made a show of swinging the sword around, fighting off imaginary attackers. I faked a big smile and asked again, "What does the engraving actually say?"

"Ask me later when we're alone." Janet was practically purring.

"I thought we broke-up this morning." I was trying to seem nonchalant.

She held up her hand to stop me from swinging the blade and moved in close. "I realized how cruel it was of me to break-up on the day of your retirement celebration, so I changed my mind . . . if you still want me."

"Just one last time?" I asked.

Knowing it was only one more time would be worse than not doing it. I'd only be thinking we would break-up again.

I was forming the words to say "No, thanks," when Janet said, "I was wrong breaking-up . . . maybe we belong together—permanently."

I wonder how she'd feel about Kay joining us?

Janet may not be the problem. You should be asking Kay how she'd feel about Janet.

Then Janet whispered in my ear, "I'll make it up to you later tonight." She drifted away, as if she were making room for someone else to approach me.

This was happening in a room full of guests who seemed oblivious to us, but I knew better. Everyone only appeared to be absorbed in serious drinking, playing arcade games, or conversations. These people were spies— they saw everything.

I wasn't alone for very long. It was apparently Hong Li's turn to approach me. Her way is so subtle that I had not even realized she was next to me until she touched my arm. She made me nervous. Maybe it's my guilty conscious about this morning's aborted launch of the Yinghuo, or maybe it's because Hong Li is one of the most highly skilled agents in the world. Whatever it was, Hong Li made me feel anxious.

"Seems you have many women admirers, my cyber warrior. I had to wait my turn in the queue to talk with you." Her voice had an understated quiver to it.

Hong Li is a tall woman—almost as tall as me—so we stand nearly eye to eye. I'd forgotten how exotically mysterious her eyes are. One moment they are dark pools, making it impossible to comprehend her thoughts, then the next, they can sparkle with a contagious humor. Sometimes they shine with an intense fire and energy, hinting at a great inner strength. At other times they can become severely penetrating, reading your mind and exposing your deepest thoughts.

Hong Li softly glued her body to mine—full length. "I also have something for you." At the moment her eyes were dark, unreadable pools, possibly with a glimmer of passion.

I don't know where she had been keeping the large, polished gold amulet adorned with sapphires and attached to a heavy gold chain, but suddenly she was pressing it into my hand. I studied it. It was about three inches in diameter by maybe a quarter inch thick. The amulet had intricate carvings that were beyond any description I can articulate. It was also something I would never wear. I'm not that kind of guy. Then it occurred to me.

The women had planned this!

I said, "I can't accept this. It must be worth a fortune."

"The amulet is possibly worth a quarter million US dollars in itself, but all is not as it may seem, my handsome lover." She gently took the amulet from my hand and twisted the ring that the gold chain passed through. The amulet opened. Her long delicate fingers extracted a small USB flash drive. The amulet was a vessel to conceal the drive.

"What's this?" I asked.

"Something that will provide the solution you are seeking. It is the companion to the other two gifts," She smiled.

"Where did you get this?" I asked.

Hong Li smiled shyly and pressed closer. I could feel her breath on my face. Slowly, almost ceremonially, she nudged her lips against mine. At that moment, no one else existed in the room. My arms snaked around her body and pinned her hard against me. We kissed. A muffled moan escaped from between our welded lips—I'm not sure who made it. I wanted nothing more at that moment than to take her up to my room and spend the next two days with her. Hong Li pulled back a few inches and said in a whisper, "Later this evening, my cyber warrior. I will tell you everything you need to know. Also, I have something more for you . . ." She turned and slowly walked away.

I was considering going after her when Jackson approached and said, "We have more company. Three black SUVs have parked in front of the garage. They look like the armor-plated type the government uses for the president and such. Right now a bunch of tough-looking men, dressed in dark suites, are spilling out and covering all directions. I don't see any weapons, but that doesn't mean anything."

My brother and his wife joined us. Tom announced, "Jackson says we have more guests. I guess it's a good thing the sheriff is still here."

A night to remember, indeed.

35

THE UNINVITED GUEST

Word of the armored SUVs had spread throughout the party, and my guests had clustered to gawk at the new arrivals through the large widows that had a view of the lake, garage, and driveway. The room buzzed with anticipation of who would exit the armored SUV. Several of the more adventurous guests approached me and asked if I needed help. I knew many of my friends were more than willing to put it on the line for me—which I appreciated—but I didn't want anyone else hurt or maybe killed, like Marie, so I announced to the whole group, "Stay inside and continue with your fun. I'll go outside and greet my newest guest."

Most of the guests continued with their drinking, game-playing, and party prattle. A few stayed near the window to watch.

Jackson grunted and then went down the hallway to a utility closet where he had hidden the shotgun with the high-explosive rounds.

Tom said, "Obviously, you don't mean us. We're going out there with you."

Terry nodded in agreement.

Janet approached our little subgroup.

I don't want anyone else hurt—especially these four.

"Fine, except I don't want to show my hand yet," I replied.

"What do you have in mind?" Terry asked.

"Come with me," I answered.

I led the small group of supporters to my library where I stored the three gifts in the very secure vault: the sword, the black squirrel, and the amulet. Then I closed the vault door and reset the locks. (I'll tell you more about the vault later).

I pulled the Colt Peacemaker from my back and double-checked that it was fully loaded. Doing so was more to prepare myself for what was ahead. I knew it was loaded.

"I told you that pistol isn't practical for a modern gunfight. You should use something more up-to-date," said Tom.

"I like this old Peacemaker. Besides, I have you guys to back me up if this gets nasty." I dramatically spun the cylinder and then slipped the Peacemaker back into the small of my back.

"What do you want us to do?" asked Tom.

I explained my plan to Tom, Terry, Janet, and Jackson.

"Let's do it!"

I marched outside alone to greet my latest guest.

I paraded directly up to the gaggle of gorillas that were guarding the three black GMC SUVs. I was trying to appear confident, but to be honest, I was scared. I figured I'd used up about all the luck one man could expect in one day, even on his retirement day. The new arrivals could be anyone, including someone who wanted me dead, and whoever it was sure brought enough muscle to get the job accomplished. My eyes darted from one gorilla to the next, watching for hostile intentions.

The first thing I noticed was that the gorillas all looked alike. They were all over six feet tall and north of two hundred pounds. They all projected a real tough-guy image with their near-military-short haircuts. They had been trained to shift their small eyes horizontally without moving their heads. Throughout the events I'm about to describe, not a single one of the gorillas ever spoke, which contributes to my theory that they were trained at the same school The Major and The Russian got muscle from. Talking is not part of the curriculum.

I stopped in front of the guy I thought to be the chief gorilla (he had that posture). "To whom do I owe this honor and pleasure?"

He gave me the high school tough-boy stare-down; I call it *Mean-Mugging*. I assume he was trying to impress me with his tough-guy-intimidation imitation.

I may be scared, but I'm not backing down from this bully.

I stood my ground and waited for a reply to my question with a smile fixed on my face. The smile was purely theatrical. I could feel my bowels loosening. The one thing that kept me from backing off was the knowledge that my best friend, my trusted brother, my girlfriend, and my sister-in-law were backing me up just out of view. Tom was carrying an M-4. Jackson had the shotgun loaded with the high-explosive projectiles. However, the cherry on my *dessert of death* was Janet and Terry. Terry was on the roof with a semi-automatic sniper's rifle, equipped with night scope. Janet was her spotter and backup. If Terry was half as good as her reputation, she could kill all these gorillas before they could get a shot off. I hoped she had the crosshairs firmly fixed on the chief gorilla right now. He looked like he was trying to decide whether he should eat me or not. From the bulk of his clothing, I guessed he was wearing body armor under his cheap suit, so she would need to make a head shot.

One other kernel of knowledge that gave me courage was that the sheriff and his deputies were still down below, wrapping up their investigation of the earlier battle.

I repeated the question, "To whom do I owe this honor and pleasure?"

The gorilla just glowered, pretty much confirming my theory that speech wasn't part of training.

The rear door of the center SUV swung open and Jacob Castello, one of the richest men in America, crawled out. He is also a very public figure and has all the requisite political connections. He was also the force behind many attacks on the historical culture of the United States. He wants to ban all religions, all prayer, replace the flag with one without stars or stripes, and even tear down the US Capital's monuments, because they were built to honor corrupt men and false ideals. As much as I didn't like this man, if he got shot here tonight, there would be hell to pay, and what happened to me or to the others would be out of the local sheriff's control.

Why would Castello show up here? We don't know each other, and I'm not a political person.

Castello walked up to me and held out his hand, "I'm Jacob Castello—"

"I know who you are, Mr. Castello."

Castello seemed a little set back but then recovered quickly and said, "Yes . . . well, I happened to be in your area and wanted to meet you and wish you a happy retirement."

"Why would you—a stranger—want to go out of your way to do that? More to the point, how do you know about my retirement?" I asked.

"I make it a point of knowing things that can increase my wealth."

The largest of the bodyguard-gorillas stepped up behind me. I could feel his presence back there without looking.

I forced a smile and said, "Mr. Castello, I doubt I have anything of value to you, but you are welcome to come inside and join the party. I ask that you leave your bodyguards outside. They aren't needed. You will be safe in my home."

"What are the police strobes lights for down the hill?"

"We had some uninvited guests earlier," I answered.

"So you called the police and had them arrested?"

"Something like that," I answered.

There was a brief pause while Castello studied me, then he said, "I apologize for showing up uninvited. Hope you won't have me arrested too." He laughed at his own lousy joke.

I didn't laugh. "Depends on why you're here."

Castello continued, "Yes . . . well, I'd like a word with you in private somewhere."

"To be honest, I'm not interested in going anywhere as long as your monkeys are with us."

The largest gorilla, standing directly behind me, placed a hand on my left shoulder and pressed down. I guess he thought the weight of his beefy appendage would make me show more respect to his boss.

"If junior here doesn't take his hairy paw off my shoulder, I'll send him to the hospital and then charge all of you with trespassing and assault. Remember, I won't have to go very far to get the sheriff." I nodded my head toward the red-and-blue flashing strobes down the hill.

Castello shook his head, and the gorilla removed his hand.

"Well trained," I muttered.

I heard the gorilla growl, but no words were formed and he kept his hand to himself after that.

Castello said, "Sprout told me you were a maverick—that you weren't a team player."

"You know my former boss? How is that?" I asked.

Castello didn't answer the question but instead repeated his request. "Mr. Wolfe, I'm asking nicely if we could have a few words in private."

I smiled. I couldn't help myself. Castello was playing perfectly into my hands. I said, "Okay, Castello, follow me. There's an office in the garage. It's not too clean, but there's no back door so all our friends here can see everyone who goes in or comes out."

"That sounds acceptable," said Castello.

I led Castello to the office in the rear of the garage. I opened the plain wood door and stood aside, gesturing for Castello to enter. He backed off and said, "After you." I walked through the doorway first. I wasn't worried about this particular billionaire stabbing me in the back while I walked through the door—at least not literally. Oh, he'd gladly see me killed, but he wouldn't do it personally. His attorneys would destroy me, or possibly a faceless sniper would be his assassin.

The tiny office was more a coffee room and tool storage area than a real office, although there was a small metal desk and a couple of metal chairs. The room was cluttered with all the odds and ends you'd expect to see in a garage office. It was also dirty. I doubt it had been swept out since it was built.

I flipped a switch, filling the filthy room with bright, florescent light. The blinding light only made the mess look worse. I also casually flipped a second switch that activated another device Jackson had installed last year. At the time, I told him he was wasting my money—putting a video camera, disguised as an oil can, in the garage—but he'd insisted. Now I was happy he had installed it.

I remained standing. "Have a seat if you wish."

Castello looked around at the clutter and dirt and said, "No, thanks, I think I'll just stand."

"So why did one of the richest men in the world personally drive all the way into the boonies to see me? It can't be to wish me well on my retirement, since this is the first time we've ever met."

"I came here to ensure for myself that you aren't a threat, and if not, offer you a deal."

"A threat? How could I be a threat to you?" I asked.

"Let's not play games, Wolfe. You know what I'm talking about."

"Do you mean a National Security threat, or something more personal?"

Castello studied me for a moment and then asked, "Is that blood on your shirt?"

"Yes."

Then it hit me. But I needed to be sure, so I asked him, "Don't avoid the question. Are you concerned that I'm a threat to you, personally, or to the Squirrels?"

"We rarely use that name any longer—the Order of the Golden Squirrel. When that name was conceived we were a bunch of immature college kids. We were making fun of the sanctioned fraternities on campus. Now we've grown up and only refer to ourselves as the Order."

He's spilling all the beans.

"So you're a member of the Order?" I asked.

"I was one of the founding members, back in the late sixties."

Bingo!

I nodded and said, "I understand how a bunch of college boys would form such a secret fraternity, but I don't understand why the Order still exists today. What is its purpose, now that you are all grown up?"

"What every organization exists for: to make money and amass power."

He isn't concerned I'll expose his squirrels—why?

I asked, "Why are you telling me all of this?"

"Because we want to offer you a position in the Order," he answered.

"Doing what?" I asked.

"Essentially what you did for the Agency for the past twenty years, but getting paid a lot more for it."

"I've done all right."

"Yes, I can see. I wonder how long you'd keep this estate if the IRS and the FBI knew how it came into your possession."

"I wouldn't concern myself with that if I were you," I said.

"But you know I'm right. If the IRS learned that you took this property as a gift for helping the British develop a military-grade attack virus that works against any government's software system, you'd not only lose this property but also go to Leavenworth for a very long time."

How does he know about the MI-6 project?

"I was on an official sabbatical from the Agency, and the assistance I gave MI-6 was sanctioned by personal order of the President of the United States. It was all legal."

"There is no written authorization to verify that the president ordered the work."

"Yes, there is. I have my copy of the document safely put away in—"

He interrupted, "—the safe in your condo?"

That's why they broke into my condo this morning!

"There will be other copies."

"Not any longer. It seems they have all disappeared, and the former president is now dead, so he can't verify that he gave you the order." Castello stared at me until the silence was becoming unbearable, and then he said, "But this doesn't have to be a problem for you. I can arrange for you to have a clear title to everything, if you would simply do a few jobs for the Order."

"For example?" I asked.

"Well, for example, you know that the Chinese Mars launch, Yinghuo, failed this morning?"

"I may have heard something about that. It's really too bad for them," I answered.

"We don't need to play games here, Mr. Wolfe. I know it was your last official project to impregnate the Chinese Yinghuo operational software and cause their launch to fail this morning. That's exactly the type of work you would do for the Order. Only as I've already said, you'd be paid much more for your work."

How does he know? That work was classified beyond top secret!

"Who would write the checks?" I asked.

"The Panzram Company," he answered.

I said, "I'd have to give it some thought."

Castello was pressing. "You would be listed as an employee of the Panzram Company. Your income would be aboveboard so you won't have any problems with the IRS or others. Also, I'd ensure your title to this property is free and clear, without any tax obligations." Castello gave me that used-car-salesman smile that said, *trust me, I'm your friend.*

Why such a hard sell?

"Why is someone of your power and wealth coming here and offering me this, personally? Logically, you should send one of your underlings to make me this offer."

"This is confidential Order business. We try to keep our Order business as close as possible. We don't like too many people knowing about it. It's our culture," he answered.

"I don't think I am the right fit for your squirrels, Castello."

A sour expression clouded Castello's face. "What do you mean?"

If you haven't figured it out yet, I'm no good at hiding my true feelings and thoughts.

I told him, "I intend to dismantle your squirrels and shine the light of justice on you personally. I want the pleasure of seeing your kingdom wither and die. You're a traitor, Castello—the worst kind. You used America's gifts of liberty and opportunity to become rich, and now you are using your wealth to destroy the very system that enabled you to become wealthy. I intend to expose you—not become your employee."

"You stupid little shit! I came here to offer you a special position . . . something that could make you wealthy! I can see now that was a bad idea. You're too fucking stupid to understand the great opportunity I've placed at your feet."

He was clearly angry—shouting the words with spittle.

I said, "Yes, I agree—you coming here was a bad idea, and I can't get over the irony of it."

"What do you mean?" he asked.

"If you and Sprout had left me alone, I would have gone quietly into retirement. If Sprout hadn't killed Jimmy this morning—"

Castello cut me off. "Jimmy Trang committed suicide."

He knows about it! How would he know? Unless . . .

I said, "Let's not play games. How do you know anything about Jimmy Trang?"

"Sprout told me." Castello seemed pleased.

"Sprout is dead, and why would he be sharing information with you, anyway?"

Then it occurred to me: Terry had been right early tonight. I killed Sprout, who killed Jimmy. I'd probably done Castello—and the Order—a favor by assassinating the assassin.

Sometimes I'm too impulsive.

I continued. "I can prove you ordered Sprout to murder Jimmy to stop him from exposing your treasonable acts against the United States. Sprout told me as much before he died." Sprout hadn't said that, but I believed it to be true.

Castello's voice became harder. "You can't prove shit!"

"Really?" I mocked him.

"I'm protected! Who do you think they will believe?" Castello was shouting. The gorillas outside could probably hear him.

I answered in a soft voice, "They will believe me when they see the video of this conversation, Mr. Castello, and also see the video I made earlier when Sprout said he was ordered by you to kill Jimmy."

"Sprout would never be stupid enough to say that!"

You're right, he hadn't been, but now I have a recording of you saying it.

"Oh, he was, and you are too."

I just hope Jackson's hidden video camera is working.

"You are unbelievably stupid! I only have to give the word right now and you'd be dead, and then I'll burn this piss ant estate to the ground."

I acted startled. "That's not too bright with the sheriff right outside."

"My men will kill the sheriff deputies too, and make it appear you did it!" Castello stomped from the tiny office.

I followed directly behind, and purposely collided with him in the narrow doorway. I used the collision to slip a small plastic chip into his jacket pocket. It was a little smaller than a dime in diameter and wafer-thin. It was a locator chip; activated by my smartphone app. I could follow him anywhere there was cell service, and for as long as he had the chip on his person.

Castello stormed out ahead of me into the driveway and shouted to his men, "Finish this!"

The order was apparently some prearranged code, because the bodyguards moved in unison.

The lead gorilla closed the distance to me. He had been standing just outside the office doorway anyway, so he was on me in a second. He spun me around so my back was to him. His right hand pressed down very hard on my shoulder. I guess he was performing some lock-up technique on me, or something, but he paused for a moment which cost him his tactical advantage. Had he been a little brighter or more skilled, I would have been in serious trouble. But he was strong—not smart—and I'd had enough of this bully.

I told you earlier that I didn't like fighting or physical violence—I'm not like my talented brother, Tom—but that doesn't mean I'm helpless. I've practiced jiu-jitsu for more than twenty years, mainly to keep myself in shape, so I am quite capable of handling a knuckle dragger like this guy. I spun around and slammed my palm into the bottom of his nose to stun him. Blood exploded from his nostrils, spraying everywhere, including all over me. At almost the same time, I reached up and grasped his huge paw that still rested on my shoulder and deftly stepped behind the gorilla, then twisted his hand and locked up his elbow. The torque threatened to dislocate his shoulder, break his elbow, or snap his massive wrist—maybe all three. I must give him credit: he didn't make a sound. Instead, he tried some feeble countermove that I was ready for. I heard his shoulder pop. The pain caused him to drop to his knees as if he was praying, but I increased the pressure anyway. I heard another faint crack emanate from his elbow. He looked as if he was about to pass out. I twisted a little more and watched his face become cataleptic. He was past pain, so I let go of his arm and spoke in a soft voice. "Stay."

Disabling Gorilla Number One had taken less than four seconds.

The other gorillas were moving as a single unit—all toward me. Only now, seeing what I'd done to their mentor, they stopped and drew their weapons. That's when my brother and Jackson appeared from inside the main house with the heavy artillery. They were a welcome addition to our little drama. They spread about twenty feet from each other and closed the distance with their weapons at the shoulder, covering the gorilla bodyguards.

I knew Terry and Janet were hidden on the rooftop, but they wouldn't make themselves known unless required to shoot someone. Terry and Janet were the two aces up my sleeve.

I slowly drew the Colt from behind my back and cocked the hammer.

Tom's voice boomed across the dark night, as he approached. "Put your weapons on the ground . . . slowly, guys, or we'll drop you."

Jackson added, "And your boss is likely to get hit in the crossfire."

Castello grunted then said, "You can't possibly think to win a gunfight against my men?"

"This ain't just a shotgun, ass-wipe," answered Jackson.

"What?" asked Castello.

In explanation, Jackson fired a round at a nearby pine tree. The round exploded and the tree cracked and did a slow-motion fall toward the lead SUV. It landed two feet from the front bumper. Suddenly, an aura of new respect radiated from the gorillas. They lowered their weapons and remained very still.

I shouted, "Shit, Jackson! You could've made your point without blowing up one of my trees."

Jackson said, "We needed the firewood, anyway."

Down at the gazebo, the sheriff had heard the explosion. We all watched one of the green-and-white patrol cars slowly drive up the road with its emergency lights flashing.

The gorillas holstered their weapons and were standing empty-handed when the sheriff's car pulled slowly to a stop.

I lowered the Colt's hammer and replaced the pistol in the small of my back. I instructed the gorilla still kneeling at my feet, "You may rise."

He slowly stood without making any sound.

I'd be crying my head off . . .

Castello snarled at his chief bodyguard, who now stood, cradling his arm. "When we get back, you're fired!" He spit the words like they tasted bad in his mouth.

I laughed. "You should show some compassion, Castello. This guy's doing the best he can. It's really your fault. You have poor HR skills. It's not his fault you hire incompetents."

Before Castello could respond, the sheriff and a deputy had arrived. They got out of the patrol car with their pistols drawn.

"What was that explosion?" the sheriff asked.

Jackson answered, "I was just showing these boys how the new, high-explosive rounds work. You remember, I showed you last month, and you said you might order some for your deputies."

The sheriff turned to Castello and asked, "Who are you?"

"I'm Jacob Castello—"

The sheriff grunted and said, "I've heard of you. You're one of the richest men in the US."

"The world," I corrected.

The sheriff smiled at me and then studied Castello's security men. He asked the gorilla cradling his arm. "What happened to you?"

Castello answered for him. "He slipped on a patch of ice getting out of the car. We were just about to take him to the hospital."

The sheriff grunted again. His eyes swept the gravel driveway. There was no ice to be seen. Then he studied my brother holding the M-4 and he asked Jackson, "Is everything all right up here?"

Jackson said, "Right as a newborn baby. These people were just leaving. Mr. Castello came to wish Mr. Wolfe a happy retirement, but he's done now, and I believe he was about to leave."

Castello's eyes shifted from me to the sheriff and then back to me. He said, "Yes, I have a meeting to attend."

"After midnight on a weekend?" asked the sheriff.

"Yes, it's a fraternity meeting. We meet once per year." Then he suddenly realized he'd said too much and stopped talking.

Sheriff Boone said, "Drive safe."

Castello opened his own passenger door and climbed in. As soon as he was seated, he pulled his cell phone and called someone. He radiated hatred at me through the still open door. Suddenly, he slammed the door shut, so I never heard what the call was about.

This is far from concluded.

Castello is a powerful and very rich man, one of the original squirrels. He is also a traitor. He knew that I knew all this, and that I can prove it. There is no doubt he would kill me to protect his ugly secret.

Next time, he'll send professional killers, not knuckle-draggers.

After Castello's three black SUVs disappeared into the night, the sheriff said, "Don't think I'm stupid because you aren't in handcuffs . . . yet. The massacre down the hill has to be accounted for in the justice system. The shabby story you've given me so far isn't going to hold up. Nobody's going to buy that the bad guys were right-wing-gun-nut fanatics trying to make a political statement against big government. There's no big government out here. The icing on your Cake of Lies is Castello showing up with his squad of thugs. It looked to me like he wanted to bury you, not wish you a good retirement, Wolfe. His showing up stinks of conspiracy; I don't like conspiracies. If you want to stay out of jail, I need to know the truth."

Jackson said, "Hell, Buford, we're just celebrating John's retirement, and these thugs keep coming out of the woodwork. It ain't our fault!"

"Not good enough, brother-in-law or not," said the sheriff.

"If you don't believe me, come inside and meet the other party guests." Jackson pointed to the wing of the house where the party was going strong.

The sheriff shook his head and said, "Not interested in your party guests. I need to know what's going on with the gunfights and thugs out here."

I said, "Come inside where it's warm. I'll tell you over a beer, or your favorite soft drink."

"I'll come inside, but I'm waiting until I hear your story before I have a drink," said Sheriff Buford Boone.

"Sounds reasonable," I answered.

Everyone followed me into the library.

36

A NEW ALLY

It took some time to convince Sheriff Boone we were the good guys. The sheriff wasn't a fool, and only by telling him the truth—minus any classified details—would I win him to my side. So I told him about my day; that is, I told him about the Order of Golden Squirrel and the Panzram Company. I left out a few chapters, such as Janet breaking up with me this morning. Also, I didn't mention Sprout's stroke, or the meeting with The Major, or The Russian, or my small part in the failure of the Chinese space program. Oh, and I forgot to tell him that we still had Planter handcuffed to my F-100 in the hangar. I didn't think he'd understand or be sympathetic about any of those bits and pieces.

On the other hand, I must say the sheriff was very thorough in his questions. He'd asked the same question two or three times, using different words or from a different perspective, but if you don't know something happened, it's unlikely you'll ask questions about it.

During the entire interview, Jackson and my brother sat quietly, sipping a beer and listening. Terry and Janet showed up about fifteen minutes into the discussion sans the sniper rifle. I have no idea where they had stashed it, and I never had a chance to ask before things got exciting again. But more about that later.

Finally, Sheriff Boone announced, "The way you tell it, you have a righteous fight against evil on your hands, Mr. Wolfe." Then he looked over to my brother and asked, "Are you really *the* Thomas Wolfe, assistant director at the FBI and war hero?"

"I'm an assistant director at the FBI . . . I served twenty years in the US Army."

"My SWAT commander told me about you. He attended a workshop that you hosted at Quantico earlier this year. He was quite impressed."

"Well, I . . ."

The sheriff turned back to me. "Your story sounds right, John Wolfe, and I figure if you have the backing of the FBI, I'm in too."

I began to protest that the FBI wasn't officially involved, when Tom caught my eye, frowned, and shook his head slightly, so I remained quiet.

The sheriff turned to his deputy and said, "We left only one patrol unit down at the gazebo. I need you to go down there and back him up. I'll arrange for a relief in a couple hours."

The deputy nodded and departed. We listened to the green-and-white patrol car's tires crunch on the gravel road as it returned to the gazebo.

The sheriff said, "I'll have that beer now."

I had a new ally.

It was Jackson who suggested, "Well, hell then, let's join the party proper!"

At the time, I thought things were beginning to look good, but this is not one of those stories where a happy, peaceful ending is promised. In fact, you may find the ending kind of frustrating. I'm sorry about that, but it's the way things happened.

Unknown to me at the time, while we were in the main house talking to the sheriff, another small army of dark forces were initiating the assault to end all assaults. This time they came in from the south. They entered the hangar and found Planter still handcuffed to the landing gear of the F-100, but more on that later. (There's only so much bad news I can tell you about at one time). Not finding what they wanted at the hangar, the evil men carefully moved up the jeep trail toward the main house. They traveled on foot because they wanted stealth and surprise, not speed.

In the meantime, we were blissfully partying with no worries; engaged in our impression of the last days of Rome and completely unaware of the dark army's approach.

37

A QUIET MOMENT WITH AN OLD LOVER

Our subgroup entered the game room: me, then my brother, Terry, and Jackson with the sheriff bringing up the rear. I suppose we made an interesting spectacle, because all the guests quieted down and turned to gawk at us. Using the lull, I introduced Sheriff Boone to everyone and asked they treat him as one of the family. Then our little parade moved directly to the bar, and I personally drew the sheriff's first cold draft beer of the night.

The party resumed.

The sheriff had barely taken a sip of his beer when Sue slid up next to him and said, "Hello, Sheriff Boone, my name is Sue. I could show you around, if you wish."

I guess she's over the sting of rejection from earlier this evening.

It didn't take long before the sheriff and Sue looked like they'd been together for years and deeply in love—or at least lust. I decided it wasn't my business. The sheriff was a big boy. Hopefully he was big enough to handle Sue. I turned away, and then the next time I looked they had vanished. To where? I don't know, and I didn't go looking for them either. They were two consenting adults, and my house has plenty of bedrooms.

After I was assured the party was going well, I slipped away to my bedroom, located on the other side of the house. I wanted to change into something more comfortable—that is, clothing with less blood and sans the stink of gun smoke. I was standing in my boxer shorts, debating whether I should take a quick shower, when I became aware that Hong Li was watching me. I don't know how long she had been there before I became aware of her. She was standing rock-still, studying me as if she were Death deciding whether it was my time or not. Even after I faced her, she didn't move or make a sound.

Maybe she was here to kiss me; maybe she was here to kill me? It could be either. After all, she owed me for helping with the 1997 Reversion. Maybe that obligation and the time we spent in the bedroom while saving the '97 Reversion was stronger than her sense of duty to her employer. Maybe not.

Make love or murder?

She was immensely qualified to accomplish either, and this was the first time we'd been alone since my arrival. Hong Li is an active Chinese agent, and the Chinese can be very vindictive—even more so than the Russians if they feel justified. I was responsible for shutting down their Yinghuo space vehicle this morning. It had been my last operation before retiring. Hong Li may suspect it was me.

When Hong Li finally spoke, her words were soft notes, a serenade recited in subdued—almost whispered—a cappella. "I am very sorry to be here under these circumstances, my love, but my primary purpose for coming is not to wish you a happy retirement. It is something much more serious, my sweet lover."

Damn!

My eyes darted to the nightstand next to the bed where I had placed the Colt. The table was at least ten feet away, and the pistol was inside the top drawer—too far away and too difficult to reach if she was here to kill me.

Don't overreact. If she were here to kill me, I wouldn't have known she was here. I'd just be dead.

I asked, "Why are you here, Hong Li?"

"My superiors are very displeased at the failure of the Yinghuo launch this morning. I am to determine if you were involved, and if so, express their extreme displeasure." She remained statue-still. Her hands were empty and in plain sight.

She's making sure I don't overreact until we've finished our conversation.

"Why are you telling me this? Why not just do what you must do?" I asked.

"I am doing what I must, my love. I have a greater duty than simply revenge against someone performing his duty. There are more important problems we must address, which creates a conflict."

What the hell does that mean?

"What?" I asked.

"I have been offered a great deal of money by The Russian if I obtain your masterpiece for him, the Perfidious Mountebank Program codes and frequencies."

Seems I have no secrets any longer.

"How do you know about the PM Program?" I asked.

"My government has suspected for several years the Agency was installing such a program in all equipment sold to foreign governments, but despite our efforts we have been unable to locate or decipher the program, so we could not prove it."

Maybe I am a genius.

In a moment of self-congratulatory bliss, I said, "It's only placed in military aircraft we sell to other countries—not all equipment, and not in civilian aircraft," and then immediately realized I'd just committed a huge security violation.

Not as smart as you thought you were.

Hong Li grasped the significance of my statement and smiled. "I appreciate you being forthcoming with me."

She's not here to kill you.

I asked Hong Li again, "Why are you here? If you simply wanted to kill me, I'd be dead by now. If you wanted me to give up state's secrets, I doubt you would approach me as you have tonight. So what is your goal?"

"I want to provide The Russian with false program codes, receive the payment he has promised, then cause a virus program to be transmitted to his clients, which will work its way throughout the terrorist organization network and destroy their communications, financial networks, and data files. After I am sure the virus has been launched, I intend to kill him."

We all knew that The Russian was selling arms and secrets to terrorists around the world. Currently, his primary clients were Middle East terrorist organizations. The Major, Janet, Hong Li, and I all wanted The Russian dead. But before he died we needed to dismantle his network—both physically and financially. Hong Li was offering an opportunity to accomplish that goal.

I couldn't stop myself from chuckling. "How do you know I want to kill The Russian?"

Hong Li said, "I am aware that your girlfriend, Janet, has tasked you with that mission on behalf of the Agency. I am also aware that The Russian has contacted you personally and offered you a great sum of money for the PM Program's codes and frequencies. I propose we join our labors and take advantage of the current circumstances to reach our mutual goals."

"For the record, Janet is no longer my girlfriend. We broke up."

Hong Li said, "That is not important, but our opportunity will be gone if we do not act."

I said, "Are you sure you want to play this dangerous game?"

"Yes," said Hong Li.

"You may get your chance. He is supposed to show here tonight."

Hong Li studied me for a moment with a sadness etched on her lips and in her eyes. "Yes, I know he's bringing a woman that he's holding hostage to ensure you cooperate. Is she your lover?"

How does she know about Mary?

I said, "Mary's not my lover."

"Then why is he leveraging her to get what he wants from you?" she asked.

"It's complicated." I answered. Then I asked, "Why are you standing across the room?"

Hong Li's smile changed to playful as she smoothly glided across the space that separated us, stopping inches from my face. "I needed you to know I am not here to do you harm . . . I am here to enlist your assistance in our common goal."

"How do I know you won't kill me after we have accomplished our common goal?"

She whispered, "If I intended to kill you afterward, I would not have given you the amulet and USB drive earlier."

"What is on that drive?"

Hong Li said, "I took it from the very beautiful Mary Killigrew after you departed from the meeting with the Russian at the farmhouse this afternoon. Ms. Killigrew told me the USB drive has the names and financial information for the Order on it. She obtained it from one of the original members."

"You were at the farmhouse when I was there talking to The Russian?" I asked.

"I was waiting in another room for you to leave. By the way, my love, you cannot trust that woman—Mary."

"Seriously," I said, feeling lame. "But how did you get the drive from Mary?'

"Mary is a confirmed lesbian, and she is very attracted to me. It was relatively easy to gain all of her secrets. I have been working on her, and The Russian, for several months."

I've been a total idiot!

"How much did The Russian offer to pay you for the PM Program?" I asked.

"One hundred million US dollars," she answered.

Same amount he offered me. He's playing us all.

I chuckled. "You've become a capitalist. Do you intend to keep the money for yourself or turn it over to your government?"

Hong Li said, "I wish to retire in the United States. To do so, I will need more money than I have managed to put away working for my homeland."

"Why the United States?" I asked.

She took my hand in hers and pulled me closer. "I have traveled to almost every part of this world and have sampled every civilized culture on the planet, and I have decided, even with its flawed system and unethical politicians, the United States is still the best place on earth to live. However, it is expensive to live here comfortably."

I said, "I cannot allow The Russian to have the PM Program codes."

"On that we agree," she said.

"You have a plan?" I asked.

"Yes, The Russian plays people against each other. We can use that." Her voice was only a whisper.

"In that case, I agree. We'll work together," I said.

Hong Li finally kissed me like only she can kiss. I felt myself responding on all levels, if you know what I mean.

Of course, at that exact moment, Janet walked into the room.

"Excuse me . . . am . . . I . . . interrupting something?" she asked.

38

FALSE FLAGS AND SAFEGUARDS

Janet's face was awash with astonishment. "After last night and then again this morning, you still have the energy for this? And with an agent of the Chinese Government! I have underestimated and apparently underutilized you, sir."

"Janet . . ." I began.

She cut me off with, "You're a retiree now. You should pace yourself—save it for when it really counts."

Hong Li said with a wicked smirk, "Oh, but it does count, trust me."

I knew I needed to get the conversation on a different track. "We were discussing a partnership with a mutual goal."

Janet said, "Some discussion! I can imagine what the mutual goal could be."

I shrugged. "You could join us," then realized that had been a mistake the instant it was said.

"I doubt even you could handle both of us at the same time!" said Janet.

Hong Li came to my rescue. "It was work, I assure you. I was about to propose a cyber-attack against The Russian's computer network by selling him the PM Program codes and frequencies, enhanced with a very refined virus my people have developed specifically for this purpose."

Janet shot me an even more disapproving look then asked Hong Li, "You know about the PM Program?"

I cut in. "She already knew! I didn't tell her."

". . . and you have built a designer virus to piggyback on it?" Janet asked.

"Basically, we have known of your program for several years, and have developed an enhancement for the False Flag safeguard," answered Hong Li.

"Oh, and you know about the False Flag safeguard too?" Janet now looked angry.

Hong Li said, "Actually, we've developed a powerful malware virus."

"The False Flag safeguard *is* a powerful virus. Yours would be redundant," said Janet.

Hong Li said, "No, your safeguard merely destroys the computer that uses the wrong passcodes. Our enhancements will also search out and target the bank accounts the user does business with. The target loses all his money. The virus then further seeks out the accounts the primary target did business with and destroys them also. The program continues to seek out more and more connections until it has found all the accounts, anywhere in the world, connected to the target account. The program will create a worldwide financial holocaust for terrorist organizations."

"How do you activate it?" I asked.

"You can attach it into your False Flag safeguard program. It will execute first, and then allow your program to destroy the primary host's computer."

"How do you identify what accounts are associated with terrorism and which are not?" asked Janet.

Hong Li said, "Our program has a complex algorithm protocol. It won't attack a legitimate business—paying for a dinner in a restaurant for example."

"Where is your program now?" I asked.

She pulled out a USB flash drive. "I have it here. You only need to install it as a subroutine of the False Flag safeguard."

Janet asked, "How do you know so much about the PM Program?"

Hong Li remained silent.

After a moment of awkward silence, I said, "I have the PM Program here."

Hong Li said, "We should install my refinement before The Russian arrives, so he doesn't suspect."

Janet almost shouted, "Wait! How do we really know this is what she claims? She could be loading a Trojan Horse program that steals the PM Program and does who knows what damage?"

"Because I trust her," I said.

Janet shot me a glare that would turn a mortal to stone.

Ignoring her, I walked over to a podium that contained a large-volume book resting on the reading pedestal. I opened the book's front cover to reveal a keypad and punched in the six-digit code.

A green LED light signaled that I had entered the correct code. I now had thirty seconds to press my right thumbprint to a sensor pad disguised as a wall switch, located about five feet away. I pressed my thumb against the hidden pad, and an overhead, recessed spotlight highlighted a door, which meant the thumbprint had been accepted.

These two steps had to be performed correctly, and within the time limits, or the system would lock itself down for twenty-four hours. It's a pain in the rear if I accidently screw it up, but a great safeguard if an unauthorized interloper tries to open it.

I opened the highlighted door to reveal a small closet like room. I stepped inside. A retina scanner was mounted on the back wall. I pressed my eye to the scanner and heard a soft, high-pitched beep, and the wall to my right slid open.

I turned to the women and said, "Please wait out here. There isn't room enough for all of us inside." I entered the small vault constructed of a steel floor, ceiling, and walls and lit by a single, caged bulb in the ceiling. The vault is as secure as any commercial bank—more than some.

Earlier, I had stored the three retirement gifts inside the vault: the sword, the black squirrel, and the amulet with Mary's USB drive. They still sat on the table against the wall where I'd left them. This time, however, I had to open the fourth gate, a hardened-steel, armored metal cabinet inside the vault—a vault within the vault. The extra level of security was required to protect the PM Program codes and frequencies.

You may be wondering why I kept a copy of the super-secret PM Program in my home. Again, I refer you to my first training officer, who told me the Agency was a very jealous lover, and someday would unjustly take a very unpleasant revenge against me for some trivial infraction. He recommended I keep a few aces—something worth a lot of money—up both sleeves to protect myself that day. I had squirrelled away the PM Program, and a few other jewels, for that purpose. If you're surprised at my lack of wholesome values and honesty, go back to the Chapter 7 and re-read the Agency's true Values and Mission Statement. It was how I was trained.

I pressed my thumb against a pad hidden on the side of the wall cabinet, and the door unlocked with a loud click. Inside was the USB drive containing the PM Program codes and frequencies, a dozen one-ounce gold bars I was saving for a rainy day, and my second Colt Peacemaker that was an exact match to the pistol tucked in the small of my back.

I removed the PM codes and frequencies drive, relocked the cabinet and then the vault, and walked over to the other side of the library, where there is a computer station that can do pretty much anything that can be done by any computer on the planet.

I inserted the drive into my computer. The security routine popped up. I performed a quick administrator's sign-on so I could access the program language itself. Then I turned to Hong Li and said, "Okay, I'm ready. Show me your virus!"

She handed me her flash drive.

I plugged Hong Li's USB into my computer. The menu popped up. There was no security sign-on procedure.

Janet's right: check for a trap before you install this.

I ignored my little voice.

I asked Hong Li, "What language is your virus written in?"

"We used the same programming language you did for your PM and the False Flag safeguard programs."

"How did you know—" I began.

Janet groaned. "We don't know what else her program does. It could destroy the Agency's computers, or shut down all US banking, or who knows!"

She didn't need to use my computer to do any of those things.

I continued working while Janet continued voicing her doubts and fears. Finally, I announced, "I'm in!"

Janet stopped complaining at that announcement.

This is one time I hope Janet is wrong.

At that moment, Jackson, Tom, and Terry entered the library together. Tom, asked, "Hey, what's up?"

I answered immediately before Janet could override me, "I was just thinking of coming to find you guys. We're making new plans, and I we'll need you."

"Sounds like fun," said Terry.

As predicted, Janet began, "I don't think it's a good idea—

I cut her off with, "Hong Li, The Russian has a very suspicious nature. How do we slip him a computer virus without him catching on?"

Hong Li said, "I have a plan."

We listened to her plan and then conspired to refine it. After we were done conspiring, it took about fifteen minutes to piggyback Hong Li's virus to my program. Now whoever used the wrong passcodes to access the PM Program would blindly default to my False Flag safeguard routine. That, in turn, would activate Hong Li's financial virus program and my killer virus in that order. It would be a one-two-knockout punch.

And then we kill The Russian.

39

MORTAL ENEMIES

They were not traveling together, and certainly they were not friends, but they arrived at the same time—one in a Lincoln stretch limousine, with an escort passenger car: the second in a single armored black SUV. I watched from the game-room window as they exited their vehicles and awkwardly acted civilized. Their respective security men were watching each other as if they expected a shooting war to break out at any moment. I had the passing thought that a shootout between them now would solve many problems. But it didn't happen that way. Instead, they shook hands, talked, forced laughs in appreciation of each other's shallow witticisms, and pretended to be old friends. Seeing them together—pretending to enjoy each other's company—was quite entertaining from a sadistic point of view. It was, of course, all a lie. The Russian and The Major were mortal enemies.

In the world of espionage—just as in international diplomacy—mortal enemies can appear to be friends if there is a mutual benefit in doing so. Such enemies can cooperate for a specific purpose and limited time; however, once the common benefit is achieved, they may turn on each other in a most deadly and final way or simply part company until another day. In this case, neither party was prepared to go terminal at this unplanned encounter, so they would act cordial.

Apparently, they had reached some sort of agreement regarding their personal security, because only four knuckle draggers followed the two icons of the espionage world as they approached the house. The remaining security men stayed behind with the vehicles.

The Major and The Russian walked side-by-side, chatting and chuckling like old friends. Watching from the window, it was clear they were very different men in every way. The dapper little Russian was considerably smaller in stature than The Major in both height and width. The difference was so vast that seeing them walk side by side was somehow hilarious. The Major wobbled along in his wrinkled brownish-colored suit and scuffed brown shoes that could have been purchased at a thrift store. The Major was barely able to transport his bulk across the few yards of gravel driveway and up the six stone steps that led to the entryway into the main house. The Russian, on the other hand, was dressed in an Italian, custom-tailored, navy-blue suit and highly polished Oxfords. He moved with a considerable bounce in his step, almost tap dancing across the gravel. He took the short flight of steps two at a time. I'm guessing he did so, not so much a result of his limitless energy, but because he knew it would antagonize The Major. The energetic Russian stood at the top of the steps, waiting impatiently for The Major and smiling as if he'd just won some important athletic contest— an Olympic gold medal for stair-climbing or something. The Major seemed to take each step as an independent, long-term task to be savored as the final goal for the evening. When The Major finally reached the top of the stairs he removed a soiled handkerchief and wiped perspiration from his forehead, even though the outside temperature had dropped to freezing.

I knew it was my responsibility to personally greet these two distinguished guests, so I slipped away from my other guests in the game room. I reached the main entrance and opened the front door to greet them. There they stood, standing side-by-side, each with two identically cloned knuckle-draggers standing at their rear.

"Good evening, gentlemen." I could smell The Russian's aftershave lotion and The Major's body odor. Neither was pleasant.

Then I saw Mary standing at the bottom of the stairs. For some reason, I hadn't noticed her before. No one was watching her and her hands were not bound. She was wearing a new outfit—sans a bullet hole. She looked striking in the navy-blue slacks, solid blue sweater, dark blue ski jacket, and Russian fur cap. She was wearing the same boots from this morning.

"Won't you please come in?" I asked. I smiled at Mary and said, "You're invited too … nice outfit."

She returned a perfunctory smile and slipped past me without speaking.

As the procession traveled along the hallway, Janet suddenly appeared at my side. I glanced back and saw Jackson, Tom, and Terry following from a discrete distance. I couldn't see any weapons, but I'm sure they were present.

The Major was struggling to keep the pace set by The Russian. I slowed to accommodate him, but The Russian insisted on walking faster, passing the others. His two knuckle draggers sped up to stay with him, until there were two divided groups. Unfortunately, the lead group didn't know where we were headed.

It was obvious The Russian was walking fast to irritate The Major. So to irritate The Russian, I slowed down as much as possible, staying back with The Major.

Let him make the wrong turn at the intersection so he is forced to retrace his steps.

Instead, The Russian stopped at the corner and looked back at the slower group, which had now spread about ten yards along the hallway. He folded his arms across his chest and tapped his foot. His expression and body language were screaming, "I'm waiting—hurry up!" But instead he said, "Which way?"

Let him wait until you and The Major catch up.

Janet spoiled my little scheme by announcing, "Left turn."

The Major touched my arm gently to stop me and said, "Mr. Wolfe, before we go further I'd ask to have a private word with you, please."

"Jackson, could you ensure my other guests find the game room? Make everyone feel at home. We'll be there directly."

"Sure . . . no problem," answered Jackson, who had been splitting the distance, attempting to place himself in mid-group.

The Russian seemed as if he were about to object.

He's justifiably paranoid about us having a secret meeting.

I grinned in as friendly a manner as possible at the dapper little man—clearly looking friendlier than I felt. "We have some private business that does not concern you, sir. I assure you I'll be available to you, for our business, soon enough."

Janet hooked The Russian's arm in hers and said, "Come with me, handsome. I'll show you a good time."

She didn't have to do that!

The Russian grumbled, but he and two bodyguards followed her. The Major and I remained behind with his two knuckle draggers.

"I thought you said a word in private." I indicated the bodyguards towering over each side of me.

"I rarely go anywhere without my security, Mr. Wolfe. I'm sure you understand."

I answered, "In that case, I wish to call back a couple of my friends— keep it even—you understand."

"You don't trust me?" The Major had contorted his face with a look of disappointment and contrived hurt. It was purely theatrical.

"No," was my simple answer.

"As you wish." The Major's yellowish eyes addressed his two security men then shifted to the hallway intersection where the others had already turned the corner. The eye routine must have been a signal his security men understood, because they shuffled down the hallway, leaving us alone.

I said, "So what did you want to talk about in private?"

"I was wondering if you have decided to accept my employment offer."

Careful . . . remember, his offers are take it or die!

"I'm inclined to accept; however, we have not talked about compensation, vacations, and other such details yet," I answered.

The Major grunted and said, "I assure you that compensation and such will be more generous than you would ask for—more than you could dream."

"Well, maybe next week we could meet under more private circumstances and finalize the details," I suggested.

The Major studied me for a moment before replying, "That will be acceptable. However, I have two courtesies to ask for now."

"Yes?" I asked.

"First, do not think that you can play me for a fool. Do not attempt to somehow mislead me into thinking you will work for me and then attempt to expose my existence and identity. If you do, I assure you the outcome will be very unpleasant."

"And the second?" I asked.

"Tonight, I would ask that you introduce me as an old friend. Just say my name is Patrick—no last name—and that I am here solely to wish you a good retirement."

"Doesn't The Russian know who you are?" I asked.

"Of course, but he also knows how to play the game."

"Do think he knows the purpose of your visit?" I asked.

"He most likely thinks I'm here to obtain a copy of the PM Program codes and frequencies and then kill you—just as he is." The Major's eyes projected an unholy gleam, crowning a sinister smile.

"Is that what you believe? Couldn't he be here to recruit me, same as you?"

The Major chuckled, as he patted his ample belly, and said, "Shall we have a drink and meet your other guests like the old friends we are?"

40

THE PARTY RESUMES

The party had come to a halt in the game room. Everyone was staring at the new attendees in silence. Most knew who the latest arrivals were, so there was a cold stillness in the room. The cold could become very hot if the wrong sentence was uttered, or someone moved too fast.

This is no good.

I stood in the center of the room and indicated The Russian and The Major, who had already selected an oversize leather chair near the fireplace—apparently fatigued from his walk, and then announced in a loud voice, "Everybody, I'd like to introduce the two newest arrivals to our little party, Dimitri and Patrick. Please consider them honored friends and guests *tonight*." I put a little extra stress on the word *tonight* then I ended in a lower volume with, "Jackson, could you give me a hand at the bar?"

A low-pitched murmuring washed through the room, and then the party clamor picked up again.

Unlike The Major, The Russian had remained on his feet, keeping his back to a bookcase and flanked by his two bodyguards. He wasn't just being paranoid. There were people in this room who would give him good reason to be cautious.

Janet stood close to me behind the small bar. I wondered briefly where she kept her pistol. There wasn't room in those tight jeans, so I was guessing she had a shoulder hostler under the sweater, but it would need to be snug—and the pistol small—because there wasn't much room there either. Tom and Terry sat on the leather sofa and played the romantic couple at the party. I knew that—like Jackson—both my brother and his wife were armed. Actually, I still had the Colt Peacemaker tucked under my shirt in the small of my back.

Probably most of the people in the room are armed.

I looked around for the sheriff and Sue, but both were still missing from action.

Sue must be giving the sheriff the full tour.

Mary appeared at the bar, opposite me. "How does a lady get a glass of wine here?" As she spoke, her eyes were constantly sweeping the room, watching everyone. I guess paranoia can be contagious. I assumed she'd picked up a new weapon someplace and that it was concealed somewhere on her fifty-billion-dollar body.

Hong Li said Mary is a lesbian—too bad.

I was considering how much fun it would be finding Mary's hidden weapon, and maybe trying to convert her straight, when Janet bumped me with her hip, breaking into my fantasy.

She asked, "Would you like me to help serve drinks?"

Janet is acting terribly territorial for someone who broke up with me this morning.

"That would be helpful."

In the meantime, Kay had casually moved next to Mary. Their eyes locked, and I think I saw fire arc between them.

Hong Li entered the room—I don't know where she had been—and cozied directly up to The Russian as if they were passionate lovers. She began whispering into his ear. I could see him whispering back. I felt a twinge of jealousy.

With Hong Li's arrival, all the players were in position, and accounted for—according to plan.

I handed Mary a glass of red wine. "I see someone else has become cozy with your boss." I nodded to The Russian and Hong Li, who were making serious goo-goo eyes at each other.

Mary responded with, "Not to worry, Casanova; that's all business, I assure you."

"I was wondering how you felt about them?"

"Why should I care?"

But she's watching them closely. Is she more concerned about The Russian or Hong Li?

From my peripheral, I saw The Russian hold up a *stay here* hand to Hong Li and set course directly for me. His agile body deftly weaved between the other guests. His bodyguards had difficulty keeping up.

I waited until I was sure The Russian was within hearing range before asking, "By the way, did you give your boss the USB drive . . . the one you made me go back into the hospital to get?"

If you remember, Hong Li had acquired that USB drive from Mary—presumably in the bedroom—and had given it to me cased in the jeweled, gold amulet.

Mary's eyes dropped to the floor for just an instant and then focused directly at me. She spit out the words, "I don't know what you talking about."

I remained silent.

"What USB drive, my dear?" asked The Russian as he wedged himself between Kay and Mary.

"She didn't tell you about the USB drive?" I asked, trying to sound surprised.

The Russian turned to Mary and said, "My dear, do you have a present for me, something that you neglected to tell me about?"

"No, I have no idea what this man is talking about," answered Mary.

She's playing everyone against everyone else.

Pull on the thread some more: see what unravels.

I said, "So tell me, Mary—I'm confused—do you work for Panzram Company or The Russian?"

The Russian answered my question before she could prevaricate her way out. "She technically works for both, but her ultimate loyalty is to me. Isn't that right, my dear?"

Mary said, "Yes, I guess you could call me a double agent. I have been working my way deep inside the Order to learn how they operate and who the managing members are."

I decided to see what other cracks I could wedge. "Then what was your goal this morning when you and Planter played that little charade with me?"

"I don't know what you're talking about."

"Sure you do. If both you and Planter work for The Russian, why did you stun him with a Taser? Now that I recall, I'm even more impressed with how Planter reacted. He gave no indication you two were together at the time. That was cold, using a Taser on your own partner."

The Russian perked up and asked Mary, "You tasered David? He didn't tell me. This was his first job with me."

I was right . . . Planter was a New Guy.

Mary laughed—I think it was genuine. "You should have been there. I think he messed his pants."

She's cold.

The Russian laughed too. "Yes, I can imagine." Then he asked me, "By the way, where is Mr. Planter now?"

I said, "Poor Mr. Planter has had a tough day, so I left him where he can get some rest. He's safely tucked away."

"Our arrangement was to return him in the same condition he left with you."

I smiled. "At the proper time."

(Remember, at the time I didn't know about the army of dark forces that had passed through the hangar and were, at that moment, slithering by foot between the trees, with the goal of ruining my party.)

The Russian leaned across the bar to get a little closer to me and said in a softer voice, "So, Mr. Wolfe, when do we conclude our private business transaction?"

It's time to spring the trap.

"You mean the codes and frequencies for the PM Program?" I asked, a little too loud.

The Russian quickly scanned the surrounding guests to determine whether we'd been overheard, but everyone appeared to be ignoring us. He said, "Yes, I'd like to make the transaction and be on my way. I've never been a big fan of loud parties."

Hong Li suddenly appeared behind The Russian. One of his knuckle daggers turned to address the Chinese agent, but then Kay slipped in behind him and placed a restraining hand on his gun arm. I quickly looked around for Janet, who was moving to the exit. Jackson, Tom, and Terry were already gone.

All according to plan . . .

I said with my best used-car-salesman smile, "In that case, please follow me to the library?"

41

THE DOUBLE-DOUBLE-CROSS

As we were leaving the game room, I stopped and indicated Mary and the two bodyguards following directly behind. "We don't need them. Let's keep this simple—just two gentlemen completing a business transaction. I have some excellent bourbon I would like to share with you while we complete our business. Is that acceptable?"

The Russian seemed to consider my suggestion and then said, "Yes, assuming, of course, your people also wait here."

I looked around, as if confused, and said, "I see no one from my camp following us."

The Russian nodded. "Very well . . . the bourbon sounds interesting."

At that moment the sheriff and Sue reentered the game room. It was obvious from their body language and facial expressions that they had become very well acquainted.

I said, "Sue, you have a warm glow about you."

Sue looked away as if I had embarrassed her.

Then I addressed the sheriff, "Help yourself to a drink, Sheriff—my home is your home. I'll be back shortly."

"Thank you, John. That is very kind," answered the sheriff. He seemed more relaxed than before—mellow.

I watched as the new couple walked to the bar, hand-in-hand. They had clearly melded. Sue had found someone.

Then my eyes caught the Major, still sitting in the overstuffed chair. He was intently watching me. He didn't look friendly. I'm guessing he didn't like that The Russian and I were leaving the room together—meeting privately. I pretended not to notice as I turned away and exited.

I hope The Major doesn't interfere.

The Russian and I entered the library alone as agreed. I closed the heavy, double wood doors to the hallway, giving us the illusion of privacy. (There were several people electronically watching, listening, and recording our "private meeting.") Then I crossed the floor to the small wet bar in the corner of the room.

As I poured, I asked, "How do you propose transferring my one hundred million dollars so that I can independently verify it?"

The Russian said, "I can make the transfer from my phone, tonight, as soon as I verify the receipt of the codes and frequencies. Shall we begin?"

He's in a hurry.

I handed him a glass of bourbon. We clinked glasses. "To you and the horse you rode in on," I said. The Russian looked like he didn't get it, so I added, "It's an old American salute, sometimes used between friends when drinking bourbon."

The Russian nodded as if he understood, but I doubted it. He took a sip of his drink, then nodded his head in satisfaction and took a second, longer pull on the bourbon.

I walked over to the reading podium, opened the front cover, and punched in the six-digit code. The green LED light signaled acceptance. Next, I walked to the wall switch and pressed my right thumbprint to the disguised sensor pad. The overhead spotlight highlighted a door. I opened the door and entered the small closet-like room.

"Should I come with you?" asked The Russian.

"No, please . . . there's not enough room for both of us. Please wait outside."

I pressed my eye to the scanner. I heard the soft, high-pitched beep, and the wall to my right slid open. "Please wait out here," I repeated and entered the small vault.

I quickly retrieved the recently enhanced USB flash drive that contained both the PM Program's codes and frequencies, plus Hong Li's virus. I was about to exit when my eyes fell on the second matched Colt Peacemaker. There was also a box of silver-tipped, hollow-point bullets next to the pistol. The first Peacemaker was still tucked in the small of my back.

On impulse, I opened the presentation wooden box and removed the second Peacemaker. Just like its twin, it was beautiful. I held the flawless, black-finished single-action pistol with genuine ivory grips. It wasn't a lightweight pistol, but it was perfectly balanced in my hand. It occurred to me that the Colt had never been loaded. There comes a time in everything's existence when its destiny must be fulfilled. Intuition told me tonight would be the night for this Peacemaker. I quickly loaded the silver-tipped, hollow-points. I hefted the heavy pistol in my hand and fantasized about emerging from the vault with both Colts blazing away. I'd cut The Russian down in an act of barbaric glory. But even if I didn't go to jail for murder afterward, killing The Russian before he uploaded the viruses would defeat our whole plan. Killing him first would be stupid! I sighed and placed the second loaded Peacemaker back in its wooden box, then reverently placed the wooden box inside the cabinet. The second Peacemaker would be ready, in reserve, if needed.

On impulse, I stuffed a handful of rounds in my pants' pocket—just in case—and then locked the armored cabinet.

The Russian called to me, "What's taking so long?"

I exited the vault and announced, "Just making sure I had the right flash drive. I'm ready to do my part. It's your turn. Show me the money!"

Be the mercenary.

"You must show me the program's directory before we go further," said The Russian.

"If you insist." As I crossed the room to my computer, I could feel the extra weight of the bullets in my pants' pockets, and I was also very conscious of the first Colt Peacemaker pressing into the small of my back. The sensations felt both comforting and uncomfortable.

I sat down behind the desk and inserted the flash drive into my PC. The menu immediately popped up, asking for an ID and password.

This is where I had to do a tap dance of deception. If I entered the true ID and Password then the real list, codes, and frequencies would be displayed for The Russian. If I entered the False Flag ID and password, my virus and Hong Li's piggybacked financial malware would be activated. I couldn't stop the malware from happening once the false password was entered. The effects wouldn't show up for about twenty-four hours, but there was no antidote, no stopping it; it would happen. And that was something I didn't want happening to my computer.

So I entered the true ID and corresponding password. The genuine table of contents appeared. Now the tap dance: show him enough of the real program to convince him it was genuine, but not long enough for him to remember any of the details.

The Russian moved in closer to look over my shoulder.

The table of contents—the real table of contents—listed the countries that military aircraft were sold to. Then under each country was a subcategory showing the dates and the types of aircraft. Each line was a hot link to the corresponding page with the codes and frequencies for a particular aircraft or groups of aircraft—all very user friendly. The idea is if a country goes to war against the United States and is using US-built aircraft against us, the Pentagon can select the type of aircraft to disable—either all military aircraft sold to that country, a subcategory, or just an individual aircraft—and make it fall from the sky. There are a few protocols to follow that I won't bore you with right now, because my editor told me I was already putting you to sleep with this minutia, and Tony—my attorney—has checked himself into rehab because of all the whiskey I've driven him to drink.

I sat back and waved at the screen. "There it is."

The Russian was smiling. "I'll need that ID and password."

I could see in my peripheral vision that The Russian had been holding his phone up—taking a video as I entered the ID and password—the valid one.

He can't leave with that information on his phone.

"Of course," I said with my best con man smile.

The Russian continued. His voice sounded stressed, higher pitched than normal. "Please write them down before we complete the transfer."

I wrote the False Flag ID and password—not the valid one I had just used—on a slip of paper and handed it to him.

He smiled and slipped the paper into his pocket without reading it.

His first mistake.

Then he shoved a compact Makarov pistol into my right ear for emphasis and demanded, "Now give me the flash drive." His voice had dropped a full octave.

I'm not a weapons expert, but I do know about this particular handgun. The Makarov had been the Soviet Union's standard-issue, concealed sidearm until the breakup in the early nineties. It is a .380-caliber—Europeans call it the "9 mm Short." It is a small but deadly round, especially if he fired into the side of my head at point-blank range.

I didn't argue. I removed the flash drive without properly performing the ejection procedure. That wouldn't matter when he loaded it into his computer later using the False Flag ID and passcode.

"There's no need to be uncivilized," I said.

"Please remain sitting where you are, Mr. Wolfe." The Russian stepped back several feet and plugged the flash drive into an adapter socket for his smartphone. Then he retrieved the note with the false passcodes and tapped his smartphone.

I couldn't see how far he took the program, but I wasn't too concerned. Once he entered the false ID and password both Hong Li's virus and my program would kick in. Nothing could stop it.

The Russian played with his smartphone for several minutes while I just sat there. He kept his distance from me, his eyes bouncing from his small screen to me and back, as if I were going to jump him or something. Finally, he said, "It appears to be genuine. I selected an Israeli F-18 that I know exists as a test, and it was there."

"Did you crash it?" I asked, knowing if he tried to down an aircraft under the false flag feature, it wouldn't work and he'd catch on.

"No, I will save that fun event for another time, when there is money to be made."

Good! It was done!

Twenty-four hours from now, any arms dealers, terrorists, or other nefarious bad guys The Russian had done business with would have all their financial records obliterated. The program would then seek out anyone those nefarious bad guys had done business with and destroy their accounts too. The Terrorist Financial Holocaust was on, and nothing could stop it now.

"In that case, you owe me one hundred million dollars," I said, still playing the mercenary.

The Makarov was still aimed at my face. "Mr. Wolfe, I am aware that you and the Chinese woman have been plotting against me. You are both too dangerous to live beyond tonight, so there is no point in paying either of you any money."

I wasn't too worried because I knew my friends and family were electronically watching this exchange.

We're headed for an out-of-control Wild West shootout.

42

INTOLERABLE LOSS

"So you're stealing the codes and frequencies." I leaned back in my chair. I could feel the Peacemaker pressing against the small of my back, but I knew I wouldn't be able to draw and shoot him before he shot me. That didn't mean I intended to just sit here and be killed without at least trying. I hadn't liked The Russian from the first instant I met him. I couldn't explain my reasons at first, but his double-cross—cheating me out of the hundred million dollars—and the Makarov aimed at my face were pushing my buttons now. I was pissed off.

As if he picked up on my intentions and wanted to put distance between us, The Russian backed up to the entrance of the library. He stood against the bookcase that covered a whole wall and framed both sides of the door. The Makarov was still pointed directly between my eyes. He wasn't bouncing on his heels now. In fact, he'd become completely still.

I allowed my hand to slip behind me. I could maybe draw as I dropped behind the desk.

"Goodbye, Mr. Wolfe." He was almost whispering.

If I could make him miss with the first shot I may have a chance . . . I had to at least try . . .

At that instant, Hong Li crashed the door open and rushed into the library, colliding with The Russian. In instinctive reaction, he fired at me, but the shot hit the wall behind my head.

She had been observing our transaction on a closed-circuit TV in a room across the hallway and had decided to join our party in person when he'd announced his intentions to kill me.

(These things only take fractions of a second to occur—longer to describe.)

I dived behind my desk.

While still stumbling from Hong Li crashing into him, The Russian turned and fired a second shot, hitting her in the stomach.

Hong Li bent over, stepped closer to him, and then fired two rounds into The Russian's chest with her own pistol.

He fired another round at her.

They were standing nearly belly button to belly button. It was impossible that either could miss at that range, but somehow both were still on their feet.

She fired again.

It was ugly.

The Russian's bodyguards rushed into the library with their weapons ready.

By now I had my Peacemaker clear. I pulled back the hammer and fired one round at the first bodyguard through the door. I shot too fast, without properly aiming, and missed. However, the heavy .45-caliber round exploded into the doorframe near his head, causing him to duck behind a stuffed chair.

The second bodyguard was right on the first guy's heels, but he hesitated. I'm guessing he was confused. He saw Hong Li firing at his employer but also saw that I had just shot at his partner. Who to shoot first? The textbook for bodyguards would tell him to shoot Hong Li first to save his employer, but survival instincts told him to shoot me first and save his own life. After all, if he's dead he can't help his boss. It was probably the first time he'd been in a real gunfight, and I guess the logic problem was more than he could solve while being shot at, so he reacted by hesitating—not acting.

His hesitation gave me time to cock the Peacemaker and fire a second round. This time I hit my mark. The large-caliber slug hit the second, confused bodyguard in the chest and knocked him down.

But that still left the first bodyguard, who had ducked for cover behind the chair. He stood to get a bead on me, but Hong Li twisted around and placed a bullet in his head before he could fire.

She is fast!

The Russian shot Hong Li again.

As I said, everything I'm describing occurred in just seconds.

Miraculously, Hong Li was somehow still on her feet and still very dangerous, even with multiple gunshot wounds. She moved like a ballet dancer—graceful and fast without hurrying. She twisted back around to The Russian and fired two more times—point-blank.

At the same instant, I fired at The Russian, hitting him in the right shoulder. The heavy bullet spun him around and propelled him against the bookcase.

Hong Li fired another round, this time hitting The Russian directly between the eyes.

It was finally over.

Hong Li's pistol slipped from her fingers, bounced on the wood floor with a thud, and slid away from her. She leaned back against the bookcase, holding her stomach as if she were fighting severe cramps, and then slowly allowed herself to slide to the floor. There she remained in a sitting position.

There was stillness in the room.

Tom and Terry crashed through the door with M-4 rifles at the ready. They separated to each side of the entrance and swept for targets.

A heartbeat later, Janet and Kay rushed in, both with pistols in hand.

A minute too late …

There was no one left to shoot. Nobody moved or spoke. The silence smothered the room. I remember having the odd thought that I was getting used to the scent of burned gunpowder drifting in the air. The smoke was almost pleasant and definitely better than the alternative of not being able to smell anything because I was dead.

Hong Li!

I rushed over to Hong Li's side where she sat with her back to the bookcase. I desperately stared into her dark, exotic eyes and saw the sadness looking back at me. She was slipping away. I could see in her face that she knew she was dying. Her wounds covered her chest and abdomen. There were so many I didn't even think of counting them. I knew there was nothing we could do in time, but I tried anyway. I pushed against one hole, which only caused more blood to rush out from another and she cried out in pain. It was hopeless. Blood was leaking from all over her body.

She asked with a hoarse, raspy whisper, "Did he download the program into his system?"

"Yes," I answered with tears in my eyes. "By this time tomorrow the Terrorist Financial Holocaust will hit."

"Mission accomplished," she said with a wisp of a smile. There was blood in both corners of her lips.

"Hong Li, we'll get you to a hospital. I'll take care of you. You'll be all right!"

"No, my love . . . everyone has a time. This is mine. Promise me you will have a good life—take a thousand beautiful lovers—and think of me from time to time." She covered my hand with her bloody, wet fingers and squeezed. Her once powerful hand was so fragile that I could barely feel the pressure. I bent down and kissed her softly on the lips. They tasted of her blood. She seemed as if she were about to say something, but stopped. She contemplated me. There was a suggestion of a frown in her eyebrows.

"Hong Li! I love you!"

Her body shuddered delicately—almost an orgasm—then her eyes lost their spark and she became very still.

The others were standing over us, silently watching. Janet placed her hand on my shoulder and pressed gently. "I'm so sorry, John."

I said nothing. I could still taste her blood where we had kissed. I would never forget that taste.

The stillness was shattered a few seconds later by the sheriff crashing into the room, waving his pistol around. "What the fuck is goin' on?" he shouted. "Where the hell did all these guns come from?"

Before anyone could formulate an answer, Jackson burst into the room with his shotgun, almost bumping into the sheriff.

Where were all these people before? Maybe Hong Li wouldn't have died.

Jackson announced, "There are over two dozen heavily armed men, dressed like ninjas, coming on foot from the south. They just passed the gazebo and are moving this way! Also, The Major and his bodyguards left when the shooting started. They're gone."

The sheriff asked, "I have a deputy and a patrol car down at the gazebo. Do you know his status?"

Before Jackson could answer, complete darkness blanketed us.

They cut the electricity.

Jackson's phone dinged, indicating a new contact by a camera. He checked his smartphone. The screen illuminated everyone's face in the otherwise total darkness.

Jackson announced, "Six bad guys are standing at the front door at this very instant. A second group is circling around to the side, toward the game room, and a third to the rear of the house . . . looks like about fifteen bad guys total. Perhaps we could ask them about your deputy, Sheriff."

Before the sheriff replied, an explosion blew the main entrance doors off their hinges. The concussion thundered through the house, knocking pictures off the walls and shattering windows.

43

MORE UNINVITED GUESTS

The bad guys had used too much explosive to blow the front door—no finesse—and the irony of it was the door hadn't even been locked. They could have turned the knob and quietly walked in. They were barbarians, but even barbarians can be dangerous.

My thoughts were broken by the fresh wave of gunfire in the hallway.

"The people in the game room . . . we need to get them to safety!" shouted my brother over the *bang-bang-bang* of gunfire.

I said, "The problem is we're cut off. The entrance is between us and the game room."

"Who is shooting who out there?" asked Terry.

The sheriff repeated his question from a few minutes ago. "Where did you all get those weapons? I thought we took them all."

Tom answered, "There's a cellar with a firing range full of weapons. When we heard the shooting in the library we ran down there and re-armed ourselves."

Then Tom turned to his wife. "Terry, that's where we'll take the guests. You take them down to the cellar—keep them safe."

"Why me?" asked Terry.

"Honey, every time we divide the tasks, you don't have to take the women's lib stance and argue you can do more. Protecting the guests is important—it's saving lives."

I stated the obvious. "We need to get past the shooters in the hallway first."

"Who the hell is shooting, anyway?" demanded the sheriff.

"I don't know, but it could be the Order," I said, then turned to Tom and asked, "You're the military tactician. We need to get to the game room and protect the guests and then defeat these intruders. How should we handle it?"

My eyes were beginning to adjust to the darkness. I could now see the others standing around me.

Tom said, "With just two M-4's and a shotgun, we need more firepower—too many pistols, not enough rifles." He held his M-4 up as a visual aide.

"It's what we have," said Janet.

Tom Wolfe nodded. "Follow me."

I shouted at him, "We're walking directly toward the men who just blew the front door! We don't know who's shooting who."

Tom shouted back, "There's no choice. We hit them hard and fast."

"But who do we shoot at if we see two different groups?" I asked.

"Whoever shoots at us first," answered the sheriff.

"Right!" said my brother.

We're sanctioned.

We exited the library and carefully moved along the hallway. It was about fifty feet to the front entrance. The shooting suddenly stopped, but we couldn't see anyone in the darkness.

The sheriff hissed loudly, "Wait! They could be legitimate police. We need to find out before we start shooting."

Tom said, "You're welcome to ask, Sheriff. You can be our official greeter, but I'd approach them carefully if I were you."

The sheriff looked at my brother, then at me, and finally at Jackson. My eyes had become accustomed to the dim light now and I could clearly see the tension in everyone's faces. I also saw several dark forms at the far end of the hallway. They were guests who had been armed and had come out to greet the invaders—the gunfight we heard from the library. The guest force had fallen back to the game room entrance. I waved at them and they waved back. I motioned for them to stay clear. I think they understood.

The sheriff said, "If the invaders were law enforcement, they wouldn't have blown the front door without at least announcing themselves first."

"Still want to ask them?" asked my brother.

The sheriff sighed, "I guess we have to be sure. I'll take the lead, but you guys be ready to back me up."

Tom nodded. "Terry, Jackson, and I have the big guns, so the three of us will spread out just behind and to the sides of the sheriff. If there's shooting, drop flat to the floor and make your shots count. Everyone else, stay back unless you have no choice. We all stay together—fight as a unit. Don't get separated. If those with a pistol get the chance, pick up a bad guy's rifle to increase your firepower."

"That's it! That's your brilliant plan?" asked Janet.

Tom smiled at Janet then said to Terry, "I predict you and Janet are going to become great friends."

Sheriff Boone stepped around the corner, into the open, and shouted, "This is Shenandoah County Sherriff Boone. Identify yourselves!"

A submachine gun answered his challenge. The sheriff was hit in the chest with the first volley, knocking him back into me. I dragged him around the corner to safety, while Tom and the others returned fire.

Kay stayed with me to help with the sheriff. She ripped off his shirt and announced, "Good! He was wearing his vest. It stopped the bullets. He'll live."

We left Sheriff Boone to recover from the hammer like impact of the bullets and returned to the hallway. By this time the gun battle was burning in earnest. Bullets were crashing into the walls and woodwork, destroying my precious home. It pissed me off.

What do these assholes want?

At that moment, as if he were reading my mind, Tom said, "These assholes are seriously trying to kill us."

I fired a single round from my Colt through the dark, gaping hole where my front door had once been. I couldn't see what I was shooting at, and the muzzle flashes had ruined any chance of night vision, but somehow the bad guys were able to see us.

Tom shouted, "Aim at the flashes. They have night-vision optics, so they can see us . . . stay down or behind cover."

Suddenly, shooters began firing from behind us with automatic weapons. The bad guys had breached the rear entrance and we were surrounded.

It was getting nasty. We were caught in a cross fire against superior numbers. They had submachine guns and we mostly only had pistols. Tom shouted out, "Ammo count!"

Terry with her M-4 answered, "Six rounds left."

Jackson with the explosive rounds in the shotgun replied, "One round!"

Tom checked his banana clip and answered, "I have about ten rounds."

The shooting hadn't slowed.

From the corner of my eye I saw Kay rush to the rear, firing at the invaders who had come in behind us. Janet was running by her side. The intruders returned fire in a flood of bullets. Kay spun around and fell to the floor. Janet was forced to dive to the floor. At this distance, in the dark, I couldn't see whether she was hit or not.

We're in serious trouble.

I jumped up to run to their side, but Tom grabbed me and pulled me back down.

"Stay down!" Tom fired four single shots through the hole where the front door had once been and we heard someone scream. Then he spun around and fired four more rounds at the shooters behind us, and all the hostile fire stopped—at least temporarily.

He's good at this.

There was complete silence. We waited, but nothing moved or made a noise from either direction.

"I don't like it," said Terry.

"Me either," agreed my brother. "But it's time for you to get to the game room and escort the other guests into the cellar, so they'll be safe."

Terry surprisingly said, "On my way!"

Tom added, "Stay with them. You can reload down there. You're their protection."

"Okay," she replied.

". . . and stay quiet," Tom added.

"You done?" Terry asked, and when Tom didn't answer, she rose into a bowed stance and silently ran to the game room.

We watched her disappear into the darkness.

After she was gone, I asked, "Where did the bad guys go? We couldn't have killed them all."

". . . not sure," answered Tom.

"Well, I need to know how Kay is." I stood up.

"Get down!" shouted Tom as he low crawled around the corner to escape the gunfire.

I was almost to Kay when Tom shouted, "Grenade!" A second later there was a terrible explosion and everything went black. I felt myself falling, except I couldn't see or feel anything, and then complete silence enveloped me.

When I woke the lights were on again. I was still in the entrance hall, but everything was fuzzy. I think there were half dozen armed men dressed in black body armor, black baseball caps, and goggles. They just seemed to be standing around. I twisted my head to see more.

The guy standing over me pulled his goggles off and asked, "You John Wolfe?"

I could barely hear the words because of the ringing in my ears. When I tried to answer, my throat was dry and raw and I only managed a muffled cough. Talking hurt my throat and came out as a croaking sound. I felt sick to my stomach—not enough to vomit, but just enough to be miserable.

I felt around for my Colt, but it was gone, of course.

The guy standing over me gave me kick, but with my other issues I hardly realized it.

He shouted to his men, "Stand him up!"

Two men grabbed me and pulled me to my feet. I stood swaying back and forth, trying to find my balance. I was completely disoriented, dizzy, and the sick feeling in my stomach intensified. The random thought that they must have used a flash-bang-stun grenade came to mind. Stun grenades rarely kill, but they will disorient and disable most people for several minutes. That would explain how I was feeling.

I knew I had to start thinking again—fast. I counted ten bad guys; all clustered in the hallway. I looked for anyone on our side. Janet and Jackson were being held prisoner, tied up. Kay was on the floor, not tied up, not moving, and no one was watching her—a bad sign.

I couldn't see my brother, his wife, or the sheriff. Then I remembered that the sheriff was probably still around the corner, recovering from the ballistic impacts of being shot in his bulletproof vest.

Maybe they found him and delivered a coup de grâce.

I had no idea what happened to Tom.

He could be dead.

My sister-in-law, Terry was probably downstairs in the firing range with the other guests. They would have weapons down there, so there was still hope.

The bad guys must have turned on every light in the house, because all the bodies were clearly illuminated, and they were everywhere. I studied Kay, lying bloodied and motionless on the floor, straining to see some sign she lived, but there was only stillness. I vowed to make these assholes pay.

"Well, you John Wolfe or not?" he asked again, breaking into my thoughts.

I fell back against the wall for support. My ears were ringing so loud I had to shout to hear myself. "What the hell are you guys doing in my home?" My voice sounded far away and raspy, as if sawdust was coating my vocal cords.

"We want the PM Program's frequencies and codes. You don't need to know anything beyond that."

Does everybody know about the ultra-top secret program?

"Are you John Wolfe?" he repeated.

I fixed him with my most stern stare and said, "Go screw yourself!" But then I coughed, taking some of the steam out of my charade of defiance.

I saw him swing, but I couldn't do anything to avoid it.

The world turned black for me—again.

44

INTERROGATION CAN BE PAINFUL

When I again became aware of my surroundings, my hands and feet were zip-tied and I lay prone on the pool table in the game room. The bad guys had turned on every light in the house. I guess they didn't want anyone popping out of a shadow and shooting at them. I turned my head and saw Jackson and Janet zip-tied, on the sofa. The good news—I think—was I still did not see my brother, my sister-in-law, or the sheriff. Also, none of the other guests were visible. I assumed the bad guys had not found the cellar/shooting range yet—the door leading to the basement was casually disguised as a bookcase. It was probably only a matter of time before they were discovered. That's when it occurred to me that this wouldn't end well if I couldn't find a way to change the course of the evening very soon.

There were a lot of bad guys. I saw over a dozen men dressed in full body armor, black gloves, black baseball caps, and goggles riding on their foreheads. Some were clad in camouflage—others in solid black clothing. The bad guys were scattered all over the room. Who knows how many more were skulking around the rest of the house? They all carried submachine guns—Uzi's, I think.

We're really screwed.

The guy who had hit me in the entranceway now stood over me. He was dressed in woodland camouflage that fit him a little too tight around the middle. He had taken off his black ski cap and goggles, revealing an ugly, scarred face, accented by a stringy, handlebar mustache that showed hints of gray. He was out of shape in contrast to the others, who all looked like trim, early twenties fighting machines. I figured the old, fat, mustached guy was the leader. He was acting the part. I decided to call him Mustache.

Mustache smiled. It was an ugly smile. "Welcome back, Wolfe. Your friends here identified you, so we can move past that question. But I need to know where the program is. Give it up, and this will be much less painful for you and your friends."

He intends to kill us after he gets what he wants.

"Who are you?" I asked again, trying not to stare at his face.

"I'm the man with the gun pointed at your head." He shoved a large semiautomatic pistol in my face for effect. "Where are the codes and frequencies for the PM Program? I know you keep a copy here at your house," he answered.

How does he know?

I tried to appear confident as I said, "You think I keep such highly classified material at my private home?"

"Yes, you're a maverick with an ego, and that's exactly what you would do." It was Mary—The Fifty Billion Dollar Woman—who made that last statement.

She had suddenly appeared holding a pistol, and it was pointed at me. Mary slipped next to the leader, and they exchanged a quick smile. They looked cozy together, like old friends. She whispered something in his ear, but I couldn't hear, especially with my ears still ringing from that flash-bang grenade.

"You're with these guys?" I was shouting, but I couldn't help myself.

"Yes, I told you I work for the Order," she replied.

The Order—not The Russian! She switched back again!

Then it occurred to me; she was telling me the invaders were the Order.

"Well, Wolfe, you going to make this easy or hard?" asked Mustache.

"Screw you!" It wasn't poetry, but I couldn't think of anything more elegant to say.

Mustache slapped me so hard that I almost passed out again. If I hadn't already been horizontal, I would have fallen. Then he turned to one of his underlings and said, "Cut an electrical wire and plug, long, from one of those arcade games, and bring it to me." He turned back to me. "Last chance to do this without an extraordinary level of pain involved."

"I like pain," was my witty reply, realizing as soon as I said it that I may live to regret those words.

"As you wish." He took the electrical cable from his minion, and using a small pocketknife, stripped the wires bare about four inches at the tip. He inserted the three-pronged plug into a nearby wall socket then waved the end with three exposed wires at my face. "Last chance . . ."

I closed my eyes in some weak effort of making him disappear, but it didn't work.

"Tear away his shirt and undo his pants. Pull them down to his knees—underwear too."

My eyes snapped wide open again.

I was naked from knees to neck in a matter of seconds. Mary stood over me, shamelessly treating herself to an eyeful.

I would have been embarrassed if I hadn't been so terrified. I tried to sit up, but several minions pinned me against the pool table.

Mustache took a moment to look me over. "Oh, Mr. Wolfe, you are nicely endowed. Don't you think so, Mary?"

Mary studied my private parts and smiled. "Oh yeah, too bad we're going to fry his package—such a shame."

These animals are not going to be my friends regardless what I do or say, and in the end they will kill me.

I looked directly into Mary's eyes and said, "Hong Li told me you are a lesbian. Why do you care about my package? I can understand your male counterpart, here. From the gleam in his eyes and the shit-eating smile on his face, it's clear he likes men more than women."

Mustache growled and raked the three bare wires across my chest in a whipping motion. Then he repeated the action in a fast one-two slap, then repeated it all again. There was a snapping-sizzling sound as the copper leads scraped across my chest—back and forth. He repeated the electrical flogging. The copper wires burned and cut into my bare skin, leaving jagged knife-blade furrows that felt like fire. My muscles locked up and my body contorted. I felt my rib cage crack. It hurt worse than anything I could recall in my life, but somehow I managed not to scream out. I can't tell you where that strength came from, except I didn't want to give these guys any satisfaction. They'd already killed Kay and probably several others I cared about. It was certain they intended to kill me—all of us—before this was done.

The only good news is the electrical shock also made Mustache's minions, who had been holding me down, jump back from the table. Apparently, the current had traveled through their hands and shocked them too.

Ah, too bad . . .

I smelled burnt flesh—mine.

"Shit, that hurt like hell!" cried one of the minions.

He should try it from here.

Another said, "Yeah, let's find a rope and tie him down. I'm not holding onto him while you're doing that."

I was sincerely happy for the reprieve. The electrical shock was overwhelming. I knew I wouldn't be able to withstand it very long. It was time to use my brain.

Separate the bad guys; make the odds more favorable.

"There's rope in the garage, outside across the driveway," I offered. Maybe Tom and the sheriff were outside somewhere. If so, maybe they could still save the day—I mean night.

"Why would you help us?" asked Mustache.

Give him a grain of truth with your deception.

"I'm just buying a few extra minutes before you start again, but I'm telling you the truth. You'll find all the rope you need in the garage."

Mustache nodded to one of the minions. "Go find rope—hurry!"

The minion nodded to a buddy. "Come with me."

That left Mary, Mustache, and maybe ten minions in the room—much better odds.

Yeah—right!

Mustache said, "Okay, asshole, you just bought yourself maybe five minutes—at the most—until they get back. You should use the time to reconsider cooperating."

"If you want the USB drive with the PM Program codes and frequencies, why don't you ask Mary? The last I knew she had it all."

It was a lie. Mary's USB contained information about the managing members of the Order, and Hong Li had gotten it from Mary and given it to me, so Mary had nothing. I was trying to pit my enemies against each other. It's an old trick I learned early in my career at the Agency: use misinformation to drive a wedge between your enemies and make them distrust each other.

"I don't know what he's talking about," said The Fifty Billion Dollar Woman.

"Then why did you have me go back into the hospital to retrieve it?"

Rule Number One of misinformation is to stay as close as possible to the truth.

"No—you lie! That USB drive had something else . . ." She suddenly stopped talking and looked around, realizing her mistake.

Mustache chuckled. "Nice try, but I trust Mary completely. She's been completely vetted."

I glanced between Mustache and Mary and said, "I bet she has."

Mustache bent over me and looked into my eyes for several moments. Finally, he said in a softer voice, "You could save yourself a lot of pain by telling me where to find the program."

I could smell Mustache's rotten breath. I think he had something with garlic, onions, beer, and dog shit for dinner. I know for certain he hadn't bothered to clean his teeth after eating. My eyes involuntarily shifted away to Jackson and Janet tied up on the sofa. I was wondering if they had some scheme to escape. It didn't seem so—very submissive.

Mustache's eyes followed my gaze. "Maybe I should be asking your friends the questions. Would you like that better?"

Janet was shuddering. I didn't blame her. She had spent her entire career in a lab and office environment, not as a field agent. As far I could remember she'd never been outside the Washington, DC, area for work. This violence was something she wasn't prepared to deal with.

Mustache put the wire down and walked over to the sofa. He studied Janet for several moments. I could see what he was thinking: she was on the edge of panic—the weak link for him to exploit.

"What is your name?" he asked her.

Janet was silent.

Mustache slapped her, making a loud cracking sound. Her face turned blood red, but I to give her credit, she didn't cry out. The impact forced her head to spin sideways and then she snapped it back, silently challenging her antagonist, but everyone in the room knew it was false bravado.

I knew I needed to do something fast, or we could all be dead. I announced, "All right, I agree—I'll give you the PM codes and frequencies if you don't hurt anyone else and let us all live."

"Why should I agree to any terms? I'm holding all the cards. My men can take all night to tear this place apart until we find what we want. In the meantime, I can be having fun with you," said Mustache.

"It won't do you any good, because what you want is locked in a vault that you will never open without me. But if you untie me and promise to let us all live, I'll show you," I answered.

"Okay, show me!" Mustache returned to the pool table and cut the zip ties on my ankles, but left my hands secured. "But if this is a trick you will be sorry." He nodded toward Janet and added, "Life is so transitory: one moment you're alive, the next . . ." He left the sentence unfinished.

My hands were zip tied in front, so I awkwardly pulled my pants back to where they should be and stood. "One more thing: I don't want her anywhere near me. She stays here!" I pointed to Mary.

I don't want her ruining this.

Mary pouted as if she had been insulted.

She's acting.

"Come on, hero, show me this vault," said Mustache as he shoved me toward the door.

45

DON'T SALUTE A FALSE FLAG

I was escorted by Mustache and four of his henchmen. I walked as slowly as possible without being shoved from behind. I was desperately searching for an idea—an edge. Mustache left the other shooters in the game room with Jackson and Janet. The two men who had gone out for a rope had not returned, but for some reason Mustache didn't seem to notice or care about that. I hoped they had run into Tom and the sheriff. My hope was feeble, but it was all I had, and it gave me optimism.

We passed the hallway intersection that led to the front entrance, or more accurately, to the hole where the front entrance once was. I could feel the cold winter air blowing through the breech. The hall and entrance areas were brightly lit, so I could vividly see the bodies lying everywhere from the recent battle. Tom and the sheriff were not there—a good sign. But I saw my Colt Peacemaker on the floor where I'd dropped it when the flash-bang grenade had knocked me out. I considered rushing over and grabbing it but then realized I'd be cut down before I got even within arm's reach of the pistol.

"Keep moving," growled Mustache, with a shove.

We entered the library.

Less than an hour ago I was here with The Russian.

Again, all the lights were on in the library. The bodies of The Russian and his thugs were in a stack near the entrance. So was Hong Li's body— surrounded in a puddle of her blood. The copper scent was overpowering. I had to turn away. I took several deep breaths to overcome the urge to retch.

"What are you stalling for?" asked Mustache. "Show me this vault!"

I didn't say anything, but took one last look at Hong Li before I slowly moved to the pedestal. I was desperately searching for a way to turn the tables on this asshole, but I couldn't see the light at the end of the dark passageway that entombed me. The situation seemed without hope. The feeling of doom pressed down on me.

"Let's do this!" said Mustache.

His four minions spread out to opposite sides of the room. They all aimed their Uzis at me.

"The vault requires a three-step process to open," I explained.

Déjà vu all over again.

"Quit stalling and get to it!"

"I'm not stalling. I can't do it with my hands tied together." I held my hands up as a visual aide to make my point.

Mustache produced a fast opening knife and cut my ties, and then stepped back several feet. The good news was his Uzi was slung loose from his shoulder and his pistol was still in the holster. I guess he was depending on his four minions for security. But my hands were now free.

The odds just improved marginally.

"Now you have no more excuses!"

I opened the book cover, revealing a keypad, and punched in the six digits. The green LED light flashed on. If you recall, I now had thirty seconds to press my right thumbprint to a sensor pad disguised as a wall light switch. Briefly, I considered stalling so the automatic lock would kick in and the vault couldn't be opened for twenty-four hours, regardless of what I did. But that would only be suicide. Mustache wouldn't believe the vault was locked for twenty-four hours and step up his pain exercise with me as well as the others. Besides, I didn't need to do that to defeat this Neanderthal. I had an ace up my sleeve.

I hope.

I pressed my thumb against the wall switch. The overhead spotlight ignited, highlighting the door. I crossed over to the highlighted door and opened it. I stepped in and pressed my eye against the retina scanner mounted on the wall. I got my eye in the correct position on the first try, but I didn't hear the soft, high-pitched beep because my ears were still ringing from the flash-bang grenade. Regardless, the wall to my right slid open. I began to step inside the steel box.

If I can get to my pistol . . .

"Stop!" shouted Mustache. "I want to see what's in there before you enter." He shoved me aside and entered the cramped room. He studied the items on the small table and then turned to the wall cabinet against the opposite wall. "Where's the USB drive?"

I said, "It's locked inside the wall cabinet. I'm the only one who can open it. It reads my biometric code on a hidden touch pad."

The leader said, "I don't see any touch pad."

"It's hidden . . . you have to know exactly where it's located to use it. That way if you kill me it's unlikely you will be able to open it."

Mustache unsuccessfully tried opening the wall cabinet and then turned to me. "Okay, you open it, but no fast movements. And as soon as you get the cabinet open, step back so I can see what is in there." He stayed inside the vault, just inches behind me.

I knew we were out of sight from the four minions waiting in the outer room.

I moved very slowly—stalling for time while I thought—but I could think of nothing that had a real chance of working other than what I was about to try. I truly believed I was about to commit suicide. I wouldn't be able to open the cabinet, grab the Peacemaker, and shoot him before he sprayed me with that Uzi.

It's hopeless, but my only hope.

I pressed my thumb to the hidden pad. The door unlocked with a click that I could barely hear because I still had ringing in my ears.

I may have permanent hearing damage.

Mustache had clearly heard the click, because he said, "Step back so I can see inside."

I sluggishly pulled the cabinet door open, using my body to block access to the cabinet—still stalling for time.

At that moment, there was a violent exchange of gunfire outside in the library.

Mustache turned and took a step through the vault door. His back was turned to me.

Move!

I opened the presentation box, seized the Peacemaker, and spun around while pulling the hammer back. Even though my ears were still ringing and I couldn't hear, he must have heard the distinctive sound of the Colt being cocked, because his head swiveled back to me. His body followed his head, and the Uzi followed his body.

But it was too late for him and I couldn't miss—not at this range. The pistol was pointed center of mass. We were less than five feet apart. I fired, hitting Mustache in the side of his chest as he spun toward me. The single heavy round knocked him out through the entrance of the vault, where he crashed to the floor and didn't move again.

The .45 Long Colt is a powerful bullet.

Those outside, in the library, paid no attention to my single shot, because they were engaged in a fierce gun battle of their own.

Suddenly the shooting stopped. My ears vibrated with loud ringing from firing the Colt in a confined space, surrounded by steel walls. The hearing damage was piling on top of the flash-bang grenade and previous gunfights. The now-familiar scent of burned gunpowder filled my nostrils. My eyes and nose itched from the smoke in the confined space. I listened intently, but my ears detected no sound or movement from the library, just silence.

I briefly considered retrieving Mustache's Uzi but thought one of his minions could be waiting out there to shoot me, so I waited inside the vault with my Peacemaker cocked and pointed toward the entrance. I waited, reluctant to stick my face around the corner.

I was still considering the safest method of exiting the vault when my brother called to me. "John, are you in there?"

46

NOT THE MARINES

When I stepped out into the library proper, I saw Tom hiding behind my desk, aiming his rifle at the vault door. He slowly rose to his feet and said something to me, but he was speaking too softly for me to hear him over the ringing in my ears.

I shouted back, "What?"

He picked up one of the fallen Uzis, inserted a fresh magazine from a dead minion's ammo pouch, and handed the weapon to me. Then he said in a substantially louder voice, "I said, we need to get to the game room. Terry may need us."

"Two of the bad guys went out to the garage—" I began.

Tom cut me off. He explained, "The sheriff and I already took care of them. The sheriff is checking on his deputy down at the gazebo and calling for reinforcements."

I surveyed the bodies piled up in the library. All four minions were dead. My brother had shot it out with them—one against four—and they all died.

Tom didn't have a scratch on him.

Hong Li hadn't moved. I pulled my eyes away from her body and said, "Looks like you've cut the odds down."

"There is still a formidable force in the game room, and Terry is about to take them on. She needs our help," he answered.

"How do you know?" I asked.

"We're in contact—two-way radio."

"Huh?"

Tom explained. "Terry and I have tiny, earbud-based two-way radios." He indicated his ear. "They have a range of about quarter mile but are so small you can only see them if you are looking for them. Terry can hear our conversation—both sides—and she's talking in my ear right now, telling me to stop wasting time and get moving. She and the others are about to emerge from downstairs and take on the bad guys in the game room."

First Jackson with his phone-app cameras and now my brother with his earbud radio ... I'm supposed to be the high tech wizard.

We stepped into the hallway and immediately encountered two men coming from game room.

They had apparently heard the shooting and were coming to investigate. Tom shot them—bang-bang—without ceremony.

We approached the entryway to the game room.

"They'll be ready for us," whispered Tom as he dropped to one knee and carefully peeked around the corner.

I was holding back about four feet, holding my newly acquired Uzi like a newborn baby. I shouted, "What?" From my perspective, he was mumbling.

Tom put a finger to his lips for me to be quiet.

There were at least ten armed men in the game room and only two of us—three, if you counted Terry. I wasn't a gunfighter. It seemed to me we were seriously outnumbered and outgunned.

I tried desperately to understand Tom, but he was talking to the wall in a muffled voice.

Finally he nodded his head, stood up, and turned back to me. "We're ready to go. On my signal, we rush ... doorway. You go ... drop ... Shoot center ... right. I'm going left ... Terry, and a couple others ... guests, are coming through ... on right ... from the center, so don't shoot at her! ... people standing ... target ... Got it!"

My ears are trashed.

I had unconsciously been watching his lips—on-the-job training for lip reading. I think I only got about two-thirds of his plan, but I nodded yes anyway and prepared for something I'd never done before.

To write here that I was scared beyond shitless should win me the Pulitzer Prize for Understatement, but there was no choice: I had to do this.

Tom looked directly at me, and I thought I heard him say, "Go!"

We rushed into the room, and I dropped to my right knee and pointed my newly acquired Uzi at the bad guy nearest me. It seemed we stared at each other for several lifetimes before anything happened. Then the room exploded with gunfire, and the smell of burned gunpowder again filled my nostrils. The bullets ripped into the wall above my head and into the beautiful leather sofa that I was kneeling behind. I was vaguely aware of someone firing at the bad guys on my right. Terry and friends had come up from the cellar, just as Tom had explained to me. Tom was on my left, crouched behind a pinball machine, firing in short controlled bursts. I—on the other hand—fired at everyone I saw standing. I'm pretty sure I hit several of the bad guys, but Terry and my brother were the real shooters. They were cleaning away the bad guys like a high-pressure water hose cleaning dirt off the patio. I pulled the trigger and the gun didn't fire—I was empty.

All the shooting stopped, but nobody moved. It was unreal. I heard someone cough in the center of the room, near the pool table. Tom shouted loud enough for even my trashed ears to hear, "Stay down until we clear you!"

He was talking to Jackson and Janet.

At that point he and Terry moved forward as if of a single mind, converging in the center of the room. To my complete surprise they hugged and then kissed.

This is no time for sex!

Before I could tell them, they got back to business. Tom waved me forward. I tossed the Uzi down on the sofa, but Tom picked it up, found another, exchanged magazines, and handed it back to me. "You may still need this. Treat it with respect."

Janet and Jackson were on the floor, looking up at us. Tom realized he'd told them not to move. He laughed and said, "It's okay to get up now."

Mary and three bad guys were still alive, because they were the only ones who had fallen to the floor and not fired a single round at us. Terry plus two others from my guest list who had volunteered to participate in the shootout herded the survivors into a corner and sat them on the floor, facing the wall. I looked around and confirmed that all the other bad guys were dead. In most cases it was easy to tell by the way their heads or chests were mutilated or deformed by the bullets. I had to perform a closer inspection on a few to be sure.

When I spoke I probably shouted too loud, based on the surprised reaction everyone gave me. "We did this: without the marines!"

"No marines—just us." Terry laughed.

Tom laughed too and said, "You seem surprised."

At that moment, Sheriff Boone cautiously stepped into the room. He was holding a shotgun, ready to shoot. After studying the scene for a few moments, he announced, "My deputy is dead, apparently killed by this scum. I've called for backup and ambulances. I'll have half the force here soon."

Finally!

The sheriff waved his shotgun at the bodies then settled on the group sitting in the corner. He looked like he wanted to kill them. He spoke into his chest-mounted microphone. "Hurry with those EMT units. Use AIRVAC if available. We have seriously wounded here." Then he asked, "Are the others still downstairs?"

Terry answered, "Yes! They're still in the cellar."

"Let's leave them down there until my men arrive and we can lock down this shooting scene properly," said the sheriff. "Also, let's cuff all the suspects."

"Don't have any zip ties," said Tom.

The sheriff pulled out a bundle of nylon ties from his side pants' pocket and handed them to Tom. Tom gave me half.

"Cuff everyone, even the dead. And disarm them as you go," the sheriff said.

I wasn't sure I had heard him correctly with my ringing ears, so I asked, "Why bother cuffing the dead? They're dead!"

"I've seen the dead rise again to invite others to join them. I don't consider someone dead until *after* the autopsy," answered the sheriff.

We stripped the dead of weapons and tied their hands behind them—just to be sure.

Tom secured Mary and the three survivors in the corner, while Terry stood guard.

We're back in control, bragged my little voice.

"Looks like we can call this soup!" said Janet.

I said, "No, there's more . . . there's a meeting of the Order of the Golden Squirrel tonight, and I want to be there." Then I turned to Jackson. "Could you go to the hangar and bring Planter back? I'm sure the sheriff will want to ask him some questions. He may know something about tonight's squirrel meeting."

Jackson seemed relieved to leave the room.

47

WHO IS MARY KILLIGREW—REALLY?

The sheriff asked, "You think this Order of the Golden Squirrel is having a meeting tonight?"

I answered, "Yes, I do. That little drama by the garage earlier was Castello's way of asking me if I wanted to enlist in the Order. He said he was on his way to a meeting. It's tonight. I thought it strange a billionaire of his stature would be attending a meeting in the middle of the night on a weekend. But when you think about it, secret meetings would more likely be held in the night, away from witnesses. Which reminds me, I slipped a tracker in Castello's pocket so I could follow his movements."

Tom said, "I'd like to go with you."

I nodded. "As soon as we discover where." Then I looked across the room to where Mary sat on the floor, hands cuffed behind her. "There may be another way to know. . ."

"What do you mean?" asked Janet.

I said, "Terry, bring Mary Killigrew over here. I'd like to ask her something."

Terry Wolfe snapped at Mary, "Stand up! Move slowly!"

Mary had difficulty standing, unassisted and with her hands tied behind her, but in a few moments she was standing in front of me.

I asked her, "So tell me, Mary, where is tonight's meeting? And do I need an invitation or secret password, or something, to get in?"

"I don't know anything about any meeting tonight," said Mary.

"Yes, you do, honey. It's time you came clean. Who do you really work for: The Russian, the Order of Golden Squirrel, Panzram Company, or someone else?"

"You're not making sense," she said.

"Well, let's try a different track. Why are you here?"

"To get information about the Order."

I asked, "For who?"

"I'm working for one faction of the Order that is trying to gain power over the whole organization. It's an internal conflict."

I laughed, throwing my head back, and said, "That's a new one! I can't trust anything you say, can I?"

Mary fabricated her fifty-billion-dollar smile and purred, "You can trust me, John. You have me in your control. I wouldn't lie to you now?"

I laughed. "Lady, you're a nightmare disguised as a wet dream."

"What do you mean by that?" she snapped with a feigned hurt expression.

I opened the floodgates of thought I'd formulated since meeting her. "First, you tell me you represent a potential employer who wants to recruit me for a job. You throw your fifty-billion-dollar beauty at me and try to charm me into giving up all my secrets. Then you Taser Planter, who was really your partner, but you pretended he wasn't. Then you try to Taser me. Then you almost got me killed trying to save your life at the hospital, but you send me back inside to get your purse and a flash drive, knowing I could end up arrested or maybe dead. Then you tell me you work for the Order, through the Panzram Company, but later you change your story and claim you really work for The Russian as a double agent, trying to get information from the Order. Then you tell me the Order is after you because you killed Kincade—a founding member of the Order—and have his secrets. Next thing I know, you've snuggled up to these murderers here"—I waved my Uzi at the men lying around the room—"who seem to have known and trusted you for a long time, and then you help them torture me." I paused for a moment to stare into her stunning, dark-green eyes. "Now you're telling me you're doing all this for one faction of the Order to double-cross another faction of the Order. I'm not listening to you anymore. Even if you think you're telling the truth, I doubt you could know the difference! You've made everything so complicated I bet even you have trouble remembering what's true and what's a lie. Do you even know who you are supposed to be loyal to—who you really work for?"

"Do you really think of me as fifty billion dollars beautiful?" Her dark emerald pools were pulling me into dangerous waters.

I answered with a softer voice—I couldn't help myself. "Yes, at first I was totally taken in by your beauty, but not any longer. I want to know who do you really work for?"

"Actually, I work for Homeland Security—" she began.

"Argh!"

48

WHERE DO SQUIRRELS MEET?

Now Mary was claiming to work undercover for Homeland Security. She weaved this intensely complicated yarn of how she was working to expose the Order. I asked, "Why did I only find money from Panzram deposited in your bank account? Shouldn't you have pay checks from Homeland Security, if you work for them?" She snapped right back that her real salary was being held in trust pending the resolution of this investigation. She claimed it was a standard procedure for undercover agents so their bank records wouldn't give them away. That's when I stopped listening to her, because anything she said was likely a lie, a trap, or both.

Luckily, I had a couple of backup strategies in mind to learn what I wanted to know. First, I had slipped a tracker into Castello's jacket as we were leaving the garage. It would tell me where he was, and if I was lucky, he'd be at the squirrels' meeting tonight. The second possibility was Planter. He worked for the recently deceased Russian, who had been collecting information about the squirrels. Maybe Planter knew about the meeting. He should be here soon. Jackson had been gone for over thirty minutes and would be bringing him back.

Why did I want to discover the location the meeting was being held tonight? I wanted to crash it.

Jackson entered the game room alone. He looked rattled. I'd never seen him that way before. He walked directly up to me and said, "He's dead— Planter's dead. Shot three times: Once in the head and twice in the heart. They wanted to make sure."

"What?" I didn't think I'd heard Jackson right. My ears were still ringing.

"Planter: they shot him while still chained to the landing gear. He was executed."

I squinted at Mary, who was again sitting in the corner. "So these are your friends?" I said to her from across the game room.

She shouted back, "No, I told you, I really work for Homeland Security. I was trying to infiltrate the Order. These killers work for the Order. I have no allegiance to them."

She has no allegiance to anyone.

For once I agreed with my little voice.

The sheriff asked, "There's another body? Who is Planter?"

Jackson answered, "These guys shot another of our guests. You can find him in the hangar on the south end of the property. There's no hurry—he's dead, and no one else is down there."

"I'm going to check it out. Keep an eye on those prisoners." He indicated Mary and the others sitting in the corner, tied up. "Also, stay here until I return. I still have questions to ask you all." The sheriff was talking into his chest mike as he exited.

After the sheriff was gone, I walked over to Mary, thinking I'd give it one last try. I asked, "So why were these men here tonight? What was their goal?"

"I don't know."

"Yes you do. You're one of them. You were snuggling up to the mustached leader like old friends. He said he trusted you completely—that you'd been vetted. I want you to come clean, lady. Tell me who they were and where the meeting is tonight."

Mary was silent—thoughtful—before she said, "All right, I'll tell you on one condition."

"What?"

"I go with you to the meeting," said Mary.

"That ain't happening." It was Janet.

The Fifty Billion Dollar Woman snapped back, "It's my job. I'm supposed to infiltrate the Order. I'm supposed to be at that meeting tonight and get the intelligence.

"For who?" asked Janet.

Mary looked at Janet then her eyes leveled on me. She said, "For Homeland Security."

Janet grunted. "You can't believe anything this bitch says."

"I'm telling you the truth—I work for Homeland Security."

Terry had been listening to the exchange. "What if she's telling the truth this time?"

"Okay, let's say for a moment that I agree to your terms. Where's the meeting?" I asked.

Mary said, "I won't tell you . . . but I'll take you there. That way I can be sure I go."

Damn! Slippery as hot grease on ice.

I said, "No, I'll find the meeting without you. You can stay here with the sheriff. I'm sure he can verify who you really are."

Mary said, "John, you're making a serious mistake. I've been tracking these people for the past three years—getting deep inside their organization. I know where the meeting is taking place, I know the routine, and I can get you inside. They believe I'm one of them. You have no chance without me."

I said, "I can't trust you, lady."

Janet added, "Even if you are Homeland Security, in the several years you've been on this case, all you managed to do is sleep with some old fart, rip off his accounting records, and then kill him. That's all you've accomplished."

Women can be hard.

Mary stiffened. "I only slept with the old guy once so I could copy the disk."

Janet quipped, "You must have given him quite a rough ride. He died."

Mary snapped back, "I was just doing the job I'm supposed to do. I had to Taser him when he caught me," she added apologetically.

I cut in. "So you lied, seduced, stole, and then murdered him."

"He had a heart attack when I tasered him. They're calling it natural causes. I feel bad about it. He really wasn't a bad old man." She was looking down at the floor, not in our eyes.

She's still not telling us everything.

"We can't trust you, but that's okay, because we don't need you." I had found my smartphone in a pile with other such devices confiscated by the bad guys when I was captured. I checked it. The locator app said that

Castello was at a place called Kincade Mountain Ski and Boating Resort. He was stationary—not moving. Assuming he was attending the meeting, the Order was having its meeting at the exclusive resort.

Janet made a few quick phone calls and confirmed the resort had been booked solid for the week by the Panzram Company and that there were no rooms available at any price.

I asked Janet, "Will you authorize a full-spectrum elect-surveil on this resort?"

"Shouldn't be a problem," she replied. Janet made the call to the Agency. "Bernie, I need a full-spectrum elect-surveil of Kincade Resort, effective immediately. I'm sending you the details now . . . Yes, it's in Virginia . . . and I want everything: hard line, cell, satellite phones, texts, email, Twitter, Facebook, Linked-In . . . even someone driving by on the highway talking on a cell phone or using their car's Wi-Fi . . . I want a full workup, everyone who is there, phone-call transcripts, text-and-email analysis, credit-card match-ups, travel arrangements before and after. Do a detailed printout report and an executive summary! Put Big John on it."

All this data is already routinely being collected by the Agency. Every form of communication known to man is automatically collected and stored—from everybody, every day. Normally it is simply collected and stored, only to be looked at if the individual becomes a person of interest. Janet was simply issuing an order to make everyone at that resort a person of interest. The already-collected information would be flagged, sorted, organized, categorized, and then put into written reports for human eyes. Big John is a super computer that can analyze data at a science-fiction level of speed and volume, using preprogrammed criteria controlled by artificial intelligence algorithms. There have been rumors that Big John has been used by previous administrations for less than honorable—political—purposes, but I have no personal knowledge of that occurring.

Janet listened to Bernie for a moment then turned to me. "Bernie wants to know the focus criteria for Big John's search."

I grunted. The enormous-capacity computer worked best when it had a point of view, or focus-criteria, to bounce data against. "Tell Bernie we're looking at a criminal-slash-spy network that is holding an executive-level planning meeting at the resort this weekend. Key topics are unknown and therefore not limited, but I expect they intend to do some massive harm to the United States, for monetary profit."

"That'll work," said Janet. She relayed the information to Bernie.

I turned to my brother. "So, are you in the mood for a little vacation—maybe bust some traitors?"

He replied, "Busting spies and traitors is part of my job description as assistant director, of the FBI's Critical Incident Response Group."

I chuckled. "Well Mr. Assistant Director, I believe this qualifies."

My brother's eyes twinkled as he glanced to his gorgeous wife. She was gleaming back at him. The chemistry between them was obvious, and it seemed their bond was stronger when they were facing danger.

Terry said, "I could use a weekend away from it all."

If I ever find a woman like Terry, I'll settle down.

49

KINCADE MOUNTAIN SKI AND BOATING RESORT

By this time, a small army of sheriff's deputies and other emergency crews were swarming the property like angry killer bees. They were photographing, mapping, and documenting the bodies before removing them—including Hong Li, Marie, and Kay. They started in the library and were now working on the game room and front entrance. My regular guests were finally allowed to come upstairs. They were held in the formal living room—one of the few rooms where there wasn't a shooting victim—and instructed to stay there until a deputy took their statement. However, before long several had quietly slipped away into the night, something many were experts at doing.

Sue had latched onto the sheriff again, and it was obvious they were going to be a couple.

Jackson, Janet, Terry, Tom, and I were interviewed again and allowed to roam freely, for now. The five of us were gathered in the library. We had spent the last hour researching the Kincade Mountain Ski and Boating Resort. We had learned it was owned by William Kincade; the owner of Kincade Broadcasting, a radio, television, internet, and movie production company. Kincade was also the man Mary had seduced, copied his computer files, and then killed.

We decided the deceased billionaire hadn't operated the resort to make money, because it was too expensive for any except the conspicuously affluent. The extravagance of the accommodations had been pushed to extreme limits, almost beyond imagination. Contributing to the exclusive nature of the resort was its size. The maximum number of guests that could be accommodated at the resort was less than one hundred. There were three levels of accommodations, ranging from extravagantly luxurious to obscenely lavish.

The least expensive accommodations were the "standard suites" located in the main hotel. They rented for $4200 per night. Each two-thousand-square-foot suite included a fully stocked wet bar, kitchen, palatial king-size bedroom and bath, a second bedroom with its own bath, living room, and a private spa on a secluded balcony with a view of the lake (all the resort's rooms had a view of the lake). An in-room, champagne breakfast with unlimited menu was also included, plus a dedicated maid was assigned to each suite, available twenty-four hours a day.

The top floor of the hotel was comprised of two luxury suites, each renting for $25,000 per night. Each of these six-room, fifty-five-hundred-square-foot suites included everything the standard suites had plus two additional bedrooms—each with its own full bathroom and private spa—plus a 'party room' for entertaining. The luxury suites also included a private, indoor lap pool, and terrace with a fully stocked outdoor wet bar. These accommodations came with two butlers and two maids dedicated around the clock.

However, for guests requiring more private and more elite accommodations, there were four "cabins" available. These cabins rented for $45,000 per night and offered a level of luxury and privacy that rivals anything on the planet. These so-called cabins were actually modern, ninety-five-hundred-square-foot villas, secluded at discrete intervals on the lakeshore in the beautiful pine-and-hardwood forest. Each villa had its own private swimming pool and spa, a billiard room, a Steinway grand piano and music room, and a fully stocked bar with a bartender. Each cabin included its own private dock, which moored two motorboats, with full-time crews standing by twenty-four hours. One boat was a very fast, twenty-foot ski boat. The other was a fifty-foot party boat with fully stocked bar and bartender. Both craft were ready for touring the lake twenty-four hours a day. Also included with each cabin were a Jeep and a stretch limo, both also on twenty-four-hour standby. The limo was available to pick up and return guests to the local airport as part of the cabin experience. In addition to the above, two butlers and two maids were assigned around the clock to each cabin. The website states, "Service personnel may be replaced and rotated at the guest's desire . . . (these personnel are) available for the guest's unlimited needs."

The one-by-three-mile private lake rests at three thousand two hundred feet elevation. Therefore, it is snowbound during most of the winter. However, there are no slopes suitable for snow skiing in the area, so the resort does not attract snow skiers, and the lake's surface does not freeze thick enough for ice-skating, so conventional winter sports are limited.

The question remained in my mind: how did the resort stay open? Very few people are wealthy enough to afford such rates, and those who are usually want to travel to more exotic locations if they are spending that much money.

Unless the advertised rates are fictitious to discourage the real public from staying. If so, how did the Kincade Mountain Ski and Boating Resort pay its bills?

Terry looked up from the computer screen and announced, "The Panzram Company has reserved the entire resort—every room, suite, and cabin—the same week for the next ten years in advance."

"They clearly want to ensure privacy for their secret strategic-planning meetings, but that wouldn't pay the bills for the remainder of the year," I said. "Who stays here the rest of the year?"

Janet offered, "I can get staff back at the Agency to dig deeper and find out."

As those words were spoken Janet's cell phone vibrated. She answered. After several minutes she disconnected and announced, "That was Bernie from the Agency. He has been ordered to pull the plug from all surveillance on the resort and instructed to delete all the information collected—everything—even the routine captures. The resort is off limits to surveillance activities of any kind."

The Agency director is a squirrel, a member of the Order . . .

"They're onto us," I said to the group. "We need to move fast. Terry . . . Janet, can you find images of the resort's staff IDs and uniforms?"

"Masquerading as service staff sounds good," said Tom.

Janet learned there were a total of one hundred staff members at the resort—more than one employee per guest, a high ratio. She found images of staff uniforms and ID badges. This was a fly-by-the-seat-of-your-pants operation, and I didn't have the facilities to manufacture them here, so we would steal what we needed on site.

Terry found the Order's meeting agenda and schedule for the weekend. She announced, "Check-in is Friday evening, and checkout is Sunday."

"A two day meeting ..." echoed Janet. Then she added, "Why reserve the resort for an entire week?"

Terry said, "Some of the members arrive earlier or stay after. This is a big deal. From what I'm reading, the members rarely come together face-to-face, even for the annual meeting. They often send surrogates. However, it appears this year is an exception because someone who calls himself the Administrator is urging the members to personally attend this year. They must have something very important on the agenda."

"I wonder what it is?" asked Janet.

"Well, let's crash the party and find out," I said.

Tom said, "How long will it take to get there?"

I answered, "It's about a two hour drive from here." Then I turned to Jackson and said, "I need you to stay here and keep an eye on things."

"I think I should come with you," he said.

"No, I need you to stay back—guard the home front. Keep an eye on your brother-in-law—the sheriff. Be ready to do damage control, if necessary."

Jackson said, "On one condition: you call me every hour, on the satellite phone, and let me know you're okay."

"Yes, Mother."

"No, I mean it. You miss a call-in, and I'm coming in, guns blazing."

"That's too strict. We may miss a call and not be in trouble," I said.

"Okay, you can miss one check-in, but if you miss the second, I'm all over you."

"Agreed," I said.

"One more thing: I want a code phrase, in case you call under duress," said Jackson.

"This is getting too dramatic," I said.

Janet cut in, "No, I think that's a good idea."

I sighed and asked, "What do you suggest?"

"If you say, 'we're having fun' I'm coming with the cavalry."

"Agreed."

It was time to launch our invasion. Our force was small: Tom, Terry, Janet, and me. We would use Tom's government car. It was a cold, dark night, and our route to the Kincade Mountain Ski and Boating Resort would take us through the most undeveloped regions of Virginia, and we had no idea what to expect when we arrived.

We were entering the darkness—plunging into the unknown.

KINCADE RESORT

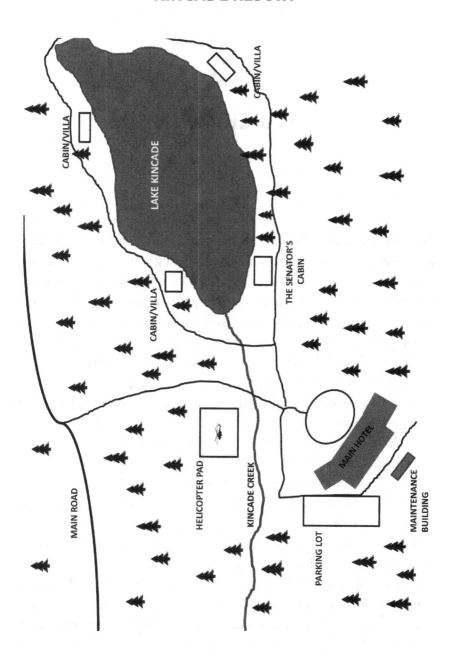

50

CHECKING IN

The resort was quiet at two thirty in the morning. The only lighting came from the safety-firelights on the stairways and the quaint, undersized streetlamps that lined the driveway and walking paths. Snow had begun falling in earnest—becoming almost a full blizzard. By sunrise there would be more than a foot of fresh snow on the ground, and the roads would be blocked. The plows would clear the most traveled roads first, so it could be two days before the road in and out of the resort was cleared. That could work in our favor. We had the squirrels trapped at the resort.

Of course, we were also trapped.

I called Jackson on the satellite phone. He answered right away, probably just waiting for the call.

"All's well. We just arrived at the resort," I reported.

"You need me there?"

"No! Call you in an hour." I disconnected.

Kincade Mountain Ski and Boating Resort's architecture reminded me of Camp David—the retreat for the President of the United States. I'd been to Camp David one time, years ago, to make a short presentation to a presidential advisor. It was a short presentation, and as soon as I completed my briefing I had been quickly but politely excused. I wasn't important enough to speak directly to the president, or to stay very long at Camp David. Anyway, the Kincade resort architecture reminded me of Camp David: heavy wood and rock, cabin-style buildings, with a touch of gingerbread here and there, creating a substantial but quaint appearance.

Except there are no American flags flying.

The Kincade Mountain Ski and Boating Resort was smaller than I had imagined when we were planning our foray. The buildings were more intimate. The lake was also smaller than I had imagined. As we drove in I could see the entire lake from the circular driveway in front of the registration entrance. The size would make it more difficult to blend in—to get lost in the crowd.

An exception to the resort's cozy ambience was the helicopter landing pad, located across a grassy meadow from the main lodge. I counted six parked aircraft. The pad area was well lit with ground-level, recessed floodlights. The lights cast bright spots, creating dark shadows and giving the parked aircraft an eerie, almost spacecraft appearance from this distance.

We pulled around to the rear of the main building and immediately saw a white-and-green security SUV, sitting at the far end of the parking area.

We'd have to deal with the security guard before entering the building.

Tom said, "That's my ticket! I'll take that guy's place. Security can go anywhere—probably has keys to everywhere."

I heard myself saying, "I'll back you up." Why, I don't know. As I told you before, violence isn't really my thing.

Terry and Janet remained at the vehicle while Tom and I approached the security SUV from the rear at different angles. When we stepped up to the front doors—me on the passenger side, Tom on the driver's side—we saw only one guard inside, and he was sleeping. We could hear him snoring through the closed windows. His arms were crossed, and his chin was resting on his chest. He was large. Even from this brief inspection, I could tell he was at least fifty pounds overweight. Because of his size he could be strong and potentially difficult to handle.

Tom smiled at me over the rooftop of the security vehicle. His breath was frosting in the cold night air. I could see he was enjoying this. My brother looked ominous.

I shrugged. After all, Tom had more experience at this sort of thing, so I'd follow his lead.

Tom pressed the door handle to open the SUV on the driver's side, but it was locked, so he tapped softly on the window.

The security guard jumped as if he'd been hit by an electrical shock. His head swiveled back and forth between Tom and me. It was actually funny. Tom waved for him to open the door. Instead, the guard rolled his window down.

That was good enough for my brother. Tom's fist shot forward so fast I didn't really see it, but I saw the result. The security guard's head rocked back against the headrest, and then bounced forward toward the steering wheel. Tom caught the security guard's head before it touched the horn.

My brother is fast.

Then Tom looked back over the top of the security SUV, and with frosty breath clouding the heavily falling snowflakes said, "Want to give me a hand on this side? He's a big boy."

My first impression about the security guard had been accurate. He was heavy. It took serious effort for Tom and me to pull him out of the front seat and stuff him into the rear deck of the SUV. He was maybe twenty-five years old, but he'd already eaten his lifetime quota for doughnuts and sweet rolls. If he didn't slow down, he'd soon be too fat for even a Santa's suit.

We secured the security guard with his own handcuffs and then used a torn T-shirt and duct tape to blindfold and gag him.

We drove the security SUV back to our car. By now the women were outside, looking out of place and cold. They gathered around the security car as soon as we stopped.

Janet peered into the rear of the SUV, "Did you kill him?"

"No, I wanted to, but John wouldn't let me," Tom answered, but he was smiling.

He has a dark sense of humor.

It was Terry who said, "Let's not stand out here until someone sees us on a surveillance camera and sounds an alarm. Besides, I'm cold!"

"We can't leave him bound in the rear of the security vehicle. Somebody will see him eventually." My eyes searched us as I spoke.

My brother said, "Yeah, and if we tie him to a tree, in the woods, he'll freeze to death."

Janet said, "How about we put him in an unoccupied hotel room. We were planning on commandeering several anyway."

Tom said, "That works! Terry, park our car in guest lot."

While Terry and Janet were parking the FBI car, Tom liberated keys from the security guard's belt. The guard regained consciousness and began wiggling and grunting—trying to get free.

Tom whispered in the guard's ear, "Shhh, we don't want to wake the evil rich people, do we? Don't worry. We're going to book you into a nice luxury suite. I'll even take off your blindfold and leave the TV on so you have something to watch if you behave yourself. Think of it as a little vacation, as long as you don't give us any trouble."

After the women returned, we left the security guard cuffed in the rear of the SUV, and using his keys, Tom unlocked the rear delivery entrance to the hotel. We were in.

We wandered through a series of service hallways and utility work areas until we found a door that opened onto the main lobby. The lobby was deserted this time of the morning. No one was working the registration desk. Janet casually walked behind the front desk and tapped the computer keyboard. Within moments she had deciphered the registration process and learned that everyone was booked into the first and third floors. The second floor was empty—ten rooms.

"Two rooms should be enough—one for Tom and Terry—one for John and me," Janet announced.

What? Did she say we'd be sleeping together again?

Janet must have read my mind, because she said, "Don't get too excited, lover boy. We bunk in the same room but not the same bed."

Tom said, "No, make it three rooms. Two should be adjoining. We'll stick the security guard in the connecting room for safekeeping. Terry and I will keep an eye on him."

Janet said, "I'll program several sets of magnetic room keys for three rooms."

I said, "No, program four manager-level key cards that will open anything. We can also use them to open our rooms."

After a few minutes of searching, Janet announced, "Security cards can only be done on the security computer."

So I said, "We also need to find uniforms and make ID badges—before everyone is awake and walking around."

Janet said, "IDs are also printed by Security."

Tom said, "It's getting late. The kitchen staff will begin preparing for breakfast soon."

Terry said, "Good! I'm hungry!"

Tom laughed. "Then we better hurry!"

So much for getting any sleep tonight.

We found the hotel security office unlocked, so we simply walked in unchallenged. There was one young guy dozing in front of the security monitors. One of the monitors showed the rear of the hotel where we had overpowered the first security guard. The young, indoor security guard had apparently napped through all of the excitement. Tom tapped him on the shoulder, causing the young man to raise his head. What he saw was me and the muzzle of my Colt Peacemaker. A few moments later he was secured by his own handcuffs and gagged using a bathroom towel and more duct tape.

I quipped, "We seem to be collecting security guards."

"Well, at least they'll have company in their private suite," said Tom as he rummaged around the cabinets and drawers until he found a bundle of zip ties and stuffed them into his pockets.

It only took our computer whizzes—Terry and Janet—two minutes to hack into the hotel's security system. The ladies quickly learned that there were three levels of access. Only management and security had unlimited access to all areas. Janet printed manager badges, with card keys for her and Terry. Then she printed security IDs and card keys for Tom and me. We could now open any lock in the resort.

Janet announced, "Uniforms! We need security-guard uniforms for the men."

Tom said, "We need to speed up. People will be waking soon, and we need to put the security guys on ice."

I asked, "What room numbers do we have?"

Janet answered, "Rooms 210 and 208, and 206—three in a row."

"Okay, first we lock this guy up." Tom nodded to the young guard we'd just tied and gagged, and then added, "and then we bring Big Boy inside before he freezes to death."

Janet and Terry went searching for security guards' uniforms while my brother and I marched the young guard up to his suite. Once inside, we insured he was properly secured, gagged, and blindfolded. We sat him on the floor and instructed him to be still. Then we quietly slipped into the adjoining suite so our prisoner couldn't be sure whether or not we were still watching him.

The ladies returned with the security guard uniforms for Tom and me.

That's when I remembered to call Jackson. "We don't want him to ride in—guns blazing—to save the day."

After assuring Jackson we were all right, Tom and I retrieved Big Boy from his security vehicle. He was shaking uncontrollably, on the verge of hypothermia, by the time we brought him inside.

I was feeling pretty good about our progress, but I didn't realize the hardest part was yet to come.

51

OUR ACCOMMODATIONS

We bound up both security guards in room 210 and removed their blindfolds but not their gags. As promised, we left the TV on—the Disney Channel. I didn't want them watching some Bruce Willis-*Die Hard*-type movie and getting ideas of being a hero. I said, "You boys behave yourselves," as I quietly closed the adjoining door between the suites.

Tom and Terry took the adjoining room 208, to keep a close eye on our prisoners, while Janet and I moved into room 206.

Janet and I took a moment to tour the accommodations. They surpassed anything I'd ever stayed in before. There was a massive and fashionable living room with large windows overlooking the lake and including a wet bar and sixty-five-inch flat-screen television above the fireplace. There was a discrete bronze sign attached to the wet bar which read, "All Beverages Complimentary." The plush, oversize sofas and chairs were made of soft velvet and would comfortably seat eight-to-ten people. There were two, very large bathrooms. Both baths had a heavy tile floor, marble countertops, and a walk-in shower with multiple showerheads and a seating platform. There was also a separate bathtub with jets in each bathroom.

It was now 0400 hours: time to check in with Jackson again. Checking-in was becoming a burden, but it was what I'd agreed to do. I told Jackson that I wouldn't be checking in again until about eight thirty because we needed sleep. He became suspicious, and it took a few minutes to convince him all was well—in other words, me refusing to say, "we're having fun."

Even though I was exhausted, I lay in bed—fully awake—not finding sleep. Nothing I tried worked. I was wide-awake and listening to Janet's soft snoring next to me. It wasn't her purring keeping me awake, nor was it my dirty mind thinking I'd like to play with her. It was my stubborn mind that insisted on rerunning the events of the past twenty-four hours. Finally, I decided since I was awake anyway that I should focus my thinking on what was ahead, not what was behind. We were about to take on a powerful criminal organization, and we needed a plan.

At the head of this powerful organization were a handful of billionaires with enormous egos. Such people will use underlings to do much of the detail work, but when it came to strategic planning or negotiating deals these men, or women, would want to be in on the action personally—they wouldn't trust others to make deals for them. Self-made billionaires think it's their planning, people, and negotiating skills—which means bullying and out-smarting others—that made them wealthy. They relish face-to-face meetings and hostile confrontations, especially when they win. Therefore, I was certain the rulers of the Order, or whatever they called themselves, would personally attend this meeting, especially if it was important. They would not be sending their lackey lieutenants.

That's when the idea came to me. I needed to observe and hear these billionaire villains firsthand. I needed to know more than what they are planning. I wanted to see what they looked like, assess their strengths and weaknesses and intrinsically know the type of people they are.

Unfortunately, high-tech electronic surveillance was not an option. We hadn't brought the proper equipment and had lost all our support from the Agency. Standing around disguised as security guards, wouldn't work either. Even if we weren't found out as pretenders, as soon as they started talking about the sensitive stuff we'd be excused from the room. I considered climbing into the air conditioning ducts and spying from inside the walls, but I hated that. During training in Baltimore, there was an exercise where we were supposed to crawl through the air ducts to eavesdrop on a conversation. My shoulders were too big to squeeze through the ductwork and I made too much noise, grunting and breathing heavily. I was so lousy at the ductwork exercise that I got caught almost immediately.

There must be a better way.

Suddenly, it was seven thirty in the morning, and I didn't remember sleeping—not even a catnap. I felt more tired than when I'd lain down. Also, I was hungry, and the room felt hot and stuffy. I got up to turn down the thermostat setting. Then I walked to the glass doors, opening to the balcony, and studied the lake and surrounding forest in the distance. It was still snowing heavily. There was at least a foot of fresh snow on the ground—maybe more.

I gently slapped Janet's foot. "Get up! You've snored enough for now!"

"I don't snore!" she mumbled.

"Yes, you do, but I've never minded."

Janet sat up, looked at me, and smiled. "That's a good sign."

I love her smile.

That's when the idea hit me: we would use the second oldest espionage technique—return to the old ways. It was spy craft that had been around, in one form or the other, since before the time of the Ancient Greeks—a proven method.

52

SECRET SPY SCHEMES 101

I'm sure you already know the oldest spy technique. It has been around since the beginning of history—Seduction. A woman (or man) seduces someone in the enemy camp (it can be either sex in today's world) to gain secrets. The target may, or may not, realize they are giving secrets to the enemy. This was the original spy technique and it is still common today. If you remember, it was how Mary obtained access to the floppy disks with information about the Order. She seduced, and then killed, the old-money guy, which makes her both a spy and an assassin.

The third oldest spy technique is turning someone in the enemy's camp—Treason. It is closely related to seduction but the motivation is different and the traitor knows he or she is being turned. The traitor is either bribed or blackmailed. This technique requires finding a trusted member of the court, someone who can hide in the open, or has access to the leader's plan. You then entice him/her to disclose secrets in exchange for not exposing some embarrassing facet of his/her life (guilty of some criminal act, child molester, cheats on spouse, etc.). Sometimes you can simply bribe the individual with gold, promises of position in the new order, or other riches. As a footnote, this category of traitor is typically executed after the war is won, even if they were promised an important position in the new order, because they have proven they cannot be trusted.

Number four (but arguably making a sprint for number one in today's high tech world) first became prominent circa 1938—Electronic Surveillance (also called elect-intel.) With the invention of wireless microphones and other electronic gadgets, electronic surveillance has become more common and much more sophisticated in recent decades. Elect-intel enables spies to take fewer risks. Today, intelligence agencies worldwide rely heavily on elect-intel. It is the primary reason the Agency exists.

You may have noticed I didn't cover the second oldest espionage technique. That's because I wanted to save it for last. It is the technique I intend to use against the squirrelly order. The second oldest spy technique is listening from concealment—Eavesdropping. Since the first army was formed, spies have hidden in covert locations to learn their enemies' plans. They hid in bushes, behind rocks, in crawl spaces, in the lofts overhead, or in false walls. There are even accounts of spies hiding inside man-size vases and directly behind the king's throne. You can also hide in the open, disguised like one of the enemy. This works best if you are mingling in a large group. This time we wouldn't be skulking behind the curtains, listening through keyholes, or crawling through ventilation ducts. Instead, we would hide in the open by pretending to be one of the bad guys. It is called Role Playing or sometimes Role Camouflage.

It would be a tap dance. We needed to be important enough have access to the meeting, but not important enough that others would expect to know us. It would only work if our legend (spy jargon for cover story or false identity) was indispensable worker bees. That would allow us to eavesdrop in the open. Our legend needed to stand up under routine scrutiny. Since the beginning of time, getting caught has meant sure death for spies. The lucky spies die quickly.

Janet returned from the toilet and asked, "What's for breakfast?"

For some reason, that reminded me that I needed to check in with Jackson. I made the call not too soon. He said he was about ready to come find us. This hourly check-in was becoming a burden, so with a lot of arguing, I adjusted the call-in to every three hours. Then I called Tom on the house phone and said we were coming over to their room.

Terry and Janet went downstairs to find us breakfast, while Tom and I checked on our prisoners. We were benevolent custodians and decided to allow them to use the toilet one at a time. It was a better option than the mess they were threatening to make.

53

RED FLAGS ON A WHITE FIELD

Our little troop of spies finished stuffing themselves with scrambled eggs, sausage, sweet rolls, toast, fresh fruit, orange juice, and coffee as I explained my plan. We were gathered in Tom and Terry's suite, at the formal dining room table.

I announced, "We'll be representatives of William Kincade."

"Why him?" asked Terry.

"William Kincade owns this resort. He is also a squirrel. In fact, he is one of the founding members of the squirrely order. It's why they hold their annual conferences here every year." I added, "I think it's the reason this resort exists: to give the Order a secure meeting location."

"But he's dead," said Terry.

"Exactly! Mary seduced him, stole information about the Order from him, and then murdered him by zapping him with a Taser. They think he died of a heart attack, so nobody is suspicious."

"How does that help us?" asked Tom.

"Because the Kincade staff will only make a token appearance for this squirrely meeting, no matter how important it is. The old man's funeral is this weekend in South Carolina, and his people will all be attending."

"What are you proposing?" asked Tom.

"We identify the token Kincade people who are attending this meeting and take their place. The earlier we identify and isolate them the better. They were expendable at the funeral, which means not important, so they probably won't be well known here."

"Sounds dangerous," said Janet.

"It won't work!" said my brother. "They'll know right away we don't belong."

I ignored the criticism. "We need to find out the dress code for the meeting and get the appropriate clothes."

Janet said, "John, you should listen to your brother. We'll be red flags on a white field."

I said, "If you all believe that, why did you come?"

The room was silent, so I continued, "Tom will be uniformed security. That way he will be able to stay close, and be openly armed. Terry will mingle as an anonymous assistant . . . try not to let anyone pin you down about who you are supposed to work for. You should be able to use your womanly skills to evade incriminating questions."

No one said anything.

Finally, Janet mumbled, "Not exactly a plan."

"If we stay flexible it'll work," I said.

Janet turned to Terry and asked, "What do I wear? I didn't come prepared to attend a business meeting—"

"—or a social function," added Terry.

I laughed and then said, "I saw a clothing store in the hotel lobby. Shall we go down and find something that fits before they open? We have a key . . ."

54

NOT JUST ANOTHER MEETING

Janet and I entered the hotel lobby from the elevator, walking side by side as if we belonged together. I stole a glance at her. She looked beautiful—maybe not better than Fifty Billion Dollar Woman, but at least as good. The best part was I trusted Janet. It felt good to be next to her as we marched across the lobby. We were trying to appear as if we owned the resort so no one would challenge us. Well, we were impersonating the owner's representatives.

The first rule of role camouflage is to act like you belong and know what you're doing. Nothing stands out more than a stranger who acts like he is lost—unsure where he's going. The second rule is to avoid eye contact, unless you want someone's attention.

We entered the conference room and circulated, becoming just one of the fifty or so faces in the room, always keeping our eyes glued to an imaginary goal on the other side of the room and walking as if we had a destination and purpose but weren't in a hurry.

This meeting was being held at an isolated resort. The participants were members of a small circle of criminally inclined, publicity-shy billionaires. Therefore, there was no need for a gatekeeper at the door—no one was checking IDs. Also, I noticed no one was wearing a nametag. That could be both good and bad. Good, because we wouldn't need to come up with a badge to look like we belonged, but bad because it could mean everyone knew each other personally and didn't need nametags. More importantly, it made finding Kincade's legitimate representatives more difficult. So we walked around and eavesdropped on conversations without being trapped into one.

There was a large, oval-shaped table in the center of the room with thirteen plush chairs distributed around its circumference. Centered at each sitting place was a Tiffany desk lamp, a black leather folder, and a set of Monte Blanc pens. Just to the right side of center of each place was a crystal pitcher of ice water. The crystal drinking glass was set upside down.

Orbiting a discrete distance out from the table were clusters of small tables and chairs that appeared to correspond to each of the thirteen places at the oval table. The important people had a seat at the table, while their staff members sat against the walls, ready to do their master's bidding.

I assumed the Kincade staffers would have seats orbiting directly out from their deceased master's vacant position at the table. My plan was to wait and see which oval table seats remained unfilled.

Janet and I made a second complete circuit of the large ballroom. Amazingly, the chatter was just as mundane as any conference of accountants or computer salesmen would be. We heard no dark conspiracy plots being seeded or confessions of where the bodies had been buried.

Disappointing . . .

The billionaires' staffers were a mixture of race, ethnicity, sex, and ages. Most were dressed in what is commonly referred to as *business casual*. The men wore Dockers and either a polo shirt or an open-collar dress shirt, no tie. Most men wore a sports jacket. The women wore either skirts or pants, with a blouse or sweater. A few women wore suit jackets. Only the older men were wearing very expensive suits and ties. I assumed they were the ruling members with a seat at the oval table.

Janet and I were dressed in business casual: jackets and pants. I also had my Colt Peacemaker stuffed into the small of my back. I didn't know for sure what Janet had stuffed in her pants, but I'm sure it was something lethal.

There was a subgroup of attendees who looked like bodyguards—big and tough. They had the same aura about them that I'd encountered several times in the past twenty-four hours—clearly alumni from the School of Speechless Knuckle Draggers. This subgroup stood near the exits, quietly watching everyone with their suspicious eyes.

We had been circulating the room for ten minutes, and I had not learned anything helpful, especially not in terms of finding the staff we wanted to replace. We were running out of time.

Tom entered the room and stood quietly at the front entrance. He wore a security guard's uniform and convincingly acted like he belonged here. I couldn't see Terry. I just hoped she had intermingled and was in a good position—a seat that would enable her to stay in the room when the meeting began.

That's when Janet elbowed me. "The man and woman at ten o'clock . . . dark-blue pants and sports jacket . . . woman's wearing a black skirt and blue blouse."

"What about them?" I asked.

Janet sighed and said, "They're the Kincade representatives."

"You sure?"

"Yes, see Terry signaling us? They're our targets."

"I don't see how you can know."

Janet shot daggers at me. "Come on!"

I took a deep breath and said to Janet's back as she was walking away, "Hope your right."

I think I heard her groan.

55

ENTICING HANSEL AND GRETEL

We slowly walked up to the indicated couple. They were in their late twenties or early thirties. Both were very attractive. The man was a little smaller than me, maybe five-ten and weighed about one hundred seventy pounds. The woman was about five-six and weighed around one hundred ten. They had similar coloring—eyes and hair—to Janet and I. That was a break. Hopefully, if not too many people had met them, we could pass ourselves off in their place. They were standing alone—another plus.

I glanced at Janet to be sure she was ready. She was actually grinning. *Show time!*

We stopped in front of the couple.

"Hey there," I said with my friendliest smile. "My name's John and this is Janet."

The woman spoke first. "I'm Nancy. This is Peter. We're with Kincade's group. Who do you guys work with?"

I evaded. "Oh, I heard about Mr. Kincade on the radio—such a tragedy. Did they determine the cause of his passing yet?"

Nancy said, "It was a heart attack. The funeral services are this Sunday."

"I'm sure you miss him," said Janet.

"I didn't really know him too well," answered Nancy. "I just started working for Kincade this year—"

Peter interjected, "I knew him well. He paid off my college loan when I started working for the Order."

Nancy asked, "Who are you guys with, again?"

It was time to isolate these two—get control of the situation—while we still had some momentum in the dialogue.

Offer the kids candy to entice them inside.

I said, "I'm glad you asked. We're here to showcase a new production device that will help the Order make even more profits. Would you like to see it? It has been a deep secret until now, but Janet and I are on the agenda to demonstrate it this afternoon." I waved my hand toward the exit. "It's just in the next room." I gave them my best trust me smile.

They seemed unsure, so I launched the clincher.

"We're looking for support in the Order. Those who help us sell the idea will be given a unit for free—a two-million-dollar value. We're expecting this device to change the way you do business forever; that I can promise you."

Doesn't candy sound good? Want a nibble? It can be yours ...

Peter asked, "Exactly what are you talking about?"

"It's better if you see it, then all your questions will clear up," I answered.

I noticed that Terry had moved in closer. I quickly glanced to the door and saw that my brother was gone.

Get the kiddies to follow you.

"Please, come with us. It'll only take a moment, and I promise you will be happy you did."

Peter looked to Nancy, they shrugged and followed us through the throng of people, past the large oval center table, and out of the conference room. No one even glanced at us during the migration. It was as if we were invisible, or maybe they just assumed we were doing what we were supposed to be doing. Either way, we had successfully gotten the two Kincade representatives away from the others without setting off an alarm.

I prattled on with meaningless gibberish to keep them off guard as I led them down the hall to the fitness room. "This involves the latest technology and has been tested and approved by the FDIC."

Peter slowed just as we reached the door. "What the hell are you talking about?"

His mother must have told him not to take candy from a stranger.

"Come in and I'll show you." I was patting myself on the back as I used my card key to open the door to the fitness room. I indicated for Nancy and Peter to enter first.

Nancy's instincts kicked in. She spun around. "I'm returning to the party!"

She bumped into Terry, who had quietly followed us. Terry grabbed Nancy's arm and said, "Please go inside!"

Nancy looked like she was building up a full-volume scream, but Terry was on the job. She stabbed a Taser into Nancy's neck, dropping the female staffer to the floor—a hundred-ten-pound sack of dead weight.

First Mary, now Terry . . . Do all women carry Tasers?

Peter must have fancied himself a martial-artist-hero-type, because he swung on me. Like I've said several times, I'm no Kung Fu expert, but I'm not exactly a novice either. I simply slid to the side, causing him to miss me, and locked up his swinging arm. That's when Terry used her Taser a second time. Peter didn't fall like his sister-in-arms, but he did tremble and lose control of his large muscle groups. That's when Tom appeared from inside the doorway and pulled Peter all the way inside the fitness room. Both Terry and Janet grabbed Nancy and dragged her into the exercise room. The door closed quietly behind us.

I reopened the door and took a quick look outside. Apparently, no one had seen the kidnapping.

The kids are in the bag.

We took their wallets. Their full names were Peter Travis and Nancy Lombard. They both lived in Charleston, South Carolina—different addresses—and both were apparently single. They had IDs as staffers for Kincade, or more precisely as employees of the Kincade Broadcasting Network."

We didn't have time to talk to them and learn more. The meeting would begin soon.

I asked Terry, "Have you found a place to sit when the meeting starts?"

She said, "Yes, vacant seats are easy to find. Several members and staffers are at Kincade's funeral."

"How did you learn that?" I asked.

"I just talked to people. You'd be surprised what you pick up in a few minutes of casual conversation," said Terry.

I said, "Okay, Terry goes first, finds her seat, and then becomes invisible. Janet and I will follow. Tom, can you handle these two by yourself?" I indicated Peter and Nancy.

"No problem," he replied. "I think we'll leave them secured in that utility closet with the mops and brooms." He nodded to a side door on the opposite end of the room. "It's too dangerous taking them upstairs—too many hostiles walking around."

I said, "Good! Join us in the main conference room ASAP. I want you close by."

"Roger that!" said my brother.

56

PROJECT UNDERGROUND STATE

We gave Terry three minutes' head start before entering the conference room. Most of the people were already either sitting at their assigned places or standing directly next to them. That made our task of finding a couple of vacant seats a little easier. Also, most were talking, so no one paid attention to a couple discretely walking through the semi-dark conference room.

The overhead lighting had been dimmed, leaving only pools of bright light created by the desk lamps on the oval table. The lighting created an enigmatic ambience in the room. The obscure environment should have worked in our favor. However, I felt as if there was an indistinct but dangerous presence watching us from the semidarkness.

Probably just my imagination.

People began taking their places. The challenge was that we didn't know where to sit, so we stalled while the others sat.

If you act unsure people will notice you.

There were three empty chairs at the oval table plus ten vacant chairs around the walls. Peter and Nancy would be sitting directly out from one of the three vacant oval chairs.

But which one?

I whispered to Janet, "Any idea where we should sit?"

"No, but we should sit down before someone pays us any attention" she answered.

"Sounds easy enough," I quipped.

We selected a vacant staffer table directly out from a vacant chair at the table. I was extremely conscious that if we committed some Order of the Golden Squirrel *faux pas*, we'd be busted, and things would get nasty real fast. But since the light was dim, maybe we wouldn't be recognized as impostures.

We sat down.

The pre-meeting buzz and small talk continued with no one sounding an alarm.

Maybe we're safe.

I calmed my breathing as I studied those seated at the oval table. It was difficult to see clearly in the shadowy, almost dark room, but I recognized several faces. They were the rich, the powerful, and a few famous. I saw one well-known New York Stock Exchange trader, a banker, a defense contractor, and the CEO of one of the biggest dot-com companies on the planet. There were also at least two politicians: one from the House of Representatives; the other a US senator—I think his name is Fetterson. Then I saw Castello and suddenly realized how stupid it was for me to be here.

He told me he was coming to the meeting.

I whispered to Janet, "I need to disappear. That man sitting on the far side of the table, at the end, is Jacob Castello. He came to the house last night and knows my face. If he sees me, we're toast!"

I studied Janet's frown while she considered a response. Somehow, she looked even more beautiful when she concentrated. I liked the way her eyebrows wrinkled.

Cut that out!

Janet whispered to me, "It's dark, and we're sitting in the darkest part of the room. Keep your face turned away and down. Don't make eye contact. Maybe he won't notice you."

Pretty thin, but at this point it's the only hand I have to play.

A dapper, medium-height man, sitting at the midpoint of the oval table, stood. I thought it funny that when he stood the top half of his body became obscured in the darkness; only his crotch was highlighted by the desk lamp.

He spoke with an aristocratic British accent, "Let's get this started, shall we? As the Administrator, until we select my successor tomorrow, I will chair this meeting—assuming there are no objections?" His voice had authority and energy.

Silence filled the room.

He continued, "Good! A reminder of our long-standing ground rule for meetings: We won't use proper names in this forum, and, of course, we will dispense with going around the room and making introductions, as most of our membership are excessively introverted and wish to remain anonymous . . . So I have been told."

Soft chuckling rolled through the room, then silence again.

"Without further ceremony, I believe the senator is first on the agenda to speak about . . . Project Underground State. Senator . . ." The Administrator sat down.

It was US Senator Fetterson, from the State of Washington.

Senator Fetterson remained seated. "Ladies and gentlemen, it is time for us to activate Project Underground State. Catalytic Activation will be this January. As you know, for the past decade and a half, we have been slowly and systematically placing our people in the media and in key government positions. We have been sowing the seeds of mistrust with each president and with the Congress—regardless of political party. These people have been influencing public opinion and will facilitate the transition of power to our provisional government immediately after activation. This effort has been expensive. We've spent nearly a billion US dollars in this effort over the past fifteen years, but we have been successful beyond even our own expectations. The current administration is unable to function at even the most routine level because it expends all its efforts defending against an endless barrage of accusations and formal charges, covering everything from sex scandals to charges of corruption and incompetence, and even complicity with our enemies. The public-approval rating for Washington politicians, in general, is the lowest it has ever been in the history of the country." He paused to judge the participants' reactions.

Silence.

Fetterson continued, "So now we are prepared to implement the final stage of Project Underground State. Catalytic Activation will push the country over the edge, creating a void in power that we will fill. Because of the mistrust and frustration that we have sowed in the past decade, the American people will welcome the strong leadership. To implement

Catalytic Activation we have obtained—at substantial cost—a small nuclear device. In fact, Bigfoot is here, at the resort, at this moment." He paused again, but this time it was for theatrical effect. Like all politicians, Fetterson was enjoying his time in the spotlight.

I could feel the electricity and excitement in the room as the participants began talking among themselves.

Fetterson spoke over the rumbling. "If anyone would like to inspect the device after this meeting, please come to my cabin. I will also be hosting cocktails and snacks, of course."

There was a wave of subdued laughter.

Fetterson continued, "However, after tonight's viewing, Bigfoot will disappear. Catalytic Activation will happen during the president's State of the Union address. As you know we will have the entire government in attendance: the vice president, both houses of Congress, the Joint Chiefs of Staff, The Supreme Court, and the other prominent leaders of our country . . . somehow, I have been selected as the Designated Survivor this year—how convenient-don't you think?" He chuckled, and the others laughed with him.

The fix is in . . .

Fetterson waited for the participants to settle down then said, "The State of the Union address will be ground zero for our Catalytic Activation. In the confusion and chaos that will follow detonation, our deep provisional government will take control. As acting president, I will declare martial law and suspend the Constitution."

I strained to see in the semidarkness and thought I could see a drool of spittle falling from the corner of the senator's mouth.

A faceless figure sitting at the oval table, with his back to me, asked, "Is it safe here?"

"I have ten of my best security men guarding Bigfoot. Trust me—it's safe."

"That wasn't my question. I meant is there danger of radiation?"

Senator Fetterson turned back to his chief of staff, sitting at the table behind his position, in the dark. "William, would you please address that issue?"

Fetterson broke the anonymity rule by saying the guy's name out loud. I guess the rules don't apply for the bosses.

William stood. He was about thirty, blond hair, blue eyes, and a trim body sculpted by consistent work in a gym. Even in the semidarkness I could see that his face was flushed—probably red. I guess he didn't like his name being said out loud in a room full of nameless faces. Still, William worked for one of the most powerful politicians in the nation—a man poised to take over the country via mass murder—and felt forced to comply.

William cleared his throat. "There's no danger of radiation leaking from the bomb. However, we must take precautions when delivering the device that it is not detected by the particle-emission sensors placed throughout the Washington, DC, area. If one of those sensors sounds the alarm, within minutes there will be hundreds of federal police swarming all over the device." He sat down.

Another faceless man opposite Fetterson asked, "Isn't there another way for us to accomplish our goal?"

Fetterson asked, "What do you mean, sir?" His voice was lower than before, but there was clearly an emotional edge to it.

The faceless man said, "I'm not comfortable exploding an atomic bomb on Washington, DC, and killing our whole government along with thousands of innocent people. In addition, we will be destroying the buildings and monuments that represent over two hundred years of our history. There must be another way."

"We resolved this issue in previous discussions. There must be a catastrophic event that creates a catalyst for change," responded Fetterson.

"I regret that I was not present at that meeting, but an atomic bomb . . . detonated in our own capital . . . could we put this to a vote of those here tonight?"

"Does anyone else feel this way?" asked Fetterson.

The room was intensely silent.

Fetterson waived William over and whispered to him for several moments. William whispered back. Fetterson shook his head and adamantly pointed at two men, who had been invisibly standing against the wall. William nodded and walked to the two men indicated. There was a short conversation. The two men moved around the edges of the room, staying in the darkness. They passed within a few feet of Janet and me and then stopped directly behind the faceless objector at the oval table.

Fetterson said, "Sir, you seem to be the only dissenter in the room. Do you insist on standing by your position?"

"Yes, I do. In fact, I believe doing this would be the greatest act of treason ever committed in the history of man. If we do this we condemn ourselves to eternal damnation! I cannot be part of it." The faceless member stood, abandoning his seat at the table, and walked from the room.

The two dark figures followed him out.

A few seconds later, we heard the faceless man beginning to protest in the hallway. "What are you do . . ." He was cut short with a scuffling and then there was only quiet.

Fetterson scrutinized the others around the oval table before saying, "I assume there are no further objections . . . good! . . . then let's move along."

The Administrator said, "Senator, I believe there is at least one silent dissenter in the room—possibly two."

"Is that so?" asked Fetterson.

The Administrator stood. "I am speaking of loose cannons that have declared war on the Order."

Fetterson nodded quietly—a secret passing between them. He sat down.

The Administrator turned to a black man sitting at the far end of the oval table. "Mr. S, would you care to address this topic?"

Mr. S slowly stood. He was medium height, dressed in a very expensive looking, tailored navy blue suit, white silk shirt, and bright red tie. When he spoke his deep authoritative voice filled the room. "There have been several recent instances that have threatened to expose our operations and disrupt our projects. It began two years ago when Vernon Crassman, one of our most prominent members, was viciously attacked at his ranch in Washington State. These same people later followed Crassman to his Thailand fortress and assassinated him."

"Who are these people?" asked someone.

"The protagonists are two brothers: John and Thomas Wolfe. Thomas Wolfe is the assassin who killed Vernon Crassman in Thailand. He poses as a high-level member of the FBI, but we think that is only a cover to give his murders a legal veil. His brother—John Wolfe—has been using his position with the Agency to spy on the Order's operations."

Fetterson said, "We have highly placed representatives in the Agency. If John Wolfe is an employee of the Agency, why don't we simply order him to stop his spying?"

A rumble of sidebar conversations. . .

Mr. S replied, "John Wolfe is not currently an employee of the Agency. He recently retired. It was only after his retirement that we became aware of his activities against us."

If they had let me retire quietly . . .

"In that case, we should terminate both Wolfe brothers," declared Fetterson.

Mr. S said, "In fact, we have already made several attempts to eliminate them both, but at each turn the Wolfe brothers have proven to be very slippery.

Another member stated loudly, "I propose we send a Direct Action Team and end this, so we can get on with more pressing business."

There was a rumble of approval for that idea.

Mr. S answered, "We have done just that, sir. In fact, last night we sent two different Direct Action Teams to kill both Thomas and John Wolfe. We had the opportunity because the brothers were together at John Wolfe's home in Virginia. We haven't heard from either team, despite numerous attempts to contact them. We believe both teams were unsuccessful."

An anonymous speaker said, "Maybe you should send in better men."

A few muffled chuckles . . .

Mr. S answered, "Those were our two best Direct Action Teams!"

That had been their best men? My respect for the Squirrels dropped a couple of notches.

The chatter rose almost to a roar.

The Administrator waved his hands. "Please—ladies and gentlemen— let's have order."

The room fell silent at the British speaker's urging. After he was sure the group was ready to move forward he said, "I believe that the senator wants the floor . . . sir?"

Senator Fetterson waited a few seconds before speaking. "The point is we cannot afford to underestimate the Wolfe brothers again. They are a threat to Project Underground State."

Another member, sitting at the table, waved his hand for attention and then said, "Are you sure we aren't overreacting?"

"Those brothers are dangerous men," growled Senator Fetterson.

Project Underground State—Catalytic Activation—*Bigfoot is a bomb: This is much bigger than I thought. And they think Tom and I are a danger to them—flattering and scary.*

Another anonymous speaker said, "I say we should suspend moving forward on Project Underground State until both Wolfe brothers, and any of their comrades, are permanently out of the picture."

The British speaker exchanged a quick look with Senator Fetterson, then with Castello. "Perhaps we are going about this in the wrong way. What do you think, Mr. C?"

"Perhaps . . ." said Castello. Then he turned in his chair and looked directly at me. "John? Do you know of a different approach that would provide a satisfactory solution to this issue?"

I stared back at him from across the room. I was speechless. Even in the semidarkness and at this distance, it was obvious that Castello's eyes were focused on me. In fact, everyone in the room was now staring at me.

I'm screwed.

Janet whispered, "We should make a run for it."

I gently placed my hand on her arm—wait.

The Administrator said, "Yes, Mr. Wolfe, since you have joined our little gathering—uninvited—why don't you take a seat at the table, so we may discuss our differences in a civilized manner, like gentlemen?"

I was dumbfounded, wordless, and scared beyond anything I can describe here.

"Come on! Don't be shy. Come take a place at the table."

I'm so screwed.

I whispered to Janet as I stood, "Stay here . . . be invisible."

57

THE GUEST OF HONOR

The Four largest knuckle draggers in the room had suddenly surrounded me. There was no point in resisting, so I smiled at the four monsters, as I stood. They seemed determined to escort me either to the oval table or to hell—my choice. I prudently chose the table. After I was settled, two monsters remained behind me. I think the other two climbed back into their tree, but I'm not sure.

I hope Tom and Terry are on the job.

The Administrator said, "Let's not forget Mr. Wolfe's friends."

I watched, helplessly, as more knuckle draggers appeared next to both Janet and Terry.

Tom has disappeared.

The Administrator said, "Ladies, I apologize for not having enough seats at the table, so we'll simply escort you to a holding room until we have decided your fate. Gentlemen, please escort Mr. Wolfe's lady friends to the exercise room and keep a very close eye on them. Thank you."

The exercise room—the same place we put Nancy and Peter. I wonder if Tom is waiting there.

The four knuckle draggers escorted Terry and Janet from the room. After they were gone, the Administrator said, "Don't look so surprised, John Wolfe. Did you really think you could just walk into our intimate little meeting and not be recognized? Which reminds me: we dearly wish for you to return Peter and Nancy to us—unharmed. Where did you store them?"

"I thought you weren't supposed to use names, but I hear names being used: Peter, Nancy, William. How can you be so careless, breaking your own rules?" I tried to sound more sure of myself than I felt.

Castello said, "You realize, of course, you just signed your own, and your associates', death warrants."

I remained speechless.

Castello laughed. "What no arrogant comebacks or smart-ass remarks? I'm disappointed."

The Administrator said, "I apologize to all the members for this unfortunate interruption, but it is a necessary function we need to dispense with at this time." Then he turned back to me and said, "So tell us, Mr. Wolfe, what did you hope to accomplish by being here, and where are the others—your brother for instance?"

Everyone in the room was still staring at me.

Yes, where are you, Tom?

I took a deep breath and spoke in a slow steady voice, "My story isn't worth telling, so if you allow us to go quietly into the night, you can get on with your business at hand," I faked a smile.

The Administrator said, "Don't be so modest, Mr. Wolfe. You and your brother have been a significant irritation for several years. Besides, you just sat through a summary discussion of our most important and sensitive operation. You can't expect to just walk out of here, now can you?"

"What do you want from me?" I asked.

"You can begin by telling me where your brother is."

"I don't know."

Wish I did.

Castello said, "This is going nowhere. We are wasting valuable time here."

"Mr. Administrator, my people can secure Wolfe's cooperation. Hand him over to me, and before this conference is ended we will have our answers," announced Mr. S.

The Administrator said, "Very well, if there are no objections we will allow our friend from Los Angeles to interview Mr. Wolfe and his lady friends."

Mr. S nodded to his aide, a tall, muscular brute with raven-black skin and even blacker shining eyes. "Gerald, will you please take Mr. Wolfe to the exercise room and reason with him and his lady comrades?"

Castello added, "We need to know who else is working with him. One more thing: see if you can get the PM Program access codes and frequencies."

The Administrator said, in typical British understatement, "It would also be useful to know where Nancy and Peter are being held, if it isn't too inconvenient."

Gerald said, "Consider it done!" as he waved at several knuckle draggers standing nearby.

They aren't short of muscle here.

The thugs lifted me from the chair and dragged me from the room. It wasn't that I couldn't walk; they didn't give me a choice. Gerald led the way. Our destination was the exercise room—the same room they had taken Terry and Janet, and where we'd locked up Peter and Nancy.

Where are you, Tom?

As we approached the exercise room, I heard a woman's voice inside, but the words were muffled. Gerald opened the door and stood aside to allow me to be dragged inside. Now I could clearly hear Terry say, "You'll be sorry if she isn't allowed to go."

Janet pleaded, "Please, I really need to go!"

The muffled, earlier voice had belonged to Janet.

"Tie Wolfe to that machine!" ordered Gerald as he pointed to a bench press machine.

"What about using the toilet?" Terry asked. "I need to go too."

"Pee in your panties!" said Gerald. "I'm not taking any chances with any of you getting loose and creating problems."

I was quickly strapped to the machine—hands only; they neglected to tie down my feet.

Maybe I can use that somehow.

I counted the enemies. Including Gerald, there were six men, more than enough to control two women and me. They had spread themselves strategically around the room. Two stood by the entry door, one near the women, and the others orbited around me.

Gerald stood nearest me. He was trying to intimidate me by burning his dark, laser-like eyes through me. He was clearly a very powerful man, both physically and mentally. I could see an intense but angry intellect burning in his eyes. To be honest, I was worried.

Gerald said, "Now, Mr. Wolfe, you and I are going to become very well acquainted with each other over the next twenty-four hours. In fact, I will become your entire universe."

"Stop the prattle and get on with it!" I heard myself saying.

Careful what you wish for.

"As you wish." Gerald stepped in and punched me directly on the nose. It happened so fast that I couldn't have avoided or blocked the punch even with my hands free.

Blood gushed from my nostrils, and I could only see blackness with thousands of little white dots floating in black space, but I was still conscious and fully aware of the pain. I think he broke my nose. My stomach turned, and I almost lost the scrambled eggs and sweet rolls I'd eaten earlier. I coughed and spit up blood. My vision slowly returned and I was about to say something smart when he hit me again—in the same exact spot. This time I passed out.

I regained consciousness to the words, "Hey, that's not going to work. You're too heavy-handed. If he's unconscious, he's not experiencing the pain or talking." It was one of the other knuckle draggers. It was the first time I heard one of them talk since we arrived. For a moment I thought I was hallucinating.

Gerald sneered. "You got a better way?"

"Hell yeah, I'll have him singing your favorite song in a few minutes."

"Right! The job is yours . . . for thirty minutes." Gerald stepped back, folded his arms across his chest, and leaned against the mirrored wall. He appeared relaxed, but his eyes still had that inhuman intensity.

The talking knuckle dragger snapped at his cohorts, "Search and then strip him—completely naked!"

They found my satellite phone and the Colt.

"Hey, what's this?" asked one of the thugs.

"It's a telephone and a pistol, stupid!" The lead thug took it away and tossed both into the corner of the room. "He won't be making any calls or shooting anyone."

Then he slowly, dramatically, reached around to the small of his back and produced what appeared to be a razor-sharp deer-skinning knife with a six-inch, fixed blade. He twisted and turned the knife so that the light reflected off the shiny blade, into my eyes. "You're going to tell me everything I ever wanted to know—everything. Shit, you'll be making up stories just to entertain me. Either that or you will lose your manhood but not your life. I promise to let you live ... without your manhood."

"No matter what I tell you, in the end you're going to kill us. We've heard too much. There's no other way this can end," I said.

Gerald grunted from his position leaning against the mirrored wall. "Maybe, but there is dying, and then there is dying. How easy or bad it happens is your choice."

Before I could come up with a witty comeback, two knuckle draggers tore my clothing off, which kind of took away my impetus for smart comebacks. I now sat naked and tied to the bench press machine. It was almost *déjà vu* from the pool table last night. Under normal conditions, if you will, I would have complained about being cold, but for some reason, the goose bumps didn't seem that important right now. Although I was acutely aware of the seat's cold vinyl sticking to my bottom.

The knife-wielding knuckle dragger moved closer—it was all very theatrical. He aimed the point of his six-inch blade at my exposed and very vulnerable parts and then slowly made imaginary cuts in the air.

At that moment, we heard a kicking and a muffled screaming from the storage closet. It was Peter and Nancy asking for attention. I, for one, was happy they had asked.

Gerald and another knuckle dragger walked over and opened the closet door. "Well, here's one of our enigmas solved," said Gerald. He nodded to his partner to cut them loose.

After they were cut loose Nancy and Peter rushed from the exercise room, I assume to tell of their nightmarish ordeal.

Gerald nodded to the knife-wielding knuckle dragger. "Please continue with your work."

The knife-man tossed the blade vertically, nearly to the ceiling, causing it to spin end-over-end. The knife fell back and stuck point first into the vinyl bench, inches from my personal equipment.

One of the two knuckle draggers guarding the hallway door laughed and mumbled something to his partner. Both men were enjoying the show—at my expense, of course.

The knifeman apparently got motivation from being appreciated, because I could see his eyes sparkling. He was reacting to the others enjoying the show. He laughed and pulled the blade free. "That was just a warm-up drill . . . something to get your attention."

I must admit it was an effective way to capture my attention.

I stole a fast glance at the satellite phone and pistol where they had landed in the corner of the room.

I missed the last check-in with Jackson.

Stupid me—I'd insisted on two missed check-ins before Jackson would come looking for us. It didn't matter; even if Jackson came this instant, I'd likely be dead by the time he got here.

58

DON'T GO QUIETLY

The knife wielder was grinning like I imagine he did the first time he had sex with a woman. It was clear he enjoyed waving the blade in front of my eyes. He asked, "Do you have anything you'd like to say before I go further? It could save you a lot of humiliation and pain if you said the right words now."

Gerald muttered, sotto voce, "It'll save us from making a mess too."

"Leave him alone, and I'll tell you everything you want to know," Janet shouted from across the room.

Janet! You still care.

Gerald shot back, "Shut up, woman! We're having fun here. Your time will come soon enough!"

The knifeman smiled. "Where would you like the first cut to be?"

I thought he'd already decided that.

At that moment, I occurred to me these guys may be gruesome masochists, but they weren't experienced at tying victims to an exercise machine. If you remember, only my hands were lashed to the frame. My legs were still loose, and this knifeman was standing within range of my foot. It was a stupid mistake for him to make, and I had no intention of going out quietly—not without a fight.

Ultimately, I wanted to shove that blade where the sun doesn't shine, but first things first. He was threatening mine, so I'd harm his. I knew I had to make the first move good because I wouldn't get a second chance. As he droned on about something or other—he liked to hear himself talk—I rehearsed the move in my mind to be sure. Then as a distraction, I answered his first question that still hung in the air—where I wanted the first cut to be.

I said, "How about you cut your own throat first?"

While his impoverished brain was trying to decipher that statement, my right foot thrust out catching him squarely in his package—*quid pro quo.* He stood frozen in place for maybe two seconds as I watched his face drain to a pale gray and his eyes lose their focus. The knife slipped from his hand, and he slowly collapsed to the floor. He lay there, groaning softly. I knew I'd pay later for doing that, but it was satisfying at the moment.

Gerald stepped in and slapped me across the side of my head with an open hand. Like I've already said, he is fast. I wouldn't have been able to block the blow with my hands free. The lights went out momentarily and my head filled with a loud ringing. When I could see again Gerald was winding up for a second swing.

Gerald was standing in the same exact spot the knifeman had been standing—such an idiot. I just repeated my trick with the same results. Gerald dropped to his knees next to his buddy.

But Gerald was strong and only needed a moment to recover, or maybe I missed my mark. Either way, there was hatred in his eyes as he slowly stood up and hit me across my face so hard that I felt the skin bleeding in the shape of a handprint. This time black spots danced in front of a white background. I felt as if I were about to vomit. I feigned unconsciousness to buy time, which was easy. I closed my eyes and my head started spinning.

Tom, where are you?

59

THE TOP WARRIOR IN THE WORLD

"He's faking. I didn't hit him that hard," said Gerald.

"I don't know. It's cumulative. Stop hitting him so I can do my work," said the knifeman, who was standing again.

Gerald grunted. "Somebody get some cold water and splash it on him—wake him up."

"Let's cut something off and see if he reacts," purred the knifeman.

"First, strap down his feet so he can't kick!" ordered Gerald.

At that moment, the door opened and Tom stepped into the room. He was still dressed as a security guard and was holding his Glock down against the side of his leg. He casually slid to the right and stopped next to one of the two knuckle draggers who were guarding the door.

Finally!

No one reacted as the hallway door automatically closed itself and locked with a loud click. Everyone remained motionless. They stared at Tom, not sure who he was.

Finally, my brother said, "Did I break up some fun and games? If you want I could come back later."

"No, please stay!" I shouted from across the room.

The two men guarding the doorway finally reacted, but they were too slow. Tom hit the nearest knuckle dragger with the heavy steal barrel casing of his Glock. The guard's head rocked sideways, hitting a piece of exercise equipment, and then rebounded into Tom's fist. The knuckle dragger collapsed into a heap on the floor.

The second doorway guard rushed my brother, but Tom was somehow a full step ahead. He seemed to effortlessly hit the guard mid-step, on the chin with a back fist. The guard dropped to the floor: One punch—out cold.

The others had been dumbfounded and unmoving, until now.

The knuckle dragger standing nearest the women pulled a pistol and fired off two wild shots at my brother. Tom dropped to one knee and fired twice. Both shots hit center of mass in the chest. The knuckle dragger was down.

There was still Gerald and two other knuckle draggers operational in the room, and now they all moved at once.

Gerald dropped behind a weight machine. He was apparently not armed.

The other two knuckle draggers pulled weapons and began firing at my brother. It all happened so fast that I'm not sure who was on first and who was on second, but there was a thunderstorm of explosions that lasted maybe three seconds then the room suddenly became eerily quiet and still, except for the tinkle of expended brass that accompanied the crash of a broken mirror hitting the floor.

All the knuckle draggers were down.

I could see spent brass lying all over the floor. Most of the mirrored walls were shattered with bullet holes. Blood was seeping from the bodies and soaking into the exercise mats. The powerful stench of copper and gun smoke gagged me. I had to fight the urge to vomit.

Gerald slowly stood. He was apparently the only bad guy who had not been hit, because he had not pulled a weapon. "You made quite a mess, but it's all for nothing. Others heard the shooting. There'll be an army here in a few seconds. He was creeping, step by step, toward Tom.

My brother just stood there, as if he didn't realize the huge, powerful man was closing the distance.

Gerald was the only person moving.

Gerald said, "I'll make you a deal. If you take your friends and go, I will give you a ten-minute head start before I sound the alarm and organize a posse to find you."

Another step . . .

Gerald was now less than five feet from Tom. I was about to shout a warning when the powerful man moved. He was a blur—inhumanly fast—but my brother was somehow faster. Tom's gun hand shot forward in the fastest movement I've ever seen a human being make. Actually, I didn't see it because it was so fast. But I saw the results. He must have slammed the heavy Glock alongside the powerful man's head, because I saw Gerald stagger backward, stumble over a sit-up bench, and back-flip to the floor. It was the fastest knockout I've ever seen or heard of.

Now I understood why people in the FBI say Tom is the best shooter and unarmed fighter they have.

I'd argue he's the top warrior in the world.

This was one time I wouldn't argue with my little voice.

"Shall I untie you?" asked my brother, breaking into my private hero-worship session.

"It's about time!" I heard myself saying.

Terry and Janet shouted in sync, "Hey, don't forget us!"

60

FREEDOM IS TRANSITORY

Tom freed the women first, quipping "Ladies first!" Then he turned to me. While he was cutting the plastic restraints that held me to the bench press, he announced, "First order of business is to tie up all the bad guys—"

I cut in, " ...I know, even the ones we think are dead."

"Right!" he smiled then reached into his cargo pants' pocket and tossed a bundle of zip ties to his wife.

"Got it!" Terry replied as she caught the bundle. She turned to Janet and asked, "You wanna help?"

"Absolutely!" Janet took a handful of zip ties and secured the two knuckle draggers at the door.

I was moving slow. My head was still spinning and my ears rang. I'm not sure if it was the slapping I'd received from Gerald or the thunder of the gunshots in a closed room—maybe both. In any case, I cleared my head as best as I could, breathing deep and slow, as I got dressed.

Despite the buzzing in my head and my broken nose, I was smiling, happy to be alive. We had prevailed and now all we had to do was to get to the car and we were home free, I thought.

Janet asked, "So what's next?"

My brother nodded to Gerald, who was still lying on the floor, unconscious. "He was right. Someone heard those shots for sure. We need to be ready for them."

"Rodger that!" Terry picked up a Glock, checked the magazine, and found two spares on the same body. Then she noticed a Taser on his belt.

"Hey, you never know, I might have use for this." She clipped it to her belt line. She now looked ready to raise some hell of her own.

Janet picked up a pistol, checked it in a professional manner, and then slipped it into her waistline.

We weren't out of danger yet.

I collected my Colt Peacemaker and satellite phone. I pocketed the phone and checked the pistol to be sure it was loaded then tucked it in my belt. It was heavy, but reassuring. I was feeling better now.

Tom shook his head and said, "You should pick up one of those modern pistols the bad guys were using."

"I'll stick with the Colt." Then I asked Tom, "So, hero-brother, like Janet asked, what's next?"

"Let's burn this place to the ground!" Terry answered in a loud voice.

"Here-here!" shouted Janet.

Tom nodded. "Stay still. I'll check the hallway. See if we've collected a crowd out there yet."

Tom slowly opened the hallway door. He peeked around the doorframe then quickly eased the door shut. "Four men, with pistols, moving this way."

Janet said, "Our freedom was short-lived."

"All freedom is temporary," I said as I looked for another escape route.

Until yesterday, I had never been in a gunfight. I had managed to avoid all physical violence during a twenty-year career in the intelligence business. Now, in the past twenty-four hours, I've become an experienced shootist.

It was my little voice stating the obvious—again.

I announced, "That door is the only way out. Looks like another gunfight."

"Maybe, but I think we can cut the odds more in our favor," said Tom.

"How?" Janet asked.

Tom didn't miss a beat. "We invite them to the party."

"You've done this before, haven't you?" I said.

Tom laughed. "Well, it does remind me of last year in Iran."

"How did you get out?" asked Janet.

"We had friends who blew the place up, and a helicopter that was invisible," answered Terry.[2]

I said, "Like I believe that!"

Tom laughed. "She's telling you the truth. If we live through this, I'll tell you all about it over a few beers, but right now I want to invite these guys to our party." He walked over to the door, boldly opened it, and stepped out into the hallway.

"Hi, guys!"

---

[2] In *Nemesis Syndrome*, while hunting for Crassman, Tom and Terry were trapped in a super-secret subterranean Iranian weapons facility. They conned and fought their way past hundreds of Iranian security forces, escaping to the surface, and finally escaped from Iran in a stealth helicopter.

61

COME INTO OUR DEN

Tom still wore a security guard's uniform, which caused the approaching bad guys to hesitate. "We can use your help. These interlopers have made a couple escape attempts. Could you give us a hand?"

"We heard gunshots," said the apparent leader.

"That's what I'm saying. We had to shoot him in the leg."

"I heard more than a single gunshot," said the leader.

I guess he can count past one.

I had edged up to the doorway, listening to the exchange. Terry had taken up position on the other side of the door. Janet had taken partial cover behind a dumbbell rack across the room. Her pistol was aimed at the doorway.

The new arrivals approached in a single file. The first knuckle dragger warily stepped across the threshold into the exercise room, his pistol sweeping left to right.

Terry adeptly stabbed her recently acquired Taser into his neck. There was the intimidating crackle of electricity. I caught him and took possession of his pistol. Terry helped me drag the stunned thug into the corner. I motioned for Janet to come over. "Search him for weapons and tie him up."

We could hear Tom outside, talking to the remaining thugs.

We dashed back to the doorway just as the second knuckle dragger stepped through the doorway. Terry punched him in the chest with her Taser. She seemed to be holding the Taser a few beats longer. For some reason, the second guy didn't seem as affected.

Taking a cue from my brother's playbook, I hit him aside the head with my heavy Colt. There was a solid-sounding thump and he went down. I caught his body before it hit the floor and dragged him into the corner, next to his buddy. "Here's another for your collection," I said to Janet who was finishing up with the first guy.

Janet lashed the second guy's hands and feet while I searched him for weapons. In doing so, I learned he was wearing a bulletproof vest, which had apparently insulated him somewhat from the Taser's effects.

I rushed back to the door, ready for our next guest.

The last two knuckle draggers were holding back, reluctant to pass through the doorway. They hadn't seen the fate of, or heard from, their comrades and they were suspicious. The talking model, who could also count past one, stood back from the doorway, seeking the safety of the hallway.

"What's going on in there?" he asked in a loud voice.

Tom peeked inside the door and shouted, "Oh crap! They need help! Get in here now!" He ran into the exercise room, allowing the hall door to begin closing.

It worked. The two remaining knuckle draggers jumped to catch the door before it closed and rushed into the room. Their pistols were up and ready to fire.

The next sequence took only seconds, start to finish.

Terry hit the leader in the neck with her Taser, but she was out of charges and nothing happened to her intended victim.

Instead, the leader swung his pistol, knocking Terry to the floor. Then he immediately swung his pistol at my brother's face but Tom faded back just far enough to make him miss.

Both Tom and I jumped forward, but there's no beating my brother at this kind of combat. He hit the leader who fell without a whimper. He was out cold.

The second bad guy brought his pistol up to fire, but I was close enough to slap his hand down again with the Colt. He dropped his gun. My brother jumped forward, hitting the bad guy on the jaw before he could recover. The bad guy staggered back but didn't go down. Tom hit him a second time and he collapsed. Now both bad guys were on the floor, not moving.

It was over.

"Disarm and tie them up," ordered Tom as he hurried to the door and peeked out to see whether others were coming.

We quickly added the knuckle draggers to our collection. That made six living prisoners not counting those upstairs in the suite.

Then I remembered I had been late checking in with Jackson. I made the call with the satellite phone. Jackson said he had been preparing to come find us. It took a few minutes of conversation, and not saying the code phrase, to convince him we didn't need him to rescue us.

What could one man do, anyway?

By this time Gerald had regained consciousness and was struggling to free himself.

Terry stepped forward, pointing her pistol casually at his genitals, and softly purred, "If you cause trouble, I'm going to shoot them off."

I was convinced she meant it. I think he was convinced too because he stopped struggling.

My brother laughed softly as he took another look outside for more potential guests in the hallway.

I moved next to Terry and said, loud enough to be sure Gerald could hear me, "If you really want to, you can shoot his nuts off anyway. He was going to let that other guy castrate me."

Gerald shook visibly. I could see the fear in those bright eyes.

I decided it was a good time to get information from him. I asked, "How many bodyguards and security men are there—total?"

Silence . . .

Terry aimed her pistol at his crotch.

He said, "I don't know, and I wouldn't tell you if I did."

My brother closed the door and announced, "There's no one else coming down the hallway right now. But I think we should get out of here while we can."

"What do we do with these guys?" asked Janet.

"Double-check their bonds and leave them here," said Terry.

"No!" I snapped, maybe a little too emotionally. "If we do, they'll be freed by their buddies, and we'll have to fight them again."

Tom said, "I agree. We don't want to fight the same battle twice."

Janet said, "We could kill them."

We all looked to her—even the hawkish Terry—with surprise.

- 300 -

Terry was smiling as she said, "I'm in!"

The room fell still, very quiet. I could see the fear in the conscious knuckle draggers' eyes. We had their attention.

I asked, "Where did that come from, Janet? You weren't like that before."

Janet answered, "Recently, I've done a lot of things that weren't me . . . starting with Sprout at your retirement party?"

The others looked to me with questions on their faces.

"I don't know what she's talking about! Do I, Janet?"

Tom broke into the conversation. "We aren't going to murder them. We'll take them to the suite and leave them tied up with the others."

"Then we need blindfolds and gags," said Janet.

It was decided.

62

LET'S NOT LEAVE QUIETLY

Tom took point, making sure the coast ahead was clear, while the rest of us herded the restrained and blindfolded prisoners. Apparently, the meeting was still going, because we made it to our room without encountering any problems.

Inside the prisoner suite, we found the captured security guards where we left them, on the floor, but squirming around in an attempt to get free. They stopped moving as we entered.

Tom stood over the group with the M-4, reclaimed from where it had been stored in the adjoining suite. Tom vaguely pointed the intimidating assault weapon at the group of thugs, as he said softly—almost growled—through gritted teeth, "I need you to stay put—no wiggling around. The alternative is you never wiggle again."

Tom makes a good impression of Dirty Harry—even looks a little like Clint Eastwood when he was younger.

That's when I announced, "These guys are wearing bulletproof vests."

"So?" replied Tom.

"So let's use them. It'll give us an edge," I answered.

"I'm not untying them to get their vests off," Janet said.

"You don't have to. Bulletproof vests use Velcro. We can strip the vests off without untying them," said Tom.

I double checked the zip-ties. After I was sure they would keep, I said, "Okay, gentlemen, these are your accommodations for the evening. We have spared no expense. You may also notice we have the Disney Channel running for your entertainment. We didn't choose the porno channel, because we thought doing so may make you uncomfortable, being tied up and not able to give yourself any relief. Also, I'm sorry to say that the bar is closed and room service is not available at this time." I walked over to the telephone and yanked the wire from the wall—something I hadn't thought to do before. I finished with, "So make yourself as comfortable as possible, and let me remind you that attempts to escape will be looked upon very unfavorably."

After one more check of the bonds to ensure our guests were unlikely to get free, our little band of interlopers retired to the adjoining suite. We closed the connecting door so the prisoners couldn't hear us talking and wouldn't know whether we had gone.

Tom sighed and asked, "Suggestions how to proceed?"

"I need a drink!" Terry walked over to the bar and began making herself a drink.

"Me too!" Janet joined her.

It occurred to me the two women were very much alike and had formed a bond over the past twenty-four hours.

I said, "Is there an ice pack in the refrigerator? I could use something for my head."

Janet inspected my face. "You sure could. It's turning several colors of blue and black . . . and there is swelling. I guess Gerald hit you pretty hard."

"More than once," I shot back.

Janet returned to the bar and found a plastic bag and filled it with ice. She came back and gently pressed the ice against my head. At first it hurt, but then it began to feel better.

"Thank you."

"You should take better care of yourself," she said softly. Then she returned to the bar, where Terry had poured them both a glass of whiskey. Janet took a long drink.

I said, "Go easy on that stuff. We're not out of the woods yet."

Janet said, "What do you mean? We get into the car and drive away."

Terry said, "I agree. We live to escape and tell our stories to the authorities. Let them finish this. We're done!"

I exchanged glances with my brother and then announced, "We're not leaving yet."

Terry asked, "What do you mean?"

My brother said, "John's right! We have one more thing to do."

The women turned from the bar and waited silently for him to explain.

Tom bowed to me. "You want to explain it to them?"

I nodded and explained, "We're going to find Fetterson's cabin and retrieve Bigfoot, the atomic bomb. We have no choice. If we don't, the next time we know its location will be when Washington DC blows up."

63

WE HAVE A PROBLEM

I held the ice pack against my head as I looked through a crack in the blackout curtains, appreciating the peaceful scene outside. The evening sun was about to set on another day and the snow had stopped falling for now. The reddish glow reflected off the unspoiled carpet of white snow that covered everything. The scene was a post card picture—beautiful.

Best of all, there were no search parties tramping around the countryside or making room-to-room searches inside the hotel. For the moment it appeared they were not looking for us. Maybe the bad guys were so involved in their meeting they didn't know we were free yet.

More or less.

My brother was standing outside on the balcony, studying the lakeshore with binoculars. I stepped out into the cold evening air and announced, "Hey there!"

"Hey!" he replied.

"Figure which cabin is Fetterson's yet?" I asked.

"Not yet."

"So, what are you thinking?" I asked.

My brother sighed. "Just before you came out here I was thinking that living in the breech is becoming normal for me."

I laughed and said, "It has been less than twenty-four hours. Where's your stamina, little brother?"

"Not just this . . . I'm looking back over the years. My life has been one battle after another against evil ever since I joined the army. This is just the latest chapter," he answered.

"You were fighting bad guys before the army."

"What do you mean?" he asked.

"Remember in your sophomore year of high school when you got suspended for beating up those three seniors who were picking on little Jimmy Franks? Dad asked you why you got into the fight, and you said, 'They were calling Jimmy bad names and picking on him, and he wasn't strong enough to protect himself.'"

"Yeah, Dad just smiled at me and said, 'Well, next time let the other guy throw the first punch so you can claim self-defense.'" Tom was laughing.

I laughed too, and then there was a moment of quiet before I said, "Well, if there is any truth to reincarnation and Karma, your next life will be totally stress-free—no problems. You'll come back as a monk who plants crops and prays all day."

Tom grunted. "That's for certain . . . I'm experiencing enough conflict for ten people in this life." Then after a moment he asked, "If I'm going to be a monk, what do you think you'll come back as?"

I thought for a moment and then said, "Either a Sagittarius, or possibly an Aries."

"Huh?"

I explained, "Well, both star signs are generally known for their uncompromising honesty regardless of the consequences for telling the truth. I've spent this life lying and misinforming everyone. Lying is a cornerstone of my profession. So next time, I'll be brutally honest to make up for it."

"Maybe you'll be a monk too."

We both laughed, even though it hurt me to do so.

Terry and Janet joined us at that moment. Apparently, they had overheard enough of our philosophical discussion to join in.

Terry said, "Well, if there is such a thing as reincarnation and Karma, I'll come back as a pacifist—no conflicts and no violence. I'll be a monk who can't even kill a deadly spider or a snake."

Janet laughed. "I'll be celibate—no sex. I've definitely strayed far from the innocent little girl I started as in this life."

My brother chuckled and said, "Well, maybe we'll all be monks at the same monastery. That way we can be together!"

We all laughed.

I caught Janet's eye. She returned the gaze. For an instant, I think she was sending me a tender message. Then her eyes shifted to my brother. Tom and Terry were kissing. The balcony had suddenly become smaller. It felt like Janet and I were intruding, but they didn't seem to care.

I said, "No time for that now, kids."

They separated but continued staring into each other's eyes. I knew at that moment what real love was. I could see it clearly with my brother and his wife.

I could see that Janet was thinking the same thing. Our eyes touched again. I felt real affection there—not the rough-and-tumble, lighthearted sex-and-fun games she and I had shared over the past couple years. It was a little scary because it was too real for me. I looked away and then back at her. Janet's expression mirrored mine. She was feeling it too—having the same thoughts—the same doubts.

Before I realized what I was doing, I stepped forward and kissed her. Doing it seemed natural at the moment.

She kissed back.

Tom said in a soft voice, "Hey, big brother, I thought you said we didn't have time for that."

We all laughed, as we watched the sun officially drop below the mountain ridge to the west.

Terry said, "Let's go back inside—it's cold!"

Inside, I began to focus on our problem again. "So, little brother, you're the master military and police tactician ... how do we handle this?"

Terry said, "Let's call the FBI Hostage Rescue Team. They work for Tom and could be here in two hours."

Janet shook her head. "I'm guessing they won't be allowed to come. The Order probably has people high up in the FBI too."

"Even if they did respond, they may not get here fast enough. All Fetterson has to do is put the bomb on a helicopter and fly away, and we have lost," said Tom. "But I have an idea."

We listened to his plan, made a few suggestions, and then agreed. We needed to move fast; while we still had surprise on our side—before the Order had a chance to move against us with a plan of their own.

There were a few problems. We didn't know which cabin had the bomb, and we couldn't just go down to the registration desk and ask. We were stumped. Also, there were six helicopters sitting on the helipad; anyone of them could be used by Fetterson to escape with Bigfoot. We had to stop that from happening.

I said, "We need to disable the aircraft first."

"Let's blow them all up!" said Terry.

"No, I think something more subtle will be better," said Tom.

"What do you have in mind?" I asked.

In the excitement I forgot to call Jackson for a check-in.

64

ONE MORE TIME, INTO THE BREECH . . .

We slipped out of our suite and strolled through the hotel lobby as if we belonged. No one challenged us during our trek. In fact, we only saw two people. Both were resort staff working at the registration desk, and they paid us no attention. We exited the same rear service entrance we had originally entered early this morning.

It was almost full dark outside and the undersized street lamps had automatically lit up. We crossed the paved backstreet, passed between the maintenance building and the parking lot, and then turned right and took a circular route behind the parking lot through the woods. At about the halfway-point, we crossed an ice-cold stream that was knee deep. After that my feet quickly became numb, especially dragging them through the fresh snow. I was about to give up when we reached the helicopter pad.

I stomped my feet on the frozen concrete landing pad, trying to return circulation.

"That stream was intense," said Tom. Then he laughed like he was having fun. "Reminded me of the survival course I did in Alaska. I nearly froze my butt off that time." He laughed again.

"Well, I never had freeze-my-ass-off survival training and I'm not dressed for this—especially in these civilian dress shoes!" I shot back.

My brother laughed again and replied, "Suck it up! You're not dead." Then he inspected the nearest helicopter: a Bell 505 Jet Ranger X. The bird was painted bright red, white, and blue with no visible corporate markings.

Tom said, "I like this one. It's almost brand new and easy to fly—also easy to sabotage. It has a ramjet engine that depends heavily on compressed air to ignite the main combustion chamber." He handed me the duffel bag containing the M-4 rifles that he had been carrying and said, "You guys keep watch. This won't take long if I can find a wrench."

At that moment, the helipad's flood lights clicked on, illuminating the aircraft. I jumped and my heart began racing, thinking we had been discovered, until I realized the lights were automatically activated by light sensors in response to dark.

I stepped away from the floodlight and opened the duffel bag, removing the two rifles. Terry claimed hers and I took Tom's. Janet had her pistol. We each slipped behind an adjacent aircraft, making a rough circle around the helicopter Tom was working on.

Tom found a toolbox in a side panel on the Bell helicopter. He selected a wrench then opened a second panel. His arms disappeared inside the aircraft. He was talking as he worked. "I'll disable the combustor by plugging up the primary air-intake-injection hose with this bullet cartridge." He held up a bullet as a visual aide to his lecture. "The bullet happens to be the perfect size to block airflow without being sucked inside the combustor, which could be disastrous . . . There now, this bird won't start, and they won't know why without a complete diagnostics. Later, if we need to fly this bird, it will only take about a minute to unplug it."

"You know how to fly this helicopter?" I asked as my eyes swept the far side of the meadow, watching for anyone approaching from the main resort.

Tom said, "I've never flown this particular model, but the Bell 505 Jet Ranger X is billed as one of the easiest helicopters there is to fly. I should be able to handle it." He closed the panels but slipped the wrench into his pocket. "Let's do the others."

Terry came over and peeked inside the passenger cabin. "It looks too cramped for all of us."

"We can make it work, or we can use another," answered my brother.

It took about thirty minutes to disable all six helicopters.

Tom was working on the last one when Janet announced in a muffled voice from the shadows, "Three men coming across the field!"

I brought the rifle up. I really didn't want to shoot anyone. Not because I'm softhearted, but because I knew the shots would alert the entire resort. There had to be a better way.

Janet said what I was thinking. "We shoot them; it'll bring the whole resort down on us."

Terry hissed from behind another helicopter. "Well, you better think of something fast, because they are definitely coming this way."

We were at the far end of the parked helicopters, so the approaching group would have to pass several well-lit birds before getting to our location. We had all found dark shadows for extra concealment.

I turned to ask my brother what he wanted to do, but he was gone.

Where did Tom go?

"Hold your fire!" I instructed in a loud whisper.

We waited.

I put the M-4 down, leaning it against the landing struts of the aircraft I'd been using for cover. I stepped into the open, with my empty hands in clear sight, but I was hugely aware of the Colt Peacemaker stuffed in the small of my back—just in case.

Where was Tom?

I greeted the approaching men, "Hi there!"

They stopped in a pool of light about twenty-five feet away.

Not too bright.

That's when I recognized the man in front—the British speaker. The one they called Administrator—the meeting's facilitator. He did not appear to be armed.

The other two men were just more faceless knuckle draggers that I seem to be encountering much too often lately, and they both had suddenly produced pistols that were aimed at me.

"Wait! Everybody wait!" I said as I raised my hands in the universal sign that I was unarmed and not a combatant. To tell the truth, I was more concerned that Terry and Janet would blow the thugs away than I was the thugs would shoot me.

Everyone was still for several seconds.

Finally, the Administrator spoke, "Well, if it isn't the troublesome Mr. Wolfe. You do seem to have the ability to slip away and then reappear under the most impossible of circumstances, sir."

"All we want to do is get away. Let us go and this will be over," I said.

"Oh, I'm sure that's what you wish, but I'm afraid that is quite impossible."

"What do you want from me—the PM Program codes and frequencies?" I asked, stalling.

Tom has to be near.

"We would appreciate your little program, but that is not our major concern, because we'll eventually get it anyway—after we control the country. More importantly, we can't have you venturing out, telling others about Project Underground State or the Catalytic Activation—can we?"

It was at that moment that my brother appeared from behind one of the helicopters they had passed. Tom quietly walked up behind the three, stopping arm's length away. He didn't bother to tap anyone on the shoulder to give fair warning like they do in the movies. He just hit the closest knuckle dragger in the back of the head. The thug fell, his face buried in the snow.

Must be my brother's trademark—one punch–one KO.

Before the second thug could bring his pistol around, Tom was already on him. He grabbed the gun barrel and twisted it, shoving the muzzle hard into the knuckle dragger's stomach. I heard a muffled shot and saw the knuckle dragger double over and fall to the ground.

The Administrator turned as if he were about to flee when Terry stepped out from behind the helicopter and said, "I wouldn't, Englishman."

The Administrator stopped and put his arms up. "All this violence isn't really necessary, I assure you."

"Anyone have any zip ties left?" I asked.

Janet answered, "No, we've used them all." She had appeared from behind another helicopter.

Tom said, "Use his belt to tie his ankles together and his shoelaces for his hands."

We bound the Administrator with his own belt and shoelaces. Then we did the same to the two knuckle draggers, even the one who had been shot.

"Sit on the ground and don't move." Tom gave the Englishman a gentle push, knocking him down onto the snow-covered tarmac.

"That wasn't necessary," complained the Englishman as he struggled to a sitting position.

Janet asked, "What are we going to do with them?"

I said, "Yeah, we're collecting quite a population of prisoners."

The thug that my brother knocked out began moaning. I bent down and said softly, "Be quiet and we won't hurt you again."

Terry inspected the man who had been shot and announced, "We have a body to dispose of. Too bad he committed suicide, shooting himself in the stomach like that."

Terry has a morbid sense of humor.

Tom sighed, letting out a long stream of air, and then said, "I don't want to haul any more prisoners back to the hotel. It's too dangerous."

Terry said, "We could shoot them."

Janet shook her head. "No, let's stuff them all into the cargo wells of the helicopters."

Tom said, "Roger that, each in a different bird, so they can't help each other get loose. It should hold them as long as we need."

I indicated the Administrator and said, "Except him; I have some questions for this guy."

Tom shook his head. "Getting him back through the lobby is too risky, and we can't question him out here."

I insisted, "He knows all their secrets, like where to find Fetterson's cabin and the details of their plan."

Janet said, "I agree. We should have a quality talk with the Englishman."

Terry said, "They're right, Tom."

"Okay, we'll take him," agreed my brother. Then he addressed the Englishman directly. "But if you give us any trouble, I'll snap your neck and stuff you into a laundry cart for housekeeping to find, understand?"

"Rest assured I will be the model of cooperation."

It took a few minutes of considerable effort for Tom and I to toss the two thugs—one dead from a self-inflicted gunshot and the other semiconscious—into the baggage compartments of two separate helicopters.

The trek back to the hotel was a reverse version of the trip to the helicopter pad, including the frozen creek. No one complained—not even our British friend—so I didn't either.

It was pitch black—no moon—by the time we entered the hotel through the rear service entrance. Strangely, the facility almost seemed abandoned, and we encountered no one as we and climbed up the rear stairway to the second floor. As we entered the suite, I said, "Close the suite's blackout curtains before turning on the lights."

We seemed to be having some good luck. It made me nervous.

65

A NO-WIN SITUATION

The first order of business was to check on our guests in the adjoining suite. We had assembled quite a collection of prisoners. I opened the door and saw Heavy Boy—the first security guard we'd taken prisoner when we arrived—hopping around the room. He was apparently looking for a way to cut his ties. He stopped his jumping dance and stared at me. His expression looked like a little boy caught stealing cookies from the cookie jar.

I turned back to the others in the adjoining suite and announced, "Hey, come look at this. The big guy has taken up dancing to entertain his buddies."

Tom came to the doorway. "Explain to him he's not to provide entertainment."

I walked up to the heavy security guard and said softly, "Hop back to your assigned place."

He hopped back across the room, but before he could let himself down easy, I shoved him hard from behind. He crashed—face first—into the coffee table. It broke under his weight. I could tell the fall had hurt him, but it hurt the table more.

"Listen carefully, all of you. The next time somebody tries to escape or sound an alarm, you all will die."

A lie, but they don't know that.

I continued, "We can't be worrying about you. It's easier if you're dead." I gave them all my best impersonation of a tough guy and then quietly left the room, closing the adjoining door behind.

Tom had been standing just inside the connecting doorway, backing me up. After the door was closed, he said softly so the Englishman couldn't hear him, "That was good. I even believed you."

We sat the Administrator on the sofa in our suite. His arms were still tied behind him.

I said, "Sorry I can't make you more comfortable, but this will have to do."

Terry stepped in. "Why are you treating him so gently? Strip his clothes off and give him a taste of what Gerald and his friends were going to do to you."

I saw fear in the Administrator's eyes. The good-cop-bad-cop game was on.

I announced, "I just want to have a quiet talk with our British friend. I'm sure we can be civilized. Now, why don't we start with your name—your real name—so I can properly address you."

My brother shouldered past me, looming over him, and said harshly, "Nice will take too long. We don't have the time. I'll interrogate him!" Tom seemed ready to tear the Administrator's arms off, not his clothing like Terry had offered.

They've done this before.

I stifled a grin and said, "Let me try first. If he doesn't cooperate, then you can have a run on him with your violent ways."

The Administrator said, "There's no need for this, gentlemen. I will freely tell you about any subject you wish. My name is Sir Jonathon Quail. I live in London but have a summer home in Manchester. My family has what you would call old money, from textiles and shipping, primarily accumulated in the eighteenth and nineteenth centuries. Our family fortune took a marginal dip in the twentieth century, during the first and second World Wars, but I am recovering nicely at present, largely due to my involvement in microcircuits. My company manufactures circuits in Shanghai and ships them to Mexico where they are assembled into various electronic devices and sold all over the world. It is really quite innovative. We take—"

"Shut up!" I heard myself say.

"Well . . . I thought you wanted me to talk?"

"Right, but I pick the topic, not you," I answered.

Easy, I'm supposed to be the good guy.

There were several moments of silence, and then I realized everyone was waiting for my first question. The problem is I hadn't planned this out very well. I was stumped. Then I thought, *Start with the latest first.*

"What were you and those two thugs doing at the helicopters?"

"I'm also a pilot. I was going to prepare my aircraft to fly out."

"Why?" I asked.

"Does it matter?"

Terry stepped in closer and said, "Yes, if you want to keep all your parts attached, it matters."

"No need for such threats. We can be civilized, young lady."

Terry said, "Well?"

"If you must know, I didn't want to be present for the violence that is about to be brought down upon you." Incredibly, he was smiling.

"What violence?" I asked.

"They know you have escaped. They have organized search parties, with orders to kill you on sight," he answered.

"Why are you being so cooperative?" asked Tom.

Quail sounded confident when he explained, "Because there is no scenario where you and your band of misfits will prevail. Even if you manage to escape the resort, you won't last more than a day before we eliminate you. You're in a no-win situation."

The room became cold—still—as we each considered the Englishman's words.

66

MONEY AND POWER

I asked, "Would you care to explain that?"

Quail began, "People: such as me and the other ruling members of the Order—"

My brother broke in, "You mean the Order of the Golden Squirrel!"

Quail softly grunted. "Yes, we are really trying to get away from that. In our more mature years, we prefer simply the Order. But as I was about to say, regardless what transpires in the short-term, ultimately, we will win and you will lose. It has always been that way, and I don't foresee it changing."

I asked, "How do you figure?"

"Money and power always wins over poverty. It doesn't matter that poverty's cause is just and righteous."

"I heard this little speech last year from Crassman just minutes before the top of his head splattered all over the ceiling," said Tom. "You telling it again won't convince me any more now than it did then."

"Yes, Vernon and I had this discussion on several occasions." Quail sighed. "Although he was a crude and barbaric man, I did enjoy our spirited talks over a glass of bourbon. I miss him to some extent."

Terry snorted. "Please don't start crying, Sir John." She had placed extra stress on his name, sounding sarcastic.

"It isn't necessary to refer to me as Sir John. That's more of an honorary title in these modern times," said Quail.

"Money and power always wins. Let's get back to that." I was interested in how he thought.

Quail nodded and then said, "Let's approach this from a perspective you may be able to identify with, something you are no doubt familiar with: recent movies of comic book heroes and villains, which are so popular in today's shallow, I-want-it-fast, culture."

Was that an insult?

He fell silent.

I felt impatient, so I said, "Keep talking."

"Take, for example, the recent movie, *Superman versus Batman*, I believe it was titled. For some obscure reason these two superheroes become adversaries. I did not buy into the plot, but their battle climaxed with Superman's death. Given Superman's powers such an outcome is not logical. Superman was clearly more powerful than Batman in every measurable way, and arguably had a more righteous cause than the dark-spirited Batman. Superman could have easily killed Batman, literally with a flick of his little finger. But did he? No, instead Superman allowed himself to be defeated by Batman."

"How does that relate to money and power winning over righteousness and poverty?" I asked.

"Well, to understand that we need to look at each of these men— who are they, really? Superman purposely did not possess material riches, although he could easily have used his super powers to do so. Arguably, Superman represents the poor antagonist. Batman, on the other hand— as Bruce Wayne—is a multibillionaire. In fact, extreme wealth is Bruce Wayne's only superpower. He uses money to buy his toys. So in the end the man with the money wins over the man without money."

Terry quipped, "That's perverted."

"It's only a movie, not reality," Tom said. "And didn't some monster kill Superman, not Batman?"

Quail smiled and said, "Semantics, and I find most fiction is based on reality—even the most radical notion has some basis in reality."

"I'm not convinced," said Terry.

Quail studied my beautiful and deadly sister-in-law, and then replied, "In that case, let's take another example. Another recent movie—I believed was titled *Avengers-Civil War*, or something like that. In this case, Captain America battles Iron Man. Captain America is not as powerful as Superman, but he's still a formidable opponent with many superman-like qualities. Iron

Man, on the other hand, is simply another billionaire who can afford a high-tech metal suit. Again we have the ultra-rich versus the pauperish-but-righteous man. Captain America was clearly the superior warrior in every category. He could have simply waited for Tony Stark to remove his tin suit and squashed the billionaire like a bug, just like Superman could have done to Batman at any time. But neither superhero did this. Who wins the battle of Captain America versus Iron Man? Iron Man. Why? Someone with no money is fighting someone with billions of dollars. The man with the money will always win, and money will always prevail."

"Those were only movies for the simple-minded, and not very well-plotted movies at that," said Tom.

"Well-plotted or not, I find they mirror reality."

"What about right and wrong? I believe that the righteous cause will prevail, even over money," I said.

"Not true. Iron Man's motivation was revenge. He wanted to murder Captain America's best friend. On the other hand, Captain America's motive was to stop Iron Man from murdering his best friend. Captain America clearly had the more righteous cause—to save a life. In Superman versus Batman, it could be argued that Batman was eliminating his competition as top superhero on Earth. Batman didn't want Superman's superior skills upstaging him on Earth. Superman, on the other hand, wanted to stop a monster from destroying mankind. Superman's motive was clearly the more righteous."

"You're saying that righteousness cannot prevail over money," I said.

"Exactly! Money always wins—even if the righteous path is backed by supermen." Quail paused. "Just like me. Just like the Order. Wealth will always prevail over poverty. Therefore, you have no chance."

Terry stepped forward and whispered, "What if you commit suicide? Would you still prevail?"

"I assure you, I have no intention of killing myself."

"Mishaps happen . . . maybe you shoot yourself in the stomach like that guy back at the helicopter pad. Then we'll see if you still want to lecture us on your money-and-power theory."

Quail smiled, but said nothing.

Then it occurred to me; *Quail is stalling.*

I asked, "Where are Fetterson and the bomb?"

Why didn't I ask that earlier?

"I believe you can see the Senator's cabin from your window, on the lakeshore. It's the cabin closest to the main building," answered Quail.

I peeked through the blackout curtains and immediately identified the huge, mansion-style log cabin sitting on the lakeshore. It was maybe two hundred meters away and lit up like Christmas. I turned back to the room and announced, "Even from here I can see security guards posted around the perimeter."

Quail was smiling. "Yes, that would be the Senator's cabin, and that's where you will find Bigfoot. I believe he and the bomb are both still there—at least for the moment."

Quail is so confident—so arrogant.

67

SNOW COVERED JUNGLES OF VIRGINIA

After tying Quail up with the others, we exited the hotel through the service door at the rear of the resort, crept across the snow-covered pavement, and again slipped between the maintenance building and the parking lot. However, this time we turned left, passing behind the maintenance building before plunging into the dark, cold forest. Tom took point. I was number two. Terry and Janet were rear guard. Our destination was the cabin Quail had identified as Fetterson's. Our goal was to find Bigfoot—the atomic bomb, not the fabled hairy creature.

My breath vaporized in the frigid night air. I shivered. This was not a fun hike. To aggravate matters, I was still wearing my city-dweller's shoes, and my feet and toes quickly went numb again, causing me to stumble on the uneven terrain. I didn't have the proper clothing for this night hike, but it was too late to go back now.

We skulked from tree to tree, without flashlights. Tom moved as if he expected someone to take a shot at us at any moment. He didn't take a direct route to our destination. Instead, he led us deeper into the dark forest, away from the resort, and then after a hundred meters in the wrong direction circled in a huge arc back to the lake.

I didn't enjoy humping the boonies—never have, especially in the dark and freezing my butt off.

I stopped and checked to see whether the ladies were keeping up. They were fine—probably doing better than me. They were both wearing snow boots. Their feet were probably very warm.

I caught up to Tom and tapped him on the shoulder. "Why this route? The cabin is only about two hundred meters from the main lodge, but we've been walking nearly a mile."

"Too much open ground between the main lodge and the lake; someone would likely see us crossing." Then he pointed to the snow-covered ground. "Even if they didn't see us cross, we're leaving a trail of footprints a five-year-old could follow. Someone could come along behind and know we were headed to Fetterson's cabin. We'd be trapped."

He was right. It would have been stupid to walk directly to the cabin across the open, snow-covered field, but that didn't change the fact I was freezing.

My brother continued, "Also, there are too many guards on the resort side of the cabin. We're going around and approaching from a direction no one expects—the lake side. I'm hoping there will be fewer guards on that side and we'll have the advantage of surprise."

My little brother moved out ahead without waiting for my response.

All those years of sneaking and peeking had given him a set of skills especially suited for what we were doing tonight. So I just grunted agreement and fell in behind.

By now I couldn't feel my feet at all which, combined with the dark, caused me to slip on an icy flat rock and land on my back. I crashed to the ground without anything to soften the fall except a few inches of snow. I thought I was going to pass out but somehow managed to stay conscious.

I've had one too many blows to the head today.

My brother came back and pulled me to my feet. "You okay?"

"I think so . . . I just slipped on the icy ground. It's friggin' cold out here. My feet are numb; so are my fingers," I answered.

"Suck it up! We're almost there," snapped my heartless brother.

Janet moved up next to me. I could only see her shadowy form in the darkness. She whispered in a very soft and sexy voice, "Isn't this exciting?"

Maybe for you . . .

"I'm a city dweller, not a polar bear. I don't like stalking the snow-covered jungles of Virginia!" I answered as I followed my brother's path. Within a few yards I tripped over another rock. This time a pine tree managed to scrape my face as I reached out to catch myself.

Janet must have thought I looked funny, because I heard her giggle.

"This is not what I call fun!" I said, and then realized I sounded like some spoiled, weak kid.

Suck it up!

"What do you call fun?" she asked.

I answered, "Sitting in front of a cozy fireplace at my Old Rock House, with a bottle of wine and a beautiful—and willing—woman."

"I think that can be arranged," she whispered, and then gave me a light kiss on the cheek.

This dangerous skulking around is turning her on!

"Quiet!" Tom pointed at a sword-like beam of light cutting through the trees ahead of us.

We were almost to Fetterson's cabin!

I was confident that Fetterson was still there with Bigfoot. We'd disabled all the helicopters at the landing pad, and according to the road-conditions app on my phone, the only road leading out of the resort was closed due to a snow-and-rock avalanche earlier today. The road wasn't scheduled to open until tomorrow.

What we weren't sure of was how many knuckle draggers Fetterson had guarding the nuclear bomb.

As we closed to the edge of the tree line it became obvious the bad guys had turned on every light in the cabin—inside and out. The harsh light radiated far out into the surrounding forest, only broken up by the trees that created long slivers of black shadows projecting away from the cabin. On the upside, the light allowed us to see the best path while still concealing our approach in the black shadows.

I could see sentries walking the perimeter. They stayed on the same path, over and over, creating a well-beaten, circular trail about one hundred feet out from the cabin.

Tom edged up to the established path and crouched behind a large tree, in a black shadow. He had completely disappeared into the blackness.

I knelt behind a tree, mimicking his tactic, and the ladies took cover in the shadows farther back. We waited quietly.

I could feel my heart pounding in my chest, and my breathing picked up. For some reason I didn't feel cold anymore, but my toes were still numb.

There must be a lesson there.

I could hear men talking from several locations. Some were very close. If they heard an unfamiliar sound or a scuffle, they'd be on us in seconds.

Then I saw a man's silhouette approaching from the cabin. His moving shadow blocked each slice of light as he passed in front of the trees. He was walking directly toward Tom's position. I smelled cigarette smoke and then saw the glow of the cigarette. The approaching sentry was smoking while on guard duty—not very professional. He stopped about fifteen feet from my brother's position and turned back to look directly into the bright lights of the cabin. It was stupid. Now his night vision would be ruined. He'd be blind when he looked back to the dark forest. I knew my brother would know that and take full advantage of the opportunity.

This is clearly my brother's element. I watched with some admiration as he closed on the unsuspecting guard, using the blackness of the shadows to cover his approach. Tom moved quietly and effortlessly. He was so smooth and silent that the sentry never had a chance. Tom dragged the unconscious sentry behind a tree, making him invisible in the dark shadows, and then used the sentry's belt, bootlaces, and jacket to bind and gag him.

Tom waved for us to come forward. As we arrived, I couldn't take my eyes off the unconscious man lying in the darkness. The women were also studying the still figure.

It was Janet who suggested, "He'll freeze to death if we leave him lying in the snow."

Tom sighed, "I'm not carrying him—he's too big."

"Jonesy, where are you?" It was a second sentry, standing in a pool of light about fifty feet away.

We faded back into the darkness.

The second sentry walked toward our position, following the established footpath. He stopped about thirty feet away and stared into the dark tree line. He was suspicious and was being careful. His eyes swept back and forth, passing right over the position where we squatted behind two large trees that had grown together. He shouted again, "Jonesy, where are you? They just brewed some hot coffee—time for a break."

Tom casually stood and stepped out from behind a tree. "Had to take a piss . . ." he said in a muffled voice as he walked directly up to the second sentry, while keeping his face turned down. When Tom was maybe six feet away, the sentry said something like, "You ain't . . ."

My brother knocked him out before he could finish the sentence.

One punch—one KO . . . again.

Tom motioned to us. After we gathered around, he said, "That coffee sounds good. Shall we go to the kitchen and help ourselves?"

68

COFFEE ANYONE?

We tied up the second guard with his own belt and bootlaces, and then gagged him with his own jacket. Then Tom and I went back and dragged the first sentry out of the forest. We stacked them both together against a tree near the kitchen door, where they would be found before they froze—probably.

Janet and I took their rifles.

Tom identified them as H&K 416s. "They're high-end weapons . . . a lot of Navy SEALs like them." Then he added, "Dependable and easy to shoot."

Tom led the way into the cabin. The outside kitchen door was glass on the top half and heavy wood on the bottom. Tom peeked through the glass but saw no one inside. He glanced back at me and shrugged. We were expecting someone to open fire on us at any moment, but it was quiet and we entered the kitchen without being challenged. It was easy—too easy—and it worried me.

I said, "Something's wrong. If they have the bomb in here, you'd think it would be better protected."

We were all now in the kitchen, and sure enough, there was a fresh pot of coffee and four coffee cups set out on the center island. Four cups: the same number as our little war party.

They are expecting us.

Terry reached for the pot to pour herself a cup of coffee, but Tom swiped all four cups off the counter, smashing them to the floor. "Don't drink the coffee!"

"What the hell?" Terry shot back.

"There's a good chance the coffee is drugged. You'd wake up with a huge headache and a half-dozen thugs standing over you," he answered. "John's right! This is all too easy—too convenient."

"A trap!" said Janet.

There were two exits from the kitchen: the one we had entered from outside and another door on the opposite side, leading deeper into the cabin. I took a step toward the far, inside doorway. That's when a burst of automatic gunfire shattered the window over the sink and peppered the wood cabinets, ripping a dozen holes just inches from Terry's head.

We all dove to the floor.

Tom shouted, "Shoot the lights!"

We shot out the ceiling floodlights, plunging the kitchen into pitch-black concealment.

There was another long burst of automatic fire that ripped through the outside door, shattering the glass. Bullets crashed into the floor and hit the cabinet next to me. Their impact sounded like a ballpeen hammer punching holes into a wooden box. Exploding floor tiles peppered and cut my already-swollen face. I rolled several feet laterally to gain better cover behind the center island, but then some eager shooter fired another burst through the window from the opposite side of the kitchen, and I almost died again. The bullets exploded in a straight line; just missing along the length of my body. A couple of rounds grazed my pants leg but didn't hit flesh. I could see the others weren't any better off. Both Janet and Terry were huddled near the stove, unable to move or shoot back because of the unceasing, incoming fire. Tom was lying flat on the floor next to the interior door. Each time he peeked around the corner several shooters would open up from deeper in the cabin, forcing him to retreat.

We waited, not moving, because there was nothing else we could do at the moment. We were pinned down. The bad guys were playing it smart—staying out of sight, shooting from covered positions, and not giving us an opportunity to shoot back. Their assault was brutal—a serious attempt to kill us.

Another bunch of bullets zipped in through the hole that had once been a window, hitting more floor tile and wood cabinets. Fragments pelted me. A piece stuck in my left eye. It hurt like hell, and I couldn't open the eye without serious pain.

This sucks!

Tom shouted, "This way out!"

We crawled across the floor to converge at the interior door. A burst of automatic fire ripped through the doorway.

"You crazy? We can't go this way!" shouted Janet.

Tom said, "It's our best chance. I go through the door first and shoot left. John, you're number two—clear the right side of the room. Terry, you're number three—sweep the whole room center, left, right. Shoot anything that looks like a target!"

"Wait! I said. "I have something stuck in my eye. I can't shoot. I can barely see."

Janet worm-crawled over and put her finger to my eye. "I can see it. Looks like a chip of tile. It's just stuck in the corner. Let me get it."

A few seconds later she had the fragment out, but my eye was still sore.

"You good now?" asked Tom.

"I guess," I replied, not really feeling good.

Janet's voice was deep and quavered as she asked, "What about me? What do I do?"

Tom didn't hesitate. "You cover our rear and act as reserve. Anyone comes up from behind—shoot them. Stay here until we call for you."

Janet whispered, "What does the reserve do if things don't go well for you?"

"In that case, you have two choices: Come in shooting and try to save our asses, or run away and save your own. It's your call."

"There's no where I can run!" she shouted.

Tom just smiled.

My brother likes this shit!

I could see the fear in Janet's eyes, but I also saw determination.

Terry was tightly gripping her rifle, staring into the darkness of the next room, silently preparing herself.

I wanted to throw up.

Tom made eye contact with each of us then hissed loudly, "Okay then, ready? On three . . . one . . . two . . . Go!" He dashed through the doorway without checking to ensure we followed.

Terry and I were on his heels.

69

TRAPPED

The light was dim in the next room, because the lights were off, but the shooting started the instant we cleared the threshold. There were two bad guys inside the large room; both sprayed full automatic as we dashed inside, but we stayed low and their rounds passed over our heads. When we shot it was more accurate—at least Tom was. The distance between us and the two bad guys was maybe twenty feet—very close. Tom punched three shots in a straight line up the first shooter's midsection, while I hit the second shooter in the upper leg. My brother immediately shifted and put two more into the second shooter's chest.

I told you, I'm not a gunfighter.

A third man's silhouette appeared in the doorway at the opposite end of the room and began shooting. Terry responded reflex fast; hammering him from groin to face with a full-auto burst. He was slammed back against the doorway facing. His weapon clattered to the hardwood floor as he slid down and sprawled across the doorway.

We remained still for several moments, until we decided there was no one else to shoot.

Slowly, my brother stood up and walked to the nearest fallen man, kicking his weapon away and checking for a pulse. He announced, "This one's dead!"

Terry and I rose. I checked the body nearest to me, while she crossed the room and peeked through the doorway. She turned back to us and announced, "I see no one in the next room.

Janet cautiously entered. "Did we win?"

Terry asked, "Want me to turn on the lights?"

"No," said Tom. "It's light enough, and there's no point in making ourselves targets for anyone outside."

We were standing in a large, formal dining room with an elegant, twelve-place mahogany dining table at its center. A huge, acid-etched glass and mahogany hutch stood against one wall. It was filled with expensive-looking crystal. On the opposite side of the room was a huge, plate-glass window. I could see an awe-inspiring view of the moon that had just peeked over the ridgeline and was reflecting off the mirror surface of the lake. The image through the window was almost too perfect, as if it had been painted on a canvas by a master.

But there is no Senator Fetterson and no nuclear bomb.

"Did Quail lie?" I asked the group at large.

"Big surprise there," said Terry.

As if for an answer to the question, a burst of automatic fire erupted through the doorway the last bad guy had recently entered. It was joined by gunfire from the kitchen doorway. We dove for cover just as a third burst shattered the picture-perfect lake-view window. We were taking fire from three directions, but no one attempted to enter the room. They seemed content with staying in place and trying to kill us off from a distance.

"It's another trap!" shouted Janet.

"Same trap—part two," said Tom as he reached up and tipped the large dining table over to provide better cover.

We returned fire.

"I'm low on ammo," I shouted over the racket of crystal and glass shattering and the hammer punches of bullets slamming into the walls and splintering the dining table.

Tom slid a submachine gun across the floor to me. It had been liberated from a dead bad guy. "Use this!"

It was another H&K 416.

He slid a canvas bag to me. "Here are some extra magazines. Don't waste your shots. Set the selector to single shot."

Janet asked, "How many do you think we're up against?"

My brother said, "At least six, maybe ten."

It was Terry who said the obvious. "We're in their kill zone—right where they want us! We need to get out of here!"

I fired a couple of rounds with my new gun. I thought I'd seen a shadow pass across the threshold of the door I was covering, but I was an instant too slow and still had trouble seeing. My left eye was burning and itching, irritated from the floor-tile chip. My shooting was not accurate. I had shot behind the target as he passed by.

Tom shouted at me, "Lead the target, not where it is now!"

The incoming fire suddenly stopped.

Tom's head swiveled back and forth and then he said, "Terry's right. We need to get out of here. We're going out through this door, into the next room and out the front door. We have a better chance if we get outside and fight in the woods. Make sure you have a full magazine in your weapons." He looked around to ensure we were with him, then said, "Same order as last time . . . ready . . . Go!" Tom jumped up and ran through the doorway with his M-4 firing controlled, single-shot action.

I jumped up and followed. A bullet shattered the doorframe next my head. Something hit me in the neck. It burned like hell. At the time I thought I had been shot. It wasn't until a few minutes later, when I had time to pull it out, that I realized it was wood shrapnel from the doorframe.

We pushed into the great room, weapons hot, as they say in adventure and war stories. This room was huge—at least twenty-five by forty feet.

My brother dropped to one knee to make a smaller target. I mimicked him.

I have discovered that in these situations, time seems to slow down, giving a warrior an infinite amount of time to deal with multiple threats and perform unlimited actions—in a matter of speaking. At the same time everything happens so quickly you don't have time to think about what you're doing. Another curious fact is that I don't remember doing some things that I must have done, like slamming in a new magazine when I ran out of bullets or diving for cover when I was being shot at, or even returning fire in some cases. Actions go into some kind of automatic action mode, and the conscious mind checks out.

Subconsciously, I was aware my brother was kneeling on the left side of the doorway, firing at two bad guys hiding behind a large piano. I was kneeling on the right side of the doorway firing at several different targets in the great room. At the same time, I was somehow aware Terry was lying on the floor—prone between us—firing.

There was a bad guy hiding behind the large bar on the right side of the room. He was my responsibility, and I knew he was going take us all out if I didn't do something fast. I flipped the selector to automatic, stood up to get a better angle on him, and let loose a *hellrendous*—as opposed to horrendous—stream of bullets. On some level I knew that I shattered the bar, the mirror behind the bar, numerous bottles of fine liquor, and most of the bad guy's head and shoulders. I'd made a mess, but he was no longer a threat. I breathed a sigh of accomplishment.

That's when something hit me hard. It felt like a major league baseball player had hit me with a baseball bat. He'd knocked a home run into the center field bleachers. I became dizzy and lightheaded, and then everything went black.

I awoke lying flat on the floor with Terry and Janet fussing over me. Terry was pressing both hands really hard into my side, about where I'd guess my appendix is. Her pushing hurt like hell, and I was about to tell her to stop when the lights went out again.

The next time I woke, my midsection was bandaged, and Janet was sitting next to me. My brother and sister-in-law were occupied elsewhere, but for some reason I couldn't understand what they were doing. I had trouble focusing my vision or my thoughts. It was as if I couldn't get my eyes or brain to work.

Janet's smile pierced the fog. "Thank God you're back! I was so worried." She kissed me tenderly on the lips.

It felt nice. I could smell her unmistakably female scent, even with all the burned gunpowder in the air.

My sense of smell is still working.

Slowly, my head cleared, and I began noticing more details. All the lights in the cabin were still out, which explained why everything looked so dark. The only light was coming from the moon shining through the large picture glass window that looked out over the lake, with a similar view that the dining room window had. I could see my brother crouched by the bar. He seemed to be watching the huge window. Terry was behind a leather sofa, near the large fireplace. Her rifle was trained on the dining room entrance we had just shot our way through.

"What happened?" My voice sounded weak and hoarse.

My brother doubled over to keep a low profile and scurried to my side. He kneeled next to me and said, "You were stupid and stood up in a gunfight, so you got shot."

"Shot?" I looked down at the blood-stained bandage that felt too tight around my midsection.

Tom shrugged. "Yeah, but I think you'll be okay . . . just lost some blood. Apparently the bullet missed a big artery in that area, which is the good news. We managed to stop the bleeding before it became too serious. But it'd be a good idea to get you to a doctor soon."

My gut was cramping and waves of pain rolled through my abdomen. Also, it hurt to breathe deeply. I had an urge to sit up, but when I tried, the pain forced me to stop, so I lay back.

This sucks!

I asked my brother, "What's the situation?"

"Well, for about ten minutes it's been quiet."

"Haven't they tried to talk to us?" I asked.

"No, I don't think they want information from us anymore. They just want us dead," he answered.

"We should return the sentiment," I said, and coughed for my effort. Pain shot up my side and down my leg. My gut cramped up.

Coughing is a bad idea.

"I need to sit up. Will you help me?"

Tom and Janet reached under my arms and slowly pulled me to a sitting position, propping me against the wall. It was strange—if I moved a certain way there was no pain, but as soon as I twisted or bent the wrong way, the pain became unbearable. Right now, it felt better to sit up.

"My gun . . . could you hand it to me?" I said, feeling very vulnerable. The H&K 416 was lying about six feet away, where I'd apparently dropped it.

Janet checked the assault rifle, inserted a fresh magazine, and handed it to me. She looked very professional at it, yet I doubt she'd ever held a gun in her hands until yesterday.

Quick learner.

Janet asked, "Are you feeling a little defenseless?"

"I guess . . . getting shot apparently does that to you," I answered.

She bent over and kissed me on the lips. It was a long kiss. Then she whispered in my ear, "Don't die, John. I want you to live."

"So do I." I was struggling to stay conscious. I guess I couldn't afford to send blood away from my head.

"Ladies and gentlemen," said an amplified voice from outside the cabin. "As you can most likely ascertain, you are completely surrounded. There is no escape. We have also disabled the cell relay tower so you cannot phone for help. You are isolated."

It was Quail with his unmistakable British accent. They had found our improvised prison suite and released the captured people we had secured there. We were back to square one, maybe worse. Now they knew we were here and had us trapped in this cabin with superior numbers and firepower.

We're screwed.

Quail continued, "If you give yourselves up now, we won't kill you. We'll hold you until after the State of the Union address in January, and then we'll let you go free. You have my word."

This is the first week of December . . .

I said as loud and forceful as I could manage, "Bullshit! They aren't going to keep us safe and locked up for almost two months, then just let us go free. If we surrender we're dead!"

Terry said, "I agree! Our only chance is to fight our way out. Get into the woods."

"Agreed!" said Janet.

That's when I became the wet blanket. "I agree, but I'm low on ammunition and I'm shot. I can't go romping through the jungle, shooting it out with the bad guys."

Tom checked his rifle and announced, "I'm low too. Five rounds left . . . how about you, Terry?"

Terry announced, "I have six rounds left."

Janet said, "I have nine rounds."

One more exchange could find us defenseless.

My little voice was annoying.

"What's your answer?" asked Quail's voice on the megaphone.

I painfully raised my H&K 416. "Tom, take my rifle. You'll make better use of it. I can barely lift it. I still have my Peacemaker if it comes to that." I reached behind my back and pulled out the beautiful single-action .45.

At least I'll die with style.

I could see the sadness in Tom's eyes as he said, "I think the boys at the Alamo had better odds."

A short burst of automatic fire ripped through the room from outside.

70

SPRINGING THE AMBUSH

Quail barked at us over the megaphone, "You must be running low on ammunition and there is no escape. Give up now and we will spare your lives. We will provide you with medical attention if you require it. You have my word."

I asked, "How does he know we're almost out of ammo?"

"Or need medical?" added Janet.

Quail continued, "The members are leaving the resort at this moment. We have terminated the meeting early, so it will do you no good to resist. The Senator and Bigfoot will be gone soon."

I wonder . . .

I decided to conduct a test. I said in a clear voice, so everyone in the room could hear me, "I'm bleeding to death. I think I was hit in an artery."

Janet squawked, "What?" She inspected my wound.

My brother and Terry also rushed over.

I put a finger to my lips, signaling to be quiet, and whispered softly, "I think the cabin is bugged. They can hear everything we say . . . maybe video too. Just go with me . . ."

Tom grunted, and then said in a loud voice, "This is bad, brother. If we don't get you some professional attention, you could die."

"I can't stop it!" shouted Terry in an anxious voice with a smile and a wink, as she pretended to adjust my bandage.

A few moments later Quail's amplified voice was booming through the cabin again. "We have a doctor out here that can render medical care to anyone who may need it, if you surrender now, that is."

That confirms it!

My sister-in-law and Janet pretended to work on me while we spoke in whispers.

I laid out my idea.

Tom asked, "Are you sure about this?"

I answered, "I don't see an alternative."

Janet asked, "Do you think they'll go for it?"

I shrugged. The movement hurt, but not as bad as before. "We'll know in a minute."

Terry and Janet remained with me, while Tom faded back toward the dining room door.

Terry announced in a loud voice, "John's dying."

All according to plan.

I groaned, "I can't see . . ."

"John!" cried Janet as she vaguely fumbled with my bandage.

It was an Academy Award moment.

Quail's amplified voice filled the room with, "So what have you decided? Don't be sorry you wasted time."

They are definitely watching and listening.

Terry pronounced me dead. "Dear, John is dead."

Tom declared, "Those bastards will all pay for this!"

Janet left my body and found a covered position behind the bar.

Terry asked in a whisper, "You've got the most dangerous part. Sure you're up to it?"

I felt weak, but I had no choice. I faked a grin and answered, "Let's do this!" I slipped the Colt under my jacket, but kept my thumb on the hammer and my finger on the trigger and played dead.

Janet shouted from behind the bar, "Hey, everyone, I found a trap door! It opens to a tunnel. Looks like it leads away from the cabin. Maybe we can use it to escape!"

She should get an Oscar for her performance.

Tom openly ran across the room to her position. After a few seconds, he announced, "She's right! We can use it to get out of here! Get over here, Terry!"

Terry made a show of scrambling across the room and dropping down behind the bar. There was no trap door. It was part of the deception—called misdirection in the espionage world. After a few seconds all three low-crawled away from the bar, finding concealment behind the leather sofa near the fireplace. They waited silently.

. . . and waited.

More minutes passed.

They aren't buying it.

I heard a footstep in the dining room. It sounded like a boot crunching broken glass. Then on the other side of the cabin, I heard the front door open. The door's hinges squeaked. They needed lubricant.

A man shouted from the front door, "Anyone home?"

Someone has a sense of humor.

"Hello," he said. "Is it alright I come in?"

There was obvious anxiety in his voice.

I guess he doesn't want to be shot.

Then a third man shouted from the broken picture window, "There's only one guy visible. He's leaning against the wall . . . not moving. Want me to put a bullet in him to make sure?"

Nuts! That wasn't part of the plan.

I was about to start shooting when I heard Quail say, "No . . . no shooting unless necessary."

Thank you, Sir Jonathon.

Quail had answered from the front door, without the megaphone.

Quail's inside the house, leading the assault personally. I didn't think he was the hero type.

I remained still, squinting through my eyelids, waiting for someone to stand over me with hostile intentions. I heard more speaking in low tones from the direction of the front door. The main force must be entering from that direction. Then I heard more footsteps from the dining room.

A pincher movement . . .

Quail shouted, "Surrender now and no one else needs to be hurt."

Four men entered from the dining room. At the same time four more figures appeared from the front entryway.

Eight! We're seriously outgunned!

They entered from both ends as a single entity, and immediately spread around the room. I saw a shadow moving through the broken picture window—a ninth shooter. I was guessing it was the guy who had offered to put a bullet into me. He was now openly silhouetted in the window, with no fear of being shot. We were covered from all directions. It was a miracle that the others had not been detected yet.

I had an impulse to shoot the guy in the window—the one who had offered to shoot me.

Wait . . . You'll probably only get one shot . . . Make it count.

I felt very exposed. Every hostile weapon had to be pointed at me. I knew if I moved or tried to shoot, I'd be riddled with bullets, so I played dead; waiting for the right moment to spring the ambush.

It didn't take long. One of the bad guys walked over to the bar and searched for the fictitious trap door.

"Hey! There's no trap door here!" he shouted to his buddies.

Another thug said, "Are you sure? They had to go somewhere."

That was our signal. I shot the guy standing nearest me. I think from my low angle, it entered his groin and exited the small of his back.

The others rose up from behind the sofa and sprayed the remaining bad guys. The ambush was over in just a few seconds. All eight were down. None of them had fired a single shot.

Silence fell hard in the cabin. I could hear my ears ringing, but nothing else. Again, the smell of gunpowder filled my nostrils. I was really beginning to like the scent.

The stillness continued. There had been no reaction from outside the room. I think we caught them completely by surprise. Then I heard someone running out the front door.

Our British friend—Quail is a runner.

A round crashed into the wall next to my head. The plaster and wood exploded like a small hand grenade, peppering my already beat-up face and arm with wood fragments. I fired an instinctive shot, with my Colt Peacemaker. The shooter silhouetted in the window had returned to fulfill his offer to make sure I was dead. It had been his last mistake. I think I heard him say, "Nuts!" as he dropped from sight.

"Nice shot," said my brother as he lowered his rifle.

I had shot the guy in the window before my brother could fire!

I actually beat my brother to the draw!

But my self-congratulatory celebration was cut short by a blizzard of bullets that riddled the room from every possible direction. Tom, Terry, and Janet dropped flat to the floor to avoid instant death. I was still propped against the wall, with very limited ability to move.

Janet shouted, "I hate this!"

Terry yelled over the continuous thunder of rounds bombarding the room, "Yeah, this sucks!"

Tom said nothing. He had moved near the window and was selectively returning fire, trying to pick off our adversaries.

My head rotated back and forth, but I could see nothing to shoot at from my position. My side hurt like hell, but somehow with all the bullets crashing into the room that didn't seem so important at the time.

Janet shouted out, "There must be a hundred shooters out there!"

Tom shouted back, "No, I'm guessing maybe ten at the most."

We're in serious trouble.

71

IT CAN'T GET ANY WORSE—CAN IT?

The rounds continued crashing into the furniture and punching holes through the walls of the great room. There was nowhere safe in the room. Columns of exploding wood erupted from the floor. I attempted to crawl behind the sofa for better cover, but my side burned and my stomach cramped intolerably. The pain was severe, but I continued crawling across the floor, praying the incoming rounds would somehow miss me.

Terry called out, "I'm out of ammo!"

Janet shouted back," I have only two rounds left."

Tom yelled, "I'm down to four rounds, but we have the weapons from the guys we just shot!"

The shooting from outside stopped. Quail's megaphone voice said, "We're not coming in the cabin again. Surrender now and live! Continue your resistance and die! What is your answer?"

Quail's back outside, nagging us from a safe position.

I managed to ask in a hoarse voice, "What do we do now?"

Tom grinned and winked at me. "Well, look at it this way: it can't get any worse."

Quail's voice blasted over the megaphone again: "If you don't give up, we will burn the cabin to the ground with you inside. Surrender and live or burn to death: it is your choice!" Leaving the megaphone's push-to-talk button on so we could hear him, Quail said, "Find some petrol to burn the cabin!"

Janet asked, "Well, now we know how it can get worse. What are we going to do?" She sounded afraid.

I'm afraid too.

Tom didn't help with his response to her question. "We could die ... but dying by fire is supposed to be very painful." He let the sentence linger in the air for several seconds, before adding, "However, I don't plan to die today."

I asked, "You have a plan to get us out of this?"

"I'm working on it," he replied.

It's just bravado.

That's when I remembered that I hadn't checked in with Jackson for at least two check-in periods. My first thought was, *Crap, I don't have the time to keep checking in with Mother, telling her I'm all right—like some teenager on a first date.*

Then it occurred to me. *All is not well. Maybe it's a good thing I haven't called Jackson as scheduled.*

But what could Jackson do? He's only one man and almost a hundred miles away. The roads are closed because of snow and avalanches. And he doesn't even know which cabin we're trapped in. He could bring the Special Forces and Special Ops community—all his buddies—but they'd never find us before the cabin burns to the ground with us in it. We are still doomed!

Quail's men weren't shooting. There was no noise coming from outside.

I put on a forced grin and said, "They're not shooting. Maybe they're getting low on ammunition ..."

Tom and Terry actually laughed.

"I doubt that," said Janet.

We heard the distinctive sound of a helicopter warming up its engines.

Quail's voice was on the megaphone again. "Hear that? That is Senator Fetterson. He's leaving with Bigfoot. We managed to repair his helicopter."

We listened as the helicopter engine increased its RPMs.

Quail said over the megaphone again, "You've lost! Give up and we'll let you live."

Bullshit!

We could hear the blades spinning faster now. The helicopter was taking off. I thought I could hear a second helicopter lifting off too, but it could have just been the engine's reverberation bouncing back and forth between the hills surrounding the lake. The helicopter circled the resort once, making a low pass directly overhead, and then the engine sound faded until we couldn't hear it. The fainter echo of blades also faded, so maybe it hadn't been a second helicopter. Just an echo ...

The resort felt unnaturally silent after the thunderous gunfire and helicopter's *thump-thump-thump* sound faded.

Quail's amplified voice broke the silence with, "So what is your final answer?"

I reached into my cargo pants pocket and pulled out the satellite phone. I hit the speed dial code for Jackson. He answered on the first ring.

72

THE ROCKET MAN

"Have no fear! Rocket Man is near!" Jackson was laughing over the phone connection.

I had the satellite phone on speaker so the others could hear. I wasn't worried about Quail listening in any longer.

"Can you hold on for ten minutes—maybe twelve?" Jackson asked.

"Do we have a choice? Where exactly are you?" I asked.

"I just departed from the Old Rock House, but I'm making great time," he answered.

I asked, "How will you get here so fast?"

Jackson laughed again. "The only way to fly . . :" His voice faded in a rush of static and we were disconnected.

I announced to the others, "Jackson says he's coming to rescue us, but he just left."

"He'll never get here in time," said Terry.

"And he's just one man," added Janet.

My brother said, "Let me have the phone."

I handed the satellite phone to Tom.

Tom punched in a number and waited a few seconds before he said, "Musashi, this is Tom Wolfe. I need you." He didn't have the speaker on, so we could not hear what was being said on the other end. They talked a few moments then disconnected. Tom announced, "My Hostage Rescue Team from Quantico is coming, but we have to hold on for at least an hour, maybe two."

"We'll all be dead by then," said Janet.

We were on our own.

I suddenly felt as if I was about to have the mother-of-all-rolling-cramps in my intestines, and at the same time I needed to vomit. I was able to resist the urge to vomit, at least for now, knowing the violent action would be disastrous, but I had no control over the cramps. They hit me like a sledgehammer, striking full force in my stomach. I had a brief thought that the violent cramps and urge to vomit was triggered, or at least magnified, by the stress of our situation, but that knowledge didn't stop it from happening. I had little control. There was nothing I could do except double over on the floor and moan. I felt helpless.

Maybe if I stood up it would hurt less.

Janet was at my side, "What's wrong?"

Tom answered, "He needs to get to a hospital . . ."

Terry came over and checked my bandage. "He's not bleeding much, so that's good news."

"Externally . . ." said Tom.

"What?" Janet looked worried.

Tom explained, "He's not bleeding where it shows, but we don't know what's happening inside, where we can't see."

Hearing this doesn't make me feel any better.

Quail's megaphone voice filled the room. "We are pouring petrol on the outside walls—all around. Surrender before it is too late."

We saw a bright flash of light as the gasoline was ignited. The cabin was burning.

I said, "Help me stand up. If I'm dying I want to be on my feet with a chance to fight back."

Tom and Janet helped me up. I leaned against the bar holding my side.

The satellite phone beeped. Tom answered and listened for a few seconds, and then activated the speaker.

Jackson was talking. "This is Rocket Man. Mark your position so I can see you from the air."

"You're flying in?" asked Tom.

The answer came as a colossal thunderclap that shattered all remaining windows and crystal pieces in the cabin. The shockwave was born from a military jet breaking the sound barrier a couple of hundred feet above the lake's surface.

"Give me the phone," I shouted.

Tom handed it to me and I shouted over the connection, "We're in the burning cabin, surrounded by bad guys—danger close—360 degrees."

"Roger that! I see the burning cabin."

I said, "Wait! A helicopter took off about three or four minutes ago. If you can acquire him, shoot him down. He's carrying the head bad guy and an atomic bomb he plans to use on Washington, DC."

"An A-bomb on DC? I don't know . . . maybe that's a good thing." I could hear Jackson laughing. There was silence over the connection then he said, "Okay, if you insist . . . I've got a whirlybird on weapons radar. Consider him bug squish."

Overhead the roar of the F-100 faded in the same direction the helicopter had gone. We heard the distinctive chatter of the 20 mm Vulcan Gatling gun firing in the distance. Then the F-100 banked and seconds later the jet was again breaking the sound barrier over the lake. He'd only been gone about forty-five seconds.

Jackson must be flying with his foot to the floor.

"Down one bad guy and his whirlybird . . ." We could hear Jackson laughing over the speaker.

I was smiling. "Thanks . . . now clear a zone around the burning cabin so we can get out. Bring it in as close as you can."

73

PURGATORY ON EARTH

The F-100 was running without lights, making it invisible as it approached faster than sound, giving no warning of the impending slaughter. The first clue anyone on the ground had that the Super Sabre had attacked was when the earth erupted into massive, twenty-foot columns of dirt, rock, and fire. Jackson had meant the pass as a psychological shock, sacrificing accuracy for brute force. He wanted to put the bad guys on notice of the hell yet to come. Somehow, even at supersonic speed, Jackson managed to hit a SUV parked near the cabin. The explosion rattled the cabin walls and lifted the SUV into the air, crashing it down onto a clump of small pine trees. The pines immediately ignited, becoming a massive, roaring column of flames. A few seconds later, several adjacent trees caught and quickly became an inferno. The jet made another pass. The thunderclap of the Super Sabre nearly shattered our eardrums. Jackson was making his passes at speeds in excess of 800 mph. The sound-barrier shock-wall was so powerful that it knocked down trees and blew out the forest fires that he had just created with the incendiary rounds—like an immense child blowing out his birthday cake candles. We were experiencing the terrifying end of the Vulcan 20 mm Gatling gun, mounted on a supersonic delivery platform.

The four of us stayed huddled in the great room, watching the fireworks through the large opening that had once been a picture window.

I later learned that Quail had run away after Jackson's first pass, but more on that later.

Jackson made another pass. This time he slowed to gain accuracy. The Super Sabre slowed to near stalling speed over the lake, as he accurately placed the deadly 20 mm incendiary missiles, at the rate of six thousand rounds per minute, around the perimeter of the cabin. Jackson was stubbornly bending the Super Sabre to his will—emulating the Warthog. He was a master at flying the Warthog, which is designed to almost hover as it places rounds into its target.

Jackson made a tight turn and fired again. The snow-covered ground and dark-green forest exploded as men were smashed and vaporized by the powerful 20 mm rounds. A three-second burst hit the remaining cars that had been parked together, turning them into flaming relics of melting metal and burning rubber. A black SUV was hit by a short burst of incendiary rounds. The armored SUV leaped into the air. Its gas tank exploded while it was still suspended above the ground. Another burst hit the tree line where several men were concealed. They had stupidly fired at the Sabre Jet on its last run. Jackson's aim was true. The trees flashed into 6000-degree white phosphorous flames. The men were vaporized.

Jackson made his final pass, this time so low and slow I could see the white star against the silhouette of the jet as it passed overhead. Jackson seemed to make the F-100 hover as fire erupted from underneath the fuselage. It was beautiful and frightening at the same time: a fire-breathing dragon, flying low and slow—protecting us from our enemies. The cabin's floor shuddered. Fireballs ejaculated from the trees and became meteors shooting into the heavens.

The F-100 banked over the ridgeline on the far side of the lake.

Jackson announced over the satellite phone's speaker, "That's all, folks! I'm out of bullets and I need to refuel … seems I was a little heavy on the throttle."

The F-100 drifted off the ridge and dropped to the lake. He was flying barely faster than stalling speed—still forcing the supersonic fighter jet to fly like a Warthog. Doing so magnified the jet's documented avionics problem.

"Headed home," Jackson announced, as he banked in a radically sharp turn, causing the F-100 to flat spin, which quickly turned into a roll and then a tumble.

I could see it happening thorough the picture window opening.

Jackson had been flying maybe two hundred feet above the lake's surface—not much room for mistakes. The Super Sabre continued its uncontrolled yawing and rolling until it impacted the far side shoreline in about three feet of water. There was a terrible, brilliant, white-hot fireball and concussive explosion. The tremendous explosion instantly flattened the trees nearest the crash site. I stood mesmerized as a blue-white shockwave rushed across the water's surface towards me. When the warm tsunami-like shockwave hit the cabin, it crashed the few fragments of broken window still in the picture opening. The shock wave rushed inside the cabin, strong enough to make the women's hair wave in the wind. A full G-Force of air pressure pushed against our bodies, almost knocking me over in my weakened condition. A few seconds later I watched as a three-foot water tsunami crashed against the shore.

I knew there was no chance Jackson had survived. It had happened too fast and too low to the ground. There had been no time for him to eject. The white-hot fireball had been too intense. I could see it all happening in slow motion, over-and-over in my mind. The image of the crash would stay with me forever.

We had to move. Flames were still dancing around the cabin, threatening to burn us to death if we stayed. The smoke from the fire was maybe a greater threat. It was getting more difficult to breathe. We could hear men moaning outside in the forest. One man's scream, in particular, dominated all the others. He ululated a horrible, uncontrolled, ear-shattering cry that seemed to rattle from the bottom of his lungs. The sound sent shivers up my spine. Thankfully, he made one last ear-piercing cry and then became quiet. Maybe his death had put an end to his suffering.

Tom disappeared outside. I could see his shadowy silhouette walking around the cabin with the rifle against his shoulder, ready to fire. After several minutes, he returned and announced, "Everyone is either dead or ran away. We seem to be alone."

I said, "We should hike over to the crash site and see if Jackson is alive, just to be sure."

Tom locked eyes with me and said, "I could tell from here that ... besides the impact ... jet fuel burns very hot ... even the metal skin melted ... Jackson couldn't have lived ... I'm sorry, John."

I nodded and said, "He saved our butts tonight."

"Yes," agreed Tom. "We owe him a debt that we can't repay."

"I know." I don't know if it was the death all around, or because I was on my feet, but I was feeling stronger.

The thunder of several military grade helicopters could be heard approaching over the distant horizon.

74

I'M TO BLAME

The three Blackhawk helicopters appeared over the ridge from the east. The huge, flat-black birds with the stenciled white letters "FBI" on their sides passed over the resort and then turned back, settling in three different locations within sight of each other. The first landed at the helicopter pad, the second sat down in front of the main building on the circular driveway, and the third landed on the snow-covered field near the burning cabin, near us. Men dressed in black, with helmets and body armor, rushed out as the aircraft touched ground. Their assault rifles were pressed hard against their shoulders, searching for hostile targets.

We had emerged from the burning cabin and were standing in the open, hands up, so they could clearly see we had no weapons. Although my side hurt and I felt weak, I was now able to stand and walk on my own. I did lean on Janet for support. It felt nice, and she didn't seem to mind. We waited quietly for our rescuers.

I'm sure we looked like a wretched bunch: dirty and stinking of blood, gunpowder, and sweat. It had been a hard day and night. I know my face was badly swollen from the beatings I'd taken in the past twenty-four hours. I could barely see out of my left eye. Curiously I was sweating, even in the cold, dark early morning air. A new wave of dizziness rushed over me, followed by nausea.

Soon they had me on a stretcher in the main lobby of the resort. An FBI medic, dressed in full body armor, was fussing over me. He stuck an IV with clear liquid into my veins. Janet was standing on the other side with a seriously worried expression on her face, except when she was looking directly at me. That's when she smiled. It was a beautiful smile—an angel casting her blessing on my sorry soul.

I managed to ask, "How am I doing, doctor?"

"I'm a medic, not a doctor," he answered. "The bullet passed all the way through—that's the good news. But you've lost some blood, so I've put in an IV to replace fluid. Once your BP comes up you should be stable."

"What's going on? Has anyone checked to see if Jackson is alive? Did they catch Quail and the others? What about Fetterson? Did they find the crashed helicopter? What about Bigfoot? Did they find it?" I realized I was talking fast, but I wanted to know all these things.

Janet answered, "They're still looking, but so far no luck on the crashed helicopter. Quail is in custody with the others. The FBI is keeping the members of the Order under guard in the conference room down the hall."

"We should question them!" I said.

Janet said, "Let the FBI do its job. They're still searching to be sure they have everyone rounded up."

"We need to find that bomb!" I tried to sit up, but the medic gently placed his hand on my shoulder and pushed me back down.

"A team is searching for the helicopter crash site—they'll find it." Then he added, "I want to get your blood pressure up, but not this way. You need to calm down. We have the best men in the world here, and if there is something to be done, they'll do it, so just rest. This is something to help with the pain." He stuck a needle in my arm. "Also, I've called in a Med-Evac helicopter. It should be here soon. Let the others do their jobs. You focus on recovering. Don't worry—you're going to be okay."

Janet said, "I want to go with him to the hospital."

Tom walked up at that moment. "I think we can arrange that . . . how you doing, big brother?"

"Did they find the bomb?" I asked.

"They found the helicopter that Jackson shot down, but it's too soon to report anything," he answered.

"How many helicopters are there on the pad?" I asked.

Tom said, "I haven't been over there, so I'm not sure—why?"

"Because I thought I heard a second helicopter taking off. I dismissed it at the time as an echo. Now I'm thinking two helicopters took off at the same time. Jackson shot one down, but the other got away."

My brother replied, "—We'll know soon."

I turned inward and cursed myself for not calling sooner for help. The SWAT team was professional and fast, but they had been at least an hour too late—maybe two. It wasn't their fault. We had waited too long to call them. The only thing remaining for them to do was clean up the mess. If Fetterson got away with the bomb, the world would be plunged into chaos. The president, the Supreme Court, the Joint Chief of Staffs, Congress, and thousands—if not hundreds of thousands—of people in Washington, DC would be vaporized in a nuclear blast. It was my fault. I thought I could handle it.

I had been stupid.

I felt strange, as if I were losing touch with the world around me. I looked up to the medic to see if he noticed, but he was out of focus. Janet was also a fuzzy image. She said something, but her words didn't make sense. It was as if she were speaking some alien language.

I struggled to ask, "What . . . give . . . pain, doc?"

I think he said, "A shot of morphine."

The world went black.

75

ONLY BAD NEWS

I woke in a hospital bed with tubes snaking in and out of various parts of my body to drain or infuse this or that—who knows for what purpose.

Hospitals buzz with bad news: "I'm so sorry, Miss Jones, but your husband passed away last night. There was nothing we could do—it was his time." Or, "Your wife has breast cancer. We need to operate . . ." For healthy people, hospitals are unhealthy places to spend time. Have you ever noticed that most of the people you see in hospitals are sick—even the visitors? Every room is occupied with someone who is a little closer to death than the average guy on the street. Another thing—since the initial session with the emergency room doctors and surgeons who stitched me up, I haven't seen a single doctor. Where are they? Aren't they supposed to be working? What do they do all day if they aren't seeing their patients? Are they playing golf? If so, they must be ready for the Master's Tour by now. Maybe they're chasing nurses? Now that I think of it, I don't see the good, old-fashioned RNs around anywhere either! Where did they all go? Maybe they're with the doctors? There must be a motel someplace nearby, full of doctors and nurses, consulting with each other's anatomies and playing "Doctor." Possibly between their coupling procedures, they occasionally call in, prescribing treatments and medications for patients they haven't examined personally since the surgery. In fact, the only medical people I've seen in the past three days are medical assistants. They sometimes call themselves technicians, but the point is, they aren't doctors or even nurses.

How do all these "almost doctors" know they're doing the right thing to the right person? They look at my wrist tag, that includes my name and date of birth, and then consult their computer monitors on wheels that they rolled in the room. (I assume the computers have replaced the paper charts medical staff previously used to make themselves look official.) Finally, they always ask my name and date of birth as if they can't read my wrist tag. That's worrisome; if they can't read how can they know what treatments to give me? Who is giving these technicians instructions? It can't be my doctor, because I haven't seen him since surgery. I figure the real threat of dying is staying in this hospital bed, being poked, tugged, injected, or forgotten by people who apparently can't read and who obviously don't know what they're doing.

If there weren't so many tubes and IV's growing from my body, I'd get up and leave right now.

You may have gathered that I hate hospitals.

I made a feeble effort to sit up but somehow couldn't find the strength, so I laid back and sighed.

Uh-oh, here comes the drug technician. I forgot her name—Sherry, or Susan, or something.

"Good morning, Mr. Wolfe. How are we feeling today?" she asked.

I said, "Well, I have no idea how you're feeling, Miss . . . I'm sorry, what is your name again?"

My voice sounds so weak. My throat is dry.

She answered, "Cindy."

I continued, ". . . Miss Cindy, but I want to get out of here."

"The doctor says three more days to be safe."

"The doctor? How does he know? He hasn't seen me for two days!"

"He's managing your case on a daily basis, I assure you." Cindy reached over and consulted the printed scale on the side of a plastic bag that was hanging over my head like the Sword of Damocles. The bag contained clear liquid that was in turn connected to a tube leading into my body.

"Looks and sounds like you could use a topping of morphine." She disconnected a small side tube, connected to the primary tube, and disappeared before I could say I didn't want any more morphine.

Why is it so difficult to talk or move?

I must have dozed off, because when I looked up again, she had already been back in the room long enough to replace the morphine supply tube and was showing me her cute round bottom as she exited. I called after her, "I don't want . . ." but my voice faded to a sub-whisper. I sounded so hoarse and weak.

Damn morphine.

I fell asleep.

The next time I awoke I wasn't alone. Mary—The Fifty Billion Dollar Woman—was standing over me. Her hands were resting on her hips in a pose that only she could strike. As usual, she looked beyond sexy. She was bewitching. She aroused me even in my seriously diminished condition. Then I looked deeper into her eyes. They were shining with fiery intensity and there was a devilish smile on her lips. A shiver ran up my spine.

She's here to kill me.

I tried to rise—to defend myself—but there was too much morphine in me, so I fell back. Then I reached for the emergency call button, but Mary casually moved it out of my reach. I cried out, but my vocal cords didn't work. The sound was so weak it couldn't be heard more than a couple of feet away.

I'm helpless.

"You don't need the nurse. You have me." Her voice was deep, seductive ... inviting. She bent down.

This is it! She's going to kill me, and I can't stop her—damn morphine!

I raised my arm to block her, but she gently weighted it down with her hand. I was too weak to resist.

Mary kissed me softly on the lips, and then kissed me again—longer, more lingeringly the second time.

How perverted; she wants to have sex before killing me.

Her burning, dark green eyes were suspended inches from mine. Her voice was a deep-toned whisper. "I'm so glad you're okay. The doctor says the bullet perforated your appendix and its secretions spread in your body. He said it was septic. You almost died but now you're going to be fine." She kissed me again. This time her lips opened and she used her tongue. She stayed welded to me for a long time.

Despite the gunshot wound and morphine, I felt myself responding.

It's got to be a miracle!

I tried to speak again, but my throat was too dry. My vocal cords only made a raspy, croaking sound.

"Sounds like you need some water." Mary handed me the plastic tumbler with a straw that sat on the side tray next to the bed. She attentively held the tumbler in position while I took a long draw on the ice water. It felt refreshing, bringing life back to my throat and vocal cords.

"Are you here to kill me?" My voice was rough but at least I could talk now.

She laughed. "Don't be an idiot! I'm here to ask you if you still want that job."

I grunted then replied, "With whom: the Order or the recently deceased Russian?"

"No silly, The Major! He wants to know if you are still interested in that position."

"You work for The Major?"

She smiled at me for an answer.

"I don't believe you. Every time we talk you work for someone different."

"It's true! What I told you about infiltrating the Order was also true, except it wasn't for Homeland Security—that's just a cover story we often use."

"You mean the people who work for The Major?" I asked.

"Yes, it makes moving around easier. Before the Patriot Act created Homeland Security The Major's agents used the FBI as a cover."

"What do Homeland Security and the FBI have to say about that?"

"Oh, we don't really tell them and when one of our agents get caught—which is very rare—we say we're with the CIA or even your old agency. Our legends are always recorded in the other agencies' personnel files for that purpose."

I laughed gently because I didn't want to bust a stitch. "Then what were you doing being so cozy with The Russian?"

"The Russian was a serendipitous side mission—a target of opportunity. He's been on our wanted list for a decade. When the chance unexpectedly showed itself, The Major told me we couldn't let it pass. So he cooked up this duplicitous scheme and threw me into the mix. The idea was to get The Russian while still infiltrating the Order, which is the real target."

"So now you're telling me The Major is your true employer. Somehow I have trouble believing you," I said.

She laughed. "Trust me—it's true. So, what is your answer—the job offer?"

"Do I have a choice?" I asked.

"Of course you do!"

"Really? It's a take it or die offer—isn't it?"

Mary gently ran her hand through my hair, pulling the loose curls out straight and letting them fall back. When she answered her voice was seductive. "If you say no, I'll leave and you can go quietly into retirement, although with less money. If you say yes, we'll be co-workers. It'll be fun!"

She lowered her flawless, gorgeous face closer. Her dark green eyes drilled deeply into mine. I could smell her hair and her perfume—or was it simply her natural fragrance? Her lips slowly, gently, sealed against mine.

At that exact moment the door opened and Janet entered the room.

"Well, seems you two are getting along just fine," she said.

I turned my head away from Mary and said, "Janet, I'm glad you're here."

Janet shot back, "I can see you're happy someone is here." Her eyes were targeting the sheets where my reaction to Mary's kiss was nearly transparent.

"Janet, I . . ."

"It doesn't matter. After all, like you said, we broke up."

"You broke up with me. I didn't want to . . ." I shot back.

"We can talk about that later . . . when we're alone." Janet's eyes were shooting Zulu Spears at Mary.

Tom entered. "Hey, brother, good to see you! How you doing?"

Mary stepped back from the bed. "You want me to leave?"

My brother shook his head. "No, you need to stay and hear this. We have a team at the crash site investigating the downed helicopter, about five miles from the Kincade Resort. The aircraft was burned so severely they're having trouble finding evidence. The aluminum body was melted from the intense heat, and the weather doesn't help. It's snowing again."

"Any indication of radiation—of the bomb?" I asked.

"No bomb and no radiation signature either. If the bomb had been in the aircraft they would expect to find some indication—at least some residual radiation."

Janet asked, "What about bodies?"

"They've found several bodies, but no ID yet—too burned," he answered.

"What about the second helicopter—any word?"

"Nothing," answered Tom.

Janet said, "That means the bomb, and possibly Senator Fetterson, are still out there, still planning to blow up Washington and overthrow the government."

Tom said, "Yes, but there's more."

We waited for him to continue.

"There was a team of lawyers waiting at the jail when Quail and the others were booked. They were released on their own recognizance almost immediately. In the meantime, Quail issued a statement through his attorney. He has stubbornly denied everything and maintains that we are the bad guys. He says we invaded his college reunion party . . . that a military jet bombed the resort and murdered many of his closest friends. He is demanding that we are arrested."

"Does anyone believe his story?" I asked.

"So far everyone seems to believe his story more than ours."

"A college reunion party?" said Janet.

Tom grunted. "It gets worse. Word is I will be suspended from the Bureau, pending an investigation and hearing by the Office of Professional Responsibility. Over 95% of cases that go before the OPR result in termination or even criminal charges against the agent. In other words, I'm a suspect now, brother."

"Do you think the Order is behind that?" asked Janet.

No one offered an answer.

Terry entered the room and announced, "You need to turn on the TV." She found the remote on my nightstand and switched it on to a news network. Senator Fetterson was being interviewed. The caption below the picture said it was a live interview.

That answers the question if Fetterson survived.

The reporter said, "Senator, there have been reports of a mass murder and shooting involving a jet fighter plane in the mountains of Virginia. Reports say you were there ... You were a witness. Can you comment on that?"

"I know nothing of any shootings or fighter planes bombing anywhere in Virginia. At the time, I was at my home in Washington State. There are a number of people who can testify to that." Fetterson sounded angry.

What an accomplished liar . . .

The reporter asked, "Sir, the reports say the FBI has opened an investigation—"

Fetterson cut the reporter off with, "I will not comment on that," and then turned his back and walked away.

The camera followed Senator Fetterson as he got into his black SUV. The vehicle drove away with the Capitol Building in the background—ground zero for next month's State of the Union address. The camera panned to the reporter, who regurgitated what Fetterson had just said, and then the picture switched to the studio's talking head, who repeated what the field reporter had just regurgitated.

Terry shut off the television.

"Look at him, denying he was even there, and they all believe him!" Mary sounded angry.

"I guess he wasn't in the helicopter that got shot down," said Tom.

"That means the bomb wasn't in the helicopter either," I said.

"Or someone got him, and the bomb, away safely before the FBI arrived," said Terry.

Tom shook his head. "I don't think so. The aircraft was totally destroyed and melted. I can't see him escaping without being severely injured. I think John is right: there was a second helicopter with Fetterson and the bomb. Jackson shot down a decoy."

"Quail was right too," Janet said.

"About what?" I asked.

"The rich always prevail over the poor, even if the poor's cause is righteous."

"Not this time!" I said. "We can prove what really happened. We are witnesses. We can testify at your suspension hearing with the OPR. They will have to listen if we all go there with the truth." I felt dizziness coming on. I'd allowed myself to become too agitated.

Damn morphine.

Tom sighed. "Even if we could somehow make the Office of Professional Responsibility believe my story, it'll be February before they hear my case. In the meantime, I have no authority."

I said the obvious, "February? The president makes his address in January!"

Terry shook her head.

Janet said, "We have a chance to stop them."

Mary replied, "I'm afraid they have too many people buried deep in the media, the government . . . in key positions everywhere."

"They can't be that powerful!" Terry didn't sound convinced.

Tom said, "Mary is right: anyone we turn to for help may be one of them. It appears even the Bureau has been infiltrated."

"Then what do we do?" asked Janet.

"I don't intend to be in the Washington, DC area during the president's State of the Union address next month," stated Mary.

I sat up and pinched the needle from my arm, pulling it free. I was done with the morphine. I swung my feet to the floor, took a deep breath, and announced, "Anyone with the power to stop them is either corrupt, incompetent, or an idiot."

Janet interjected, "Pretty much sums up the current Congress."

I tested my legs. They were wobbly but I could stand. "Therefore, it falls to us—in this room—to stop the Order."

"Right!" agreed my brother.

76

THE GOLDEN SQUIRREL

Janet drove me back to the Old Rock House from the hospital. It was good to be home and to feel safe again, even though I saw damage everywhere that sparked ugly memories of the gunfights and deaths that occurred here just a few days ago. I would hire a contractor to repair the house, but not until after we brought Fetterson to justice and found Bigfoot. Stopping the Order was top priority now, before they blew up Washington DC.

After I had a few days to recover, Janet and I planned to join my brother, who was going to attempt to put together a task force to find Fetterson and the bomb.

But for tonight, Janet and I would follow the doctor's orders: I needed to rest, and Janet agreed to play nurse. We were enjoying a glass of red wine and being cozy in front of the fireplace—a temporary respite. Frankly, I needed the rest.

I studied the gorgeous woman sitting next to me. The hardship Janet suffered in the past week had only caused her to blossom into someone extraordinary. She had become a new woman—stronger, smarter, and even more beautiful than I ever realized she could be before. Her beauty came from the inner strength and confidence that had emerged from her ordeal. Seeing her metamorphosis made me realize how much I loved her. The best part was she had decided she didn't want to break up, and that she loved me too. Janet had become my new girlfriend.

We sat quietly, staring into the dancing flames in the game room fireplace.

Janet said, "When are you going to look at the three gifts we gave you at your party?"

"What's to look at?"

"Well, the sword has an important message on it, and you need to read the care and feeding instructions for the squirrel."

"I thought the squirrel was a joke, or something."

"Let's find out."

The library was tattered by the bullet holes and damage from the battle that had occurred there. It was an abandoned battlefield—sans the bodies. There was a large dark stain inside the library's entrance—Hong Li's blood.

I took a deep breath to collect my courage, stepped over the threshold of the library, and then performed my vault-opening ritual. I was seriously aware of Janet's presence, so close in the confined space. I could smell her seductive scent, and I felt her brush against me from behind. My mind temporarily forgot about the three gifts. I turned and took her into my arms and kissed her. She kissed back. I pulled her tighter against me and allowed my hands to wander. She pressed hard against me and we forgot everything for a moment.

Suddenly, she pulled back and said, "Business first . . . then maybe we can finish the kiss if you feel strong enough." There was a little grin etched across her face.

I was disappointed, but I complied. All three gifts still sat where I had placed them the night of the party. "So what do I need to know about these gifts? I already know the amulet contains Mary's USB drive with secrets about the Order. What's special about the sword and the squirrel?"

She said, "Look at the sword closely."

I studied the handle, the guard, and then the blade. It was undeniably a beautiful weapon, but I saw nothing significant. "What am I looking for?"

"Read the blade again."

"It's Latin—I can't read Latin."

She sighed and enlightened me. "The sword's name is *Gladius de Virtute*, which means 'Sword of Power.'"

"Very poetic."

"Yes, and then it says *Nolite Mortem—Pacem.*"

"Which means?" I asked.

"Stop Death—Peace."

I shook my head and said, "Okay, I'm dense, so explain it to me."

Janet said, "Hong Li liberated this sword from one of the founding members of the Order." We believe it holds the key to stop the bomb from detonating. It was the Order's motto when they first organized as an off-campus fraternity. We think it is a code—or password—to stop the bomb."

I asked, "How do I use it?"

"I won't know until we see the device itself. But my guess is there's a computer that controls the timer and detonation mechanism."

First, we must find the bomb.

I said, "What's the squirrel for?"

From the way she rolled her eyes and snorted, I could tell she thought I was an ungrateful idiot. She said, "Read the care and feeding instructions."

I flipped the heavy statue over and read the instructions on the bottom. It said, "Preheat oven to 475 degrees and place in a deep pan on bottom shelf for thirty minutes."

We took the statue to the kitchen and baked it as directed. When the thirty minutes were up, I opened the oven and found a gold statue standing in a pool of melted, black plastic.

Janet was next to me. "You need to remove it from the pan before the plastic cools and becomes solid again, but be careful; it's hot!"

"Is that solid gold?"

"Yes."

"Why? I mean why give it to me?"

"It will take money to put the Order out of business."

"Where did you get this?" I asked.

"Kay—your sweet MI-6 agent—stole it from the Order. She never told me all the details, but I know she came across it during her assignment in DC when she uncovered the corrupt senator selling British secrets a few years back. The senator was also a member of the Order. He was custodian of the golden statute. It was the Order's mascot—riches are what they worship—if you will. She told me it was fitting we use their own riches to defeat them. That's why she coated it in black plastic as a disguise, and then gave the statute to you—to cover your expenses."

"They all died because of the Order," I said softly. "Marie, Hong Li, and Kay had all been trying to shut down the Order of the Golden Squirrel. They were working on the case before I even knew the Order existed."

Janet said, "Yes, and we can't let their deaths be for nothing."

"I won't!" I promised.

77

SPIT IN THEIR EYE

Four o'clock the next morning, six US marshals and four FBI special agents, accompanied by a full SWAT team, showed up at my Old Rock House. It was easy for them to enter the house, since my front door was a large hole. They simply walked into the master bedroom, politely woke us, and then professionally arrested us and placed us in chains. They were very efficient. The head agent informed me I was under arrest for sedition, murder, and terrorism. Janet was arrested on the same charges. They searched the property with great attention to detail but somehow did not find my secret vault, so the gold squirrel and other treasures were not discovered. When I asked for an attorney, I was told we were being held incognito and without legal representation, allegedly under a special provision of the Patriot Act of 2001, reaffirmed and strengthened by the 2006 Patriot Act amendment.

They put us in a windowless van, so we couldn't see where they were taking us, but it seemed like a long drive.

After we arrived at our destination, they sat me in a metal chair, with my hands chained to a metal table. Both chair and table were bolted to the concrete floor. I was in the proverbial cell-like room with the one-way glass covering a wall. My interrogator had been grilling me for some time about the current whereabouts of my brother and sister-in-law. All his questions were about Tom and Terry Wolfe. Apparently, my brother and sister-in-law had disappeared, and the FBI, Homeland Security, and every police and intelligence agency in the country were having no luck finding him. The head agent would only say they had disappeared, and he was asking me to help find them. I explained to my interrogator that it was more urgent to stop the Order's plot to blow up Washington, DC, during the president's State of the Union address, but he didn't want to hear about that. He was only interested in the location of Tom and Terry Wolfe.

After I realized my interrogator was either corrupt, incompetent, or an idiot, (maybe all three), and I would get no help from him; I adopted a blank stare and remained silent. I didn't even listen to his questions any longer.

My thoughts lingered on Janet. I know she was doing the same wherever they were keeping her right now. My mind flashed on images of Janet's heroics over the past week. I knew she was the one. I decided if we ever got out of this alive, I was going to ask her to marry me.

First, we have to survive this ... and the bomb.

The head agent broke into my thoughts by sticking his face inches from mine and shouting. His spittle showered my face. It was repulsive, and I think he did it knowingly. Maybe something they teach in Rubber Hose 101.

"Don't you want to save your brother's life? There is a nationwide search for Thomas and Terry Wolfe. They are posted by the FBI as the most wanted man and woman in the United States. They're both tagged as armed and extremely dangerous ... which means it is legal to shoot them on sight! But you can save their lives by telling me where they are right now."

I made eye contact with my interrogator. "You should be scared. Have you bothered to read my brother's file? The US military and even the FBI consider him the most dangerous warrior on the planet. But the good news is he's our only hope. He's the only one capable of stopping the Order before it blows up the capital."

"Bullshit!" The interrogator straightened and stomped to the other side of the small room. He cast a hateful face back at me, but said nothing.

I think I'm getting to him.

"Don't you care?" I asked.

He blinked. I could see he was processing the information, but he had been tasked to learn just one thing from me—the whereabouts of my brother. It was the only objective of this questioning.

It occurred to me that the Order had the almost perfect scheme, and they had deeply padded the government with their agents to insure they could not be stopped. It was perfect except for one thing: they had not counted on my brother and his wife getting away.

People always underestimate my brother.

I saw a crack in the interrogator's demeanor. I decided to drive the wedge in a little deeper. "I hope this facility is located far away from the capital, because if it isn't, we'll all be burnt toast when the president makes his State of the Union Address. I've lost track of the time. How long is it until the president speaks?"

The interrogator didn't answer.

"When he does, you'll know I was telling the truth, but it will be too late then."

I guess I finally got to the interrogator, but not the way I had hoped. He hit me on my face—the sore side—the exact same place all those other knuckle draggers had been hitting me. The left side of my face was still very tender. I think I felt blood trickle down my cheek, but the chains were locked to the table, so I couldn't bring my hand up to check. Instead, I waited while a wave of vertigo passed.

I'm not getting anywhere with him.

There was only one response I could make.

I spit in his eye.

FROM THE NEXT BOOK

STATE OF THE UNION
ADDRESS: GROUND ZERO

... Johnson's eyes swept the room, and then settled on Wolfe. He announced with a disheartened tone, "This meeting is adjourned. Return to your respective agencies." Then in a quieter voice, "Tom, we need to talk in private."

"Can it wait a few minutes? We haven't worked out roles and responsibilities for the task force yet."

"No, this meeting is adjourned!" Johnson repeated; louder and more forceful this time. He addressed the group, "I have been authorized to instruct you to return to your individual agencies immediately. Leave the briefing folders here: do not take them with you. Also, you are to forget what you have heard here. This meeting, and its content, has been classified Top Secret—Complete Blackout. It is not to be discussed anywhere with anyone—not even your supervisors or between those who have attended this meeting. This meeting didn't happen and you didn't hear anything that was said here." Johnson paused to be sure the message had taken, and then added, "Any violation of this order will result in disciplinary action and possible criminal prosecution. There are no exceptions!" He made eye contact with Dr. Aberrant. "That includes you, sir."

Johnson turned to Tom Wolfe and said, "Follow me!" then marched from the room without waiting to see if Wolfe would follow.

The faces on the agents showed shock. They were clearly stunned.

Why the Top Secret—Complete Blackout order? If there was a bomb about to be detonated in the Capitol, it's our responsibility to stop it.

Wolfe could see the frustration on the veteran agents' faces. Personally, Wolfe was beyond frustration.

Was Johnson—Chief Assistant Director of the FBI—a member of the Order?

Tom Wolfe asked Judy Lang and Mike Musashi, "Would you pick up the briefing folders and take them back to my office? I'll be along as soon as possible."

Judy Lang said, "What's with Johnson? I've never seen him act this way before."

"I don't know, but I think I'm about to find out ... talk with you later— let you know."

Wolfe waited by the white board, watching the men and women migrate from the room. They were mumbling softly among themselves about what they had just witnessed—already violating the blackout order. Wolfe suspected more than one of them would tell their immediate supervisor about the meeting.

I hope so.

Dr. Aberrant glanced at Tom Wolfe as he quietly slipped a briefing folder under his sweater, behind his back. No words were spoken. He left the room.

At least the top echelon of the Pentagon will know.

Judy Lang and Mike Musashi collected the briefing folders the agents had left on their seats. Musashi counted the folders and announced to Wolfe. "Six folders are missing."

Wolfe nodded his head with only a hint of a smile on his lips.

More than the Pentagon...

"I think you miscounted. We didn't bring that many folders. We have them all. See you back at Quantico," Tom Wolfe answered.

Musashi and Judy Lang quietly left the room.

Tom Wolfe erased the white board Dr. Aberrant had drawn on, and then made one last sweep of the conference room to insure nothing had been left behind. He turned off the lights and exited.

Ed Johnson was waiting for him just outside the doorway. Johnson grunted, shot a glance at the corner in the ceiling where a camera was watching them, and silently led Wolfe down the hall to a smaller meeting room.

After the door closed, Johnson's eyes again darted to the ceiling in the corner of the room—another camera. Johnson's voice was uncharacteristically stiff and formal. "This conversation is being recorded and may be used as evidence against you in the future, if deemed relative in any legal proceedings. Effective immediately, you are suspended from all duties in the Bureau and stripped of all authority. You are no longer an Assistant Director or a Special Agent of the Federal Bureau of Investigation. This suspension remains in effect pending a possible review and final disposition by the Office of Professional Responsibility. You are ordered to surrender your service pistol and credentials to me at this time." Johnson stood silently, waiting for a response.

Wolfe didn't react.

The two former friends stared at each other.

A full minute passed in complete silence.

Finally, Wolfe realized that Johnson was actually waiting for him to surrender his pistol and credentials before anything more was said or done. Slowly, Wolfe drew the pistol from his shoulder holster, removed the magazine, and ejected the round from the chamber. He gently placed the unloaded weapon on the table in front of him. Next, he removed his gold shield and ID card and dropped them next to the pistol.

I can't believe this is happening.

Johnson sighed, as if he were relieved, and then said, "I am instructed to tell you that you are not to return to your office or attempt to communicate with any Bureau employees, in any fashion, until the review is concluded. Do you understand what I am saying?"

Thomas Wolfe nodded.

Johnson said, "Please give a verbal response."

"Yes, I understand what you are telling me, but I don't understand why this is happening? What's going on, Ed?"

"I am not authorized to discuss the details of this action with you. I do recommend you obtain the services of an attorney, because further action is being considered. I have been instructed to escort you off federal property at this time."

"Instructed ... by who?"

"I'm not at liberty to disclose that information—sorry. Please follow me." Johnson collected Wolfe's credentials and weapon and walked out first.

Wolfe quietly followed his former boss down the long corridor to the elevators. Johnson pushed the down button. Again, Johnson's eyes darted to a camera near the ceiling then back to the elevator doors.

They waited in silence.

The doors opened. There were two federal employees inside the elevator, so the trip to the ground floor was also made without speaking. The doors opened and Johnson quickly set course to the 10th street exit without checking to see if Wolfe was following.

Johnson stopped outside on a large stone portico that was raised above the street level and enclosed with squared-cornered pillars spaced at four foot intervals around the entire circumference. Johnson waited for Wolfe to join him. The two men paused at the top, looking down the two-tiered concrete stairs that emptied onto the sidewalk and street below.

An icy cold wind raced between the buildings. The bitter cold cut through Wolfe's sport jacket, causing him to shiver. He closed his lapels over his chest to block the wind, but it didn't help.

Four very large men dressed in black long coats, over navy blue business suits and black ties, appeared next to Tom Wolfe. Two moved in behind him. The other two took up positions—one on each side. A fifth man stepped directly in front of Wolfe and pulled back his jacket to reveal a US Marshal's Star mounted on his belt. Next to the star was a holstered Glock pistol. Wolfe looked past the marshal, standing to his front, and saw two more clones standing on the sidewalk at the bottom of the stone steps. That made seven U.S. Marshals.

Johnson moved away from the formation and stood against one of the concrete pillars that enclosed the large portico.

"Put your hands behind your head ... fingers interlaced!" commanded the lead marshal.

"Am I under arrest?" asked Tom Wolfe.

"Yes."

Ed Johnson delivered me to these marshals.

ABOUT THE AUTHOR

Walt Branam has worked in aerospace and served in combat as a commissioned officer, US Army, Infantry. He has led researchers on wilderness expeditions to locate and photograph dangerous and rare animals. He was the leader of a special government task force to bring high tech, white collar criminals to justice. For the past decade Walt has worked as a consultant to private industry. He now writes full time.

Printed in the United States
By Bookmasters